THE ANIMATORS

THE
ANIMATORS

A NOVEL

KAYLA RAE WHITAKER

RANDOM HOUSE | NEW YORK

Published in the United States by Random House, an imprint and division of Penguin Random House LLC, New York.

RANDOM HOUSE and the HOUSE colophon are registered trademarks of Penguin Random House LLC.

Library of Congress Cataloging-in-Publication Data
Names: Whitaker, Kayla Rae, author.
Title: The animators: a novel / Kayla Rae Whitaker.
Description: New York: Random House, 2016.
Identifiers: LCCN 2015049662 | ISBN 9780812989281 | ISBN 9780812989298 (ebook)
Subjects: LCSH: Female friendship—Fiction. | Women animators—Fiction. | Women motion picture producers and directors—Fiction. | Life change events—Fiction. | Psychological fiction.
Classification: LCC PS3623.H56265 A36 2016 | DDC 813'.6—dc23 LC record available at http://lccn.loc.gov/2015049662

International edition ISBN 978-0-399-58958-4

Printed in the United States of America on acid-free paper

randomhousebooks.com

2 4 6 8 9 7 5 3 1

First Edition

Book design by Susan Turner

For Warner

THE ANIMATORS

PROLOGUE:
INTRODUCTION TO SKETCH

INTRODUCTION TO SKETCH WAS HELD IN PREBBLE HALL, A BUILDING PRO-
fessor McIntosh called "Ballister's dirtiest secret" during our first
class. Prebble was an ancient, pipe-clanking fortress on the edge of
campus with heating problems, leaky ceilings, and those 1930s wall
radiators we used to melt crayons on in grade school. "You pay fifty
thousand dollars a year to attend this institution," he said, "and they
stick you in a *hovel* for four years. It's because they *hate* art."

The tuition comment didn't hold much weight for me. I was on
scholarship. My peers talked about skiing in Aspen and summers in
the Hamptons. Ballister was their safety school when Stanford and
Duke eluded them. They spoke with the opaque, offhand world
knowledge of the privileged. My first weekend there, I watched a girl
at a party barf into a five-hundred-dollar Coach purse. Terrified of
the cafeteria's clamor, I had taken to eating three meals of ramen
noodles a day in my dorm room.

I went to Ballister because of the visual arts program, because they'd given me their Poor Appalachian Kid scholarship, and because it was as far away from home as I could manage. I had chosen art because I needed something to make use of the bright lights that had existed in my head for as long as I could remember, my fervent, neon wish to be someone else. In high school, I sampled my way up and down the artistic spectrum methodically, like the good student I was, hoping I'd land on something that sparked me: I sketched, I constructed shadowboxes, I threw some rudimentary pots, trying a little of everything, committing seriously to nothing. Too scared, at that point, to put myself at stake for fear of failure. The revelation, maybe, that I had nothing to give. I had yet to encounter anything that made the risk seem worthwhile. I came to Ballister hoping that being there would put an end to my floundering. That I would finally buckle down and find what I was supposed to make, and that it would *mean* something.

I had taken the Amtrak train twenty-two hours out of Maysville, Kentucky, to the tiny upstate New York town in which Ballister was located. Ballister was, I was surprised to learn, not too terribly removed from Canada. My parents' geographic sense of the north wasn't much better than mine. They didn't believe me at first, when I told them I was five hours from New York City and hence out of harm's reach. Before I left, my father cleared his throat and thumped me on the back like I was another man. My mother gave me a fierce hug, something with a degree of pain to it, and said with her chin hooked over my shoulder, "Don't you come back pregnant."

My parents met working in a factory that made lawnmower parts. The brand's claim to fame: George Jones had once drunkenly straddled its luxury model while pursued by the Texas State Police. They were resigned to their jobs, to each other, and to us, their children, who had all the fish sticks and Nintendo we needed. They watched *Wheel of Fortune* with three feet of space between them on the couch. They fought often, and loudly. Neither had gone to college; they hoped I would become something useful, like a CPA.

The closest I had come to finding something that lit me up was in a summer gifted-and-talented program, just before my senior year. In an art course there, I made a graphic novella of the night my mom threw an ottoman at my dad, laboring over how the glass patio door shattered, shards tumbling in an arc of beauty into the green holler bottom below. I painted a textured oil backdrop to simulate the night air wadding itself into a tornado: the Horror of '89, which touched down that very night in regions of East Kentucky, West Virginia, and the golden triangle of Kingsport, Johnson City, and Bristol, Tennessee. The instructor, upon seeing it, complimented me but grimaced. Said, "I like the little cartoons, but how about we fit your skills into a more serious framework?" And pushed a pamphlet for architecture school at me.

McIntosh scared me as much as the rest of Ballister did. He was a serious artist, or had been at one point—a sort of eighties gallery darling whose decline had acted as a chute into teaching, a profession for which he had no real passion. "Oh yah, McIntosh is *intense*," said the senior VA major who'd given me a tour at orientation. But McIntosh was more than just intense. He was a carnivore who loved to eviscerate freshmen, a real crinkle of joy seaming his mouth as he did. We were instructed to bring a sketch to the first class for discussion, and McIntosh made a blonde with perfect posture, daughter of a D.C. diplomat, tear up when he put her sketch of a woman striding down a crosswalk on the projector. "I want you to pay attention here," he told us. "This is a case in point as to the importance of exactness in your line work, and the price paid when you become sloppy." He took his laser pointer, made circles around the figure's smudged face. "What a *deeply confusing* expression. This woman looks *constipated*. Was that your intention, Margaret?" He put his laser pointer down as she began to sniffle. "Well, don't feel discouraged. This is *Ballister*. There's always room for one more prelaw student." I felt lucky when he glanced at my sketch—an old lady who'd ridden the train with me until Charlottesville, Virginia, asleep with an opened bag of Planters in her hand—wrinkled his nose, and said only, "In bad need of discipline."

During the third class, McIntosh put another one of my assignments up on the projector. It was a sketch I'd done of a dog chained to a stake in a yard. I didn't realize it until it was on the wall, but the yard appeared to be on the side of a mountain. It took me the distance from my chair to the screen to realize it: I had drawn Kentucky. I looked at what I'd done, glowing large in front of the class, and felt homesickness wrapping itself around my throat, my eyes growing hot until McIntosh said, "Good. Some rather inspired pencil work here, and here."

It would be the only nice thing he would say about me all semester. I was shocked out of crying. Everyone turned, subtly, to look.

The only person I'd spoken to on campus for more than fifteen minutes was a boy from Kansas named Zack. Zack was also a VA major and was obsessed with M. C. Escher. Accordingly, I was in love with him. I incorporated his form into the bright lights of what I supposed my future would be, staking all my hopes on him. My drug of choice at eighteen: the quiet devouring of boys in my head. In the secret back pages of my sketchbook, I had even drawn him.

Zack was also in McIntosh's class. My eyes automatically drifted to the left, where he sat at a neighboring table. If I hadn't looked in that direction, I might not have seen Mel.

She was perched at a high table with her upper body craned over the desk, wiry arms and legs folded like a praying mantis, looking at me through frayed blond bangs. One dirty Chuck Taylor pressed the floor, bouncing nervously. She looked sleep-deprived—rumpled clothes, an evident ink stain on the knee of her jeans, little lines around her eyes the rest of us didn't have yet. This was the girl over whom McIntosh went into raptures the first couple of classes—she was, apparently, his sole exception to inhaling freshmen. Session one, she brought in a sketch of a man on a front porch, raising what looked like a mug in the shape of a cowboy boot to his lips, and there was this *look* the man was giving, so salty you could almost eat it. Funny and sly and even, in the cocked eyebrow, a little angry that someone thought they could spy on him like that. "Ex*pression*," McIntosh trilled, rocking on his heels. And we could see it, too, even if we didn't know how to say it—it was excellent. Steady, confident lines, delicate shading. It was work that had a good enough idea of itself to be playful.

Her second sketch was a color-smeared cluster of kids in torn T-shirts, safety pins, snarls, all collectively clobbering the hell out of each other. Punks, genuine enough to make me lean away in awe. The look was harsh yet soft, dreamy and glazed, curves creamy. The group fought as a cloud of dust, the result of their scuffling, rose above their shoes. "A little overboard with the blending," McIntosh said, "but the *look* of it is really something. And there's a degree of fun here, too, yes? Some daring? Who were these people, Ms. Vaught?"

"Just some kids I hung around with this summer." She had a funny voice, deep with the puncture of broken glass. It made me look up for a second before I went back to my sketchbook.

In my first weeks at Ballister, I kept my ambition secret. I wanted so badly to be more than what I felt. I wanted to be *good*. I wanted to be great, even. But I was cowed by the knowledge that everyone else here did, too—people who'd come from bigger places and better schools than I had, people who'd traveled and had training and experiences and seemed, in a strange way, more like *people* out in the *world* than I'd ever been or, I feared, ever would be. Seeing their work—good, bad, comparable to mine—only ever made me think of what *I* could do, if I could do it better, and not with a sense of confidence or competitiveness, but fear.

When I looked at Mel's stuff, I felt something different. I didn't know how to quantify what I was seeing in words, but I could feel it. She was naturally, easily good, and when I saw things she had done, I felt a curiously pleasurable pressure at my middle. It was an expansive, generous feeling. Before I saw her, even, I saw what she did.

Class ended. I watched Zack pick up his backpack and head out the door in the direction of the dorms, and saw one of the girls in class who did work I called, in my head, *Hallmark crap*—beatific faces, brave seascapes—catch up to him, blond hair bouncing against her coat.

Then I heard that broken-glass voice next to me. "Nice work up there today."

I turned. Mel was pulling a denim jacket over her skinny shoulders. She smiled, ticked her head back in recognition.

"Thanks," I said.

"I like seeing McIntosh clam up," she said. "Like, when something floors him and he doesn't have any Sorbonne stories in response and he's forced to just shut the fuck up. Doesn't that give you joy?"

"I do like it better when he's not talking."

There was a cluster growing behind us—Margaret, the diplomat's daughter, a boy named Edward whose mother was some sort of photography bigwig at *Vogue,* and a girl from Mexico named Reva whose family was rumored to run a drug cartel and who was wearing a bracelet studded with what I assumed were real diamonds. Just a few in the parade of intimidation that was Ballister. They'd all been pulled in by Mel; were surreptitiously following her, in fact.

"We're gonna try this bar downtown," Mel said. "Wanna come?"

My sister had given me a gift before I left Kentucky. She'd never had much use for me—for most of our lives, the fact that we were related was her chief shame—but when I accepted the scholarship and we both knew I would soon leave for a place she'd never been, she began to look at me with new, slightly awed regard. The night before my train was scheduled to leave, she tossed me a little square wrapped in paper and said, "Here's your going-away present."

It was a fake ID, a very poor one, but in the days before holograms and magnetic strips, it was laminated and had the Kentucky Commonwealth logo on it, so it would do fine. The brunette in the picture looked nothing like me and was named *Nicole Cockrell.*

"Let's see your fakie," Mel said on the way to the bar. She leaned over, pushing her horn-rims to the top of her head. I was struck by the way she smelled—like men's deodorant, low-grade and spicy. She pulled her fake out, we compared—she was *Jocelyn Stone*—and she went, "Heh *heh.*"

It was mostly me Mel talked to that night. The rest of the art kids eventually left, but we stayed, huddled at the bar with Miller High Lifes. "They can't hold their liquor yet," Mel said, wagging her hand at the door. "Kiddies." I didn't tell her that I could count on one hand the number of times I'd gotten drunk.

I saw the corner of a brightly colored book sticking from her bag. *Deadbone Erotica*. On the cover, wonky neon lizards cavorted with large-breasted Amazonian women.

I plucked it out, looked it over. "What's this?"

Mel raked her hand through her pageboy. It was the longest I would ever see her hair. Two weeks later, she would hit it with cerulean Manic Panic and walk around Smurf-headed until Christmas. Then she shaved it all off and bitched about the northern winter teabagging her scalp.

"That's fuckin rad is what that is." She leaned over and tapped the *Deadbone* cover. "You *like* comics." It wasn't a question.

I flipped through. It was drawn in a bubble style: weird, druggy shapes. I had just started paying attention to method, color, how things were rendered, the technical shit they wake you up to in school that you can't help but see everywhere after. The comic was alive, bright and blasted. But there was something else drawing me in—the yellowed paper, the deep, musty smell. It was like cutting down a tree and counting the rings within. A creepy awareness of the years passing.

"I bet you're more of a Warner Brothers fan, though." Mel tilted her beer at me. "I can tell. From your stuff. You do that thing, too, where there's this, like, acknowledgment that *crazy* exists. Like it's out there and pretty close by, actually, but you don't have to draw it for us. We get the hint."

"I used to watch some Looney Tunes," I said slowly, trying to gauge whether I was about to say something of friendship-disqualifying weirdness.

"Right on."

What I didn't tell her: I actually spent *every* Saturday morning watching Looney Tunes, then the uncensored, wartime Merrie Melodies marathons that aired on weekend afternoon cable. Nazi smashers, vintage high-speed chases through Technicolor deserts. I could still remember how offended, how personally *smote*, I was when

Nickelodeon first censored those cartoons: blurring or blocking the oversized pistols, the entire screen fuzzing at the shot that made Daffy Duck's feathers fly. I was already a purist. A devotee, of some sort.

The dust clouds in Mel's picture. Those were WB takeoff clouds, to be sure. Funny and a little bit eerie at the same time. I knew I'd seen them somewhere before.

But saying this would have felt like speaking volumes. It was more effort than I could expend, for how afraid I was of chasing Mel off. So all I said was "Yeah, they were awesome."

"So do you draw comics?"

"I used to. And then I went to this summer arts program. And the prof there told me to study architecture."

I said this with difficulty. Mel was hellfire and balls all over, I could already tell. She'd never let anyone talk her out of anything. I felt my face burn.

But she just said, "That sounds character-building," and then mimed ramming a straw through her eye.

Then, "Is your name really Sharon Kisses?"

"It is until I have the money to get it changed."

"Dude, *no*. Your name is mind-blowing."

"My name is a confirmation that my parents hate me." I burped. "It's Scottish. And it's terrible."

She gave me a long look while managing to swig her beer. "How'd you end up here?"

"You mean at Ballister?"

"Yeah."

I shrugged, embarrassed. I told the truth when asked where I was from, but I always considered lying first.

"You're Southern," Mel said. "Obviously."

I pressed my hand to my mouth.

She laughed. "Try to hide, but you can't. Whereabouts?"

"East Kentucky. About a half an hour from West Virginia."

She whistled through her teeth. "Wow. I knew there was evidence of white trashiness in you, but Jesus H." She lifted an eyebrow. "Might your couch have been covered in plastic wrap?"

I put my hands on my face in mock surprise. "However did you know?"

She smacked her palm on the bar and cawed. "I *knew* you were good people. That's what I like to hear, man." In her other hand, she dangled her bottle with two fingers, like she was used to holding a beer. "*Fluted notes* of white trashiness. *Nuances* of crackery, hillbilly goodness."

"Hey now." I shook my fist at her.

She clapped me on the back. "You're good people," she repeated.

I fumbled for something to say. I already had the sense that Mel's brain ran faster than mine. "Thanks."

"Note I said *nuance*." Mel held a finger up. The bartender took it as a motion for another round. Mel shrugged, accepted. "You're lucky, dude. We were full-on trash. No nuance. Just the thing itself, staring you down."

I was going to ask what she meant, but she said, "You ever seen *Heavy Metal*? That futuristic cartoon from the eighties?"

"No."

"Your stuff in class kind of reminded me of it. Want to go watch it?"

She wanted to hang out. The first time I would actually *hang out* with someone in college. My stomach blossomed. "Okay."

"Cool. I'm in Hagen. We can walk over."

We chugged our beers. She motioned to the bartender and pulled a wallet from her back pocket—the first woman I'd ever seen who carried her wallet in the rear. We paid and hoisted our backpacks onto our shoulders, then she said, "Hold up." Rummaged through her bag, came up empty-handed. For the first time that evening, she looked anxious. "I can't find my sketchbook."

"I'll bet it's back at Prebble. Let's go check."

The doors to Prebble were wide open, the janitors buffing the linoleum. We walked past them, unseen, and up to the art studios on the third floor. Mel's sketchbook was lying on the podium. She grabbed it with an audible sigh of relief. "God *damn*, I thought I lost you," she said, and flicked through. She stopped, mouth screwed to one side.

"What."

"That son of a bitch. He went through it." She peered closer. "He *graded* it. McIntosh fucking *graded* my private sketchbook. Look." She pointed. "Correction lines. Check marks. In ink. See?"

She opened to a sketch of the interior of a 7-Eleven, rows of stiff, shining potato chip bags on a wire rack. In the corner off to the side, a baby screeching with crazed eyes, faint yet present—not the picture's point, but a facet of its landscape. *Lovely,* McIntosh had scrawled.

She turned the page. Instead of a sketch, she'd fashioned a make-shift storyboard. A Shakes the Clown type doing coke lines off what appeared to be a *Country Living* cookbook proffered by a tired-looking call girl. Square two: Shakes straightens, one finger slyly held to nostril. Square three: gazes to the audience, eyes wide. Square four: a cacophony of light and noise, Shakes gigging his feet out, screaming, *"SQUEEEEEE!"* A pig's head floats in the corner, wink-ing, the cheerful harbinger of doom. The tagline below: *This Is Be-tween Me and the Voices in My Head.*

I liked it even better than the stuff she brought to class—it was looser, less restrained, the style sharp yet just loopy enough. But un-derneath, McIntosh wrote, *Why are you wasting your time with this?*

Mel stuffed the book into her bag, took a look around, and nod-ded at the locked room tucked into the classroom's rear. McIntosh's office.

"Got a bobby pin?" she asked me.

I picked through my bag, handed one to her. "Come on," she said. "Let's see what he's hiding in there."

She knelt down, snapped the bobby pin in half, then bent it and stuck it into the lock, tilting her head to listen as she jimmied.

I looked over my shoulder. "Maybe we should come back later?"

"It's the ten-to-six. Those guys aren't the least bit interested in what we're doing."

The lock gave with a weak click. Mel held the pin up, trium-phant. This was, I was quickly learning, my balancing point with Mel—her ideas gave me a queasy feeling in the pit of my stomach, but I went along with them anyway.

McIntosh's office was dingy even in the dark, with only a small window facing the woods to the college's south. There was a crack in the wall coming from the spot where he'd nailed his Princeton diploma; from somewhere, we could hear a steady drip.

Mel yanked open the desk and began sifting through. "Okay. Cough drops. Tea bags. Pepper packets. Metamucil. Oil pencils. Shit. Okay." She opened another drawer. Pulled out a canister of Maxwell House. "Oh *ho*. Hold the *phone*." Wiggled her eyebrows. Lifted out a baggie.

"What is it?"

"It appears," she said, "to be the dankness." She brought the bag to her nose, inhaled. "Yes. That is middle-aged, professional-grade weed." She unzipped her backpack and dropped it in. "You get high?"

I scratched my nose. There was a beat before I admitted, "Haven't tried."

Mel let her hands fall to her sides. "Aw, Sharon. You're gonna love this. You're gonna let the world happen to you, and you're gonna *love* it."

IT WAS BALMY OUTSIDE, one of the last few seventy-degree halcyon days in September. We camped out behind Prebble with a bottle of Woodford Reserve we'd also found in McIntosh's desk. I watched, fascinated, as Mel parsed seed from stem on the back of her sketchbook.

There was no way McIntosh could report the theft, which, we agreed, gave our steal the flavor of deceit. Not that it would have made much difference. McIntosh would be fired a few years after we graduated. I would encounter him not long after at an opening at PS1, saying, "Hey, Professor McIntosh, how are you?" And he would gaze at me, drinker's rosacea creeping into his cheeks, and he would hiss, "You. Are a living example. That the world. *Is unfair.*"

Never again have I been as pleasantly stoned as I was that night behind Prebble with Mel, so high without shame or baggage. After a brief bout of paranoia, the night took on a crisp, golden quality. I felt the top of my skin lift off. The weight that had been sitting on top of my throat since I had arrived began to release. Time stretched, grew thin and gauzy, all fuzzy endings and beginnings. I can't tell you how long we played roly-poly down the hillside, kicking off to land in a heap at the hill's foot. Or how we made our way to SuperAmerica to stare at the Hostess cakes until the cashier said, "Girls, either buy something or get out," and I gingerly picked up a pack of Ho Hos as if it were a living thing. Or how long Mel laughed when I tried to light the wrong end of a cigarette. And I cannot recall how we made our way back to my dorm room to find my roommate, a girl from Binghamton even more homesick than I was, mercifully spending a long weekend back home.

We were half-finished with the whiskey and had almost smoked through Mel's cigarettes. "This is cool," I said, tapping the cover of *Deadbone,* which I'd dug out of her backpack again—we were already pawing through each other's things. "Where'd you get it?"

"Comic book shop." She took it, paged through. "I rode Greyhound up here and this book got me in trouble. Guy across from me saw me reading something with boobs on the cover and took it as an invitation to bone. Had to fend off advances from Atlanta to Cincinnati. It's like, hey sports fan, do you *not* know a dyke when you see one?"

I tried to look nonchalant. I'd heard one of my more redneck uncles use that word in tones of absolute poison to describe his ex-wife. After my missing aunt Marilyn, Mel Vaught was the second lesbian I'd ever met.

"I took Amtrak," I said, recovering.

She picked up a Ho Ho. Inspected it but did not eat. "Yeah. I thought about Amtrak, too. But the bus was easier. Mom's out of the picture, and I lived with my aunt, who's great, but getting up there, you know? Couldn't really do the trip. I told her I'd be okay on the bus. Which I was, mostly. With the exception of Stiffie McGoo."

"My parents couldn't get off work," I said. "I read a lot." *Guh. Lame,* I thought. But Mel just nodded. Took down the Ho Ho in two bites.

"So where's your mom?" I asked her.

"Jail."

"Really?"

"Oh yeah. She's in there good, too. She had a parole hearing last summer and she thought it would be a good idea to send the judge a great big bouquet of fuck-yous right before. I think she called him a 'punk-ass bitch,' if memory serves? Charm for *miles,* lemme tell you."

Mel said this with a weird, offhand cheer. I still wasn't entirely sure she *wasn't* joking. But I looked at her through the smoke and I saw something in her eyes, something strapped and grim I only saw in kids back home, the really poor ones. Holler kids who wore flannel shirts from the Family Resource Center, ones from families with too many kids to feed or parents who were crankheads, at their best when they were absent. The *hard times* kids.

I realized, with a start, that Mel was one of them. I wasn't, not really. But she was, nevertheless, the closest thing to myself that I'd found at Ballister.

She must be drunk if she willingly told me that, I thought. Letting her guard slip. And this, I already knew about Ballister—the place was all about putting your guard way, way up.

She must have sensed what I was thinking, because she flopped over the side of the bed, upside down, and laced her hands over her belly. "Ballister's weird. But it's like my sketchbook, man. I have to draw what I *have* to draw, and if it's where I'm from, so be it. And I have zero fucks to give about what McIntosh or anyone else has to say about it. I'm not interested in spending the rest of my four years trying to defend how I got here. I'm *working.*"

She burped, closed-mouthed. Pointed at me. "So it's okay to say where you're from, Kisses. All right?"

I'd been caught. I nodded.

"So what are you planning on doing with your stuff?" she asked me. "What's next."

"My stuff?"

"Your work."

I rubbed the back of my neck. "Well," I said, "I don't really know yet. I was kind of hoping I'd figure it out here."

She nodded. Waiting for more.

"Like, I know there are things I want to make," I continued. "But I don't know how they're going to get made yet. You know? Like. I don't know." I scratched my head. Shrugged.

"It's okay," she said suddenly, splaying her hands out in a surrender gesture. "I didn't mean to put you on the spot, man. It's not a big deal. I'm just nosy as fuck."

"That's cool," I told her.

"I'm gonna be an animator," she said. "I thought that might be your thing, too, judging by your stuff. You'd be really good."

"Really?"

"Yeah, man. *Animate.* What else is there?"

I felt lucky that Mel was talking to me in the first place, had *chosen* to talk to me. If she believed in something, it had to have credibility. I shook my head anyway. "But you're so talented," I told her.

She laughed. Pawed, still upside down, at a pack of Zebra Cakes. "I don't think they let you do it if you suck. Here. Lemme see that sketch from class today."

She rose, made a grabby hand at my backpack. I pushed it to her and she rummaged through. Fished out the sketch and held it up, studying it, chewing thoughtfully for a moment. She tilted the sketch toward me. "Imagine your dog," she said. "Right here. See, you've already got the beginnings. The sort of hazy quality here, right around his feet. The paws are where they are now, but you've made this, like, tension. There's this *potential* to move. You were thinking about his next step, even when you were drawing him like he is. Weren't you?"

She gestured to the paws, the wavery sense of them I spent hours getting just right. It was true. It was what I thought about whenever I sat down to draw something. The story. Where has this been? Where is it going next? I'd never said it aloud, but somehow Mel had known.

"It's the greatest thing you can do for something," she said. "Giving it movement. Possibility."

She handed the sketch back. Looked at me very seriously for a moment, considering me. She said it again. "You'd be really good."

I held her gaze, unsure of where to take all this. Finally I lurched over her, snatched the Zebra Cakes, and crammed one in my mouth. I stared at her. "I fotched me your Ding Dong," I told her.

She giggled. "*Fotch*. Holy hell, what'd you do, roll around in a big pile of *Hee Haw* before you came to college?"

Mel twisted over me and reached for her backpack. Pulled out a handful of VHS tapes. Handed one to me. "Put it in."

I slid it into my roommate's VCR. Mel closed her eyes, smiled at the heavy, comforting click of it snapping into the gears. "That's the best sound in the world," she said.

The screen blinked dirty gray. A sinister, heavy-eyed duck, a methy Daffy, wears a trench coat in an alley. A lady rounds a corner, he flashes her. She screams. He turns slowly to the viewer, something in his movement a little jerky, a little slow, and grins. You can almost see the frames flicking to make the shift. "What is this?" I asked Mel.

"*Dirty Duck*. 1974. Offshoot of that whole *Fritz the Cat* San Francisco alt-comic thing. R. Crumb and all that."

I had no idea what she was talking about. But I nodded anyway.

"I've always kind of liked how it looks. It's gritty. I like how you can see someone, somewhere, actually *drawing* this. You know?"

I nodded again.

"Have you ever seen *The Maxx*?" Mel said.

I started, nearly knocking over the can we'd been using as an ashtray. "You've seen *The Maxx*?"

Mel grinned at me. "Of course," she said. "That show was, like, a milestone, if you had cable and were a weird kid. Are you okay?"

"Yeah." I leaned over, wiping up ashes with tissues.

The Maxx was my favorite show, that summer I was ten, in the days of our house's fuzzy, unreliable cable. Not something my parents would have let me watch, had they been paying attention. The story of a superhero living in two separate but real dimensions: a grimy, dangerous metropolis in which he is homeless, and a wild jungle landscape in which he battles dark forces to protect his jungle queen, who in the city is his traumatized social worker.

It aired late-night when kids my age were supposed to be in bed. Alone in the living room while everyone else slept, I consoled myself in the light of the TV.

"Well, shit. I knew you had good taste," Mel said. "I got it. Let's break it out, man."

She found the tape, slipped it in.

The screen lit with the eerie off-black of prelude. The hairs on my arms stood up. It was like being in the room with a ghost. The screen crackled, two or three lightning bolts cutting through the high fuzz of the analog. Mel had taped it from her TV.

I was suddenly back in my parents' house, alone in front of the Magnavox, back when television had an end: the time of night at which it, and by extension we, went off the radar. The CBS affiliate played the national anthem, the flag rippling in the sky over idyllic shots of farmland and mountains. And then, the screen cuts to the green, creeping Doppler radar, the dread at the dead, single-note tone of sign-off.

It was while watching the show that the idea of being any kind of artist first occurred to me. Being wrapped in that story was the furthest I had ever been away from myself. That something could lift me out of my skin like that was a revelation. When I watched, I was able to *discorporate*—a word I would learn, and love, later on. I wanted that portal for myself, strange and private and good.

I felt tears come to my eyes. I turned away slightly, rubbed. Mumbled something about contact lenses.

Mel nodded. Kindly looked away. "Finding stuff by accident," she said. "That's how most people get started, I think. I stole *Dirty Duck* from one of my mom's boyfriends, back in the day. Someone gave it to him as a joke, because it had cartoon fucking in it. But I loved it as soon as I saw it. Started drawing right then."

She removed the last two cigarettes from the pack. Lit them both. Handed me one. "Instant love," she said. "That's how it works."

We sank into a cozy little vacuum, Mel and I, watching. I don't know if it was the cartoons themselves, or watching them with Mel, but that night was the closest I had felt to knowing what I wanted from my life. She was the first person to see me as I had always wanted to be seen. It was enough to indebt me to her forever.

I STIRRED ON MY dorm room bed with my first legitimate hangover, feeling like I was going to throw up on the floor. I saw the fuzzy outline of Mel sitting in front of the television, clicking through channels. I reached for my glasses.

She turned, hair matted. "Wakey wakey, eggs and bakey," she said.

"Did you even sleep last night?"

"I don't sleep. Not really."

We rose and walked slowly to the Student Center. Campus was silent. Through the glass panels of the center, we could see undergrads in ones and twos, eating cereal around the canteen.

Mel cleared her throat. "Listen. So, uh, let me know if you ever want to work on something. You know? Like partner up? Do some cartoons?"

It was a strange, shy moment. We didn't look at each other—she stared at the ground, sort of shuffling her sneakers. I glanced over my shoulder at the center. It was quiet until I said, "Yeah. Okay. Why not?"

Mel grinned, bobbed her head. "Awesome. Yeah, you have a good head for this stuff, I think. Okay. We can get together and, you know, brainstorm. Like maybe this weekend?"

"Sure." I nodded toward the center. "I better go throw down some weak coffee and a Hot Pocket before I croak."

"Right on," she said. "See you." And she flapped back toward Hagen, platinum hair dodging and weaving. I watched her walk away for a minute before turning and going inside.

OUR FILTHY DIRTY PARTY

WE'RE HIDING IN THE POWDER ROOM AT THE ST. REGIS HOTEL. This is what working in what amounts to a rat's nest for the past decade has done to us, I think, looking at our reflections in the mirror. Ten years in a piece-of-crap studio in the armpit of Bushwick with full view-and-sound of the JMZ train, giving ourselves humpbacks craning over our drafting tables, Camels drooping from our mouths, passing expired packages of Peeps back and forth in the dark. The work has made me forget *how to act like a person.* We're not fit to go out and socialize with the fancy people, all Cheetos-stained hands and dilated pupils.

"Here." Mel hands me her pipe, the one shaped like a squirrel she picked up from a troubled-looking Village store that sold cheap dildos and off-brand candy. "Chug it," she demands. "Pull on that motherfucker like you *mean* it."

We, the recipients of the American Coalition of Cartoonists and

Animation Professionals' Hollingsworth Grant for our first full-length feature, *Nashville Combat,* are due onstage in less than an hour. And while we're happy—nay, grateful—this is not exactly our crowd. Hence, something to take the edge off.

I straighten, check the mirror again. We look better than usual. Damn near swank, even. I've managed to squeeze myself into a cocktail getup, wires and clips strapping boobs up and in, stylized girdle crackling my ribs like potato chips, all with my *sort of maybe* boyfriend, Beardsley, in mind, despite the fact that I haven't heard from him in over a week. We are known entities for what we do, which, specifically, is make "small, thoughtful cartoons and out-of-mainstream animation shorts intended for a thinking woman's audience" as mentioned in *The New York Times, BUST, Bitch, Dying Broke and Lonely Quarterly, Shitburger Review,* et al.

Mel's in a tux, hair all butched up, specs folded away in her pocket. She's the dashing one. She's crafting a joint for later, running her tongue along the adhesive side of the rolling paper. Pulls the joint away and begins to twist with her fingers. Looks at me in the mirror. "What."

"You look like a dykey George Burns."

"Words hurt." She slips the joint into her breast pocket. "You look pretty, *Sharon.* How's *that* make you feel?"

"You lie."

She throws herself on the love seat, legs splayed, fiddling with her bow tie. "ACCAP is a poor acronym, don't you think? Sounds like hocking up a wad of snot."

"I'm sure they have enough cash not to care." I adjust a bra strap, shift the girdle, try to breathe. Mel gestures for the squirrel. I hand it to her.

She takes a hit, straightens to hold the toke. "Sit down and relax," she says on the intake.

"*You* relax." I snip at the air with a bottle of Febreze I find under the sink. The St. Regis is too classy for its own good. I feel like we're hemorrhaging money just standing here.

There's a knock at the door. Mel bellows, "In use!"

"Guys, open up. I need a minute with you two."

It's our agent, Donnie. Short for Donatella. She took us on as clients after she saw our first cartoon, *Custodial Knifefight,* online when we were in college. A crossbow is posted beside the Wellesley diploma above her desk. She says the word *cock* a lot, but in the pejorative, when something goes wrong: "This isn't worth *cock*." She chews nicotine gum and drinks a steady stream of Diet Cokes. A can of it is sweating in her hand as she steps in, wearing a slate-colored pantsuit and a pair of heels that cost more than our studio rent. Her hair, the same length as Mel's, is glossy and feline, combed back. She crinkles her nose. "Are you two smoking up in here?"

Mel says, "Nope."

I look at the floor and whisper, "Yes."

Donnie rolls her eyes. Our relationship with Donnie used to operate largely by email, but she's recently begun accompanying us to parties, functions, giving us advice on what to wear, how to speak. She's grooming us for bigger times, and we've been tripping behind her all the way, playing the part of the brilliant, wayward animators, letting her attribute our fuckups to artistic preoccupation—both a kind assessment and a lie. "Just have some coffee when you come out, okay?"

Mel salutes. I feel my face go hot, nod.

Donnie puts her handbag on the vanity and checks her lipstick. "You two wouldn't happen to be hiding in here, now, would you?"

Mel slips the squirrel back in her pocket. Shoots her cuffs, wrings out her shoulders. I see her hands tremble slightly. "Please," she says.

Truth is, all this good luck has made us both a little gun-shy. When Donnie told us we'd won a Hollingsworth, it was like she pulled an atomic bomb from her pocket and flicked it on the ground. The grant is $350,000. We've just spent the past decade throwing ourselves into the blinding headlights of our work, wondering if it was ever going to happen for us, wondering if it wouldn't be the smart thing to quit. Eating meals and drinking coffee at our drafting boards, getting by on a podunk grant here, some freelance work there, the inheritance Mel's aunt left her when she died once saving us from eviction. Increasingly convinced that our lives, as they were, were as good as they were ever going to be.

The Hollingsworth is almost *too* good. There's the feeling that it's either saved us or ruined us. We walk into the night knowing that, cult status or no, *Nashville Combat*'s on a limited run, and grants don't mean shit unless people actually go out and see this thing. It's hard to escape the feeling that if we don't come up with an amazing idea for our next project, it could all end here. So cautiously, carefully, we dress up and take the subway to Manhattan. Toddling with pants down into our uncertain future.

Donnie caps her lipstick and turns to us. "Ladies," she says. "They're waiting for you out there. Time to join your party."

I REMEMBER THAT NIGHT in flashes—whether because I was drunk (possible) or because that's just how I remember everything now (also possible).

In memory, I am a spectator, watching the tops of our heads bob through the banquet hall. Mel leads the way, the only person I've ever seen who walks like the theme from *Sanford and Son* is playing on a loop in her head, through a crowd of clean-cut patrons and artists wearing Chucks with nine-hundred-dollar suits, their dates in silk boutique dresses. Getting our picture taken with Donnie and collective reps and foundation officers. Mel with her mouth open, hair bleached and cowlicked all to hell, me a sad-sacked, big-tittied Haggis McBaggis with unspeakable split ends. Playing off each other when introduced. It's the Vaught and Kisses Show: I'm the straight man, Mel's the wild card, we joust, we get laughs.

I take an occasional look around for Beardsley. Mel glances at me, irritated, knowing who I'm looking for. Mel believing in the night, believing that I should be having a better time.

We're hustled backstage and put in a dark side wing to wait for our walkout. I can see the snub tip of Mel's nose, her long, sensitive fingers reaching out to toy absently with the end. Her hands make her the best draftsman I know, deft at the old-school, minute-by-minute sketches on which our work is built, the kind the old Warner Bros. studios once glorified. Had Mel been born sixty years earlier, and a man, she would have been a star: a prewar, chain-smoking, dame-ogling cartoon auteur. Not to say she's not comfortable in her own skin, but one gets the sense she's forever strumming on a wire in there, constantly trying to escape from some secret seam. It occurs to me, looking at her in the dark, that I may be the only person to see this, the only person able to get close enough to Mel Vaught in the wild to see the quivering underbelly.

I hear her let out a shaky breath. She's nervous. I reach out and make her take my hand. One of the board members is speaking on-stage.

"Their first full-length feature, *Nashville Combat,* is a true tour de force: equal parts angry and tender, funny and sorrowful, demonstrative of a thoughtful, skilled craftwork. Like its creators, the work seems older than its years. Vaught and Kisses have made known their allegiance to the ink-and-color tactics prized by classic animators, and the content of *Nashville Combat* is as compelling as its look— a story of modern womanhood, gay identity, family, criminality, and the travails of a late twentieth-century childhood. The vessel for these issues is co-creator Mel Vaught, who transcends autobiography to make something entirely new with her story of growing up poor in the Central Florida swamps with a delinquent mother who is incarcerated when Vaught is thirteen years old. It is dark, yet brilliantly funny, well crafted enough to let the light shine through the cracks."

The lights dim. A screen behind the podium flickers.

To us, the opening credits of *Nashville Combat* are like the voice of a friend. We know it immediately. We worried over the first two minutes for months, trying at least twenty different approaches before settling on the final cut. "What's the best way," Mel kept saying, "to get someone's heart rate up? Make them feel like someone's hovering just over their shoulder? *That's* what we need." We used distortion to fuzz the initial frames, making it look like a bad conversion from analog, like the old stuff we love, something best seen in a piss-drenched movie theater forty years ago, seats knifed to bits, carpet stained, a man with no face in a trench coat two rows behind you. The landscape is all smeared pastels, ink blobs—a dirty bizarro world, part *Ren & Stimpy,* part *Clutch Cargo,* part seventies German cartoon porno.

I can feel every year that has passed since we met in the first thirty seconds of the movie. All those nights in college we spent sketching, talking Tex Avery and the old school, dissecting everything from *The Simpsons* to Krazy Kat, tracking down lovely old Nickelodeon bumpers and watching them over and over, taking notes, finding out about production companies, learning how to track other artists, their techniques, their tics. We pored over all the gritty American International stuff, all the *Fritz the Cat* and *Heavy Traffic* we could handle. The grainy, ripped-off VHS and Betamax tapes I picked up on trips to Manhattan from hole-in-the-wall comic book shops and porn retailers back when a good chunk of the Village was still dangerous. The beginning of our work life together, the 2001-to-2002 school year, tinged with rising terror levels and TVs blaring, a raw feeling around the edges of everything. The first night we met. I look down at my arm. The hairs are standing up.

Onscreen, a skinny kid with a yellow bowl cut walks through a gas station. *My mom went to prison when I was thirteen years old,* the voiceover says—the voice being Mel's, of course; no one else could replicate that rippling, broken-glass sound. *I was probably lucky I didn't go with her.*

The kid's hand grasps a pack of Skittles and slips the candy into her pocket. Cut to an old guy at the counter, coffee-ground stubble on his cheeks, scratching at his newspaper with a pencil.

Cut to a shadowy form in a trucker hat meandering in the next aisle. A swath of light comes down just far enough so you can see his eyes, wily and blue, glint knowingly. *Meet Red Line Dickie,* the voice continues. *As far as Mom's boyfriends went, he was actually okay. He tolerated me, because he found me useful.*

The kid walks the next aisle, pockets a battery. Red Line does a little nod. They do a separate stroll for the door. Then, off-frame, the unmistakable click of a shotgun's safety being switched. The rumble: *"Tell your brat to empty his pockets."*

A close-up of Red Line's mouth: luscious, cruel lips, yellow teeth. Jaw unhinging softly as he bellows, *"Run!"*

The scene fragments, goes sharp and bright. There's the sound of shots fired—the frames go crimson at the pops—as Red Line and Kid Mel scrabble to a waiting truck. They throw themselves inside. The truck takes off.

Didn't even have time to tell him I was a girl, Mel's voiceover says.

In the motion of the truck, Red Line whips off his hat, reaches out his hand. Kid Mel smacks a bunch of batteries into it, then slowly removes the Skittles from her pocket and tips the contents, careening in the light, into her mouth. *Red Line taught me one of the most important lessons I ever learned,* the voice says. *Never work for free.*

"Mel Vaught and Sharon Kisses," the announcer says. Someone pushes us out, and there we are.

I've seen the footage: the way Mel steps up to the mic, blinking, eyes almost rheumy under the lights (we are both breathtakingly stoned), hair blinding white, and me behind her (looking really good, actually, I can see that now; mouth painted red, hair piled high, *giggling*). She's handed the Hollingsworth platter. Speaks briefly, gestures to me. It seems, on film, that I need to be beckoned, that I don't want to speak. She has to pull me in, hand on my lower back: *Go.*

In the recordings, I don't look anything like how I felt that night, so well concealed am I below the layers of manners and makeup. I don't trust myself to diverge from the script. I can't be funny like Mel; God knows if I tried I'd blow my load on a knock-knock joke. So I make my remarks short: *Thank you, you don't know how much this means.* Something forgettable, something *I* forget right after I watch the video. But whatever it is, I mean it.

W E SKIP THE OFFICIAL after-party and take it back to the powder room for half of Mel's joint on the way out to the real party, in Bushwick. I put my hair up, tug it back down. Muck up my eyeliner, glance in the mirror to find I resemble Alice Cooper. Redo. Descend into the subway to sweat it all off.

It's Friday night. The L train is full of surly girls in minidresses and young, loosened-tie professionals. We hang from the pole entering the tunnel, letting our bodies sway with the train's stops and starts. Walk in companionable silence in the dark.

This party is in our honor to celebrate the grant. Our friends know how to throw down in varying, encompassing ways; Mel is not the only one who knows how to dance with the monkey, though many would argue that she does it best. We're mostly artists here, animators and editors and ink-and-color guys. Our friends have all brought their friends, writers from DC and Marvel, a few novelists watching from the periphery with slow pink eyes. There's the grad students we get for scut work, extra tracing and color help: Jimmy the Fire Maniac, quiet Indian John Cafree. Our digital team mills around the drinks table, giving us the two-finger hello in unison. Surly Cathie the sound tech is talking shop with an engineer named Allan Danzig, who claims to be third cousin to the musician. They all holler and wave.

And then there's actual applause. It makes me jump a little—the room rippling with whistles and hoots. All our friends are here, and they're happy for us. My stomach breaks into blossom. I forget the reception, I forget about Beardsley. Something wonderful has happened, and we have enough people in our lives who are made joyful by our success to fill a room. I am lucky, I think, with a stab of shame. I don't remember that enough.

Our draftsman buddy Fart approaches. I asked Mel once what his real name was. "That is his real name," she said. "Franklin Ambrose Randolph Turner. How's *that* for an acronym."

Fart grabs me in a bear hug and swings me off the ground. His Gregg Allman beard presses into my face. "Hey, boss," he yells, then reaches out and noogies Mel hard. "Congratulations, assholes!"

The factory is a former fax machine assembly site. Fireworks someone brought back from down South are whistling off the roof. We're in Barren Brooklyn, all chain-link fences and loading docks and aging signage.

From the roof, the Brooklyn–Queens Expressway is a dark river humming in the distance. A Black Cat spins and pops, tossing sparks. Someone breaks a bottle—not intentionally, not yet, that won't start until Mel is blackout-boot-scootin-boogie wasted. This is merely a party foul, the night's first, and the people yell thusly.

Mel grabs someone's top hat, slaps it onto her head, and lights a couple of sparklers. "What it do, baby," she hoots, jutting her hips alarmingly at an intern. A crowd circles her, bespectacled NYU and Brooklyn College kids, a few transplants from the design school in Rhode Island, all cradling fireworks. Mel's pretty, prettier than me, but the asshole act quashes any signals she accidentally, incidentally puts out. One night at a bar on the Lower East Side, a guy told her she looked just like that actress from the nineties, the one in *Tank Girl*. "That blond punky thing," he said slovenly. Mel told him he looked like Ned Flanders.

"Someone's losing a finger tonight," I say.

"It's not a party until body parts are separated." She wrings her hands at me, Italian-grandma-style. "So *sock* it." Hands me a bottle rocket. I give it back. Two of the interns have cigarettes tucked behind their ears in knowing imitation of Mel, who tends to have this effect on the young. She begs tribute. I see at least one bleach-blond cut on a guy who was brunet last week; a lesbo haircut on a man turns out to be unremarkable.

I point to a bottle rocket. "Sorta close to a residential area, are we not?"

"Not *that* close."

"Ridgewood's like three blocks that way."

"So?"

The interns look to me expectantly. "So?"

"Look at you." Mel grabs my face. "So concerned. Let's give her a hand. Sharon Kisses, everyone." She smooches me hard and smacky on the forehead, scampers away. The interns run after her.

I leave Mel on the roof with her followers and go downstairs to see if Beardsley has arrived. No dice. I meander, taking a deep schwag hit from a passing bong, retreating to the drinks table to fill a coffee mug from a box of merlot. The party has become its own entity; we have been forgotten, the room has filled with strangers, each younger and thinner and hipper than the one before. Shit. I'm already itching to escape.

Soon after Mel and I started working together, I realized my virtue was in my constancy. Mel is smarter than me, but I *know* more than she does. I have a knack for cleanliness, perfect portions. Chronology, arc, storyboarding—those are my areas of expertise. I'm the one who builds the narrative, keeps us on its track. But sometimes I get tired of my role in this partnership. Mel's having all the fun—she has no issues with these horseshit hipster parties—while I'm the steady guy, taking care of the admin stuff, making the appointments. Cleaning up the messes. It is a central truth I've both known and feared for years: The heart-and-soul skill of it all is not something I do as well as Mel, who is still the best I've ever seen. All that goofing off and fucking around belies the focus within. In her own hidden way, Mel is the most serious person I know.

I worry it's written all over my face, when people see us together in places like this. Mel's the *real* artist. I'm tagging along. In weaker moments, I actually allow myself to feel envy. God knows I don't want her life, her particular burdens, but her talent, what she makes look effortless. As if everyone could do this shit, and do it tomorrow.

I feel instant guilt. She's your best friend, I tell myself. If you were wiped off the face of the earth tomorrow, she's the only one you are sure would miss you.

Mel reappears downstairs with a blender full of her special Robitussin cocktail, an unspeakable combination of gin, cough syrup, fruit brandy, gummy bears, God knows what else. As many different things as she's snorted, swallowed, injected, and inhaled, Mel still goes for the drugstore option first, her favorite kind of high, that smooth, out-of-body tussin lift—that feeling of cruising through the softened world. More people stumble in, holding out wine-spackled party cups. A few simply open their mouths and crane back while Mel pours and shuffles to the ridiculous vintage mix someone's put on: throwbacks to the first Bush administration, grade school, the

Running Man. She does the Axl Rose Snake Shimmy, the Ian Curtis Crazy Arms, the Wayward Pizza Boy. "Do *you* want a slice? Do *you* want a slice?"

Suddenly everyone's dancing, frenzied. A bizarre, sweaty Prince impersonator vogues very, very hard in the midst of bystanders. Fart gets down on all fours and Mel rides him around the room, screeching, "Lookit me! I'm Roy Rogers!" Her iPhone flies out of her pocket and hits the floor with a glassy crack.

There's an excited scramble when someone puts on Guns N' Roses. Mel stops, puts her hands in the air for "November Rain." Her jam and hers alone. Gives me the double-gun salute. *You know,* she's saying. *You. Know.*

How do all parties get to this eventual point for me? I've spent one of the best nights of my life checking the door for someone who never came. I'm not supposed to be at the margins anymore. I am thirty-two years old. This shrinking feeling was supposed to have been absolved by now.

I put my cup down and slip away.

On the street corner, I fish out a cigarette. I think I'm alone when I see movement from my periphery.

A couple is entwined nearby, vigorously making out. They move their faces apart when they see me. The girl grapples with the guy's belt loops, talking into his ear. Stops when he stops. Says, "Who?"

I look away politely. Dig around for my Bic.

The taller figure steps away, looking in my direction. When I glance up, I see the chin, the stubble outlined against the streetlight at the corner. It's Beardsley.

The girl is small, raggedy-cute. She shakes her hair out of her face and looks over her shoulder, irritation scrunching her nose. Half my size, easily.

I take a deep breath and run back into the building.

I skip the industrial crank elevator, last service date *10.4.92,* dart up the stairs. Back to the party, which has dialed down a few decibels; Danzig spits Robitussin into a corner, yells, "That shit is *vile.*" Indian John is throwing up out a window while Surly Cathie pats his back, rolling her eyes. Mel materializes from the crowd. Opens her arms as she comes toward me.

"I have to go," I tell her.

"Why? This party's fuckin rad."

My face crumples. It is a college moment, public and embarrassing. "Beardsley's outside. He's with someone."

Mel grimaces and ushers me into a side room, closing the door. It's an ancient workspace, a metal table pushed to one wall, a couple of bolt-legged stools nearby. A yellowing map of the five boroughs is nailed to the wall, one corner listing off. "Okay," she says. "Tell me what happened."

I give her the rundown while she props herself up on the table, arms crossed over her chest. When I'm done, she sighs, rubs her eyes. "Well, this confirms it," she says. "Beardsley is a bottom-feeding cocksuck."

I fold at the middle and cover my face.

"Sorry," she says. "Sorry sorry." She pats me on the back. "I'm sorry. Were this not such a good night, frankly, I'd go out and stomp his ass. But then that would be all we'd be able to remember." She guides me to a stool, presses her mug of Robitussin shake into my hands. "Sharon. It's okay. To be honest, I didn't think you guys were, like, official or anything. Which I thought was a good thing. Because that guy's a toolbox."

"You didn't think we were serious?"

"You slept together, what, like once? Right?"

I let out a sound, rub my face.

"I'm sorry," she repeats. "Fuck. That wasn't the right thing to say."

Mel's always hated Beardsley. She hasn't liked most of the men I've dated, but Beardsley she gave her special ammunition, slinging shit he was too dumb to take as anything but good-natured when it was, in fact, genuine hostility. "I just get a sour feeling from that guy," she told me once. "He's so obvious. You're talented, and he wants it to rub off on him. He's trying to dig it out of you with his cock."

She leans over, glasses at the end of her nose. "Sharon. Don't do that thing you're doing right now."

"What am I doing."

"That *thing*. You know what I mean, man. That *down the rabbit hole* thing." She makes her fingers walk down a flight of stairs, doing a little Johnny Carson gaze at me, lips screwed to one side, then claps her hands and makes a raspberry fart explosion with her lips. "You're gonna needle this down to dust in your head. I am telling you, it's not worth it. Not every guy is worth an atomic explosion. Zoom out. He's nowhere near the price tag you're hanging on him. You need to *not* do this with your night. Okay?"

I nod, trying to breathe.

She pinches me lightly. "You gonna spend your party hanging out in here?"

I roll my eyes, wipe my nose. "Everyone in there knows this grant is all you."

I see her mouth scrunch as she scoots back on her chair. "Bullshit," she says quietly. "I hope that's not what you're really worried about here. You're the best there is and that's the whole story, sugar booger. I can't keep telling you so if you don't listen."

Chastised. I lean over, try to put my head between my knees.

"Let's hang out here for a minute. I need to try to fix this thing anyway." She produces her iPhone, now in three pieces, and empties her pockets: a knot of rubber bands, a Swiss army knife, a square of putty. Pushes her glasses on top of her head and starts with the bands, nimbly snipping them into ribbons. I watch dully as she braids three bands around the phone, binding all pressure points. She jabs the power button. Nothing happens. She cusses under her breath. "We may have to share your phone for a while," she says grimly.

Here's the hard truth, if you are a woman: Being an artist, even a good one, doesn't get you dick. Your stock may rise, but there is no corresponding spike in tail. Other than the lesbian contingency, of course, we're all screwed. On the world will spin while every hair on my snatch goes gray as a mule.

I know what I'm up against here. I'm *dumpy*. A guy like Beardsley, well bred and moneyed with a wardrobe frayed in all the right places, was always out of my league, even in spite of his wannabe-artist status—a year at Brown, a transfer to RISD. Glowing credentials, but no finished products to call his own. Nothing with the flight or abandon of what we do.

Mel flicks at her phone, sighs. "This thing is shot." But she springs her knife open to the screwdriver hidden in the side, replaces her glasses. "At least tell me this. What is it about him, in particular, that's getting to you?"

More truth: I have an infatuation problem.

It's not just Beardsley. It's all of them. I've felt this for a hundred other men—the rush of the encounter, the way my stomach heats and bubbles, the adrenaline, the urge to run five miles and move my bowels and puke at the same time. It's a frenzy for the story and what it could be. The ability to escape from my life, the chance at a grand renovation of self within another person. It's the sense of possibility, so good it feels like it will salvage everything. How hard it is to beat the dream. How it traps you. It's embarrassing. It's lonely. It's unsatisfying. It's impossible. At day's end, I just want a life where I'm laughing and eating and coming *all the time*. I could do this for the rest of my life—this rise and fall, defined increasingly by what I cannot have.

If I told Mel all this, she would understand. She gets the chase, but she lives it in front of the drafting board; the prey is the idea. I feel it, too, when we're working long hours, hot on the trail. But the work alone has never felt like enough for me.

There's a knock at the door. Surly Cathie pokes her head in. Smirks at Mel. "Baby break her phone?"

"I'm a fan of that mustache you're growing," Mel tells her. "It's a real vag-grabber."

"That guy from *Time Out New York* is here. Maybe you guys should go talk to him before you're too sloppy to put a sentence together."

When Cathie sees me sniffling, she makes her face go blank and drops her eyes. Mel stands and stretches, tossing her iPhone onto the table. "Thanks, *hon*." Turns to me. "I got this. Have a smoke, calm down. Come back out and we'll make Fart buy us tacos from the truck."

Mel closes the door behind her. The room is quiet, the only sound the thumping of the stereo system rattling the metal door in its frame.

When I'm sure I'm alone, I heft my shoulder bag from the floor and sift through until I reach the bottom, where I know it will be— a beat-to-hell, unruled eight-and-a-half-by-eleven Moleskine sketcher's diary, the first I ever bought, now held together by a fraying Goody hair band. I put my head down and listen for a moment to make sure Mel's not coming back before I open it.

I need to see the List.

I call it the List, though it is, in form and function, no list. It is not itemized; it's barely chronological. It is a junk drawer, my offal pile, my brain-gnawing archipelago of fuckery. My greatest ongoing work, to be completed never.

The List is a secret compendium of every man with whom I have ever fallen in love.

It began as a comfort project in the wake of the great Zack-from-Kansas rejection of December 2001 (a dismissal that bit because it unfolded in exactly the manner I had expected it to—he was spotted, unawares, making out with the Hallmark blonde at a party; I ran off, thus beginning a long and distinguished history of scuttling away crying). The idea was born of a combination of grief and the brand-new sense of enterprise that being in college, Mel's collaborator, and newly committed to being an *artist* had given me. I decided I would draw him out of my head and make it so good I would be done with him.

Rubens's primary medium was not oils but women—the pale, peaked bodies of well-fed girls. My medium is dick. The men are the impetus: from the fifth grade, when I was in love with Teddy Caudill, the List's patron saint, to the present. Every floundered crush and ill-advised infatuation is documented. And the hot, rock-hard rejection, ever present from age thirteen on: my love life, as it is, largely a spectator sport. Once I drew one, I had to draw them all: I did the same for the next guy, and the next, and all the ones who came before. The

List deepened, became richer and more fetid. Like the best projects, it grew its own horrible legs.

The man is always in the middle, captured in realistic strokes. Mel once told me my style reminded her of R. Crumb, his ability to sketch accurate form in feature and proportion yet maintain a few merry cartoon elements—thick, goony smiles, a bulbous nose. I've paid good-natured attention to sneaker toes, gummy iPhone cases, the horned edges of boutique specs. Some smile. Others slump. A few glance off the page accusingly, as if aware they've been pinned for observation. Stats dance along the edge: ACT scores, favorite books, shoe size, names of exes. Breakup method. Jack is at a Coney Island shooting gallery, gaping, surrounded by snarling stuffed chimps and bears. Pavel splays in the booth of a Midtown coffee shop, leg bent, knee cocked up; his hamburger opens up on his plate, teeth visible, readying to bite him. Steven stands in front of a crumbling factory in Bushwick, the windows of which are screaming.

But about ten pages in, the List becomes something else, veers into even darker, more alien territory. Unseemly things appear. A knife in a bed of flowers. The tip of a rifle emerging from a page's edge. One begins to see things they immediately wish they hadn't, the snuff film you should not have watched by yourself: next to number 58, a long, dark oak chest, the shadow of which stretches over half the page, a snake dripping out over one side.

Above number 69, a lock set into wood stares out, an eye with no pupil.

Around number 5, a series of tiny hands; on each, a solitary finger broken.

The head of number 32 floats in a sea of blackbirds, neck and shoulders disappearing behind flutters of dark wings.

Number 87 lost in a forest in which each tree is the torso of a woman, growing from a stump.

Number 43 drives a dark minivan down a mountain road, hundreds of arms drooping from the windows, the front bumper a set of teeth.

This is what I am compelled to draw. The things that come to me out of the dimness, what I see on the inside of my eyelids after press-ing them with my hands, my automatic writing. The List is the thing I make for no one, in a place no one can see; a dark, constant discov-ery. Even on days when I can barely stand to look at it, it is one of the few things in my life that enthrall me.

Teddy Caudill makes appearances throughout—as gatekeeper, or bystander, or both. I have trouble recalling his face after so many years, but I sketch him with tenderness—his blond head tilting, arms outstretched, as he sails heavenward from a trampoline; he leaps over a flock of geese. He looks on, a tiny head in a locket, at numbers 14, 27, 81. His hands peel an orange in one panel, his sneakers, grass-streaked and worn, crumple in another. The lost ideal: Teddy, my whisper of peace.

It's all pencil, my first, best method. The pages have achieved a satin quality, thick and polished. I've encased some of the brittle early sketches in plastic, sewn loose pages together with thread. There are multiples of some, revisions I could not help but execute, all done with the utmost care. No eraser tracks, no stray pencils markings. No hackery. Pristine.

I can feel myself circling some untouchable, hidden part of myself in this; the danger is part of the allure. God knows what's hidden in there, what I might find if I dig hard enough.

For a while, I told myself that the List was a maybe-sort-of proj-ect instead of a compulsion. Something Mel and I might turn into a cartoon, if I ever got the guts to show it to her. But I knew what the List was; or, at least, how it felt. In a word: predatory. Upending these men, placing them into a story that was not theirs but mine, and a murky, troubling story at that. It has never been seen by any-one else; it is not meant to be seen.

In her weird, exhibitionist's way, Mel likes the *intimacy* of what we do, of placing herself at the center of what we make. I love the work for the opposite reason: for the ability it gives me to abandon myself, to escape the husk of my body and fly off into the ether. I know a day of work has been really good when I have to look up from the board and recall who I am and what I'm doing.

That very few of these guys actually made it into my life beyond the pages of this book constitutes a failure, something I wasn't able to do like normal people. If hope is desire with expectation, then the List is a hopeless thing. I desire blindly, with wild, flinging abandon, but no aims, no goals.

It has—at least—a form.

I sketch Beardsley quick, as I saw him tonight in the streetlights. I have plans for him. Rising up from the center of a lake, in robes, humped fish surrounding him like coyotes. There, I think. Now you really are mine, Beardsley. You stupid shit.

There's a thin, clear light coming through the room's dirty window. It's dawn. I'm still looking at the sketch when my phone rings. I pick it up without looking. "Yeah."

"Is this Sharon?"

"Yes."

"We were given this number by Dana at Independent Artists Agency? We're looking for Melody Vaught."

My watch reads seven-thirty A.M. I look up. Mel's iPhone lies cracked side up on the table. "Her phone's busted."

The voice hesitates. "We haven't been able to get ahold of her, and we really need to." I hear the twang now. Shit. A collections agency. "I'm calling from the Central Florida Women's Correctional Facility clinic regarding Kelly Kay Vaught?"

I stare at the wall, totally useless, until it hits me: Mel's mom.

"Ma'am? Are you still there?"

"I'm sorry. Yes, I'm still here. What about Kelly Kay?"

"Ms. Vaught passed away yesterday evening. Melody is listed as her next of kin."

The woman gives me a phone number, an address, stresses Mel's need to be there to identify the body. I feel like my ears are stuffed with cotton. We hang up before I realize I did not ask how she died.

I wonder if Kelly Kay had seen *Nashville Combat*. I wonder if she died knowing that her daughter made a movie about her. I wonder if she died while her daughter was on a stage, accepting an award, blinking blindly into the bright lights.

FLORIDA

I TELL MEL IN THE DARKNESS OF A CAR SERVICE SEDAN THAT HER MOTHER IS dead. I can't see her face, only the pinched white shape of it in the passing streetlights. The inability to see her, more than anything, makes me afraid.

"What?" she says.

I scrabble. "I'm so sorry."

I see her mouth open, her chest rise and fall a few times, hands opened long and pale on her lap. She lets out a sharp sound, something close to a laugh, but she's not smiling. "You're kidding," she says. "Right?"

"No."

Chest goes up, down, up. "You're sure."

"Someone at the agency gave them my number. I think they tried you. Your phone."

She runs a hand through her hair and exhales hard. I smell a combination of rum and Robitussin. "Shit. I forgot about my fucking phone."

"Yeah."

She blinks, facing the road. "What happened?"

"You know, I feel really stupid. I didn't ask. They said something about complications before surgery?"

"She was going to have surgery?"

"Apparently?" How long had it been, exactly, since Mel had last spoken to her mom?

I go to hug her, but I get as far as grabbing her hand and stop. I use my other hand to fish out smokes. We both light up when the driver says, "No smoking in the car."

"Just let us out," Mel tells him.

We start walking down Knickerbocker, Mel a few yards ahead. "Mel," I call. It's early morning. Everything has a gray unreal quality, usual boundaries knocked aside. I grab her hand again.

She repeats, "Are you *sure*."

"Yes."

One corner of her mouth jerks. She puts her hands through her hair again. Mutters, "Jesus Christ."

We get to the studio and we're hit with the smell of our home—mildew, coffee grounds, ink. It's a mess. Clothes strewn everywhere, non-photo blue pencils rolling off the table onto the floor, cigarette butts at the bottom of High Life bottles. Mel pulls out her duffel bag. I watch her bang around the room for a moment, throwing things—underpants, socks, a bottle of Teacher's I didn't know she had—into it. This is Mel's way: not mood swings but peaks and valleys, control and then controlled fury and then uncontrolled fury. But the air this morning is different, precarious and swollen with blood. We're coming up over the mountain now. She can't find something she's looking for. She bangs around, muttering, "Son of a whore," and I ask her, "Can I help? What are you looking for?" And she just shakes her head and mutters, "It's fine, it's goddamn *fine*." And there's more thuds and a tennis shoe is thrown at the wall, then a sketchpad, then a bottle of contact solution, then she kicks the wall and screams,

"Fuck," and then she ducks into the bathroom and stays in there for twenty minutes.

I go outside, head churning, to crouch on the sidewalk and smoke. I call Avis and rent a car. I hear the lady in the basement apartment moving things in her kitchen. I watch the traffic glow, beads falling down a string on the BQE.

It occurs to me that if Mel has any family members to call, I don't know about them. There are times when, after more than ten years, I'm not sure I know Mel at all. But I do know enough to leave her alone right now.

Finally she comes downstairs, duffel packed, hair combed back, the bottle of Teacher's sloshing in one fist. She uncaps, takes a pull, hands it to me.

"Well," she says. "We should probably get out of town."

I PUT THE ADDRESS for the Central Florida Women's Correctional Facility on the dashboard and take 278 out of the city, cross the Verrazano, and hit the New Jersey Turnpike. Pass the power plants glinting in the sun, then surge into the countryside, everything too bucolic for an hour outside New York City. Mel is quiet, drinks, fiddles with the radio a bit. We make it our business to not talk about where we are going or why. I look down when we reach a Pennsylvania town with a long German name and am surprised to find myself still wearing a cocktail dress.

We gas up and pull into a Rite Aid. Mel troops alongside as I grab a basket, toss in Chex Mix, vitamin C, Dexatrim. She scrunches her nose, waggles the pills at me.

"I've larded up," I say. "Some have clearly taken note."

"Some people wouldn't take note of their own ass with two hands and a flashlight. Pardon the expression."

I grab a bottle of orange juice and push it into her hands. She looks at it doubtfully. "No sale, dude."

"You'll drink it and you'll like it."

I hear her mumble something about taking a big ole bitch injection as we approach the counter. A woman of maybe seventy with blue hair and a large silver cross around her neck picks up our basket. She scans slowly, turning the pills upside down, searching for the bar code. I train my eyes on the rows of Winstons and Pall Malls over her shoulder, feeling Mel wavering behind me. Between Brooklyn and this Rite Aid, she's managed to get herself completely soused, even more than she was last night.

I swipe my credit card. Too slow. The cashier looks to me, glum. "You need to swipe a-giyin."

"Did you know," Mel says loudly, voice garbled. "Did you know my mom didn't want me to be an animator?"

I smile tightly at the cashier. I've heard this story before. "You've said."

"She thought it was weird," Mel continues. "No, actually, you wanna hear what she really said? She said it was a *faggy* thing to do. Brilliant, right?"

The cashier's eyebrows lift. The receipt prints. She reaches for a bag.

"I mean, she's one to be giving career directives," Mel says, gathering steam. Here we go. The vitriol too nuclear to go in *Nashville Combat,* following us into a Pennsylvania Rite Aid. "Like she had any perspective outside of which brand of cream works best on recurring chlamydia."

The cashier freezes and stares at Mel. An open plastic bag hangs loose in her hand.

"We don't need a bag, thanks." I push Mel toward the exit.

Back in the car, I pop a Dexatrim. I'm an old pro at speeding and staying up all night to work. I figure driving across seven states shouldn't be much different. Mel's asleep before we hit West Virginia. I'm grateful. I still don't know what to say to her—what would matter, what might help. Mel's not in the habit of spilling guts. The only thing to do, for now, is to keep moving forward.

I'm freaked enough that my driver's hands have taken me down the interstate path I know best—through Pennsylvania toward Ohio—before I realize my mistake. It would take too long to backtrack; the only solution is to charge forward. During one of her stints of wakefulness, I confess to Mel what I've done. She merely wipes her nose with the back of her hand, lets the hand fall with a smack down to her thigh, and shrugs.

"Well, she's not going anywhere," she says.

We press down Ohio through Cincinnati's river valley and into Kentucky by the afternoon. Mel dozes on and off through three interstate changes, finally stirring on I-75. "Trivia," I say. "We are less than five hours from the birthplace of Abraham Lincoln. And less than three from mine."

"Rad." She closes her eyes. Resumes snoring.

I stop for gas again south of Lexington, throw her a pack of four-dollar Benson & Hedges. She blinks, looks around. The land has exploded into bright green elevation. Trim roadside acres lined with white slatted fences. Two men in Carhartt jackets and boots tend to a sleek, knobby Thoroughbred.

"Iddint that pretty," Mel says. She lights two of the smokes, sticks one in each corner of her mouth, barks, "I'm a walrus." Passes one to me. Her hand shakes.

Suddenly I am back home. First time in Kentucky in at least four years. I'm filled with unease, a horrible sixth sense hanging like gas since we hit the state line. I've always had the feeling that here, less is possible for me, that even the cars move slower.

I flick. The two men and horse retreat. The mountains are a jagged EKG on the horizon.

"It's like a postcard," Mel says.

I turn the engine. "Yep. Can't find a job but it's a goddamn Currier and Ives print everywhere you look."

"I take it we won't be stopping."

"We've got places to go."

"You sure? Don't want to see your mom or something?"

"Hah *hah*."

She shrugs. "All right, dude." Pitches her smoke, curls against the window, and goes back to sleep.

• • •

WE ARE WAVED THROUGH a security checkpoint and around the main facility, down a long concrete path to a separate building with a sign reading only MEDICAL SERVICES / FLORIDA DEPARTMENT OF CORRECTIONS. At the entrance, another checkpoint. We walk through a metal detector. A grim female security guard pats us down and relieves Mel of two airline-sized bottles of vodka. "I'm coming back to get those," Mel calls out. The guard narrows her eyes and throws them into a box. We are admitted.

Walking into the prison morgue is like entering a school, or a hospital: same industrial-grade lighting, same speckled linoleum, same two-piece office chairs skittering across Berber carpeting. I smell coffee grounds and the spike of bleach cleaner. It is all disquietingly *public*.

"Can I help you ladies?"

The woman at the desk is heavy, her makeup dark and slick. Kohl liner wings both eyes. A glittering cross hangs from each earlobe. There are rings on her fingers, mammoth QVC jobs. She smiles wide and easy at us.

Mel shifts beside me, but I refuse to speak. "I'm here to claim someone," she says finally. "Or, uh, someone's body, actually."

The woman purses her lips in sympathy. "Of course. Can you give me the name of the deceased?"

"Kelly Kay Vaught."

The lady gives her keyboard a few taps. "Okay. Are you a relative?"

"I'm her daughter."

"Melody." The lady straightens, reaches out to take Mel's hand in both her own. "I'm Lisa Greaph, the mortician on duty here. We're so sorry for your loss."

It's there on the name placard: G-R-E-A-P-H. I look at Mel. But Mel is distracted, slow. Her eyes trail from Lisa Greaph to the gray double doors behind her.

"If there is anything we can do in terms of guiding you through interment options, just say the word." She grasps my hand. I catch a whiff of White Shoulders. A framed cross-stitch of "Footprints" sits on her desk: *All that time, I was carrying you.* "Are you also a relative?"

I take a deep breath. Mel cuts in. "This is my partner." There's an uncomfortable pause. "My business partner. She can come with me, right?"

"Of course." Lisa Greaph gives me a warm little wink, turns. "The morgue is just through here, if you'll please follow me."

The double doors open to a white cinder-block hallway. Lisa Greaph sashays in front of us. She is dressed in head-to-toe plum muffled by a lab coat. She looks like a hairdresser suited up as a doctor for Halloween. "It's a little drab in here, I know," she says over her shoulder. "I've got a mind to petition to make this place a little airier. But we're a state facility. Gotta do what the big guys say."

Mel mumbles something under her breath. "It's okay," I say loudly.

Lisa Greaph smiles at us. It occurs to me that I can smell Mel. Pathos: corn dogs and Camel Lights. I wonder if Lisa smells what I smell.

She turns to Mel. "I worked in a salon before this." Called it. "And I'm glad. I have to use so many of those same skills here. A lot of ladies in the facility didn't maintain good diets or receive regular exposure to sunlight. And passing on takes the natural color from a body, you know. But I have to say, you wouldn't have to do much to pretty your mama up. She was gorgeous."

Mel snorts. "Looked better before she started doing crank."

Lisa Greaph hesitates. Her lab coat swishes. "Life's not easy," she says finally. "We do the best we can."

"Or not," Mel says.

I take Mel by the shoulder. I don't know if I want to shake her for being such an asshole or rein her in to keep her from bolting.

At the end of the hallway, another set of double doors. Lisa Greaph removes a large ring of keys from her belt, plucks one out with a shining fingernail. She pushes. There's a cold blast of air. I immediately think of nursing homes, the unmistakable scent of something nasty wiped up and scrubbed down. The lights are still fluorescents, but dimmed down a shade, like something's swallowing the power.

A stainless-steel table stands at the room's center. On the far wall, steel cabinets and a row of sinks, each large enough to bathe a small child. A series of dark tubes and hoses curls along the wall above them. One of those eyewash stations from high school chemistry.

To our left, rows of metal drawers with handles at their centers. It occurs to me that they are just about the width of a pair of human shoulders when Lisa Greaph, latex gloves straining over her fingernails, steps over and tugs one open.

It rolls out soundlessly. There's a table attached to the drawer face, about three feet wide. On it, a body draped with a blue sheet.

Lisa Greaph turns to Mel. "We just need your confirmation that this is your mother. Then we'll go from there."

We both freeze. No one's willing to go any closer until Lisa steps gently between us and pulls the sheet down with both hands.

It turns my stomach cold to see Mel's face in the still, slightly blue one on the table. Same nose curved at the end, cheekbones rising up Cherokee-style. The profile's gaunt, but it is obvious she was once beautiful, that she probably carried that beauty like women who know how pretty they are do—boldly, casually, ungratefully. A few lines crease around the eyes, deeper than sun wrinkles.

Her jaw is shut, but the possibility for movement is still loosely, dangerously there, as if her mouth could open at any moment. Several silver hairs cling to her temples. Her clavicle is a wide, knobby V, descending to meet points under the sheet.

Will I have to do this one day? Maybe not. It will probably be my sister. It's the women who do this job. My brother will be excused, left to wait in a living room elsewhere, television flickering on mute in a time of crisis. In order to spare me from being awakened in the middle of the night, they will call me the following morning. None of them know me well enough to know I'd probably still be awake.

I think of my dad's funeral, how he looked in his coffin, the strange way his lips were spread over his mouth. He'd worn dentures for years and was ashamed of this fact—never let anyone see him without them. They'd flown from his mouth in the accident, which happened my sophomore year at Ballister. The EMTs had misplaced them in the hurry to get him from the wreckage into the ambulance, and the mortician had no choice but to seal his lips over the void. It was the deadest-looking part of him, the only part that kept me from hoping he would wake up.

I step behind Mel and let her look.

"Is this your mother, Melody?" Lisa asks.

I hear Mel swallow. The back of her head is still. "Yeah."

The sheet is draped back over the body. The drawer wheels shut into the wall.

Lisa Greaph reaches behind her and produces a fat sheaf of forms. When Mel doesn't take them, she tucks them under her arm and says, "Why don't we step out? I'll make coffee."

There is a dim carpeted alcove off the entrance outfitted with a coffeemaker, a Xerox, and an elderly snack machine reading TOM'S! Lisa flicks a button. The sound of the drip cuts thinly through the room. We all stare at it for a moment before I gesture to Lisa's fingernails. "That's a very striking shade of purple," I say.

"Thank you!" She brandishes one hand, plump hip riding out cheerily. "It's my favorite."

"What's it called?"

"They called it Purple Rain at the salon."

"Nice." I turn to see if Mel will catch my eye this time. She doesn't.

I dig out quarters for a pack of Nutter Butters while Lisa Greaph spreads paperwork over the table, explaining the release forms, remains custody, marking the places requiring signatures. She gives Mel a copy of the death certificate. She explains the term *septicemia*.

Mel flips and scribbles. Says suddenly, "How long was she in the hospital?"

"After she was brought in? About four days."

"Was she awake for any of this?"

"For the first three. It was quick. That's probably why they didn't call you before. She asked that they not bother you."

Out of the cabinet, Lisa produces a round porcelain sugar bowl and a creamer with a mother-of-pearl spout. She gives each a quick wipe with a napkin before placing them on the table. "One of the outreach programs here at the prison is a crafts class. I teach it sometimes. On the second day, she was feeling good enough to ask for her yarn and needles. It's in the notes. Then the day before surgery was planned to repair some of the damage, she fell into a coma. Sometimes ruptures are delayed by bed rest, and then bothered by the least little thing. They think that's what happened. Even four days after the altercation."

"Altercation?" I ask.

"The wound happened during a fight." Lisa's eyes go wide. "Did the office not mention that?"

Mel leans back in her chair, legs splayed, rubs her eyes with one hand. Her other hand lies stretched toward her cup.

Lisa shakes her head. "That office. I swear. I wouldn't believe it, but they've actually done this before. I'm so sorry, Melody. I don't know exactly how it happened. The prison files separate reports for incidents, and you could find out from there. It was a puncture, I do know that, in her midsection. And it was made with a handmade instrument. Probably something with lots of little nooks and crannies that could do damage." She trails off. "She was just so sweet. Just as nice as she could be."

She pours. I raise the cup to my lips. This is not office coffee. This is a special reserve, something subtle and sweet Lisa Greaph has held back. I look at Mel. She's gnawing on her upper lip, coffee untouched.

"She knitted?" she says.

"Oh yes. She was getting good, too."

Mel is quiet. Then she says, "Do inmates have access to TV? Is there a satellite here or something?"

"There is a TV in the common room," Lisa says. "But no satellite. It's only network channels and then some other things, PBS and

QVC and Telemundo, mainly. I only know because the girls complain about it during craft class."

"Huh," Mel says. She picks up her cup, studies it, gnawing on her lower lip. I know what she's thinking, but I can't bring myself to ask for her.

She takes a deep breath and does it herself. "Did I mention that Sharon and I are filmmakers?"

Lisa smiles. Shakes her head.

"Well, cartoons. We make cartoons. We're animators. I, uh, hadn't been in touch with Mom in a while. I was curious as to whether she might have seen something we just made."

Lisa tilts her head in thought. "Well, I can't recollect many cartoons being shown on movie nights. That's out in the courtyard, during good weather? Most of the gals like romantic comedies. You know. Reese Witherspoon and such."

I have to stifle a giggle.

"What was the name of your all's movie?"

"Nashville Combat," Mel says.

"I don't believe I've heard of it, but it sounds interesting. What's it about?"

"It's about Kelly Kay." Mel traces her cup with one finger.

"Well, my goodness. That's every girl's dream, isn't it? To have a movie made about her?"

"It's about her being a whore," Mel says.

"Oh." Lisa's smile fades. I expect her expression to cool, but the look is soft, one of distinct pity. I shift in my chair. "Well, I'd say if you never told her about it, she never ran across it. The girls have Internet access, but only for short times, and mostly to email friends and family and what have you. Maybe she saw it there. But I don't know."

Mel closes her eyes briefly, then opens them. Grabs the pen and scrawls her name on the last page of the stack, unseeing.

Lisa looks back and forth between us, hesitating. "On the bottom of page five, there's an information box where it tells you how to contact the prison and get a copy of the report. It's only for family members. It takes a few months."

"You know what, we should go." Mel grabs the folder Lisa set out for her. "Thanks for, you know. Everything."

Lisa stands. "I hope you ladies didn't have far to come. Whereabouts do you live?"

"New York," I tell her.

"New York *City*?"

"Yes ma'am."

"Well, bless your heart." She gives my hand a squeeze. Turns to Mel, shakes her hand, then reaches out and grabs her by the arm, looks into her eyes for a long second. "I don't mind telling you," she says, "but I've got a feeling about you. I surely do." She pats her arm vigorously, still staring. "May the Lord bless you and keep you, Melody Vaught."

Mel coughs. "Right back at you." Turns and heads out the door.

I trail behind. Lisa touches my shoulder, purple fingernails glinting. "I'm glad she has someone to take care of her," she says in a low voice.

I cram the Nutter Butters into my bag. "Huh?"

"Bye-bye, now." The door swings shut.

We walk back to the car. The sun is round and low and hot. It hurts to face west. The soil is sand, crunchy under our shoes. There is green only in small patches, strong and spiny.

I look sidelong at Mel. I can't think of anything to say that doesn't sound dumb. The sun shines behind her head, her lips and jaw sharpening against the glow.

I swing over and bodycheck her, shoulder to hip. She walks through the stumble, grimacing a little at the ground.

"I picked cremation," she says.

"I think that's a good choice."

"Yeah. Well. I didn't feel like digging any big fucking holes in the ground anytime soon." She kicks gravel. "We got a platform now, should we ever need it. *Nashville Combat Two: Shanked in the Spleen.*" She laughs. It's a thin, glassy sound. "Come on. We were both thinking it on the way down. Right? Probably pulling some dumb bitch's hair trailer-park-style when she got stabbed. And it killed her. That's stupid, man." Mel's head bobs in time to her steps. "It's *embarrassing,* is what it is. I spend this whole trip ripping myself apart. Thinking about how she suffered. About how we hadn't talked in, like, years. And I made this thing about her and I have no idea how it might have made her feel, to watch it, you know? But now? I don't have a single solitary fuck to give, man. You live a stupid life, you will more likely than not have a stupid death. I get to mine her life for all it's worth now. That's what I get out of this." Her voice catches on something. She stops.

"Mel." I reach out, grab her hand, her shoulder.

She strides forward, shaking me off. "I'm gonna get those little bottles back. I'll meet you at the car."

I watch her slump away. We'll get a motel room for the night, then drive back tomorrow, back home for a few weeks. Then, on to the press tour. Taking our little show on the road. Maybe it's better than the alternative—anything to avoid New York for a while. Mel's big, dirty playground, where I could lose track of her far too easily. I shield my eyes, open the car door. I back away from the smell.

WHAT WE DID TO NPR

WHEN I FIRST IMAGINED WHAT IT WOULD BE LIKE TO GO ON TV OR radio, I pictured the glamour clichés first: tall buildings, busy people, a long-sought grace and knowledge occurring to me as soon as I had a spotlight trained on my face and a boom mic over my head.

But I climb the subway stairs at Forty-second Street and realize, with a loosening of bowels, that this level of comfort and smoothness will *never* occur to me. I'm about to go on NPR and I feel as stupid as I did yesterday.

I'm slightly relieved to find New York's public radio affiliate in not a high-rise but a dark, squat building from the sixties. There's a point, living here, at which you stop being the transplant, the tourist, and become something else. Not a New Yorker. God, no, never that. Just wearily, testily *deft* at being here. Strangely comforted by darkness and grime. A doorman keeps post with a crossword puzzle and wags a hand at me when I enter.

It's been an eight-week, ten-city promotional tour since Florida, a blur of more sour-smelling rental cars and threadbare hotel comforters, the feeling of never having slept enough and always having eaten too much. I'm not in great shape. Sore, chunky from our time on the road, ass melding to the driver's seat of a low-end Chevy, sepia-toothed from smoking too much, slamming McGriddles and Mountain Dews from the grief of it all, promoting *Nashville Combat,* which has been called both "regional psychodrama" and "token manipulation" by critics. It's been discussed as a class struggle piece, a work of fourth-wave feminism, dark comedy worthy of an Oscar, a gross failure, a triumph. We have been condemned *and* applauded and we don't much care either way: We nearly piss ourselves every time we see our names in print.

And we have twenty minutes until we're due on NPR and still no sign of Mel. None at all.

My phone vibrates. I wince—I won't be able to hear a phone ring for another six months without the fear of bad news on the other end—but it's a text from Donnie:

> *You just hit number 100 at the box office for the summer season. That's an INDIE ADULT CARTOON with LIMITED BACKING in the top 100. This is HUGE! You'll have LOTS to talk about on Glynnis!*

I haven't seen Mel since we landed at JFK three days ago. I try a few numbers: Surly Cathie hasn't seen her, either. Indian John lost track of her the night they saw the Reverend Horton Heat at Mercury Lounge. Directs me to Fart, who I call until his voice mailbox is full. She never replaced her iPhone. Of course.

This is not good. The NPR interview is important. The host of *Art Talk,* Glynnis Havermeyer—critic, writer, figure-about-town— was keen to meet us after she caught a screening of *Nashville Combat* at the Angelika. Donnie might have worked for months to get us this interview, harping hard on her connections, plying Glynnis's assistant, a snotty little reprobate named Fenton. But Glynnis booked us *herself*. It is an embarrassment of riches.

I turn and spot Mel weaving across Sixth Avenue. When I see the screwy little tilt to her head, my throat ices over with dread. She's fucked up, maybe a third loosey-goosey. But she's upright. And spruced: sneakers unscuffed, vest buttoned, a mid-eighties blazer of the Brooks Brothers variety. The shadow of a black eye traces the left side of her face.

"Morning," I tell her.

She cruises over and spanks me on the ass. The doorman glances up. She winks at him. "Don't worry, she likes it," she says. Jabs the elevator button.

"I take it whoever you spent last night with didn't wake you up for this."

"She woke me up to *bone*. I remembered this on my own. What kind of unprofessional dickbag you take me for?" She slings an arm around my neck and jostles me companionably.

"Still no phone?"

"Nope. But what can you do." She shakes her leg, jingles the change in her pockets, cracks her neck.

I'm developing a talent for getting impressions of Mel's hangovers via osmosis—variety, intensity, source. It's like getting something gooey caught in my antennae. This morning, the vibe is hard liquor spiky with something else, something like how I imagine burning batteries must taste. I lean in, smell: low-level rummy with, yes, something sweaty and metallic underneath. I grab her chin, peer into her eyes. Visine'd but too fat around the pupil. Pretty skittery for the here and now.

"What are you on," I say quietly.

She rolls her eyes. "So suspicious. It's *no bueno*, Kisses, the way you're on my dick all the time."

"Don't call me that."

I debate telling Mel about the box office returns. It's good news, but I'm beginning to question for whom. I look at her rummage through her pockets, a slight sheen of sweat making her face shimmer, and add up all the good things this summer that just seem to lead to less accountability, not more. An effect I suppose I should have known in theory. But you can know almost anything *in theory*.

"Did you know Fart's roommate works for *Mad*?" Mel says.

"I don't care."

"He also enjoys smoking crystal."

"*Jesus Christ*, Mel."

"I know," she says. "It had been a while, but hot *damn*. I mean, *woo*." She narrows her eyes. Whispers, "*Woooo*."

"I can't believe you."

"Oh, come on. I smoked it by accident, and then I was like, well, okay. Let's *do* this. Let's *ride* this gravy train."

My voice rises before I can catch it. "Who have you been hanging out with?"

"Dude. These guys were strictly amateurs. Lots of Xbox to be played. Nary a Hells Angel to be seen."

I lay my head against the elevator and moan.

"I'm *fine*," she says. "I'm on the downhill slope, man. Perfect time for an interview. I'll sleep it off this afternoon."

"Are you telling me you didn't sleep last night?"

"Disco naps. I'm great, I'm telling you. Let's do this thing."

"Just hold it together," I say, clenching and unclenching my fists. "Please."

"How about cooling it with the directives, little lady?"

"They might ask about your mom. Did Donnie mention that to you?"

"I got the email," she says, rolling her eyes. "It's fine. I got this. Okay?"

The bell dings. The doors slide open. Fenton is waiting. "You're late," he hisses.

"No, we're not." I point to the clock. "We're right on time."

"From my perspective," he says, "you are unbearably, *undeniably* late. Now, come on." He actually snaps his fingers at us as he turns on his heel. "We've got to get you two mic'd up."

"Gonna get *you* mic'd up," Mel mutters. She imitates Fenton's mince for a few steps. "Hey, Fenny, you lost weight?"

"No."

"You look, I dunno. *Smaller.*"

"It must just be in your head." He whips out his phone. We can see over his shoulder there's nothing there—no new messages, no schedule pop-up. He fucks around with it anyway, thumbs knobbing.

Fenton stops at a set of double doors posted with QUIET PLEASE! RECORDING IN PROCESS! We push through to rows of cubicles, clear glass, nubby metal soundboards. Stations are separated into DJ booths, where bespectacled women and hunched men gesticulate, then wait pensively through message breaks. Sound guys motion for guests to speak up, pipe down, cut off.

Fenton turns to Mel. I get a mental projection of him at six, class tattler, getting off on chalk dust and fluoride treatments. "I heard you were drunk at a panel discussion and acted like a *fool*," he singsongs.

FENTON IS REFERRING, OF course, to the Midwestern Women in Film Conference panel back in July.

It was a shitshow. Mel was fifteen minutes late, of course, and as she ran onto the stage, interrupting someone's very serious answer to a question about the state of feminism in the modern documentary, she thumped me on the shoulders and whispered loud enough for the mic to pick up, "Sorry, dude." The audience laughed. We tried to laugh with it. Mel was still drunk from the night before. It was obvious. Painfully so.

When the moderator asked us our first question—"Why cartoons?"—Mel burped and said, "For all the bitches."

Pretty fitting answer for a question that stupid. But it got more laughs and, from the other end of the stage, an audible snort. I knew without looking that the snort came from Brecky Tolliver, producer and creator of the *Obsessives* series, mini-documentaries detailing the lives of female collectors and connoisseurs throughout the country. Not our cup of tea—the last time we tried to watch, we just ended up slinging empty PBR cans at the flat-screen—but Brecky is a big deal. Two-time Hollingsworth winner, Vassar grad, confirmed lesbian, smug as the rug's snuggest bug. "Quiet work that manages to make itself loud," *The New York Times* decided. It didn't sound like a compliment to me.

Brecky hates Mel. Likewise, Mel thinks Brecky's a fuckwit and has never attempted to conceal this opinion. "I've never seen her do or say anything genuine, man," Mel said once. "She's got this ridiculous streak of sanctimony. Everything she does, she makes a *point* of doing it. *Look at how urbane and sensitive I am.* Trying to have a conversation with her is pointless. It's like trying to chat with a monkey who's masturbating into a mirror."

Brecky's snort set Mel off. "Yeah," she said, and pointed at Brecky. "Check that out. Brecky gets it. *Breckinridge* knows the score. Don't you. *Breck.*"

Brecky rolled her eyes. But Mel had her in her crosshairs. "You should do an *Obsessives* on cartoon groupies, Brecky." To the audience: "She'd have lots to say about it, because *she loves me*. Brecky *loves* me. She wants to do me in the *ear*. Isn't that right, Brecky?"

Brecky smirked. Unable to come up with some witty rejoinder, she simply leaned back, crossed her legs, said, "I don't think so." But it was too late. She had asked for it. Now she was going to have to sit there and take it until Mel ran out of steam.

She fixed Mel with a withering look. "Can we get back on track here?" she said. "Can you answer the question? Please?"

Mel let her face go slack. Pointed at her, then at herself, then back at her, beaming. The audience giggled. The moderator laughed, said, "Okay, let's refocus here—"

"Lemme give her some sugar," Mel mooed. "Lemme give Breck some *sug*. Come on. Come *owon.*"

Brecky sighed, kind of did that fake-laugh-lip-bite thing—she's too well bred to tell Mel to fuck off, that's her problem—and so Mel didn't stop, just snaked herself up and danced over, crooning, "B-hole pleasures! B-hole pleasures! It's *easy like Sunday mawnin*! Come *owon*!" And she whipped her shirt off, sports bra yellowed, belly button a rude outie under the lights, and commenced to rub the shirt all over Brecky, slathering her general area with furious, fake affection, twirling the shirt over her head while the room disintegrated. Making certain no one would be able to look at Brecky for at least a week without thinking of her as the B-hole Pleasures Girl.

It was *insult humping*. Mel invented *insult humping*. And it *worked*. A tagline covering the panel in *ReAnimator: The Cartoonist's Source* the next day: "Vaught Takes Her Shirt Off, Twists It Around, Spins It Like a Helicopter."

Yeah. So that's how *that* went.

I approached Brecky after the panel. A few of her interns hovered around, giving me the stink-eye. Brecky flicked them away with one hand. "Hey," I said to her. "I'm really sorry about that. Mel gets a little weird sometimes. I hope she didn't make you uncomfortable."

Brecky arched an eyebrow. "A *little weird*. Well, that's one way of phrasing a public violation like that, I suppose."

I smiled. It felt like passing gas.

Brecky held a hand up—dismissing me or excusing me, I have no idea—and said, "It's fine. She's having a rough time right now, I understand that. I was very sorry to hear about her mother, by the way."

"We appreciate that."

Brecky pursed her lips. "You know, I was impressed by *Nashville Combat*," she said. "I hear it's kind of your baby. Her story, maybe, but your project."

I tried to mask my surprise. Where had she heard that? Had people been talking about me? Brecky thought it was *my baby*. It was nicer to hear than I wanted to admit. "It's a joint effort," I managed.

Brecky nodded *okay, okay,* like she was doing me a favor. I was suddenly less sorry that Mel tried to hump her head. "You're talented," she said. "Mel is, too. But she's a liability."

Brecky rose, gestured for me to follow her to the corridor. I glanced over my shoulder—Mel was being mobbed by students, signing DVDs—then followed Brecky out. When we were alone, she turned and said quietly, "I was curious as to whether you were working on any solo projects these days."

"What do you mean?"

She shrugged and bit her lip, making it obvious she was holding back. Lifted her gaze to search for the right words. "We're making room in this sort of . . . well, you might call it a *collective,* I guess, for a couple of like-minded people making art. We all share a space in Hell's Kitchen. Sometimes we collaborate. You've come up in some discussions. Did I ever tell you I read your college thesis?"

"Ah, no." The thesis I wrote on the side while Mel and I were producing our first shorts. A prof at Ballister liked it so much, he sent it to *The Journal of Alternative Modern Art,* where it was published the year after I graduated: an exploration of anthropomorphic animals in countercultural animation of the 1970s.

Brecky read my thesis? What the hell. "Where'd you find it?" I asked her, trying to sound casual.

"*Alt Journal.* I've had a subscription for years. I thought your approach was really interesting. The attention paid to those Soviet animated shorts? And those Ralph Bakshi films in particular. *Love* him. I've never understood all those R. Crumb disciples giving him shit. Animation is *not* comics. Totally different medium. Anyway." She waved her hand in front of her face. "I know you have obligations right now. The project you'll be doing with Vaught for the Hollingsworth."

Our nonexistent project. Our horribly nonexistent project. "Uh huh."

She cleared her throat. "But I should say something up front, to avoid awkwardness later. We're not really looking to bring Mel in. We're a little more low-key, as an organization. And collaborating with Mel Vaught sounds like more than a full-time job. I mean, she's good. Super-talented. *Unseen* kind of talented. I think it's unfortunate that a lot of the attention being paid to your movie is more circumstantial than merit-based."

Was that a dig? That was a dig.

"She has a lot going on. Wouldn't you agree?" She looked at me meaningfully. "Baggage-wise, I mean?"

I kept silent. I wouldn't shit-talk Mel. As good as it might feel, I couldn't do it with Brecky.

"Well," she said, "in any case, we're fans of yours. We like the way you think. We like your work. And we wanted to open the door to you."

She reached into her breast pocket and pulled out a business card. "Let me give you one of these. It's a bit *douchey*, I know, having these things, but my contact info's there. Just think about it, okay? Keep me in the loop. Let me know how you're doing."

I rubbed the card between my fingers. Silky stock, thin but gauzy. It was the feel of the thing that counted. It surprised me that Brecky knew this. I looked around for Mel as I put the card in my pocket. "I will," I told her.

"I DON'T KNOW WHAT you're talking about," I tell Fenton. I follow him into the studio and put my bag down.

"Just wanted to confirm," he says. "I'd hate to think of our guests being falsely slandered."

Mel leans out, gives Fenton a loud, sharp kiss on the head. He shrieks. "It's because you're in love with me, Fen Fen. I *get* it." She brushes past him into the sound booth.

He turns to me, mouth open. Fenton likes to talk. We'll be hearing about this later, whispered aloud at a party with me conveniently in earshot.

The sound guy holds up something that looks like a Walkman. He attaches it to my hip. I feel his fingers against my pant seam. My face heats.

A few minutes later there are heels clicking down the cubicles: A short, stocky figure appears through the window, swathed entirely in gray silk. "Uh huh," she says to someone. That voice. We freeze. That's her. That's Glynnis Havermeyer.

My palms are sweating. I flex my hands, drop the note cards I'm holding. Bend over to pick them up. It's *happening*. I can't help it. This is how I view the events in my life: This one will be the narrative's peak, the game-changer. And it will be incredible if I *just don't fuck it up.*

The door opens and there she is, in the flesh. Brief silver glasses, dark lipstick. Hair dyed a red so rich it's nearly purple. Exactly the way a well-read punk should grow up to look. She's smiling. Fenton glares at us over her shoulder.

Glynnis turns. "Fenton. Why don't you take a break? Have some coffee."

"I'm fine," he says. And I swear to God, he *cuts his eyes at us,* the spiteful princess at the eighth-grade cotillion. "I don't need a break."

"Maybe the ladies would like coffee?" She lifts her eyebrows at us. Wonders never cease: She hates Fenton, too. "Thank you, sir." She shuts the door.

"That coffee's gonna be thirty percent pee," Mel says.

Glynnis laughs, offers her hand. I can already see it: She's one of those people who robs the room of all its oxygen. I want her to teach me to do that. "Ladies. So good to have you here." She turns to me. "I take it you are Ms. Kisses."

"Yes."

"I recognize you from your flashes in *Nashville Combat.*"

The best I can do is *"Heh."*

She reaches out, takes Mel's hand. "Mel Vaught, without a doubt. Your depiction of yourself is quite on the nose, I have to say."

Mel slips her hands into her pockets, lets her hair go shaggy in her eyes. She's playing bashful now. "All I gotta do's draw a broom with a bunch of yellow hair on top. Not much to it."

Glynnis laughs again. I start to lighten. *This is actually going okay.* "You know, the two of you are such a compelling couple, visually. Blond and brunette. Svelte and curvy. Contrast is the thing that draws the eye again and again. Though I suspect you already know that." She removes the wrap from her shoulders and drapes it across her chair. It gives off fragrance: the woods, something sweet. The lines in her face, unseen when she's on television—a talking head on

VH1, those interminable book talks on C-SPAN—are visible. But other than that, she looks scarily like her public self. "At the risk of sounding frivolous, that you're interesting to look at should help when you do *Charlie Rose*. They've booked you for Rose, right?"

Mel and I look at each other.

Glynnis covers her mouth with her hand. "Whoops. They haven't yet. I play canasta with one of the producers. Try to act surprised, will you?"

Mel wiggles her eyebrows at me. *Canasta*.

Glynnis sits down across from us. "All right, ladies, here's how this will go. I'll give a sort of intro to you and to your work. We'll concentrate on *Nashville Combat,* since it's still in theaters. We'll use the question roster sent to you last week. Try to keep it as natural and conversational as possible. I'll try to posit the questions in such a way that they sound spontaneous. Okay? Let's go."

She slips on a pair of headphones. The sound guy appears in the adjoining room, waves at us, does a countdown with one hand: five, four, three, two, one.

A green light comes on.

"Welcome to *Art Talk* this Saturday, August first. It's been an exhilarating summer in theaters, not least because of a plethora of small, intensely personal projects finding their way to the big screen in a movement reminiscent of the indie push of the early to mid-1990s. Once again, audiences are leaning toward the warmth of grassroots. The biggest buzz of the summer belongs to cartooning team Mel Vaught and Sharon Kisses, creators of what many are referring to as the little cartoon that could, *Nashville Combat.* Though by no means is this film *little*—it is, to quote *Spin*, 'a spitting, twitching tour de force of epic freaking proportions,' building buzz through an incredibly loyal, energized fan base. *Combat* is the story of Mel Vaught and her childhood with a negligent, drug-addicted mother in the Central Florida swamplands. It is smart, funny, visually arresting, and absolutely unflinching."

I glance at Mel. She is sitting straight in her chair, adjusting her headphones. Her expression does not change when her mother is mentioned. I close my eyes and see Lisa Greaph, her long purple fingernails pulling open the drawer.

"Vaught and Kisses take as many pains to craft an honest story as they do building the stunning visuals that have taken the cartoon world by storm. And their fans have responded in kind. Witness the Reddit subthread devoted to renderings of Mom, the movie's cranky, crank-smoking heroine, to which fans have posted their own versions in macaroni, coffee grounds, and most memorably, a painting composed of broad strokes of tinted K-Y jelly. Absolutely a testament to an audience eager for a movie like this, and for the partnership of Vaught and Kisses, a sign of breaking through to a greater audience. Ladies, welcome to the program."

We splutter ourselves stupid while Glynnis beams at us with the assurance of someone who actually believes in what is happening. "Now, earlier this year, you were granted a prestigious Hollingsworth Grant, worth over a quarter of a million dollars. Congratulations. What's next?"

She looks to me. My throat shrivels. I nod.

"She's nodding, ladies and gentlemen," Glynnis says.

I go, "Huh."

Mel pokes me. "That means yes," she says. "In the language of the lima beans." Opens her hands, shakes her head: *What are you doing?*

Glynnis likes this. "I'm seeing some partnership going on right now. You two have worked together for over ten years, correct? Do you want to tell us how you collaborate?"

I scowl at Mel. Maybe I should just be honest and tell everyone that me cleaning up from the night before has become our truest form of collaboration. Me getting Mel out of bed. Holding her hair back while she pukes with the height and depth of a longshoreman. Keeping her from brawling with anyone before noon. Making sure she doesn't fall out of a chair in front of an audience or drop equipment that cost me so much I'll have to forfeit my firstborn should I actually meet a man who's not chased off by my stink lines. And pretending she doesn't reek of gin and the tang of last night's waitress, lured into her hotel room with promises of Jell-O shots and *Full House* reruns.

I clear my throat, trying for a sort of professional "erm," and pluck at the waistband of my pantsuit. "We do it all as a team," I manage. "From the first storyboards to editing."

"I'm interested in hearing about what your storyboards look like. You're clearly art school grads, but with a taste for candy, it would seem—obvious cartoon fans, with that sense of fun and danger coming through in your work. I see *Ren and Stimpy* there. I see nineties-era Klasky Csupo there. I see Ralph Bakshi there. Can you fill us in on how this aesthetic influences the way you storyboard?"

She looks at me. My throat freezes right back up. Shit. Shit *shit*. I was prepared for this—the academic questions, the tech stuff. And now I can't talk. Glynnis, Mel, the sound tech, they're all watching me freak out.

And so she looks to Mel.

Mel kicks back, crosses her legs, adjusts her tie, and says, "Well, we wanted to do something more honest than those retrospective memoirs that make everything so saccharine, you know? And Sharon and I both watched ungodly amounts of television as kids. Just brain-slaying, vision-doubling hours of TV. Cartoons included. Drawing in that style was just the ghost that emerged when we started to dig. It didn't feel like a conscious decision. I mean, childhood is pretty much ground zero for stories, right?"

"Yours in particular was very storied," Glynnis says. "Can you tell us about the main players in *Nashville Combat*?"

"Uh, it was me, my mom, and a whole string of Mom's boy-friends. It's basically my upbringing until her arrest when I was thirteen."

"Can you tell us why she was arrested?"

Mel rolls her eyes upward as she ticks off the list. "Bunch of stuff. Possession, intent to sell, intent to prostitute. That's right. Only in Florida can you charge a woman with the *intention* to whore herself out."

I press my lips together. It's a slip, not a big one, but a slip just the same. This is where it all starts to come apart. I can feel it.

But Glynnis chuckles. "This is a very place-oriented film. Some have gone as far as to categorize it as regionalist. Would you agree with that assessment?"

Mel shrugs. "Nah. I mean, it is where it is because that's the memory. I don't think we really set out to tell about the place."

"But you've clearly chosen to make it a focus," Glynnis says. "We're hearing the term 'white trash noir' thrown around here. We're hearing a lot about 'redneck pathos.' How would you respond to the way in which this movie is being sold?"

Huh. Is it just my imagination, or was that a tone of displeasure in her voice? And what the hell does she mean, *being sold*.

I cough. She turns to me. "We won't deny the setting," I say, my voice shaking. "It makes sense. Mainstream America has a big fear of the rural. If this story isn't rural, then it definitely takes place at the margins of the suburban. The line separating what's developed and what's still wild—that's more interesting to us than the regional aspect, I think."

I lean back and take a deep breath without looking at Mel. That actually felt okay. Thoughtful, precise. Not totally vapid.

Glynnis leans in, gazing at me. "*You're* a bit of an enigma, aren't you," she says.

I laugh, startled. So does she, a stilted-reaction sound. "No, really," she says. A smile creases her mouth, but her eyes remain still. "One wonders, upon watching, if *Nashville Combat* is the product of shared trauma, in a sense. Did you find some of your own experiences surfacing in the film as well? What kind of stake did *you* have in the making of something that was so personal for your partner?"

The rest of the room falls away. This was definitely not in the questions the producers sent. And her tone—it bears the unmistakable note of a throw-down. I thought she *liked* what we were doing. I was almost right. She likes what *Mel* is doing. She is challenging me to tell her what it is, exactly—if anything—that I do. I am being asked to explain myself. Glynnis is staring at me.

I open my mouth. Nothing comes out. There's a horrible cottony stillness for a good three seconds before I feel Mel stir at my side, just now waking up to the room. She jumps in: "Are you kidding? Kisses is the boss, man."

Glynnis goes back to her with a lopsided grin. It's genuine—not what she gives Fenton, or me, but something secret and hidden. They're the only two people in the room again.

I have ten pages of notes sitting on my desk back at the studio, the weeks of worry and preparation I've put into this interview. My freshman year at Ballister, I listened to Glynnis's podcast (and she was one of the first to post podcasts, at the very tip of the aughts) on the mammoth Dell I'd just bought for college. Listening to Glynnis always gave me the sense of driving around the periphery of a large city at night, lights made brighter by the darkness surrounding—exotic signage, alien parkways. I ran over the dummy questions, I practiced my best, thoughtful *erm,* my radio laugh. Thinking, *Glynnis will love me, will love* us. Never imagining I'd need to practice a defense against an ambush, against *What was your stake in this?*

I expect Mel to say something more here, something more directly in my defense. But she doesn't.

"Fair enough," Glynnis says. "But the question of setting"—she wags her finger back and forth between us; I've suddenly reappeared—"relates tangentially to a very old argument as to the nature of animation, which still has trouble defining itself as a mature genre. When subject matter veers toward the complicated or dark, as I would say it does in your film, it seems many will pull back out of a belief that the cartoon rules of content have been violated. Which brings us to a difficult point in the story of this movie: the death of Kelly Kay Vaught, the archetype for *Nashville Combat*'s Mom."

A high-pitched shriek of gas comes from my midsection. The mic picks it up. Glynnis glances at me. Then back to Mel.

"This must be an incredibly tough time for you, Mel," she says.

"Yeah, well," Mel says, "it's, you know, never easy to lose someone. Even if you hadn't been in touch. Which my mom and I weren't, not really." She pauses. Where is this coming from? "Still a weird place to be in."

"For those of you who don't know," Glynnis starts, and then

recounts the entirety of the whole grisly Kelly Kay fiasco—the prison
scuffle, the wound. I sneak a look at Mel. Her face is neutral. I see the
pink lining of her left eye jump slightly.

"Had you discussed the movie with your mother?" Glynnis asks
gently.

"No," Mel says. "She didn't even know about it. Like I said, we
hadn't talked in a while."

"Some have suggested, how would one phrase this, a *complicated* relationship between the depiction of Kelly Kay in this film and
the events surrounding her death. What's your reaction to this?"

I grit my teeth. Mel crosses and uncrosses her legs, sniffs deeply.
"What, that guy from *Salon* who wrote that story? That what we're
really talking about here?"

"Well, if you want to address that—"

"I have no problem addressing that. It was a ridiculous argument. It was bullshit."

I reach out to touch Mel's arm.

Glynnis throws her hand out toward me. "Let her finish," she
says.

I shrink back.

The *Salon* story was on the ramifications of what the author
coined "reality fiction"—stories based on real life, real people, actual
events—and how these works affected those on whom the characters
were based. Discussed were a writer with a recent novel detailing a
breakup with an ex-girlfriend who, in turn, claimed her business suffered as a result of the book, and a woman who'd written a television
show about her spectacularly ruinous marriage who did not deny
that her handsome divorce settlement may have been inflated as a
result of the publicity. *Nashville Combat* was the article's centerpiece:
a film so personal, and so troubling, that it *may* have precipitated the
death of its inspiration, provoking a fellow inmate to beat her, either
due to celebrity or infamy.

It was a reach, by any definition. But it was also a huge blow. An
incredibly damning story in a respected publication with high page
views. We all told Mel to not let it bother her; Donnie suggested an

Internet ban. "Fuck it," Mel said, flapping her hand. "It's so much chatter. Doesn't matter." But it bothered her, I could tell.

I scroll to the quote on my iPhone and toss it into Mel's lap, then give Glynnis the evil eye: *See? I can be useful.*

Mel picks up the phone. "*If this movie is remembered at all in fifty years, it will be recalled as a snuff piece . . . less a work of art than a shock treatment, lacking in nuance or complexity.* Okay," Mel says, "look. Without getting too precious about it, art is what it *is*. And to use a work as a scapegoat for the crazy things people do is real, *real* shortsighted. So the next time he stages a goddamn puppet show with the ladies he *rows crew* with, let him slice the hell out of whatever *he* writes and retain whatever sense of superiority he can get out of it. Just because the movie made him uncomfortable does not give him the right to create some ridiculous causality between two events. I can't help it if shitheel here walked in expecting *Toy Story*."

Glynnis smiles.

Yeah. It's *real* interesting when Mel flies off the handle, isn't it, I think. "But there were other reviews," I cut in, leaning forward to make Glynnis look me in the eye. "People who appreciated the movie's honesty, its undiluted quality." *Rein her in,* I will Glynnis. *Control this interview, you patronizing twat. I know the landscape of Mel's impulses and she is* not *on level ground right now. If something rubs her the wrong way, she will blow. And when it happens, it's fast. It's a T-bone at an intersection.*

Mel recrosses her legs. Her left foot jounces *up up up up up*.

Glynnis changes the subject. "Let's talk a little bit about your technical approach. Some have said that your decision to not use advanced CGI is—what's the word here—*contrarian?*"

"We actually use CGI," I correct her. "It would be hard to be a two-man operation without it. We use it in conjunction with traditional cel-by-cel tactics. And we do it because we believe in the technique, and we like the results. Period."

Mel cuts in. "Lemme tell you something," she says, and her voice is high and fast, still amped from the *Salon* story. "The time those guys who call us *contrarian* spend yapping is time we spend busting ass old-school. It's like, *Well, suckle my nuts, look at Johnny Seven-Figures using Maya to make a twenty-million-dollar movie.* You know what? Fuck that. Johnny Seven-Figures is copping out of what makes him a cartoonist. He is compromising. If you get your meat from a bad cow, you're gonna get a bad burger, you know what I'm saying? We are slaving away over the drafting board eating that burger *medium rare* because *we know our butcher,* Glynnis. And I don't care if that cow rolled around in a kiddie pool of its own poo-poo, it's a risk we're gonna take. I will *eat it* because *we do this honest or not at all.*"

Mel leans back in her seat, takes a breath.

Glynnis is frozen in her chair. "Well put," she manages.

I look over at Mel. Mouth, *Who the fuck is Johnny Seven-Figures?*

Glynnis turns to me, and in the bright, loud voice of someone changing the subject: "Your name is quite the draw, Sharon."

For fuck's *sake.* How many times do we have to go through this. I grind my molars. "It's. Scottish."

"It's awesome, is what it is," Mel says. "I spent two hundred bucks changing my name legally from Melody to Mel and she gets to be *Sharon Kisses* for free."

"I wish I could change it," I mutter.

Mel chortles. "She'll never change it. It gets her tail. Men *shit* when they hear the name Sharon Kisses. For serious."

Mel's voice dips, goes hoarse. She's Drunk Mel now. Glynnis pushed her by talking up that goddamn *Salon* story. Now she's acting out. Overcompensating. When Mel feels sad—and right now it strikes me that Mel is, in fact, very, very sad, and has been this whole summer—she tries to make up for it by manufacturing joy. I was a moron to hope there was any way of walking into this *pretending* to be sober.

Glynnis gives a nervous titter. My hand wraps around the microphone perched in front of me. I try to see if I can lift it. It's nailed down.

Mel slaps my knee. "It's cool. I got my demons, too. When my mom got knocked up with me, she was real dandy to do a DIY abort job because she was too cheap to go to the clinic, right? And she heard somewhere that an excess of vitamin C could kill a baby in utero. So she took a metric butt-ton of C, like orange juice injections straight up the cooter. As an adult? I almost never get sick. True story. Almost made it into the movie, that bit. But it just ended up making sweet, sweet love to the cutting room floor."

She's throttling her microphone now, too. I can see it loosening off the dash, unknowingly making purchase while she talks.

"It's *true*," Mel says. "It's near impossible to overdose on vitamin C. You just end up shitting it out."

Glynnis nearly chokes.

"Try that with other vitamins. Vitamin D? You'll end up with a giant purple eye. Vitamin A? Testicles like pumpkins. But C? Just sluices on through, babe. Like me."

Mel leans over the table and the microphone rips from the dash. There's a spark, that electrical spit of a device cutting out. The sound engineer jumps up, waving his arms.

Mel says, "Crap."

Glynnis freezes. Looks at me. And for the first time in the interview, I laugh. I laugh, and I don't know what it means or where it's coming from. But for once, I'm not forcing it.

"Oh ho," Glynnis says. "You *two*. I think we'll wrap it up here."

DON'T TALK ON the elevator. The silence trails us out onto Sixth Avenue.

"I don't know what your problem is," Mel says. "She liked us. Aside from the broken mic. Why are you so moody all of a sudden?"

"My interpretation of a good interview is one where you don't talk about how much tail I do or don't get."

"I was trying to guide her away from that stupid *Salon* article because I was sick of talking about it. It's called a *joke*."

"It wasn't funny. No one thought it was funny."

"Well, congratulations. You've finally kicked your sense of humor into submission."

We go underground. I lead us silently to the Brooklyn-bound track. The news has been threatening a heat wave all week. The air presses down on us. We wait.

"All right," Mel says. "Fine. Don't talk." She walks to the edge of the platform, leans out to look for headlights. Jingles the change in her pockets. Finally tugs her Moleskine from her bag and kneels down. The picture spools out quick and dark: an enormous Hispanic lady in a muumuu. I glance down the platform. The lady is there, flapping a copy of *The Watchtower* at her face, unaware that Mel is drawing her.

Mel rears back, takes a long look at what she's done. Retouches something small at the top. I look over. Little men dressed as bank robbers run from the lady's ear. The lady stares dead-eyed into space. Below her, in bubble letters:

DER.

Mel scratches it out. Tries again:

DURRRR.

I unclench my jaw long enough to say, "Why didn't you back me up when she said that thing about me being an *enigma*? About what *kind of stake* I had in this? What the fuck was that?"

"She wanted to know more about you because you are interesting, Sharon," she says. "Not that you make that easy for anyone."

"We're supposed to be a team. You would have remembered that if you hadn't walked into NPR so fucked up your blood alcohol level could have powered a commercial jet."

She snorts. "If your writing was that colorful, I wouldn't have to live and die in the studio every day." Her mouth clamps down in regret as soon as she says it.

"I'm sorry. This, coming from someone who hasn't worked a day in two months?"

She lifts her arms, lets them fall to her sides. "The studio's not the most welcoming place right now. There's not much I can say to you that doesn't piss you off. I can't win. This is why people don't get married."

"This is why people like *you* don't get married."

"Well, hell's bells. I could have told you that." She's standing now, pale and sweaty. I can see cracks in her lips.

"You're an alcoholic," I tell her.

"Oh, come on." She flaps around in a circle. "Shut *up*, Sharon."

"No one except an alcoholic gets up and makes Irish coffee at eleven in the morning. No one except an alcoholic gets wasted and strips at a panel discussion. Normal people don't do that. People with drinking problems do that. And I think the movie pushed you into a bad place. I regret having any part in this."

"I don't see you turning away the checks we're getting. I don't see you turning down NPR interviews. But hindsight's twenty-twenty, isn't it."

"I have a standard for how I should be treated," I say. "And you just went *way* below the line."

She rolls her eyes. "Where's this standard with the dipshits you date?" Draws a smoke out of her pocket. Lights it. There aren't many people on the platform. She gets a few dirty looks, but only a few.

"You started out charming Glynnis," I say. "She liked you, not me. But then you ran it into the ground. She's probably lucky you didn't take off your shirt and slap the sound engineer with it."

Mel leans over the platform again. "You're never going to let that go, are you."

"If I left," I say, "no one would blame me."

"You can't *do* this without me," she says. "You know you can't."

It knocks the breath out of me. It's a long moment before I can even speak again. "There are people who would actually appreciate working with me," I tell her. "Do you know how many calls I've deflected from Brecky Tolliver this summer?"

Mel opens her mouth. Shuts it. Crosses her arms over her chest.

"Yeah. Ever since the panel discussion. She tried to hire me while you were buzzing around hitting on coeds."

"Wow," she says. "Look at you, whipping Brecky out like that. What, are you trying to make me jealous?"

"I'm letting you know where you stand," I say.

"Typical," she spits. "You're doing this like a total *girl,* parading it around. You gonna pick another dyke to buddy up with, Sharon? Someone you don't have to compete with?"

It's mean—a meanness she was searching for, somewhere down in the dregs of herself.

"You know what," I say quietly, "why don't you keep the ugly shit to yourself for once instead of pouring it out all over me. I'm tired of this."

Mel blinks at me, breathing hard. Then lifts her hands. Yells, "You know what? Fuck this." She starts for the stairs, cigarette clamped between her teeth, and bounds up, her back growing smaller and smaller until she's gone.

HER NAME WAS STARLA

MEL DISAPPEARS. I SPEND THE WORST HEAT WAVE NEW YORK CITY has seen in a decade—blacktop oozing apart, old people collapsing on the subway—lying in the midst of her cigarette butts and half-gnawed Charleston Chews, purposefully avoiding our workstation. I throw my back out lugging the air conditioner into my bedroom, throw it out some more carrying the TV in there, and set up shop eating popsicles, sweating, and attempting to overcome the situation with lethargy.

It's been over a week of this when Donnie calls. "Would you like to talk about it?" she says.

"No, I'm good."

"I'd like to talk about it, frankly."

It's ten in the morning. I know without seeing that Donnie's at her desk, a can of Diet Coke sweating by her elbow. NPR had its edited way with the aired Glynnis segment, but an unedited version, illicitly nabbed from someone's hard drive, made its way to Donnie almost immediately after. "I just—I'm not even sure how to begin to ask the questions I need to ask right now, Sharon."

"She wasn't that bad before the interview. I swear."

"Sharon, if Mel wants to strip down and dance the rumba at a panel discussion, that's bad enough. But it doesn't get much worse than doing a nosedive on Glynnis. This is—this is another distinction altogether. But why am I explaining any of this to you? You *know* how bad it was. I could practically hear the sound of you cringing over Mel ripping the sound equipment apart."

"I don't think this is entirely fair," I say. "Shouldn't you be talking to Mel?"

"You're not wrong. It's not fair for me to ask you to babysit. But that's how we're rolling these days, apparently. Even more so now with the grant. People are watching, Sharon. Taking notes. This is your *job*."

I sit up. "Wait. What do you mean by that?" This is where it comes out, I think with a pang. This is when Donnie confirms what Glynnis made me even more afraid of. That my job is Driving Miss Mel.

"I mean that both of you have a responsibility to carry out your share of public relations," she says.

I relax. "Oh."

"Don't *oh* me. Market this to the best of your ability. Don't embarrass yourselves. That's all you have to do."

Jesus. "Right."

"Agreeing with me doesn't mean cock unless you carry it out. Keep her in hand, Sharon. It's this or stuff her into rehab. If she would even go. Which she would not."

"Okay."

"Have you two had a serious talk about her behavior?"

"Attempts have been made."

"She'll listen to you before she listens to anyone else. Let me suggest trying again."

And with this, I hope she's done chewing me out, but she's just drawing breath. "Whatever you all do with the Hollingsworth, it better be good. Otherwise, I'll be in a choke hold to do something, you know. Disciplinary."

"Well, we're not talking to each other at the present, so we're cleaned out on the ideas front."

"*Sharon.* Are you kidding me?"

"No." I flop back on the couch. I'm so tired, I can't find it in myself to give a shit. "She probably shouldn't hear any of this from me."

"I'm drafting an email to her as we speak. This need not be sugar-coated. I do not want to hear about Mel publicly stripping, destroying sound equipment, or wantonly making out with defenseless production assistants in Florida."

I groan openly. I forgot about the Florida conference—a small liberal arts college holding a festival of Florida-centric work. Weird Florida history, Florida fiction, Florida noir (which is, apparently, a thing). They're screening *Nashville Combat,* hosting a Q and A. They were really gunning for us. Called Donnie and laid down all kinds of sexy talk and more money than what we're used to seeing for this kind of thing, frankly, so she fell all over herself to book us.

"Your flight's on the sixteenth," she says. "You signed a contract."

"How much is it, again?"

"Four thousand each. Not including travel."

I curl into a fetal position. "That's a lot."

"And all you have to do is muzzle Mel and be your lovely self. Talk about this beautiful thing you've made. You don't have to talk to each other, aside from the Q and A. You're professionals. You can at least do that much. Keep it civil for fifteen minutes and then we have a discussion about where we all go from there. Okay?"

I hang up, pop a couple of ibuprofen for the low-grade headache I've had for most of the morning, and curl up on the couch, running my fingers through three days of hair grease. Click on Netflix. Light up a joint. Try to disconnect.

Brecky's documentary series is on my "Recommended for You"

suggestion list. If Mel and I ever call it quits, I guess there would no longer be a reason to consider Brecky my mortal enemy. The reality of my social stance without Mel occurs to me. Connections shouldn't count, but God knows they do. And I will need them. I keep thinking about our fight: *You can't do this without me.* It robs me of appetite every time. I'm not accustomed to thinking of myself in the singular; it's a new, chilling experience.

I run a bath, light up another joint, put on some *Ren & Stimpy* to even myself out. I sink into the cold water and try to trace it all back. What happened to Mel this summer? How did we get out of hand together so fast? I think of the beginning of the tour, when we were still booking two separate hotel suites and she just passed out in mine night after night. How I was the only one to see how torturous it was for her to sleep, how she kicked and muttered and cried out. How watching the movie—something she once loved—turned her to ice, how she drummed her fingers on her knees at the opening credits, wincing; how, when the audience laughed, she pulled a flask I didn't know she had from her pocket and slumped down in her seat to take a pull. I felt guilty admitting to myself how much I loved seeing people see the movie. How, when the audience laughed, I could feel myself flush and get wet, squirming breathless in my seat, glad I wasn't a dude or else I'd pop a raging boner every time someone paid me a compliment, while Mel had to get high before meet and greets just to get through them. By the third or fourth screening this summer, her eyes were perpetually pink after eight P.M., no questions asked.

None of this is supremely new. Mel's always liked to unwind, drink, smoke, smoke up. She's a good-time girl. It's the look on her face, more than anything, that makes it different than before; a sudden preoccupation when she's still, the way she snaps in irritation when asked if she's okay: "I'm *fine. Jesus.*" As if she's been caught at something.

The undercurrent, rarely discussed: We did not ask Mel's mom's permission. *Nashville Combat* rides the line between memoir and fiction; we used a facsimile of Mel's mom, a her-but-not-her, as the movie's focus, though it's understood that this particular line between fiction and reality is all but nonexistent. Distribution's legal team told us slander was a hard case to prove if you changed names, where they worked, who they dated. "She doesn't give a fuck what I do," Mel maintained mildly. "You shouldn't worry so much."

But wouldn't she want to know? I asked. Doesn't she want to know what you're doing in the world?

"Like I said," Mel repeated. "She doesn't give a fuck."

But during the tour, I could tell she was thinking of that *Salon* article. Rolling the question over and over, like a pebble in the mouth.

We had planned to use the few weeks we had in New York before the tour to brainstorm, but she stopped working at the studio. Started taking her laptop and sketchpad to a bar in Bushwick called Dixie Mafia. I tried to join her there but accomplished nothing, sipping G and Ts and eyeing the male bartenders woefully. We haven't had a productive day since Kelly Kay died. It marks the first time we've been blocked in a few years. Just trying to work feels stifling. Futile.

The women have multiplied. There have always been a lot—Mel has a way—but now there are more, and they are more fleeting. It used to be that Mel's horndog would only really come out when she needed to unwind after a bad day. Like when we got shot down for a Hollingsworth the first time we applied—she wanted to drink, then fuck, then drink, in that order. She likes brunettes; in homage to her Florida roots, she's drawn to women with deep tans. She's rarely had girlfriends serious enough to bring around the studio, but now she doesn't date at all. She prefers darkness, inebriation, speed. A near-dawn visit to someone's apartment to shed clothes, bump bodies, fall asleep.

One morning, when I'd left her at Dixie Mafia the night before, she came into the studio sporting a brand-new black eye. "What happened?" I asked her.

She winked her good eye at me. "Her name was Starla."

It's all happened so fast, the transition of Mel's hell-raising from preoccupation to main attraction, that I keep asking myself if I'm not blowing it all out of proportion. If I'm really seeing what I think I'm seeing. But you don't work with someone for over ten years without getting some overflow, knowing a little of what they know, feeling a little of what they feel. I can feel the dark rushing at Mel's center, the guilt that's gnawing her raw. It rips me in half to see something she loves hurt her so badly. I wonder if this is why we can't come up with a good idea. If she's scared to work. And, if she is, what I can possibly do about it.

AUGUST 16. I WAKE up with another of the headaches. I've moved from ibuprofen to Percocet. I shake one out of the bottle I have stashed in my underwear drawer, swallow it with flat Diet Coke, and call a car to JFK.

I've just settled myself into the Delta terminal when Mel bops in, dirty duffel bag slung over her shoulder, sporting—unforgivable—a fedora.

The past two weeks have forced me to realize how narrow my life is without Mel, how unpopulated. Things got so bad, I delved into my phone directory to see who else actually lived in my world. You have other friends besides Mel, I told myself. Go out and see what *they're* doing.

I had eleven contacts in my phone. Three of those were distribution.

Donnie—a sort of friend, kind of, I've always *felt* the closer to her, of Mel and me—promises to set up a lunch when she gets back from her San Francisco work trip. Fart and the interns are out; they are firmly entrenched in the Mel camp. I get the furthest with Surly Cathie, who sounds like she's wrestling a hyena when she answers the phone. "What are you doing today?" she pants. "Feel like taking some urban junkyard photos? Professional opportunity." She moves her mouth away from the receiver before shrieking, "Get off my frigging stoop, you shitassed brats." Back to me. "Buncha elementary school kids. I hate summer."

We end up out in South Edgemere, on the very edge of Queens, rolling slowly along abandoned streets the city stopped maintaining a decade ago. "Well, come on," she says when I linger on the stoop of a house with a dangerously sagging roof and a pentagram painted on the wall. "Get in and get your feet dirty. You smell that?"

"It smells like people who have left."

She smiles and closes her eyes, the same way she does when she gets a sound take exactly right. "Oh God, yes. *Totally* gone."

The day ends when I hear growling from behind us and turn to see a large, filthy German shepherd advancing, ears back. He's joined by another dog, and another, and a few more. Soon, there's a pack. Hunting us.

Cathie just rolls her eyes. Says, "Shaggy bunch of bitches. Gotta show em who's boss or they'll track you. Eat your skin right off."

"What?"

She steps in front of me, reaches into the waistband of her pants, and produces a Colt .22. Screams, "Okeydoke, cunts, who wants to be first?" She shoots into the pack. They scatter.

Mel and I have never ignored each other for this long. The feeling is worse than I would have expected—a horribly slow sinking sensation. It feels strange to miss her, to be afraid for her. What she might be doing, who she might be doing it with. Worrying that she's in danger. So I'm almost glad to see her, flapping a crooked line toward me like she hasn't gotten enough sleep, until I see her roll her eyes at me.

"Son of a bitch," I grumble.

"Come up with something more original," she says. "Everyone calls me that."

"I'll bet they do."

She gestures at my sunglasses. "What's the matter. Has staring into the blinding light of Brecky Tolliver's vag burned your retinas?"

"Leave me alone," I say, raising my voice. An old man reading a Louis L'Amour novel looks up, glares at Mel.

"My pleasure," she says, and slinks away.

She reappears right before the plane takes off, the last to board. Donnie ordered our tickets together, of course, and the plane is full—the only seat available is the one next to me. She asks the Louis L'Amour guy if he'd be willing to trade seats. He looks up coolly, turns to me for a once-over, then looks back at Mel. Sneers, "I don't think so."

. She settles in, giving me a preemptive dirty look before we sink into a weird, pained silence. I'm a little ashamed of myself. Hurling the Brecky offer at her was a low blow.

In the narrow heat of the plane, my headache spikes, starting at the top of my skull and shooting down my spine. I put my head against the seat in front of me and squeeze my eyes shut. I can feel Mel looking over at me, wanting to ask if I'm okay, not letting herself. Eventually she tucks her earbuds in and stares out the window.

Before takeoff, I get up and stagger to the tiny aircraft bathroom and vomit into the metal toilet, then sit, head in hands. I feel the plane totter back and forth for a moment before I rise and walk back to my seat.

When we land, Mel ducks into a bathroom. I slip out to the taxi line.

So this is where over a decade of work together puts us, I think as the car winds through Florida. There is a heat wave here, too, but no one seems to notice. I slide down in my seat and close my eyes behind my sunglasses, counting down the seconds until I can take my next Percocet. We're not far from where Mel grew up. I get a good color bar of Nascar and poor dentistry and pythons swallowing Pomeranians before stepping out of the car into the Super 8 parking lot and catching an eyeful of those pink grubby outdoor motel room entrances favored by serial killers and speed freaks.

Mel's taxi is just behind mine. She wordlessly crosses the courtyard. I struggle with the lock on my door as she opens her own and smacks it shut.

As soon as I step into the room, my headache explodes.

It's like being shot, the pain pushing out from the untouchable middle of my skull, racing down my spine. It hurts too much to scream. My knees give out. I fall onto the floor. I rock back and forth. I try a fetal position; I paddle my feet. I move everything except my head. It hurts so much I can't catch a decent breath. The pain is deep, nuanced; it has *character*, it's so forceful. Something is wrong. Something is really, really wrong.

I manage to grasp my purse and beat the door open, vision doubling. The sun blinds. I cry out, take a couple of staggering steps, fall onto the pavement.

She's close by. I smell the warm, rotting scent of weed. "Sharon." Footsteps. *"Sharon."* She crouches down, puts her face next to mine. "What's wrong."

I try to gesture at my head. My arm is lead.

There's a pop. The hurt fuzzes. It doesn't lessen, but it moves slightly away. I'm on the roof now, outside my body, hanging above it all. I see the back of my head, the oily roots, love handles dimpling my waistband. Mel is on her knees beside me, joint smoldering near her on the ground. Sounds soften, light blurs. It's a tussin buzz, but thicker—the fear and discomfort are there somewhere, but only in theory. It's a sweet, whole feeling, a relief to escape from my body. I have *discorporated*. At long last.

I watch my mouth move a little, see my tongue quaver. "Aah."

Mel leans in. "What?"

She grabs my arms and I'm pulled back down. My legs are scissored underneath me, the drilling behind my left eye swells. Numb: my chin, the back of my head. My left side.

"Aah ooh oye?"

Mel shakes her head, squints. "I don't know what the fuck you're saying."

My hand is a claw. I lift it, slow, rake at my purse. It tilts and spills.

Mel reaches out, plucks my collar open. She cups my forehead, chin, then slides her arms under me. "Okay. To the hospital. Let's go." She spots a taxi idling across the pavement. Says, "Hold on." I feel her move away, hear her footsteps. She returns, hefts me up. Calls, "Over here." She slams my motel door shut and drags me by the armpits across the pavement, arms and legs dangling. Balances me on the trunk, one arm holding me around the waist.

I hear a guy say, "Is she drunk or somethin?"

"No," Mel says, "something's wrong. We need the nearest hospital right away."

She struggles to open the car door, wraps her arms around my waist, and dumps me in. The car rocks. One of my legs is slung over the gearshift. She crouches beside me, breathes, "Christ."

"Nuh *guh*," I say.

"What?"

There are holes in the air. I want out so bad. I can't go from being up there to being back down here. I start to cry, mouth open.

"All right," Mel says. "Just hold on."

The ignition splutters, I hear that same guy's voice cuss and jerk at it for a moment. "What's wrong," Mel says. Her voice breaks. She's scared. "What is it?"

The guy says, "Just hold on." There's cranking noises.

Mel looks down at me. She is peering into my eyes, first one, then the other. "I *knew* something was wrong," she says.

The car finally moves. I burble and roll onto my side. The sound drips out of everything. Mel's lips move at me, pink press and unpress, everything down to its gradient. Shades shift and move apart. I feel the car buck over a pothole. Ink spots. I can't feel my face.

I pitch over and vomit.

"Stop the car!" Mel yells.

The taxi swerves to a stop. She leans over, lays her cool hands to my forehead. Her voice is a frequency, lines wavering, jumping. Cellphone a dark egg in her hand. Her thumb works. Everything goes black.

WE HAVE TO START FROM WHEREVER WE ARE

NAKED IN A BED. PEOPLE MOVE OVER ME. LIGHTS BLAZE HALOGEN. Fingers turn my arm, press for a vein. A prick and the pain scales down, bright red, maroon, pink. Sounds hook themselves together but do not make words. Mel bleats. Someone informs her that freelancer's insurance will not cover an MRI and I hear her say, "Well, son of a *bitch*."

MORE GARBLED BACK-AND-FORTH AROUND me. Someone I'm vaguely sure is Mel. Other people.

I try to pick out curves, get an anchor on where I am. I'm back watching the board in Principles of 2-D Design or Program Layouts 1, and figuring out being smart isn't the same as being good is just as scary the second time around. Mel's hand grabs mine.

I'm in a long tunnel. I wonder if I'm being operated on, if they're going to, if they are right now, the sheet tented over, someone's phantom hands inside me, manipulating. The black sand of anesthesia, the tin smell of blood. I wonder if I'm dead, or dying.

Mel talks low through the fever dream: *I never told you* and *I never knew* and *I only wish* and *please*. And she cries, mouth open, spine a soft C.

WAKE UP TO silence.

Mel's sitting next to the bed, cross-legged on a chair, her knee sticking out like a doorknob in denim. She's hunched. Reaches up to wipe her nose with her wrist. Opens her mouth to exhale like she's recently wept. Her eyebrows suddenly prick with interest. She's studying something. I see her mouth gape a little wider. Whatever she's reading, she's into it.

I try to lift my arm, can't. There are things on my forehead and neck and chest and something over my mouth. I hear machines beeping, air streaming.

I turn my neck slightly to the left. It takes effort. It hurts. I see her rake her hand through her hair. She mouths something silently. Blinks. I squint and spot what she's reading. Panic twists my throat. She's got my sketcher's journal. The one I don't show to anyone.

She's reading the List.

She finally lifts her head to look at me. When she does, I am positive it is with an expression of betrayal. It's finally happened. After ten years, she has found me out.

But she starts, sets it aside. "Holy shit," she says. "You're awake. Are you awake?" She stands and rubs her nose, breathing hard. "Sharon."

I stir.

"Don't do that," she says. "You're hooked up to a lot of stuff."

I can't keep my eyes open. "Sharon," she repeats. "Can you hear me?"

I see the frayed Goody hair band that keeps the List together twisted on the table. The darkness swallows me whole.

W HEN I WAKE AGAIN, I am alone. The sun glows through the blinds, high and hot. *Florida.*

The television's on. I squint. The *Today* show. There's Matt Lauer talking into the camera. Behind him in Midtown Manhattan, grinning tourists are saying hey to everyone back in Missouri and Texas and Arkansas.

I make a noise and suck in my breath. It's a croak. My voice feels like driving on gravel sounds.

I turn my head to look for a call button, a phone, something. It's work. My neck is fossilized. In the hallway, a wheelchair moves at a clip, propelled by a kid with a crew cut. A nurse swishes by in purple scrubs. *Lisa Greaph.* But it's not her.

I lift my right arm. The elbow pops painfully. Skinny. Not mine. I put my hand to my face, press my jaw. Nothing. I can't feel it.

I can move my legs a little, the right better than the left. There's the rustling of plastic. It's a tube, trailing off the side of my bed. It goes into a clear pouch. I feel flayed open between the legs.

On the side rail, a button reading NURSE'S CALL. I pick up my bad arm with my good arm and mash the button with my knuckle. A moment later, there's the cork-beat-cork of sneakers. A nurse pops up, smiles thinly at me. "Well, look who's awake."

She comes over, hands on her hips, checks a monitor. The liquid in the bag tied to the bed slat is the color of Gatorade. "You know how long you been out on us? A whole *week.* That's right."

I try to speak. My mouth is melting down my face.

"What is it, hon." She leans into me, puts her fingers on my arm, cool and dry.

I realize the bag of pee is mine and start to cry.

"Oh, hon," she says. "Don't you cry. Your friend is gonna be so happy to hear you're awake. We're gonna call her right now."

• • •

MEL COMES JOGGING INTO the room at lunch, her hair sticking straight up, blond grown out to the tips, glasses smudged. "Aw shit," she yells, "Kisses is back!" She lifts her arm in the air, comes at me, slings onto the bed, then remembers herself and hugs me gingerly. Tobacco, engine oil, something else—the faint, woodsy tang of oil pencils.

For the first time since I woke up, I'm happy to be conscious.

IT WAS A SUBARACHNOID hemorrhagic stroke, caused by an artery on the brain that broke and bled. There's no one reason for this; the causes are myriad. The doctor disinterestedly ticks off the risk factors: You binge-drink? You smoke? You take speed? You stressed? Family history of fatasses and alcoholics? Yes, yes, yes. I'm told I should have gone to the hospital back in Brooklyn, when the pain started. That I could have died on the plane.

The bleeding was mild to middling, even, not as severe as it could have been. I was, apparently, very lucky. I will regain a lot. I could become fully functioning again. Maybe. The doctors are quick to insist that they don't know when, and they don't really know how much "almost full use" is. I am told we will "spur on natural neurological recovery with rehabilitation efforts."

I take all this in numbly; the doctor on call, an infuriatingly strapping man named Dr. Weston, might as well be reading from a textbook. I keep swiping my good arm across my face, positive that spit's coming down my chin. Mel takes my hand. "This is all good news," the doctor says, and I'm inclined to kick the fuck out of him: *Really?*

"You will need to work very hard to get your life back," he says. "And we need to proceed cautiously. Because you came very, very close. You were inches away."

• • •

I CAN'T USE MY left side. That, they don't need to tell me.

A speech pathologist visits with flash cards. The pictures are clear and crude—milky carbon renderings of cats, dogs, goldfish. Awful *Highlights*-grade illustrations. She asks me to read the words, but there are no words there, just hieroglyphics. That shit is not a *word*. "What is this," she says, and I shrug: It's *nothing*, lady.

I want to tell her, I'm thirty-two years old. How could this have happened? Why did it happen to me? But all I can make are useless consonants: *kkkkk* or *phbbbb*. My face feels like it's dripping off my skull. It's a big part of the problem, my mouth not working. When will I be able to speak again? Who the fuck knows? Not the pathologist. "Try again," she says. "Cuh-aah-tuh." She is close to retirement and smells like lunch and whatever fabric she's wearing: tomato soup and flannel, broccoli and polyester. She makes me cry on a daily basis. "Do it again," she says. "Again. Again."

THEY ALLOW MEL TO visit in the evenings. "How's it going with Broom-Hilda," she says, referring to the speech pathologist. She brings graphic design and sketch journals, some books. When she sees those go untouched, she begins bringing in DVDs: *Wallace and Gromit, Beavis and Butt-Head. Pet Sematary.* "I forgot how much I missed Walmart," she says. "God strike me fucking dead, but it's true. This golden bit of cinema was in the discount bin for two bucks. *Two*."

My stroke is so sweepingly terrible, it has acted as our eraser. It has hit the reset button on Vaught and Kisses. We will never again mention the fight in the subway, or the plane ride to Florida. It has been wiped from our history. Now there is just this—her, me, and the hospital.

We watch TV. Mel talks. I motion with my good hand, my bad arm like a bag of sand. The entire left side of my body feels heavy and waterlogged; not mine. There's a new weakness overall, a new, ungainly, haphazard feeling. She does not make fun of me. She's either restraining herself, or she's too scared by what she sees. "Are you hurting?" she says when I wince. "Do you need something? I could ask the nurses."

There are two seams around her mouth that I haven't seen before. I'll drop something—a cup of water, and once, her phone—and the lines will deepen. My right side's off, too. I try to handle a pencil in front of her. I fist it, manage to write my name, then drop it. The blood drains from her face.

She has not asked me about the List yet. I am grateful.

After many afternoons spent thinking about it, face to the ceiling, I decide that it is something for which to ask for forgiveness. This is the person with whom you have lived for the past ten years, I think. We've never tracked who spent what on equipment, or groceries, or furniture. We wear each other's socks; on several occasions, we have used the same toothbrush for weeks, confused as to which belonged to the other. When one of us is in the shower, and the other has to pee, we just saunter in and do it. In summers, when the window air-conditioning unit cuts not even a breeze through the eighty-degree fug of the studio, we strip down and work in our skivvies, without a thought. There's the joint credit card—and to share your *credit rating* with someone is the ultimate, blind commitment.

Our investment was so great, in fact, that it was largely thoughtless, a given—even the blank spaces that we both assumed, in theory, existed in the other. Minutiae, maybe, about her mom, or one-night stands, girls with hidden faces who never came around. But the List is an albatross. Not telling her about it was nothing less than a decisive deception, made all the more egregious by the fact that it was something I had *made,* was *making*—which, for our kind of people, is the truest extension of the heart.

And now this same person is sitting with me. Ignoring my craven hospital nakedness, the catheter, the smells and sounds of my illness, with not one word of complaint.

Sometimes I catch her staring at me, knee jiggling, and I imagine she's thinking about it, wondering if I'm the person she thought I was.

I'm wondering the same thing.

• • •

W E'RE WATCHING A RERUN of *M*A*S*H* when she asks, "Do you remember me talking to you? When you were out?"

I put two fingers up: a little. My chest burns with worry. This is it. This is when she asks me about the List. The fear prickles my body, waking me up. When she's silent, I wheel my hand, not able to stand it: what about?

"I said I'd clean up, if you woke up." She looks studiously at the TV. The color in her face is high. She's embarrassed. "I meant it," she says.

I nod. She sees out of the corner of her eye and exhales. Changes the channel.

M Y LIFE IN THE hospital is a lot of little horrors separated by sleep. Sleep is my refuge. Everything exhausts me—my exercises, lessons with Broom-Hilda, eating. I'm happiest when I can sleep through being changed. I don't want to be conscious for that. I look down once between my legs to see a nurse wiping out my crotch with the neutral, slightly irritated expression of someone paying their utility bill.

I hurt constantly. My back hurts. My ass hurts. My head feels like it's stuffed with gauze, and in the middle of the gauze a seeping, leaking sting that never stops.

Visiting hours are up at eight-thirty P.M. Mel lingers as long as she's able, tucking in blankets, drawing blinds, fiddling over turning off the TV. The nurse kicks her out, administers my last morphine dosage of the day. Kills the overhead.

I pray for the first time in years. I pray to pass the division between this time and whatever comes after. I pray for the ability to put all of this in the past tense, to put down the darkness that has clung to me for years and has finally swallowed me whole, inhabiting my body, robbing me of the things that have given my life joy, meaning. I pray to cross the gulf.

• • •

BROOM-HILDA COMES IN AT nine-thirty the next morning with a stack of flash cards. "Ready to go to work?" she says.

I take a deep breath, and then another. I try to say no and it comes out as a moan. I feel my face—the working side—start to crumple.

She sets her bag down with a thud. Looks at me with lips pinched. A tough-love look, hard and dry. "This will get easier, Sharon," she says. "But we have to start from wherever we are. Okay?"

Maybe I shouldn't be surprised to freak out, I think, watching Broom-Hilda's shoulders work as she parts the curtains and unpacks her bag. Maybe it's a good sign to freak out. A glimmer of recognition. A sane, sensible *what the fuck* coming through all the unreality. It's the kind of thing I would say to Mel. If Mel were here. If I could talk.

I used to have such confidence in my mind. I had faith in the life I had created for myself—the serviceable, productive outer persona, and my inner life, the one I could only inhabit in my head. I prided myself on my ability to control the two. Now both have collapsed.

I would give anything to be able to speak. To write, to draw. My old self grows faint, moving in and out of darkness.

ONE DAY, WHEN I'M not concentrating too hard, I feel my eyes suddenly click into focus. The letters pop out at me: C-A-T. I know what they are. I wonder where they've been. I reach out to finger the cards, grateful to the point of tears.

I try to tell Broom-Hilda, *I can see the letters now,* but I'm still grunting and drooling. "Good" is all she'll say. But this marks the day when the lessons begin to move a little faster, with a little less pain. Consonants snap off between my teeth. I push the dead side of my lips up with my fingers.

My first official word is said during therapy, working with one of those muscle-building handsprings. I drop it on the floor and, without thinking, go, "Shit."

•   •   •

THERE'S A BIG INTERVIEW with Brecky Tolliver in *Paste*. *"The longer I'm in this business,"* Mel reads aloud, *"the more I internalize my own process. It's a protective mechanism. By discussing my process, I find I'm killing it."* Mel rolls her eyes grandly. *"I will say that it's important to ask yourself throughout your process: Is this* important? *Is it* relatable? *Have you fine-tuned your bullshit detector?"* She flaps the magazine down on the table. "If I were Brecky's bullshit detector I'd be going off constantly. I'd run the fuck out of batteries."

I study the arm where they keep taking blood, a map of blue and green bruises. I draw a deep breath. Manage "Yep."

Mel's face lights. She forgets about Brecky for a moment. "That's good," she says. "You sound awesome."

I roll my eyes. Try to smile.

"I just hate how sanctimonious she can be," she continues. "She has this holier-than-thou way of trying to mystify what she does, make it this exclusive practice the rest of us are too dumb to get. Which is sad. I mean, what good is it to do this for a living if you can't share it with people? If it doesn't bring people together?"

I shrug. Raise one palm skyward.

She folds her knee up and rests her chin on it. Looks at me knowingly. "You don't want to work with her," she says. It's not a question.

I don't move. There's no signal or hand motion I could make to tell her what I'm thinking. That I might be lucky to work again, period.

WHEN I'M ABLE, I ask Mel what she does with her days. She has moved our stuff from the motel to a swampland house, posted for rent with a yard sign. She tells me about a makeshift drafting table she has constructed in its living room from a broken table and some plywood. "For when we start working again," she says.

I ask for a mirror by holding my hand flat in front of me.

I know right away from the look on Mel's face that it's bad. That there's a reason I haven't been allowed a mirror to see my reflection.

"Sorry," she says. "I don't have one on me."

I point to the bathroom.

She looks uneasy. "I don't think that's a good idea."

I slump my shoulder, put my head to the side: *How bad is it?*

"You're fine," she says. "I just know how you are. If you're not looking like you just had a blowout and a facial, you'll stress about it. One thing at a time, okay?"

I jab at her arm.

"How about you can see yourself in the mirror when you can get your ass up and get it yourself? How about that."

I'm getting angry. I turn away.

Finally, she sighs. "Goddammit. Fine. You *pretty* girls, your vanity is unbearable, you know that? Hold on. I'll fetch you your motherfucking mirror."

She disappears into the bathroom, emerges with a small compact. Hesitates for a moment before putting it into my outstretched hand. I linger, too, before training it on myself.

It's even worse than I expected. It's the me-but-not-me, the palsied, bizarro world me. My pupils are dilated, giving me a goggling, slightly deranged look. There are purple patches below my eyes, like I've been clocked hard from both sides. My head has been shaved, leaving the whole bald, small, misshapen. The entire left side of my face slopes down—my eye, my lips spilling to the side, badly cracked. My cheek hangs loose, like someone's let the air out. I reach up, touch my jaw. I can barely feel it.

"They had to shave," Mel says. "They thought they were going to have to operate at first. But it's already growing back. See? Look at you, blondie."

When I start to cry, only the right side of my face moves.

"Hey," Mel says. She reaches out and takes my head in her hands. "You're getting better every day. I know you can't see it, but I do. Don't do this, Sharon."

I've never been a knockout, but God knows, I was glad for what

I had. I have been someone who has made her living from sketching the exterior, as well as the interior, of *things*. I have made a livelihood from the appeal of the visual. It's hard to ignore the shallow scream in my head: *I am totally unfuckable.* I was already a failure with men, before this. This is the point from which I will never bounce back.

Before she leaves for the night, Mel leans over the bed and gives me an awkward, one-armed hug. "You're beautiful, shitbritches," she says. "Don't cry."

I sniff her shoulder. Camel Lights, something mealy and warm. Fabric softener. But no booze.

I'M HAVING TROUBLE RECALLING words. Broom-Hilda encourages me to get back to work so I can rebuild my synapses. "The connecting fibers of your brain," she says. "Think of them as interstates. They help you get from one thought to another. We're repaving them."

Someone brings me a sketchpad, a pack of colored pencils. I spend an entire morning staring at a blank page. Gripping a pencil with my fist like a kindergartner, I manage to draw one dark, square apple.

"HOLLINGSWORTH PEOPLE CALLED," MEL tells me on her next visit. "Uh huh?"

"I said you were getting back on your feet. Same thing I tell Donnie when she threatens to fly out."

I wriggle my nose, adjust the nasal clamp. I'm still hooked up to oxygen. My hands are getting stronger, more flexible. I can finger things well enough now to pick my nose and ears. Sometimes I find myself doing so involuntarily in front of Mel, who thinks it's hilarious, yells, "Pick a winner, dollface."

When I first woke up, Mel asked me if I wanted to call anyone. Another reason my gratefulness trumps any residual anger I might feel toward her: Anyone else would have called my family on their own initiative, but Mel knew better. How can I stay mad at her when she so totally and completely *gets* it?

She asks again. "You sure you don't want me to call your mom or something? Well, I guess you'll be able to do it yourself pretty soon. Doc says you're an overachiever at the rehab stuff."

"No."

"You sure?"

"Yep."

She shifts in her seat and sighs. "Sharon, I feel a little weird not calling. I mean, I understand, obviously. But you had a *stroke,* dude. Don't you think they'll want to know?"

I shrug.

She kicks one leg up to hook around her knee, braids her hands together above her head, and sighs. She looks good. Laundered and showered. She visited a salon and had her hair rebleached. "Well, all right, boss. If that's the way you want it, then by God, that's the way you gots it."

I reach out to the control panel to shift my bed up. My legs twinge as the mattress elevates. I cry out. "What's wrong," Mel says.

I gesture. She jogs out of the room, returns with a nurse holding a clipboard, who leans in to adjust the morphine.

I have been in the hospital for five weeks. Our first Hollingsworth pay installment is months away; all our savings are going to pay the rent on our empty studio in New York. Here, my room has a window view onto the parking lot and, beyond that, the green: lots of sharp, low shrubbery, patches of soil that peter out into sand at the margins. When the window is open the smell is rich, bacony; I pantomime the question to Mel, making a frying pan motion only she would understand. "Salt," she says. "Ocean's not far."

I close my eyes. When I open them, there's a new, rosy glow to the room's edges. The morphine is taking over. I feel myself sliding toward sleep, relieved that Mel is here. I want to keep her in the room with me for as long as I can.

"Lite-Brite," I say.

She chuckles to herself. Removes a small nail clipper from her jacket pocket, worries it over her thumb. "She wants to hear the Lite-Brite story," she mutters.

The Lite-Brite story is the part of *Nashville Combat* that really gets to people. It was posted on YouTube to promote the movie; it's the scene people send to their friends, and when it's shown in theaters, the crowd erupts. Mel had her way with the scene, reverting to the twitching, trip-wire expressions of the opening credits. And the tones: bombastic, intense. The fruit of the hours Mel spent nerding out over her color key game, a massive shade chart occupying the screen of her desktop Mac, aiming for that grainy, ghostly seventies neon, the look of K-tel record sleeves and ColecoVision graphics. After all, isn't that the future we envision for ourselves: all brighter colors and dramatic graphics, everything at its ultimate zenith?

It's still best, however, to hear Mel tell the story herself.

"Say it as a full sentence," she prompts.

I take a deep breath, start it slow, trying to imagine every letter. "Tell the story."

The clippers *snick-snick*. "Okay. So Nanny—that's Mom's mom—got me a Lite-Brite for Christmas, right? It was awesome. I can still remember what the plastic smelled like, pulling it out of the box. Nanny wasn't around much when I was older. She and Mom had a falling-out over Mom taking her clothes off for money, because Nanny was a born-again Christian. In some ways. All my older cousins, their parents worked all the time or were just fuckups who had dropped them at Nanny's and took off. So they were always running around her place and she was constantly yelling, *Don't you tetch my grape juice* or *You tetch my grape juice what's in the fridge and I'll smack you black and blue.*"

I giggle, my legs twinging. She's getting to the part I love.

She finishes with her nails, steps down to the edge of my bed. Takes hold of my foot and begins, gingerly, to trim the big toe. It's an odd feeling: her hands warm, that cool, unsheathing sensation of nails trimming off. I wouldn't expect it to be soothing, but it is.

"It was actually boxed wine. Like this big, generic thing of boxed wine. If there's one thing that improves the blood of Christ, it's having a mugful during *Donahue,* right?" Mel palms my clippings into the trash can. "Anyway. I had just learned to read, and I could write, a little. My cousin Arnie taught me to write the word *fuck.* He said that *fuck* was the worst thing you could say to someone. So I started leaving little messages for Mom in the Lite-Brite."

"Like what?"

In the movie, Mel's mom is canoodling with her boyfriend on the couch when, out of the corner of the frame, a small, yellow-haired Mel slowly rears her head, holding a Lite-Brite, the marquee rising into view: *FUCK YOU MOMMY.*

It hurts to laugh, but I do anyway.

"Yeah. Or *FUCK OFF MOMMY.* Or, you know, *BUTT.* Once, the word *FART.* I was a kid of super-classical tastes."

I laugh harder. I knock my oxygen tubes loose. Mel leans over and readjusts them. Goes to work on my other foot.

"She never saw them, though. Not until this one night when this guy she had over saw it all lit up and laughed himself stupid. But because *he* liked it, because *he* thought it was funny, *she* liked it. Which wholly and completely took the fun out of it. Which was when I quit."

"Sad," I say.

"What. That she didn't care, or that I quit?"

I hold my hands out, waggle them: both.

"Yeah. Well." Her grin fades down to something small, reflective. She tosses the last of the nail clippings away. Tucks the blanket in around my feet.

In the movie, there's a short follow-up scene to this story—the next morning Mel's mom crawls out of bed, sees the Lite-Brite, and in a face-twisting fit of rage, she throws it out the window, where it is quickly claimed by the trailer park's feral cat pack. Mel's mother has absolute murder in her eyes during the cut. It's weird and abrupt, as a scene; amid all the noise, it is governed by a pregnant sort of silence.

It always made me wince a little, seeing these parts. But Mel doesn't change, watching her mom destroy her Lite-Brite over and over. Sometimes she laughs. The joke is our default, even when it feels like we're beyond the point of making them.

THE FIRST TIME I try to walk on my own with the twin beams in the Exercise Room, I shit my pants.

First I'm upright, straining, putting weight on my right arm in exactly the fashion I've been warned against, and then the gates release and it's over. The nurses know right away. "Okay," they say, "okay." I'm hustled back to my room to be changed.

I keep my eyes closed while an orderly lays me down and undresses me. I try to picture myself somewhere else, my humiliation as distant object. It's at least the tenth time this week someone has seen my vagina without the intention of having sex with it.

I tried not to cry when they removed my catheter, after I woke up. It didn't work. It doesn't work when I'm being changed, either.

I AM BROUGHT A copy of this month's *Animator's Digest*. They did an interview with us right before the panel discussion. We are photographed in the studio, Mel in oversized flannel and Docs, nineties-style, feet cocked up on the desk, a pencil between her teeth. I am positioned behind her to hide my gut chub and double chin. The version of me who could walk and talk and feed herself, who could cry with both sides of her face.

I keep thinking about that picture as the MRI takes me into the tube, its machinery sliding me into the dark. *Mel Vaught and Sharon Kisses in their studio, Brooklyn, NY.*

Our Kotex commercial airs the same week the article is released. We were hired to design something "pad-centric" when *Nashville Combat* was in postproduction and we were subsisting on lentils and six-packs of PBR. We were instructed to steal some thunder from tampon usage with a "fun, lighthearted spot" showcasing the company's new Super Light Close-to-You sanitary napkin. "Isn't that a Carpenters song?" Mel said after they approached us.

We like to work backward, usually starting with a character's essence—the look, the feel, the sound. The shit they'd say. The way they walk—is it a swagger? A tiptoe? A duck shuffle? Do they have an inner-ear infection, a bum knee? Only then, when they have a *body,* do they make it to the lightboard. Some imagine themselves quickly, with slippery ease; they cannot wait to be born. Others, not at all. This is a tough one, because it's a *thing*—or, moreover, a product—we have been hired to sell.

When we're stuck, like we were with Kotex, we talk it through. We retreat to the far end of the studio to toss a dirty pink Spalding ball Mel bought from a bodega back and forth. There's something about watching the ball's arc through the air, feeling its contact with the hand, that does something for thought. Ideas seem to come easier, the underlying wisdom of process and plan appearing in flashes, silver minnow bellies in the waters of distraction.

Mel tossed the ball in the air, let it drop, swooped down to cradle it. "I don't know if I want to do this," she complained.

I clapped my hands, held them up to make the catch. "It's thirty thousand."

"Dude, we just finished a fuckin movie. I'm tired. Come on."

"We need the money." I wound up, then threw it soft, a perfect parabola. "I need you to want to."

She caught it, kept it. Jumped up and down. Rubbed her eyes. "What do they want," she bleated.

"You know what they said. *Glorify* the Kotex. They said *empower* the Kotex, if memory serves."

"So basically we're trying to market a half diaper for grown-ass women here."

"Exactly. So think. How do we *empower* pads?"

Mel turned. Tossed the ball against the wall. It thocked, came back. "Make em fight."

"I'm not sure we should make them living things."

"Or should we? Dude. *Vampire* Kotex."

"Gross."

"Or this. Ladies and gals, on their cycles, in a brawl. Wearing super-absorbent Kotex while throwing down." She winged the ball up the wall again, harder. "One of em swinging a chain around like, *YAAH! Kotex: Soak Up the Rage!*"

"Softer tagline, maybe?"

She ran a hand through her hair, squinted into the middle distance. Said slowly, *"Kotex: As Tough as You Are."*

And there it was. We blocked the commercial quickly, posting a fierce little storyboard in a night, pacing out the images. Me re-arranging the frames to form a tiny, ten-second arc ending with the tagline in voiceover, hovering over it for a couple of hours before calling it good. Mel started inbetweening the next morning and I joined in, letting the sketches pile and multiply.

Later that week, Mel called a bunch of people over to record sound, Surly Cathie directing, me feeding them cues and beer. Making the sound of a shitstorm is no big deal with equipment as bad as ours; for the purposes of a fight, with feedback slicing in and out, working with crap really paid off. For some of the scenes, we piled into our closet to yell and punch against our winter coats. Surly Cathie and Fart and the interns got loaded and made war cries at each other. The night ended with Fart putting his nutsack through an uncooked pizza crust, flashing the interns, and almost breaking our lightboard by flicking the button on and off and screaming, "It's a disco inferno!" All in all, one of the quickest, cleanest projects we've ever completed.

And now the commercial is airing late-night on Cartoon Network. Mel flaps around, an unlit cigarette tucked behind her ear, and gathers some nurses together to watch: It's a girl-on-girl gang fight in squiggling, exciting neon, loud and short and sharp. Lots of big hollering, vermilion yelling mouths, magenta tongues. It's good. Short but precise, clean, alive. *Kotex: As Tough as You Are.* Everyone claps.

It hits me how badly I want to get back to work, how much I've been missing it. The anticipation before a new project. Envisioning it in the confines of your own head, intangible, a whiff of itself, two steps from a daydream. Then, through work and love and sheer fucking will, it becomes real. If you're lucky, what you've made will be better than anything your flimsy imagination could have put together.

I want to see Mel work again. The way she looks at a sketch when it's done—raking her hands through her hair, cracking her knuckles, muttering, "All right. Next." I live for that moment. Live for the way seeing her work makes *me* want to work, and work more, work better, work more deeply.

I suddenly miss it so fiercely my stomach cramps. My eyes start to water.

Mel leans in. "What is it?"

I shake my head.

"Are you on *your* cycle? Wanna fight?" She crumples her empty soda can in her fist, wings it gently at me. Says low, "Seriously. You okay?"

The nurses file out, patting me on the shoulder, agreeing that it was unlike any other Kotex commercial they've ever seen.

Mel waits until we're alone. Looks hard at me, says, "You sure you're all right?"

I nod. She takes a deep breath, and for a moment I'm positive she's going to ask about the List, request that I tell her just what the hell she found, exactly, and what it means. What I've been doing.

But she doesn't. She gives me a soft noogie instead and, closing the blinds, leaves to let me go to sleep.

THE BOYFRIEND PARADE

I BECOME A WARD FAVORITE BECAUSE I'M GETTING BETTER. DOCS POKE their heads in to say hi. I have regular nurses who are cheerful, ginger with the needle when they take blood. Two of them, Agatha and Jessica, teach me how to roll over by demonstrating in the room's other, empty bed, folding their hands over their chests and saying, "Come on, honey, just shift that weight from one side to the other. Use your arm and use your butt."

We are in discovery mode—testing the waters, trying to gauge how *damaged* I might be. We won't really know the full extent for years, I'm warned. Not really. Jessica is on one side, Agatha on the other, telling me *come on, just one more push,* and I swing and roll, almost falling off the bed and pissing myself. They clap.

The first day I get up to pee on my own is an event. Passing a bowel movement, and then passing a movement without requiring help wiping, is a double event. I watch reruns of *The Simpsons* while using my hand clench, squeezing, breathing. I try to stretch. Grit my teeth through muscle spasms. Food still spilling from my mouth. Bad back, precarious pelvic floor. I have never been more aware of my body than in this period of weakness. I look out the window onto the parking lot, the salt air seeping in.

The nurses station me in a chair, blanket thrown around my legs. One of the orderlies, Carl, takes the screws off the bedside table and props it against the wall to form a makeshift drafting board. In thanks, I draw, at his request, a naked Homer and Marge performing a sweaty, strenuous doggy-style. "Make that ass tight, you know what I'm saying?" Carl says. "I mean, get them titties to swaying."

I try to zero in on the lines, the sense of flow. The end product is not great, would be discouraging were it not for the clean, sweet feeling of completion. My fingers are weak, my wrists tremble, but after a week or so I know where the line is going when I start to trace. Some part of me is relearning how to anticipate.

Soon I'm sketching for all the nurses and orderlies. Most bring in school photos of their kids. I start to read a little: newspapers from the waiting room, back issues of *Time* and *Rolling Stone*. Speaking is slow, frustrating. Some words return faster than others, old friends. Others wait for me just over the edge of the cliff, never to materialize.

Mel takes my sitting upright as a sign that work can commence.

The next visit, she plunks her dirty pink JanSport at her feet and looks to me for a moment, biting her lip. "Brainstorm?"

I try to look purposeful. I've put a sweater on over my hospital gown, in an effort to feel more like a person, less like a patient.

Mel is our fire-starter, the flint against the stone, sparking with ideas. She's started a hundred projects she's never finished. Puppet Parliament. An all-lesbian version of *Oklahoma!* Each idea better than the last.

But I am our finisher. I make us Finish Shit. I stake faith in the outline, designing the checklist needed to complete the day. I can carry my weight of design tasks, sure, but I am the only one who makes us beat the path to the storyboard and back to sketching, and that's always what counted, at the early stages. Checking our notes, posting details for later addition around the Mac. I mind the story, knowing that the story will serve as the supporting beams upon which our little men will dance; all that which, under Mel's fingers, will come alive.

But what can I mind now? With only half my words on a good day, my drawing hand like a latex glove filled with sand. We look at each other apprehensively. We wonder how this is going to go.

"Okay, man. Let's hit it."

Mel flips open her work journal and starts jogging out the also-rans, trying to see if something will stick. Lesbian *Oklahoma!* redux. Pass. A stop-motion version of the 1994 Stanley Cup finals, with the New York Rangers playing the Vancouver Canucks, in which the players are giraffes. No reason other than it would be fun to put together. Maybe. A fake nature documentary about strange animal sex practices (mosquitoes—but fucking! manatees—but fucking!) called *A Metric Butt-Ton of Love*. A saga of a time-traveling chimp titled *Time Monkey!* A short about a drug dealer operating out of a defunct porta-potty in a park on Staten Island. Some horseshit we came up with about what it would be like if cats learned to drive cars (a lot of accidents and fires and yowling). On and on. No, no, no.

Mel is squinting at me now, chewing her bottom lip. Her hair is sticking up in the back. She's been patient. She's getting tired. I'm getting tired. Thinking is hard work. Talking is harder.

And then she snaps: "Okay. I'm fuckin *dying* here, man. What about your journal? What about some of the ideas in there? What *was* that, anyway? Why haven't I seen it before? Who's Teddy Caudill? Can we talk about this? There were a shit-ton of ideas in there. The thing is *bleeding* ideas. I mean, it's raw, man. What the fuck *is* it?"

Despite myself, I marvel at Mel, at the way the world she and I inhabit together works: When I am physically unable to disclose something, she remedies my lack, goes out and finds what I'm thinking anyway.

I stare at her, dumbstruck. She lifts her hands, shakes them. Yelps "Come on!"

I take a deep breath. Then another. I can practically feel my face going green. Just the thought of talking about the List, telling the whole story, feeling the words as they form and leave my mouth, robs my entire body of oxygen. I burp deeply.

Mel rises from her chair. She knows the look on my face. "Oh no," she says. She goes for the trash can, hauls it over to me just in time for me to empty my lunch into it.

When I'm done, I say very slowly, teeth clenched, "Stop for today."

She nods. Reaches out and taps my head. "You know," she says thoughtfully, "when you're angry, your intonation levels out. Broom-Hilda should totally use this as a therapy tactic."

MEL COMES BACK FOR visiting hours the next night. Instead of asking about the List again, she says, "It's nice out. I bet they'd let you take a walk."

I've just been issued an aluminum cane, a big one that descends into spider legs for reinforcement. Mel keeps pace with me, matching heel for toe as I hobble to the elevator and out the sliding door.

It's dusk. The sky fades from pink to purple to blue overhead. Visible stars. There's a flower garden at the side of the hospital. A small brick path leads from the ambulance drive to a couple of stone benches. When we arrive, I turn, position myself, and grasp Mel's arm to lower my seat down, knees cracking loudly. "Fuck," I whisper, wincing.

"Are you okay?" she asks.

"Yeah."

Mel reaches into her shirt pocket and produces her Camels. "So," she says. "I'm sorry if I hassled you too hard about the journal. Guess I got excited when you started drawing again. Got carried away."

"It's fine."

"Did not mean to make you hork. How are you feeling?"

"Just had a stroke. No jazz hands yet."

"Heh." She exhales a plume of smoke. "There's that knife-sharp wit. You're still sparky." She flicks ash into the grass. "You know what I've been thinking might make a good project? The stroke. I mean, that'd make a hell of a story, right? You're going to have to relearn a lot of your skill set. Why not make that, you know, *the* project? Could be really interesting."

I make a guttural sound. Shake my head. Say, "Don't want people to know."

Mel coughs softly.

"What."

"Avoiding the Internet, I see."

"What."

"I kinda hate to tell you this, but word's out. Thirty-two-year-old artist, at the top of her game, has a stroke. It's sort of made you famous."

"Fuck," I say.

"That the only word you know anymore?" She raps my head gently. "You're so brilliant, your brain exploded, superstar. *Nashville Combat* was so real it made you stroke *out*."

I look down. My knees are skinny beyond recognition. I go, "Guh." Shake my head.

"Is that a no?"

"No," I say, slow and strong.

She let it drop for a moment. We watch an ambulance cruise up, turn off its lights. Go still. Then she says, "Making the movie was hard. I'll give you that. Probably the hardest thing I've ever done. Couldn't do anything else, work on anything else, until it was all finished. But then it's out in the world. And it's *yours*. Closest I'll ever come to giving birth. It's yours, too, you know. It's as much yours as it is mine."

It makes my face heat, to hear this. Makes me feel bumbling and sheepish and warm to hear Mel praise something I do. Every time.

She puts her head down, rubbing her neck slowly in thought. "There's this weird thing people tend to do, I think, when they're working something that hard," she says, "where they'll kind of disassociate. And that worked, some days. Just separate your feeling self from the rest of your head and plow through. But most of the time, I hated my life then. I lived in the only way I knew how, and honestly, I only got a couple of ways. When your day is filled with digging through all the interior shit you could never handle otherwise, your nights are going to consist of trying to get away from the day. And I will admit that I went overboard. With the drinking and stuff. It messed things up with you. It messed up a lot."

I think: *discorporate.*

She gives her Camel one last pull—her second, lit off the first— and crushes it under her heel. Tilts her head from side to side, stretching, then slumps over, props her chin on her hand. Says quietly, "You could be dead right now. You know that? This has been—I don't know, man. When it happened, they weren't sure you weren't going to be a vegetable. And when they told me, you know. That you might not come out of this. It was like, fuck. Too late."

She swallows hard, nods at the ground. I think of the night we watched our Kotex commercial. She misses what I miss, too. Our life. Working.

I don't know what to say. I reach into my bathrobe pocket, bring out the spring-bound hand clench. I squeeze it with one hand, then the other.

"And look at you," she says. "Almost two months later, you're walking. You're talking. You're drawing. This is an opportunity to do something big. Don't you think this is the time to be brave, and make something scary and new and incredible?"

"I don't feel like me," I say. I point to myself. Try to say it with my hands. Give up.

"But you will," she tells me. "I know what you're capable of. You *are* this story, man. We got some good ideas, but this is the best."

She pauses.

"Whatever you become, whatever you decide," she says finally. "*That's* the story."

"What will I be."

"Better. Stronger. Faster." She gestures to my hands. "See? Holy shit, look at those hands. Those are choking hands."

I swat her on the back of the head.

She laughs and stands, tan and muscular, to stretch. Her cheeks have filled out. She's been eating again, smoking less. Taking runs. "Want to hear something weird? I started getting the shakes watching *Nashville Combat*. During panels and stuff."

I nod. Say, "The flask."

She tilts her head back, unsurprised that I saw. "That's one way to deal with the shakes." She holds her hand out. "Got something for you out in the car. Come on, Mamaw."

I take her hand, heft myself up, and we shuffle to the rusted Mazda she bought for four hundred dollars the week after my stroke. She wrenches the trunk open and grabs a box. Holds it out.

I fumble with it, hands trembling. She gently reaches over and pries it open for me. It's a new MacBook Pro, sleek and silver and heavy.

She carries it for me as we walk back inside and step into the elevator. "My advice," she says before she leaves, "if I'm in a position to give it. Start brainstorming stuff. Just write shit down without thinking about it. Plug in as many details as you can. You'll be surprised how little things turn into big things. Okay? Just try. It's like exercising."

I stare at the MacBook sitting on my bedside table, a lump in my throat. It's a sweet, honest gift. I can't remember the last time someone bought me an actual present.

"I will try," I say.

T HEY GIVE ME A release date of two weeks into October, not so much because I'm ready to be out on my own but because, after almost two months, the insurance is running out. Dr. Weston manages to tell me this with a straight face. "It's not the best of circumstances," he says. "But you're ready for outpatient work now. It's as good a time as any."

Now that I will be shifting to "outpatient status," I figure I should finally call home.

Without letting myself stop to reconsider, I pick up my room phone and dial the 606 area code. It's the speediest physical thing I've done in weeks. My body remembers the number to my mother's house in Kentucky better than it remembers how to hold a pencil.

Mom picks up on the third ring. "Hello?"

Let me give you an idea of the way my mother talks: When she says *washrag*, it comes out *warshrag*. The name *Kent* is two syllables: *Kee-yent*. And she is loud. She is *very* loud.

"Hey," I say slowly. "It's me."

"Well, hey yourself," she says, with only a slight lilt of surprise. "Been wondering where you've been at."

There have been times, in the past couple of years, when I let myself lapse, phone calls to home spaced a month, six weeks apart. But each time Mom picks up to learn that it's me, it's this same mild voice, as if I'm calling from the dentist to remind her of her yearly cleaning.

I take a deep breath. "How are you, Mom?"

"Oh, tolerable. Been having some bad storms down here. Sump pump broke again."

"Sorry. That sucks."

"Well, we're making do. You know." I picture her holding something—a strainer, a cigarette—that she has to put down so she can lean over the breakfast bar in the kitchen, by the phone jack. "I expect we'll manage. Y'all getting some of this stuff up where you're at?"

"I'm not in New York," I say. "I have something to tell you. And I am going to say it all at once. Okay?"

Silence. Too glib for her taste. "Uh, *okay*."

"I'm in a hospital in Florida. I had a stroke. I've been here about two months."

More silence. "Well, how'd *that* happen?" There's a note of accusation here, a high tone on the word *that*, the *happen* low and knowing.

"It was an aneurysm. It broke. There was bleeding."

"Aneurysm," she says. It's half a question.

I heave a sigh. "Yes. Aneurysm."

"Well. You all right?"

I put my head in my hand. "Yes. I'm in the hospital."

"Why Florida?"

"That's where we were when it happened. We were working."

"Florida," she says thoughtfully. There's a lull of a few seconds. Talking to Mom feels like jogging with an intentionally slow partner. Every few strides, I have to run in place and wait, or go back for her. Yet it's clear: This effect is *my* fault. *She* feels the imposition. "Iddint that where your friend's from?"

"Yeah. We were here for work. She's with me."

"Huh. That's good." I hear a lighter click. Mom was once a Newport woman but has, in recent years, switched to Dorals. I close my eyes and see her Toyota Tercel, littered with green-and-white foil packages in various states of fullness. "Well. I'm glad you're all right. That musta scared you. Scares me."

"I'm okay."

"Well, if you're lookin for me to get down there, I don't think I can until next week or so. They're workin me pretty hard up to the cleaner's."

"That's okay," I say. "I have good news, too. We got this fell—fell." I start over. "A big arts grant. We get to make another movie."

In the middle of a fight once, my mother told me that I was the only member of the family harebrained enough to get a scholarship to a *big fancy school* and then waste it by "drawing pictures all day."

"Congratulations," she says mildly.

"Thanks. You sound so happy. I love how proud of me you are."

"Now, don't start with that shit. Just quit right now." There's a thud, a sharp intake of breath. She cusses. Says, "Hold on."

"Mom—"

"I said hold *on,* dammit."

There are bangs, then a muffled, feminine voice behind her. My sister, Shauna. She and her husband and kids live next door to our mother—same holler, nooks one alongside the other accessible by the same road. A thick grove of pines and brambles on a slope separates the two properties. Shauna's kids used to scramble over the rise until last summer, when my nephew was bitten by a copperhead and had to be rushed to the emergency room.

Mom and Shauna have a soft back-and-forth. The diphthongs give me goosebumps. "Sa-yed. Nah-owh." The broadness of the word *time*. Sounds I didn't realize I'd forgotten. I tear up and feel like an idiot.

Mom's back. "You wanna talk to your sister?"

I do not want to talk to my sister. "Well, I don't want to—"

"Here she is." She cups the mouthpiece, says audibly to Shauna, "She's right here. Come on."

Some protest, then Shauna's on. "Hey."

"Hey."

"Mom says you're sick?"

"Yeah."

"What happened?"

That same note of blame. I let my head fall back into the pillow. Jesus, Mary, and the fucking *donkey*. "I had a stroke."

"Oh my *God*. Are you okay?"

"Getting better. It was small. I was lucky."

"Well, that's good. You sound all right."

"Thanks." I pluck at the blanket, glance over at my sketchpad. "It was an aneurysm. It broke."

Shauna makes this *huh* sound between a laugh and a grunt. "Um . . . hope you feel better?"

"Thanks, Shauna. Shit."

"Come on. You know what I mean."

"How are the kids?"

"Oh, they're good," she sighs. "Caelin is bugging me to get Glamour Shots cause she saw our old ones."

I smack my hand into my forehead. Forced to wear false eyelashes at age seven. Just one in a long list of household abominations. "You gonna do it?"

There's a moist chomp: whitening gum. My sister's a dental hygienist. Her teeth are horribly perfect. Straight, bleached, gums tight and pink. "Well, if she wants to do it, *Sharon,* I don't see nothin wrong with it."

"Good job."

"Whatever. I gotta go."

"Okay."

"Come down and visit before Mom has a shitfit. Okay? *Bye.*"

THE DAY BEFORE MY release, I dress myself. My hands tremor, my left side slumps, but it's something I can do now, provided I sit while putting on my pants, lifting one skinny leg into the opening, then the other, and then, when the waistband is at a high, safe level, rise to pull them up. The first morning, I went at it standing and ended up rolling around on the floor in my granny panties.

One positive: My stomach is now flat. I poke, fascinated. Neat. It ain't a six-pack, but by Christ, I can see my navel for the first time in five years. I've subsisted on starchy hospital food during my stay, re-acquainting myself with Snack Pack and lukewarm Sprite, greater comfort than a mother's teat. And still, I've lost nearly sixty pounds, mostly muscle mass. I am to take supplements, drink Ensure, do my strength exercises. I run my hand over my head. My hair's grown back, thin and milky. There's been a blonde in me all along. I would enjoy looking in the mirror more if one side of my mouth didn't drip down my face.

I walk to the window and smell the air, closing my eyes. Car exhaust and minerals and salt. It's the smell of being in unfamiliar but comfortable limbo. Florida is, for now, easier. In New York, I would never stop being reminded of my body's new frailty.

My suitcase is packed, waiting for when Mel picks me up the next day. On top, my new laptop is closed.

I pick up the laptop and start for the blue Word icon but find myself opening Firefox instead. I grimace. I used to be better about this: buckling down, not even letting myself check my email until I got my hours in. But the curiosity has been digging me raw.

I take a deep breath and type in my name. There's our Facebook fan page. There's the Tumblr that Mel updates with bloody clips from old grind-house movies and (occasionally) our stuff. Then I see results:

Nashville Combat Creator Hospitalized After Aneurysm

Nashville Combat Creator in Serious Condition

Mother of Nashville Combat's Vaught Dies After Assault

The Burdens and Responsibilities of the Memoirist

Skip, skip, skip. At the bottom, an old press release from *ReAnimator* for *Nashville Combat,* clip included. It's the trailer arrest scene—that's exactly how it was labeled on the storyboard at the beginning of things, when *Nashville Combat* didn't even have an ending yet: *Trailer Arrest.*

I pause, remembering the day we came up with the idea for this section. Mel came into the studio late one morning after dropping ketamine and playing *Street Fighter* on NES all night, thumbs still twitching, absently chatty. Said, "I saw a hooker getting off the JMZ and she reminded me so much of my mom I almost asked *her* for money."

I was at the drafting table, shoeless and sockless, an enormous cup of coffee in my hand. Just kind of fucking around. It struck me, when she said this. Before *Combat,* Kelly Kay—and Mel's life in Florida, anything more extensive than what she'd told me the first night I met her—had been an incidental and rare topic of talk. It just didn't come up much. And sensing blood there, or the possibility of blood if I brought it up at the wrong time, or in the wrong way, I didn't press.

So I was interested. "How so?" I asked her.

Mel tilted her head back. "For the obvious reasons," she said.

It was something I'd suspected for years—what Mel's mom had done, exactly, for money—from stories, little hints. This was the first time Mel had actually confirmed it.

"But she had boyfriends, right?" I said. "What did they think of that?"

"Boyfriends and prostitution are not necessarily mutually exclusive," Mel said. "But that probably had something to do with choice in boyfriend."

She began going through them one by one, naming years, events, strained Red Lobster dinners. There was, it seemed, a perfect mathematical equation to Mel's mom's boyfriends; the overall assiness of each was a squared multiple of the one who'd come before him. Finally, we hit on the subject of Red Line Dickie and the summer he taught Mel how to help him steal from Walmart and various gas stations in their town.

I said, "So did it ever strike you as odd that your mom and I share a middle name?"

"Hee." Mel laced her hands together and put them behind her head. "That old Southern sound pattern. First name two syllables, middle name one. Like 'shave and a haircut.' "

"It's as much my fault as the rest of my name." I rose, throwing the Spalding from palm to palm, wiggling my eyebrows at her: Get up. I liked this Red Line idea, but it was going to take some badgering. It sometimes did, when she worked hungover.

She picked herself up with a grunt. I tossed the ball to her.

"What was he like?"

She caught it. "He was a big fat bastard."

Toss, *piff* into the hand. Toss, *piff*. Toss, *piff*. "Big fat bastards are fun to draw."

"Not this one. He was boring."

"Tell me how he was."

Mel winged the ball. I reached up on my toes to grab it. After a moment: "He was smart, but he didn't use his smarts too efficiently. Smart but crude. You know? The kind of asshole who thinks Benny Hill is funny. The kind of asshole who puts ketchup on his steak instead of A.1. Sauce."

"I put ketchup on my steaks."

"Well, you're kind of an asshole."

I rolled my eyes. "Give me an example. Come on. Something physical. He was big. Right?"

"Big like fat," she said. "Hairy like seventies hairy. Jesus. He used to make eggs in his tighty whities and you had to look away to keep your appetite."

I wound up for the pitch. "That Pete Rose Jockey ad from the seventies. Ever seen it? Just Pete and his skivvies and a baseball bat. And enough chest hair to smother a litter of puppies."

Mel sank to her knees, laughing. She slapped the floor. "Oh shit," she said. "That's it. That's Red Line. Give him the bowl cut and we're there."

We decided to place ourselves in the narrative, in parts, as its makers—why not be as honest as possible with whoever is watching? In the finished film we, unseen, are running this dialogue in the audio while the shot focuses on a blank canvas. In double time, my hand reaches out and starts to draw. The form takes shape and moves, just stop-motion pencil and paper, cool and rudimentary. A parade of boyfriends emerges: Brett with the nasty stache, who owned the sand bar; Dale, the creepy professional clogger; Alan in snakeskin boots, who bloodied Mel's mom's nose for her refusal to change the channel (there's an arc of blood there, and I think of the ottoman cracking our patio door, my mother heaving as she released); Red Line Dickie, the man himself, who nurtured Mel's talents as a young, petty shop-lifter.

Mel's dad was out of the picture. She had a vague notion he was in Texas running a pool scam. *I met him once,* she says in the voiceover. The point of view pulls away. We see me and Mel in the studio, me craned over the drafting board, her slumped in an easy chair, chewing on a cuticle.

Cutaway: I sketch Mel with a beard, holding a pool cue. *And?*

She pulls back her thumb with an expression of distaste. *He was a short man.*

The boyfriends fade into the landscape: the Florida swamplands. Mel's voice describes brown alligators stinking of raw sewage, clapping their mouths at marshmallows children tossed into the water, boats with mammoth fans whirling at their rears like they've drifted out of old MGM shorts. There are foot-wide lilies the color of fire, the hard shells of hypercockroaches. The boy next door named the rats scampering through his front yard. When one eventually bit him, he had to have rabies shots in the stomach and butt, becoming the neighborhood cautionary tale. *Rule number one: Don't befriend the rats,* Mel says. *They don't see the difference in the hand and what the hand is feeding them.*

The scene fades to a rusting blue trailer in a watercolor landscape. Lights flash from the windows. Indiscriminate yelling. The trailer rocks on its axis. *Let me dispel a common belief,* Mel says. *Double-wides can be pretty sweet, if you keep them clean. But ours was a wreck. Stuffing spilling out of the furniture. Food out everywhere. We'd have had rat warfare on our hands if it weren't for the cat pack.*

Zoom in on a swarm of shifty-eyed cats, tumbling over each other, biting, mewling in a freak-out chorus. *Had a whole family of them living down underneath the trailer. There were always like ten at a time. Some would get run over or eaten by alligators or tortured by mean kids, but they just kept replenishing themselves. They were unstoppable. I used to feed them popsicles.* Kid Mel holds a dripping orange bar out to a skinny gray kitten. The kitten nibbles, then begins to glow.

Then a screech: *"Melody, leave them fuckin cats alone, they're diseased!"*

Enter Mel's mom. We drew her to fill the trailer: hair, boobs, huge pink lips. We made a background track in the studio of nonsensical babbling, like a cassette tape running on hyperspeed, to play in the home scenes, to create a nonstop presence of *Mom* in every scene. *Mom was this itty-bitty woman,* Mel says. *Brief-looking, you know, like maybe five foot one, but God, she had this enormous rack, and these ropey little arms, and a lot of horsepower when it came to beating ass. She could land punches like a goddamn windmill.*

There is a lingering shot of her mother loping through the house, cutoffs falling down her lower back, rim of neon panty peeking through. *It was a few years before I discovered what my mother did for a living.*

And here, the men return, different this time, floating in and out of the front door. *They'd stay an hour or two, then leave. And I began to notice that, after they left, we suddenly had cash again, and we could go to Pizza Hut, or to the store.*

The situation was obvious to Mel, who'd just started plowing through Elmore Leonard and any other troubled-looking paperback she could get her hands on: They were *paying* for *sex.* She could hear them falling around in the bathroom in the wee hours, would awaken to find a lifted toilet seat, a few cigarette butts (*not* her mother's brand) floating in the bowl, and a fetid brown smell left by some large, strange man's meditations.

Trailer interior. Bright maroon background. Slack-jawed trucker dude adjusts his belt: *"You gon gimme a ride up the road?"*

Outside shot: The trailer door slams open. The trucker dude is chased out onto the lawn, dodging thrown bottles, magazines, coffee mugs, while a crowd of agitated cats accosts his legs going *mow mow mow mow mow.* "I ain't your fuckin chauffeur," her mom yells.

Second interior shot: Mel's mom, hair enormous, sits on their couch, a thick cloud of ganja smoke overhead. A circle of stoned dudes, red-eyed and loose, hoots at MTV's *The Grind. She did other stuff for money, too,* Mel continues. *She sold run-of-the-mill skunk weed, worth maybe five bucks for every twenty charged. Smattering of shrooms and coke, when she could get them.*

"Those guys were the reason I didn't try pot until the summer before college, by the way," Mel told me later. "They made anything look dumb. They could make open-heart surgery look stupider than hell."

Next shot: Mel, slightly older, watches from her bedroom window: A throng of police follow two plainclothes cops who posed as buyers. The scene is played out in shadow, with Mel's mom struggling, then wrestled into handcuffs. Kid Mel, dragging a suitcase behind her, being led into a police cruiser. *She went into custody,* Mel says. *And I went to live with my aunt on a swamp farm.*

In the movie, I snicker.

Don't laugh, fucker.

Sorry, it's just—it's a swamp farm.

Something occurs to me. I reach out and pause the clip.

Mel didn't want to do *Nashville Combat,* at first. She said she didn't think the idea was strong enough. But I kept haranguing her. I loved the stories she told about herself. I thought they were awesome. Funny and detailed and strong. I pushed her, like with Red Line— sketching it out with touches I knew she'd like, and then giving it to her to crack up over. One day I showed her the sketch I did of her as her dad, bearded with a pool cue. It made her laugh so hard she had to bend at the waist to let it out. "All right, *Sharon Kay,*" she con- ceded. "Maybe there's something there. But Mom. This is how you do her face."

She craned over, hand twitching, then straightened. A clear face, obviously beautiful but grimacing, staring at me from the page.

"Funny thing," Mel said. "The prettier the face, the fewer the details. Fewer lines, less sketch time. Not as complex as an old lady. Or a dude. Any dude."

Nashville Combat was the biggest thing we'd ever worked on, and the most personal. We both had the sense that the project was an extension of ourselves. A sense that it would become our shared his- tory for as long as we were immersed in its making—that I would give up my own personhood for a while and double down in Mel's, for as long as it took to finish.

It was the most energized I'd ever seen Mel. She spent hours talk- ing into a handheld recorder, rehashing old stories, grasping to recall each possible detail. She sketched school lunches: the olive-green plastic tray, the pizza, the chocolate milk, the corn. What her mother tended to wear around the house in 1989 (brief cutoffs, occasional Def Leppard T-shirt), what Mel herself wore on the first day of third grade (Reeboks, same Def Leppard T-shirt). She went online, found the make and model of the double-wide in which they had lived, and contacted the company. They explained that her particular model, River Blue 973, had been discontinued, but sent the blueprints with their compliments. We started with the details. Two years of work, the story stemming from the little things, then growing out and out.

But when the project was done, I left it behind. At day's end, the story was Mel's—a narrative of how she got from point A to point B, and, now that she was at B, how to get shed of A as completely as she could. The telling of the story was the furthest she would ever travel from her old self—to stepping outside that world and, from a safer distance, watching. It was a project I'd wanted to start because, callous, I thought it was *funny;* for Mel, it was much more. And maybe she knew it, because she was the cautious one, the one who knew that the next step we took could be into a pothole.

The last scene of the excerpt lingers on the trailer as the sky grows darker. *You know,* the voiceover continues, *it would be nice if we were defined, ultimately, by the people and places we loved. Good things. But at the end of the day, there's the reality that we're not. Does the good stuff really have the weight that the weird stuff does? What makes the deeper imprint—all the ridges and gathers—on who we are? Do we have a choice?*

I let the scene go dark and stop. There's a fluttering in my middle now. It's enough to make me lean over, close out of Firefox, and open the blinding light of Word.

WASPERS AND SNAKES

"WELCOME HOME," MEL SAYS.

It is the crappiest one-story house I've seen in a long time. Two bedrooms, a grimy kitchen, a bathroom with a filthy water heater in the corner. The deck is the house's saving grace, looking out onto a backyard lining a swamp. The grass here is sparse but dark, pocked with sandy soil running down to a grove filled with spiny overgrowth, wild and tangled all the way to the water's edge. The leaves closest to the bank are as long as my leg.

In the living room, Mel has assembled a makeshift studio. Two drawing boards assembled from plywood stacked on two old desks with coffee tables turned on their sides to make the angled sketch surface. It's been cut, hammered, and polished to a glimmer. There are pencils, inks, oils, rolls of easel paper. Onionskin she got from God knows where.

We're renting the place from a guy named Jesco, who thinks it's hilarious that we're from New York and doubly hilarious that we'd want to live in this house. He laughs and shakes his head every time he encounters us. "So this is the other'n," he says when he meets me. "The other *cartoony* gal."

"Uh, yeah."

"From *New York City,*" he wheezes.

"We're transplants," Mel explains. She's told him this before. "I'm from here. She's from Kentucky."

"Uh *huh.* So you're a *wildcat,*" he says.

I shrug. "Sure."

"I tell you what. Y'all are crazy to want to live in this piece of shit."

"It's short-term," Mel says. "Sharon here needs to rest and recuperate."

"Well. I wish you'd take the place with ye when ye go."

The rent is two fifty a month. When the toilet breaks our second week here, Jesco installs a porta-potty at the side of the house and outfits it with lime for sprinkling and a flute of plastic flowers. "Watch out for the waspers," he tells us. "And the snakes. We gotta horren-dous snake problem. They like high grass, and they like womern. Always slitherin round the womern. So y'all watch y'allselves."

Mel's attentive. She stays in the hospital lobby when I go to physical therapy, and we do the grocery shopping after: fruit, sandwich makings, cases of vanilla Ensure. In the evening, we take to the deck with ginger ale in tall glass bottles, watching their necks cloud as the stink and steam rise from the swamp. She rations cigarettes out to me, never more than three per day. "No weed yet," Mel says. "I read up on it. You smoke up right now, it could make you slow."

"Who says."

"Encyclopedia Brown, babe." She looks off, squinting at something down in the bushes. "I've cut back myself. Only after hours, now."

"Seriously?"

She looks offended. "Well, it won't *kill* me."

Now that we've settled into our temporary life in Florida, I need to give Mel an explanation about what she found in my journal. She's been patient: looking carefully at me when she thinks I don't see, opening her mouth, drawing breath, then abruptly going shut, holding herself back from the question she was going to ask.

Being sick has given me an excuse to keep it to myself. But I owe her this. Without knowing how, quite, or why, I owe it to her to tell her. I owe it to myself, I think. Had I slipped under completely—those few terrible moments under the bright lights, the self deeper than my body wavering on the dividing line between something known and something deeply, nauseatingly unknown—it would have been an unforgivable omission. Never telling anyone else about Teddy. Our summer.

I start approaching my lingual therapy sessions with this goal in mind. Get enough words back to finish this unfinished business so we can get on the other side of normal. So we can get to work again.

One night, out on the deck, I start slow. "I need to talk to you about the thing you found."

Her eyes go wide. She nods, still peering out into the yard. "Yes," she says.

"I should explain," I say to her. "I need to—I mean, it's kind of hard to, you know. Tell the whole story. But I want to."

"I *was* curious," she admits. Cracks through the weird silence, here, to give a partial grin. Trying to lighten it all up. "Yeah, man. What the hell kind of project was that?"

"It's not exactly a project." I take a deep breath. I feel a cold prickle on my skin, a dampness under my arms and behind my knees. The prospect of saying it all out loud is sending my body into revolt.

Mel leans in. "You okay?" She studies my face. I'm still shaky, still weak enough to warrant caution. "We started out pretty early today. You had therapy. If you want to go to bed early, I totally understand. There's nothing we *have* to do tonight."

"No," I tell her, gripping the armrests. "I need to do this."

Her fingers go for her breast pocket. She fumbles out a smoke. It occurs to me that she might be a little shaky, too. About what I might tell her. What she might have found. That she senses what's coming. When I reach over to grab a smoke for myself, she doesn't protest.

I take a deep breath.

TEDDY'S HOUSE

I NEED TO TELL YOU ABOUT THE DAY I SAW MY HOUSE ON THE *CBS Evening News*.

There's a difference between seeing your town on the national news and seeing it on the local. Anyone who grew up with a television containing no flyover states—nothing that represents where and who you are—will know what I mean. You will come to assume that where *you* are is not part of the greater whole.

Because of TV, I was keenly aware that there were other places, bigger places, where words were said differently, where people moved more quickly. I imagined an outline of America with only a few bright points within, the rest a hazy, slightly sinister filler. The outline spoke very little to who I was, but God knows, volumes to who I wanted to be. Which was, in a word: elsewhere. I could expect a weird, second-hand familiarity on the local news. The accents of the weathermen, the muted on-set colors. Sometimes I saw things on the local that I had seen myself first, and not through the vainglorious eye of TV: Interstate 64, Rupp Arena. A particular Walmart in Grayson where we shopped for school supplies. It seemed more opaque than real TV; seemed, somehow, to have cost less money.

But seeing your place on national TV, there's a sense that you've been incorporated into the world. And of course, context—how you and yours come into that world—means everything.

I was, as a kid, very much alone. From the adults monitoring me, criticizing me, giving me little more than a compulsion to shut out as much of the sanctimonious, supervisory world as possible—I would never, as an adult, really have a boss—to my peers, who made stiflingly sure to thin me out of their ranks as quickly as possible, my isolation was defining. It was not only how I thought of myself but how others thought of me as well. The other kids *hated* me. My own sister loved to tell me this, loved to be the carrier of sour information: what was said about me on the bus, who did a great impression of the way I walked, who wanted to kick my ass. When I asked her why—genuinely wanting her direction, a way to fit into life in our town—all she yelled was something she got off a high schooler's T-shirt: "If you cain't play with the big dogs, stay off the porch."

My parents liked my siblings more, a suspicion confirmed by nicknames, tones of voice. They *understood* my sister and brother. I baffled them. They were awed, but not made proud, by the test scores I brought home. They found the pictures I drew strange.

My kid life was a more or less constant state of humiliation, the feeling that my skin didn't quite fit me right and that everyone could see it.

"SERIOUSLY? YOU DIDN'T HAVE *any* friends?"

Mel is sitting up straight, legs stretched long and crossed in front of her. She is staring out into the yard, unseeing, the way she does when she is listening.

"Not really."

"That's really sad. You didn't have, like, rowdy little neighborhood dudes to break stuff with? Or little bitch friends who invited you to sleepovers to make fun of you?"

"No. Didn't even qualify for that."

"I did," Mel says. "Her name was Nancy. She invited me to her tenth birthday party and then told the class I was a lesbian." She gives me jazz hands. Sings, "She *knew*!"

"So what'd you do?"

"Peed in her closet."

"I've told you about Faulkner," I say. "What it was like there. Kids like me didn't really have friends." I shrug, uncomfortable, rubbing the back of my neck. "I don't know. Maybe I just repel people."

Mel rolls her eyes, shakes her head. "It wasn't you," she says. "So you didn't have friends. So what. What'd you do to pass the time?"

LOVED TV. I spent more time with TV than anyone. TV was my personal practice, my prayer, my companion—as much as I could get from after-school Hanna-Barbera reruns to *The Late Show* and all that followed. I was made crazy by the idea that I would miss something important: even the pauses, the snow-outed channels, the storm-time screen-skipping. I fell asleep in front of TV and gleaned from it the same intimacy I one day would from sleeping next to someone—the gurgles and clenches of their stomachs, their leg jerks and mutters. I was convinced that, despite all its noise, it would miss me.

But: I had one solitary friend during this time. His name was Teddy Caudill. Treasured, because he was my only one. And though I wouldn't know it for years, he was my first love.

It was a love that did not occur to us physically. It had a body in the way children handle each other when they do not yet know intimacy—closeness without electrical current. In the summers, his arms and legs tanned, the hairs turning to red gold. He smelled like sand, and sweat. Once, when we were pretending to be cats, I licked his face. Only later did I remember to be embarrassed: *Wait. That was not a thing to do.*

It was, in this way, unspoiled.

Teddy and his dad were our next-door neighbors. Teddy was a little strange himself, which was probably why we were friends—our force fields complemented one another. We spent whole summers crossing each other's yards, tracking kittens through the rotting woodpile, going to the creek to see how fast it took the water to turn our feet orange. Our family had just purchased a VCR, a Quasar, and I made Teddy watch tapes and tapes of all the TV I recorded: a cartoon showcase I adored called *Liquid Television*. *Count Duckula*. My favorite music video from MTV, an eerie stop-motion Claymation spot by a band called Tool that both frightened and excited me. "But wait," I kept saying, rewinding, pressing *play*. "Let's watch it again."

And he would. Teddy was patient, a weird enough quality on its own. He would listen to me jabber for an hour entire about Looney Tunes or *Harriet the Spy* or how much I hated my sister and say maybe two sentences throughout. But he clearly paid attention, his eyes on me, soft, bright intelligence behind them. He was the only person in my life who actually *listened* to me. Once, when I skinned my knee, Teddy slowly and carefully drew out the bits of gravel caught within using my mother's tweezers. I cried, and it hurt, but I trusted him.

*"*I LOVED THAT VIDEO." Mel shifts in her chair, ashing her cigarette. "One of mom's boyfriends, this guy Kurt, really liked me because I liked Tool. He gave me a Tool tape for my birthday. He would have made a cool stepdad."

I marvel silently. This isn't as bad as I thought it was going to be. In all my anxiety, I somehow forgot that it was *Mel* to whom I would be talking. Mel who would have questions, who would smoke and down Diet Cokes and tell me about peeing in some girl's closet. "What happened?" I say.

"Pretty sure Mom stole from him. Big shock. So, Teddy was like you. He was a weird kid."

"Well, he wasn't weird so much as just—" I get a mental image. Teddy, eating lunch one day that summer at my house. PBJ and Doritos. His skinny shoulders pulled slightly back, concentrating on his sandwich. When my mother had given it to him, he whispered a thank you before polishing it off like it was the world's most savory T-bone.

"I don't know," I say.

Mel turned her body toward me, cupping her chin in her hand, looking slightly away. "I'm glad you had someone," she says. "Thinking of you back then. With no one. It's sad."

This makes me laugh.

I can see her smiling. "Are you laughing at my empathy pains? Fuck you, Sharon."

"No no. That's really nice. You're a retroactive pal."

Mel shifts, sighs, lifts her eyebrows. "So." She flicks her Camel hard pack open, chooses a cigarette. "Tell me. When does it all hit the fan?"

I SUSPECTED SOMETHING OUT of the ordinary was going on with Teddy. It was in the way he picked through the world, watching everything like it might come down on top of him. He tapped on doors. He looked in the windows before entering his own house. He washed his hands over and over until they were nasty, waxy-clean. He bit at the chapped parts of his lips until they bled. This was a kid who operated on the basis of caution, like he had learned things that made him watch out. I wondered, in quiet moments, what was wrong with him.

I thought maybe his house was to blame. Teddy's house was openly filthy; the carpet hadn't been vacuumed in years, was sticky with ashes, pop spills, and in some places crisp, fragmented dog poop, courtesy of Teddy's mother's Pekingese, Coco, with whom she had left and not returned the year prior. But there was something else in there, something strange I could feel on my skin, a muffled line of electricity that prickled my arm hairs whenever I was alone with it.

My house wasn't exactly *good*—it was a fighting house I came from—but Teddy's house scared the shit out of me.

Even when it was just the two of us, I wouldn't go into any room without him. I made him come into the bathroom and turn around while I peed.

The only other person I'd seen there since Teddy's mom left was Teddy's dad, Honus Caudill. Honus Caudill was big and red-faced and I could hear him when he breathed. His work boots were crumpled by the door, dark at the instep. The length of his shoe was three times mine.

Sometimes I would hear low noises coming from deep within the house. I asked Teddy about it once. His mouth fell into a straight line and he said, "That's my dad," and that was all.

Honus Caudill scared the shit out of me, too, but if asked, I wouldn't be able to explain why. Yet another thing that refused to exist, because I didn't know the words to prove that it did.

Once, we saw him cleaning out the van he drove, a rusting, silver Dodge Caravan I could see limping up the side of the mountain when he came home. It was so old, its rear opened with two doors splaying out instead of a hatch rising skyward. Teddy walked slightly in front of me, head down as we passed his father sitting there, the van interior dark, cleaning solution and a roll of paper towels at his feet.

This all happened the summer before sixth grade.

We went to Teddy's after my sister tried to lock us in a closet. We had settled on the living room rug to play Scrabble when I noticed a small, gummy spot near the floorboard. Unlike the rest of the spills, it looked like someone had tried to rub it clean.

"That's where Daddy came last night," Teddy whispered.

I didn't know what he meant. So I pointed to a dog poop stain nearby and said, "And that's where he went. Hah hah."

Teddy was quiet.

I confessed sheepishly, "I don't know what that means."

"You don't know what *coming* is?"

"No."

"It's when a man watches dirty stuff," he says, eyes still on the stain, "and his wiener gets all hard, and he rubs it against something or he slaps it against his hand, and then white stuff like shampoo comes out of it. That's *splooge*. That's where my dad *splooged* last night."

I had no idea what to make of this. It sounded like a lie. Way too far out there to be something people actually did. But Teddy didn't lie. That, I did know. He wasn't the kind of kid who lied because he thought it was funny, or because he was bored. Teddy's dad wasn't at home that afternoon. The house was still. No one had turned on the TV yet.

Finally I said, "Ew."

"Want to see where he keeps his dirty stuff?" Teddy asked.

I didn't. I really didn't. Every fiber of my body was clamoring, even then, to run out that front door and pull Teddy with me. But I stayed. And I nodded.

Teddy went to the bedroom at the end of the hallway and opened the door. I followed him, heavy with the feeling somebody was watching me. I felt weird even entering my own parents' bedroom, uneasy at the stack of *Redbook*s on my mother's nightstand, the fifth of Jack Daniel's my dad kept in the headboard meant for books.

My belly churned as I stepped inside and took it all in. Noticed a crack in the window, the sound of the mammoth air conditioner chugging, the red blanket jumbled on the bed with clothing and a few dirty dishes in the folds. The pale stains dripping from ceiling to carpet. The ashtrays scattered throughout, all full. My senses were sharp and bloated, afraid. I couldn't explain it, would have felt stupid trying to, but I felt, all over, like my body was trying to take off without me.

There was a stack of magazines by the bed. I craned my neck to look. A lady in a bikini, bottom hiked high in the air. *Barely Legal College Daze: Hot and Horny Coeds of the SEC!*

The room stank. Mushrooms sprouting, bleach and rock salt. "What's that smell?" I asked Teddy.

He turned. "That's what splooge smells like."

"What makes it smell like that?"

"I dunno."

And for the first time since I had known him—which had been my whole life, or nearly—Teddy slipped, the light flattening behind the eyes, going pale below his hair. I had never seen a face collapse like that before. I might have called it sad, but even then, it seemed bigger than just being *sad*. It occurred to me that he brought me here because he couldn't be alone with whatever was in this room. And it scared me. I didn't want to know what Teddy knew.

I wanted to make a grab for his hand, what girls did when something scared them, but my sister's voice tore through my head: "That's so *gay,* Sharon." I stepped closer to him instead, pressing my arm into his.

A big oak trunk, the kind my mom used to store quilts, sat at the bed's foot. Teddy reached his hand underneath, pulled out a key. He slipped it into the lock and turned once, twice. It opened. More magazines. These were different, printed on rougher paper. There was one called *Bananas;* on the cover, a lady crouched, legs wide open, so wide you could see her privates, and in her—I didn't even know what to call it, not the place you peed from, the *other* place—she had a banana stuck in there. On the next page, a man and a lady. The man's mouth was on the lady's breast. She had his thing, long and purple, in her hand. Her head was tilted back.

It was dirty, but it was exciting, too. It would have been better to have looked at it somewhere that wasn't Teddy's dad's bedroom. I felt the beginnings of a heartbeat between my legs.

Teddy picked up another. *Dangerous Girls. Sexxxy Girls Getting the Punishment They Deserve.* The girl on the cover was in a bra and teeny skirt. She was tied up, wrists and legs roped together, a rag stuffed in her mouth. Blood trickled from her nose. She looked scared. It didn't look like something that belonged on a magazine cover.

Whatever was beating between my legs slowed, then died. Teddy laid the magazine facedown on the floor.

He pulled out something in a moldy plastic baggie. "It's weed," he said. Produced a glass fish with a hole in its tail. "And this is his pipe." He put the fish to his lips and demonstrated, pretending to draw from it. He gave it to me. I did the same.

There was one more package in the trunk.

Teddy looked down into his lap. "We should stop."

"I wanna see," I said.

And I didn't. I really didn't. But it was an impulse I couldn't stop, the snake curled inside me. Even then, I could not stand a closed door.

He didn't look up. I could see his front teeth worrying over his lip.

"You can't tell anybody," he said.

"I won't."

"I mean it, Sharon." His voice went up a little. "Really this time."

"I promise. I really do."

He sighed. Drew up the bag. Handed it to me.

Inside were Polaroids, the kind that were already becoming old-fashioned. I held up the first one: a little girl. It took a moment to register what I was seeing.

She wasn't wearing any clothes. She was on her side, splayed, like she was asleep. The flash made her body stark white; the rest of the shot fell into darkness. In the second picture, someone had turned her over. I could see how skinny she was—if not for the long hair, if not for the lack of penis, she might have been a boy. It must have been summer. There was a line of sun on her hip where her bathing suit had been. Something I would remember later, when the rest of this had fallen away. The sight of a tan line would send an ice-blue spark up my spine.

I didn't know what I was seeing, but I knew it looked real. And it was on a Polaroid. The kind used for pictures of my family at Christmas and on birthdays and in the snow. Something fell and tore in my middle.

My fingers kept moving, flipping through the stack on their own. Another little girl asleep, sprawled on her back, arms and legs thrown out. There was a hand in this picture, coming from the photograph's edge, reaching for the girl's form. The terrible feeling in my stomach heated and stretched and I was suddenly afraid I was going to need the bathroom.

"I don't want to look anymore," I said, louder than I meant to. Looked down. My hands still grasped the pictures.

Teddy reached out and gently took them from me, then dropped them into the bag. We were both sweating. "I'm sorry," he said. And he sounded like he meant it.

I didn't care what my sister would say about it. I reached over and took Teddy's hand.

I couldn't eat or sleep for days after. My mother took me to Dr. Ingram, who pressed on my belly, listening, his eyes gazing into space. It was impossible to get away from myself. Whenever I closed my eyes, I was in that house, seeing those pictures, smelling those smells.

I never entered the Caudill house again. As much hell as we collectively caught from my sister, I had Teddy over to my house to eat, spend the night, jump on the trampoline, and live out the rest of that summer. I kept him with me for as long as I could. I swore I would never let him out of my sight.

And then, before school started that August, Teddy was gone. His mother came for him. He moved to Louisville, and he grew up there. When he moved, the memory faded into almost nothing, leaving only the dark place in my head where it once sat, and the feeling that I'd been marked, but I didn't know by what, or how.

It took a long time, but I was able to convince myself that the afternoon never happened.

MEL HAS FOLDED HER body forward as if to protect a tender spot at her center, a wincing, thirty-degree angle she reserves for when she is ill.

When she looks up at me, her eyes are big, blank; they seem separated from her face. And I see something I have never seen before in Mel: self-removal. Inside, she has fled. The ability of anyone who has ever been on the receiving end of something violent to grasp the details that remind them of their humiliation—smells, colors, sounds—and blur these details so that they become foreign, someone else's property. It is a cultivated skill, requiring time, experience, unspeakable mental real estate. It is, for the desperate, the only chance to leave what happened with the part of yourself that is still yours.

Children learn it. Boys, but more often, and more closely, girls. When girls learn it, they learn it for the rest of their lives, inventing two separate planes on which they exist—the life of the surface, presented for others, and the life forever lived on the inside, the one that owns you. They will never forget how to make themselves disappear.

Mel breathes slowly, with effortful depth, as if instructing herself. Her lips part. She looks elsewhere. I do, too. If she cries—something I have never actually seen her do—I'm not sure I won't flake apart completely.

There's a lot that can bring two people together, it occurs to me. They may, unawares, have entire conversations that do not take place in words. They may never know, themselves, what is admitted, what is declared. What binds.

She doesn't say anything for a long, empty moment. I pull my sweater around myself, shiver, make a face. I've sweated through the fabric.

When Mel speaks, her voice is low and flat. "Did he hurt you."

"No," I say immediately.

She looks at me, finally. I can see the color of her eyes; not often visible through the lenses of her glasses. They are green tonight, veiled with a tired gray.

I repeat, "No."

Even as I say the word, I feel a twinge in my midsection. I don't have the heart to say it: I am the least qualified person to answer this question. How well do I know my own mind, the wormy crannies of my memory? My particular blank space, so white and unknowable that it hurts to look directly into it?

• • •

GREW UP. I left home for good. My exit was a foregone conclusion. I pursued my life as if it were the loose end of something I abandoned at birth and, at eighteen, set out to reclaim. I became an artist because I wanted to make a world in which I was not the pursued but the pursuer; because I needed to *discorporate*. I struggled. I was afraid I wasn't very good. I was jealous and lonely. I was frequently sad.

But even as my mind forgot, my body never did. I felt my animal hackles rise when in a room with large, silent men. I scrabbled for closeness, feeling myself shut closed like when the time for intimacy came. It made me sweat to have my picture taken. I never shook the feeling that what I had seen somehow made me dangerous, that there was something I needed to keep moving to avoid. I felt a fear like hunger; it promised to swallow everything.

But I propelled myself forward, a struggle that often felt like cutting my way through neck-tall weeds. I met you. And it felt like the struggle got a little easier.

MEL HAS FOLDED OVER again. She doesn't speak.

WAS SITTING AT my drafting table one night, by myself, working on something particularly dumb—sketches of demented dogs in pimp costumes for a cartoon strip I would never start called *Small Potatoes*—and I was letting the *CBS Evening News* play out behind me on a small TV I'd bought at a yard sale because the prefab antennae and channel dial, the kind that goes *tok tok tok,* reminded me of the old set my family had when I was a kid. And Dan Rather mentioned a child pornography bust in East Kentucky, where the supplier of illicit materials, a napper of small girls, appraiser of unspeakable objects, had been arrested by the FBI. And on the tiny screen I saw my old holler and I heard the name Caudill pronounced *Cow-dihl,* and I saw the very edge of the house in which I grew up at the screen's corner and realized the name of my hometown had not crossed my lips in an astounding number of days. I dropped my pencil.

I recalled when I slept alongside TV, glowing in my house's sullen dark, and knew *that* was my first real relationship, not Teddy. Because when TV dropped this nasty surprise on me, I felt betrayed. It ripped me open, caused the kind of deep, raw rivet torn when someone you love deceives you.

And for the first time in a decade, I saw myself with Teddy, crouched by that trunk. I saw, in my mind, his hand dipping into the dark. I made it to the wastebasket just in time to vomit.

There are some things you can never bring yourself to say, to yourself, to anyone: the dank, off-color details that define you. Secretly, for years, I had the distinct confusion as to whether I was in the audience or if I was, in fact, the photographed. And that, I couldn't tell—even my dearest friend, who of anyone would know how it saddled my already overlaced heart.

My restless Internet wanderings inevitably led me to track down those old photos, evidence seized from the porn ring and censored for public view, eyes and genitals blurred. I examined them one by one, sweating, in tears. I gazed at one for a very long time. I thought I recognized a prom queen in her face, a country clubber, or maybe a wild girl who cut class with her friends, smoking cigarettes behind the ag-tech building in her boyfriend's Carhartt jacket. Graduates of my county high school from anywhere between 1997 and 2002. Women with my history, my life. I think I pin it down. But I can never be sure.

PUSSYFOOTING

MEL BURIES HER HEAD IN HER HANDS. SHE RUBS HER EYES FOR A moment, goes still. Rises. Stares out into the swamp.

I feel my throat tighten. I'm afraid of what she's going to say. What she might tell me about what *she* sees in what I've just told her.

She shakes her head slowly. "I always knew there was something," she says. "Don't ask me how."

I look down. My hands are involuntarily picking lint balls from my sweater. "You did?"

She turns, giving me her ultimate nonplussed look. "You may not know this about yourself," she says, "but you've got a serious gift for self-containment. You run a pretty tight fuckin ship, presentation-wise. Kind of freaks people out."

I feel myself light up, like I do every time I hear an outside assessment of how I seem. Weirdly gratified, I say, "I don't feel contained. Pretty much ever."

"Well, I know you," she says. "The stronger all this shit is brewing and beating in there, the calmer you are on the outside. Until something like Beardsley happens. Remember? At the party? Whenever you freak out like that, I wonder what's *really* going on in there. Something big, to make you hemorrhage like that."

She stares back out into the yard, blinking. Says, "Hold on."

Jumps up, runs into the house. Bangs back out with the Moleskine. She sits, gingerly rolls the hair band off the book—it touches me how carefully she does this—and fingers through the pages, searching. Finds what she's looking for.

She holds a page up—it's one of the sketches between men, a placeholder that developed from a doodle. An entire landscape of something sharp and dark and glistening, a thousand bullets on a blank field. Zoom out: stubble on a man's cheek.

Another interlude: a sheet of girls' faces, disembodied, all with open mouths. The eyes have been taken out. Not merely left out but removed forcibly, by blurring. Censored.

A door yawns open, hanging weakly from the hinges. Within, darkness. A vague shape moves just beyond, approaching.

A field of bare girl-kid backs, slouched, exposed, the heads bent down.

Snakes emerging from the face of an old Magnavox floor set.

Two hyenas scream at each other.

Girls birthed from the mouths of coyotes, slick and cold and unclothed. Mel points: On the first, the remnant of a tan line circles her hip.

Mel replaces the pages. Gently closes the book.

She reaches into her breast pocket for her smokes. Picks one out, lights it. She does all this in small, careful strokes, then puts the pack on the grimy little glass-top patio table between us, lighter on top. Does not protest when I draw another one out for myself.

"You were trying to tell the story," she says. "You were trying your ass off."

I put the cigarette to my lips. It takes me three tries to light it. I can feel Mel looking at me from the corner of her eye.

I go quiet for a minute. Considering the unreality of someone else knowing this story. Now there are three: Me. Mel. Teddy. I say, "Teddy."

Mel hums knowingly. "Our golden boy. Your number one."

"My number one?"

She shrugs. "He's one lucky motherfucker. If someone drew about *me* the way you draw about *him*, I would want for nothing."

I shake my head. Take a drag. "Teddy is still ten years old to me. Like he's in suspended animation."

"I'm sure he's not," Mel says. "I'm sure he's an adult, like we are. Out somewhere living a life. Imagine what *his* book must look like, right?"

"If he has one."

Mel ashes. "I do like Teddy Caudill," she says, sort of grudgingly. "Just from his page. Because he's drawn with a cat. And a Nintendo controller. And a freeze pop."

This makes me smile. "I liked him, too," I say. Inhale deeply, cough out the smoke. Ash my cigarette. God, this is good. I missed smoking with Mel.

She taps the book. "I gotta tell you, Sharon. This is some of the best work I have ever seen you do. I know that's probably not the most appropriate thing to say, in these circumstances. But this shit is amazing. I mean, really incredible. It was enough to make sleep difficult for a few nights."

That does it. This hits me in the very solar plexus of my weepiness. Another side effect of the stroke. I'm a regular Weepy Wilma. I fall apart over the stupidest shit. ASPCA commercial? Out of tapioca? Missed the toilet on my last piss? Cry, cry, cry. But it feels so good to have someone else know about this. To not have it jammed up inside me, clammy and tight. To talk about it, and to talk about other things as well. As if it were normal. Just another topic.

The crying is loud and sudden and I don't cover my face. I just crumple up and bawl it out.

Mel is horrified. She freezes, smoke in the air.

"It just feels good to—" I take a deep breath. *"T-t-talk."*

"I—yeah, man," she says slowly. "I mean, we always could have talked about this. I wouldn't have judged you or anything. It would have been fine."

I shake my head. No, I want to say. We couldn't have talked about it before. I wouldn't have known how.

All I can manage is to gasp, "It *hurt*."

Mel grinds her cigarette, lifts her arm, and gathers me into a gentle noogie. "Yeah, dude. That's a hurtful thing. Anyone would hurt." She coughs. Wavers falsetto, *"Everybody hurts—sometimes."*

I sock her in the gut.

THE NEXT WEEK IS a revelation. Talking about the List, Honus Caudill, the pictures—it's our new normal. We talk about it like we talk about what we need to pick up from the store. It's not something I ever imagined I could put into words.

But Mel, as it turns out, has plenty of them.

"I mean, I knew you used to draw your guys, back in the day," she says. "I always thought it was, like, this revenge exercise or something. But holy hell, that, like, *compendium* of stuff, this deluge, no blank space whatsoever? It's like another universe. I've never seen anything like it."

We're out on the porch again, in the evening, Florida fug lifting in time for twilight. Blue into indigo. I'm squeezing my hand clench, gritting my teeth against the strain.

"But what I love about it," she says, "is that it's not about the dudes. It's about everything around them. It's like what it must be like to be inside someone's head. All your memories and figures sort of running together. It's about *you*."

I rub a mosquito bite on my forearm. I'm getting anxious. Mel's moving too fast for me to keep up. I have a suspicion about where this is all going. "Not a big deal," I mutter.

"Oh, but it is a big deal." She unfolds her legs from under her and crosses them thoughtfully, propping her head on an elbow. "You're no time-waster. Nuh uh. You wouldn't have put so much time into it if it wasn't important." She narrows her eyes, gazing into the swamp. "You were *charting* something. That's what I think. Like some sort of fucked-up measuring wall where you put the kids to see how tall they are."

What I most remember about my stroke is the strange way my quiet and my active brains seemed to blur, crushing the levee between night and day. Those first few months of recovery seemed like a steady flow of dream, punctuated by moments of crystal-clear pain. I often wasn't sure whether I was asleep or awake. I found myself muttering private thoughts aloud. Which is how I open my mouth and say crustily, "How deep the hole goes."

Mel looks at me, face lit. She puts both hands in the air with a grin. "You said it. *How deep the hole goes.*"

I cover my mouth. She puts her hands down. Pauses, then says, "I can't help but wonder what it would look like *moving.*"

There it is. "No," I say, shaking my head. "No no."

"Oh come on. Don't say no yet." She rises from her chair. "Getting a pop. Want one?"

She steps inside. I lean in and prod at the numbness in my leg, irritated. I wonder if I lie down, act like I'm going to sleep, she'll leave me alone. There are two hammocks on the deck. After a single sweltering night on the threadbare couch, I sleep out here, with Mel. It's nice—the locusts, the sound of trickling water, frogs.

She emerges with a Coke and an unlit joint hanging from her lips. Looks to me questioningly.

"No," I repeat.

She nods thoughtfully. She was expecting this. "Can you tell me why?"

"I have re. Reh. Shit."

"Reservations?"

I nod.

"Can you explain?"

I wish I had it together enough to cut the problem to its center. To lure the secret things with which you coexist out of the shadows of your brain, revive them, try to shape them: *It's too dangerous.* Mel, of all people, should know this. And I'm no Mel. What might it do to me?

What I come up with: "Too hard."

She looks down, nods again. Scratches her chin with her wrist. The chiggers are out.

"Let's think of something else," I tell her.

She shrugs, but I can see the disappointment in her exhale, the way she sits back in her chair and spreads her legs wide. "Okay," she says. "We'll keep brainstorming."

BUT AS I'M GETTING ready for bed, I keep thinking about it: She said it was my best work. She said it *interrupted her sleep.*

Then I think of one of the sketches I saw from my book, of a long, horny hand emerging from the frame. No shit you couldn't sleep, I think. I couldn't sleep for an entire school year after that.

(THERE IS NEW GUILT now. What good I could have done, to have told someone. This should have happened to someone who had *people.* Parents to whom she could have made confession. Teachers. Friends. Other than Teddy, I had no one. The guilt is a sleeping giant, something that sets my entire self to trembling when it wakes up.)

SHE CORNERS ME IN the living room while I'm watching *Cowboy Bebop* on my new laptop. "I got something to show you," she says.

I take a deep breath. "Do you."

She reaches behind her, produces a poster board. Unfolds it. She has made a List mural.

"What do you think?" she says.

It is the sensation an animal might have upon encountering a fast-approaching car. My mind freezes, shrivels into itself. I have just enough time to heft myself up, run to the kitchen, and croak my dinner into the trash.

"Aw Jesus." She folds the poster board. "How many times am I gonna make you do that?" She follows me, grabs some paper towels. I roll my eyes and take them. A runner of spit hangs from my lower lip.

"You've got a wino's stomach these days," she says.

I give her the finger.

"There's some ginger ale out in the car," she says. "Want me to go get you one?"

I nod. Anything to get her out of the room.

When she's gone, I spit once more into the trash can, then take a closer look at the poster, breathing hard. It's two stapled together, about four feet by four feet, covered from edge to edge. Had it been any other project, I would have liked what she's done here: She borrowed the style from the *Cheap Thrills* album cover R. Crumb did for Big Brother and the Holding Company. That same comic quilt wheel, full and chaotic. She's split the whole into cells. Each man to a box, details inserted in tiny cursive, stretching out and out like insane tentacles. She took photo bases for her sketches from the Internet, probably Facebook. The figures are not caricatures but her more realistic work, faces lined and wizened. In one panel, Jay Hasbey, number 19, cradles a kid, his or someone else's, I don't know. He is surrounded by crows. One sings, *"ACT score 35."* Another trills, *"NO FAT CHICKS."* In another, cartoonist Pete Said, number 28, is shuttled back a decade and a half by a strident lack of Internet presence, taking a wide-eyed, puffed-cheek hit from a massive 1999 bong, long and sinister, a screeching face carved into its end. Up the bong stem, in calligraphy: *Night terrors.* For Brent, the bellicose probate lawyer, a professional head shot from his firm. Written down his tie: *He said you freaked him out.* And there are more: candids from *GalleyCat* and *ReAnimator.* It gets worse in the New York years. These are people we know, people in our professional circles who document themselves on Twitter and Tumblr and Instagram, and there's a surfeit of material for them, more than anyone would ever want to know.

Beardsley is last, the photo recent, from a party. He's laughing, chin doubled above an opened shirt collar, arm at a northward angle, thrown around an unseen someone. A goblin with one raised eyebrow peeks out from his armpit. Thought bubble: *"broke up via text message. ☹."*

Seeing the List split into pages was bad enough. But seeing the List in its entirety as one sprawling landscape, going from year to year, spreading out and out, is so much worse. I am rocked by its vastness—so much want, so much deprivation, everything I hungered for from age thirteen on. The sheer numbers and the wealth of detail make me queasy. There are so many. So many.

Did I see any of these people for who they were, when I wanted them? When you need something so huge that you lack a clear objective, you will make do with whatever is there. It's a story of consumption. Forever a vessel, filled with one man, then another. Why couldn't I have wanted something nobler than someone to fuck me?

Mel busts back in, ginger ale in hand. "I've been thinking about it," she says, "what it might look like. What we could do with it."

"No."

She holds up her hands. "Wait a sec, just hear me out. What if we don't do, you know, the List as *is*? How about we play around with the idea of all these dudes and do, like, a compendium piece, a sort of *Thirty Two Short Films About Glenn Gould*. Or a story where this List, I don't know, sort of forms an alternate universe where like an ur-version of all these guys have to live in a house together and form their own weird Jonestown cult. The Cult of Sharon! Or, wait, no. They have to *marry* each other. A hundred-dude marriage. And they form a secret society that lasts for centuries. Kind of like the Masons, but. You know. *Kinkier.*"

Dead silence.

"Or something else. Something that makes it *yours*. You know? Mess with it. Turn it around. Get weird with it." She sighs, runs her hands through her hair. "Make it so it doesn't sting as much. It could be great, Sharon. It could be really good."

I feel the anger bloom, red and pleasurable. It takes something like this to remind me: Mel is an exhibitionist at heart, a pusher of tensions in unnatural, explosive directions. She has ambushed me, when my defenses are at their lowest. I can practically feel the synapses in my head firing and missing.

She wants to make a *movie* about my strangest, most vicious, most masturbatory headspace, reveal it to an entire population, throw in some fart jokes, and call it good.

I rise. Say, "I think it's time for my enema." I leave the room.

LATER THAT NIGHT, I find myself back in the living room, looking at Mel's mural. At first I just want to relive my anger: *I can't fucking believe she did that, the* balls *on that woman.*

But once I start looking it over, I can't stop. I keep going back to the upper-left-hand corner—the single-digits, back in the day. There's a man I don't know up there, squinting out. He is wearing suspenders. I look closer. Mel has taken special care around the eyes, the delicate lines around the mouth. A cat perches on his shoulder; there is a wallpaper of popsicles behind him. I look closer, my breath catching. *Teddy Caudill.*

Mel creeps in around midnight, holding a root beer. A tattered copy of *Dolores Claiborne* is tucked into her armpit. "Hey," she says.

I lift my hand.

She sits next to me, opens the pop. "Who you looking at?"

I point.

She bobs her head, takes a swig, expression pinched. "Our man. He wasn't hard to track, you know. I found stuff about the trial online." She pauses. Looks at me looking at her sketch. "What do you think? Is it accurate?"

"I dunno. Haven't seen him in twenty years."

We stare in silence, the poster board in front of us.

"I'm sorry," she says. "You know me. I see something exciting, I get all over it. I didn't think about how seeing something like this could be a mindfuck for you."

I trace my finger over Teddy's face. The line of the jaw. The temple. The hairline. "Forget it," I say. "It's fine."

S HE SAID IT MADE *her lose sleep.*

S HE WON'T LET IT go. The one thing I have kept from her, over the course of our ten years–plus as a team, has captivated her. "I know you always say structure first," she says, "but I think we have to go with whatever we have right now. Try for scenes. Something to flesh out."

"It's funny. How you're talking about this like we're going to do it."

She's standing by her mural, biting her lip. I come up behind her.

"Why are you so interested in this?" I ask her.

She shrugs, tilts her head. "Because it's interes*ting*," she says.

"That's the best nonanswer I've ever heard," I say. "Really. Why are you so hell-bent on turning this into a project?"

"I'm trying to figure out where you were, all this time," she says. "Where *were* you? What were you doing?"

It hangs over the room like an accusation, gray and gassy.

"I was here," I say. "I was with you."

She puts her hands on her hips. Leans in to peer closer at a panel. "Were you, now."

I T BEGINS WITH ME telling myself: I'm humoring her. But the fluttering in my insides, the heat in my face, says otherwise.

A project always begins like a pimple on the back of the neck. You can't see it, but you can feel it, rising just under the surface. And it drives you crazy. It swells, gains definition, becomes visible. The bigger it gets, the more it presses into the back of your spine. The more it presses, the less you can focus on anything else. Working on it every day is just a way of scratching the itch until you've finished its business and it slowly starts to shrink back down.

I keep my sketchbook by me all the time. I remind myself to be patient. Work in whatever way I can, whenever I can. I let myself draw all the dark, snaky things that occur to me until my wrist gives out: a large Magnavox. Shag carpeting. A driveway with dandelions growing through the cracks.

Teddy. It's the set of his chin that's driving me crazy. I can't get it right. Not yet, anyway.

SHE WANTS ME TO unzip myself and spill my guts. She wants new lists—the men I've been with, the ones I've wanted but couldn't have, how often I think about them. The stories I imagined coming from them, and the ones that actually did. Traits, physical characteristics. Who are they, when boiled down to ten seconds of screen time? Where was I? What was I doing? Brooklyn? Ballister? Which apartment, studio, project?

"Ever thought about how the List and the stroke might link together?" she asks me.

"Still trying to get the hang of holding a fork again."

She shrugs. Pops the top off one of my Ensures. "Sorry," she says.

"It's okay. So I take it you have this idea where you link them together."

"Maybe." She takes a sip. "Damn. These sumbitches are tasty."

I spend my mornings drawing, or trying to draw. It's slow, frustrating work that feels keenly and, in a way it never has before, like *work*. The skills are coming back but sluggishly, like they're resisting. I can anticipate now, but the anticipation doesn't always mean my hand follows through. There's no line integrity. My fingers tremble. Two or three hours before lunch is the best I can do. Any more wrings all the energy out of me. I produce sketches that look like they were done by a homicidal pigeon.

"Well, you gotta work through the dead ends," Mel says. "Just sketch. Draw whatever comes to you. Get in there. Don't pussyfoot around."

"WE SHOULD ACTUALLY GO there, you know," Mel says.

"Go where."

"Kentucky. If we go there, we might get a better idea of what this thing is actually supposed to be. That's the story's cradle, man. It's crucial."

"Not a good idea," I say. We're in the living room, Mel hunched over the drafting board, me massaging my weak leg. "For several reasons."

She turns to me. "What color were the shutters on the outside of your house?"

I stall, digging into the big muscle of my calf. I get a glimpse of what she's been working on. A pack of enormous deer, staring out, malevolent. A List-like quality to it. It's contagious. "I dunno. Black, I think?"

"You have to *know*, man. It can't be fuzzy."

If I weren't still recovering—if it didn't still take me a solid ten minutes to get dressed in the morning, if I weren't still limping so heavily I needed a hospital cane just moving around the house—I'd fight harder. But I don't have all my ammo back. I'm still at a loss—slower in arguments, pokier making connections between things.

I remind myself: Mel has shown genuine patience. That's against her true nature. She's willfully changing herself merely by sitting there and shutting the hell up.

"Making a trip just for that is not necessary," I tell her. "We can figure this out on our own. Let's not get the family involved. You know? Making this—*thing* you want to make will be hard enough without piping my mother into it."

She pokes me in the side. "Nuh uh. I want me some Missus Kisses." Yells, *"You think you're better'n me?"*

I roll my eyes. Peel the top off a dish of rice pudding.

"We have to," she presses. "You know why? If you didn't have that afternoon, with Teddy, in his dad's bedroom, we wouldn't have *this*." She reaches out and taps the Moleskine, the now ever-present Moleskine, Goody hair band in place. She refuses to be separated from it. I once saw her carry it with her into the bathroom. "The List is the fallout, man. How did this make you what you are?" She flicks her lighter, wags her thumb through the flame. Shakes her hand to cool it. "It's about solipsism. It's about wanting. Hunger. It's about how we get what we need, how we *make* what we need, and why we need it."

"Safe to say you've moved on from your slapstick *Thirty Two Short Films About Glenn Gould* idea."

"Did you ever notice your crush numbers went down when you were working on a project?"

I shrink back, surprised. "No."

"I did a count by year. When you weren't busy, you had to find a way to *make* yourself busy." She wags her finger faster through the flame. "It's about holding stories. It's a control thing. A self-protection thing. I—I don't know why it took me so long to figure out." She gets up, starts to pace. Doing that thing where she cups her hands and pops them on top of each other, snapping her fingers. "The story's not about guys on the List. It's the List itself, the stuff underneath. And that starts in Kentucky. You, your parents. That fucked-up little house. Those *pictures*. That shit was so damaging, your brain had to hide it from you. You can't tell me that's not a part of the story. That's *the* story. And *Teddy*. Oh my God." She rakes a hand through her hair. "He's in this thing *so deep,* man."

I stew for a minute before I say, "I'm glad you've had such an awesome time figuring this problem out for yourself, but this is not a *story*. This is something that happened to me. This is something that is still happening to me."

"That's why we have to go."

I shake my head.

"Sharon. This is something people feel but can't find the words to talk about. That was your first, best lesson: *It really is better to be someone else, isn't it?* Someone who hasn't seen what you've seen or felt what you've felt. And you wanted it so badly, you found a way to give it to yourself. For a long time. Putting yourself in these stories."

"Yeah. And it's done me *so* much good."

"I disagree. You have an overpowering imagination," she says. "But it's a gift you've had to pay for. That's a story that needs to be told. So tell the fucking story, man. Do the footwork. Don't just fight a fight you know you can win."

"You've never met my family," I tell her. "You don't know what they're like."

Mel peers at me. "You know what? I can handle the Kisses family, dude. Bring it on."

M Y CELL RINGS THE next morning. "Sharon?" Mom wavers. The hairs on the back of my neck stand up. I know that tone. Here comes the explosion. I was wondering when it was going to happen. I take a deep breath and push my oatmeal aside.

"I'm *sorreee,*" she bleats.

I drop my spoon. It clatters to the floor. Son of a whore. Picking it up is going to be a three-minute operation. I stare at it, frowning.

"Sharon? Say something, honey."

Today is the first time I have ever heard my mother say the word *sorry.* She has never apologized, or rephrased, or softened. Usually when she screwed up, she just let us stay out, or keep the car longer. She's bad for letting stuff marinate. Angry rebuttals delivered two months late, silent acquiescing three weeks after argument. Prime example: She was the portrait of reticence at Dad's funeral. A few appropriately timed tears, eyes rimmed with red. Two months later, Shauna found her in the backyard setting fire to a pile of Dad's belongings, screeching and sobbing at it to *burn quicker, goddammit, burn QUICKER.*

It's her practice to take in what you tell her rapidly, then give a response that makes you wish you hadn't told her anything in the first place. A rift between you and a friend, a breakup, the details of a fender bender. For your trouble, you'll likely get an irritated (and humiliating) "All *right.* Good *God.*" This isn't a biased opinion. This shit could go on her headstone. Anyone in the family will tell you the same.

"I'm here," I tell her.

She chokes. I picture her clawing at her nose with a Kleenex. The TV, a new flat-screen since the old oak tube set blew up, on mute in the background. "When you called me, I shoulda—I shoulda gone down there to that hospital *that instant.*"

"That's okay," I say. "You were." Blank. Fuck. She was *what.* "Busy?"

"A mother should never be too busy to visit her sick child in the hospital," she wails. "I saw Dr. Ingram this morning and he said what happened to you was real serious. He said you're lucky to be alive."

"That's nice of him."

"Sharon."

"I didn't die," I say. "I'm okay."

"Are you sure?"

"Yeah. I'm sure I'm not dead."

"You don't sound right. I thought you didn't sound right when you called."

"That's because I just had a stroke."

"Here I am tryin to talk to you," she says, "and you keep gettin smart with me."

"Sorry," I say. "I am getting better. I have speech therapy and physical therapy. It's work, but it's better."

"I been prayin over you," she warbles.

I have to stop and think about what's making me angry about all of this. The word finally occurs to me: *sentimentality.*

"I been prayin over it, and I made lots of mistakes. I know that now. Specially with you, and you turned out so good."

"Thank you?"

"We didn't even go up when you graduated from colletch. What's wrong with me?"

"I don't know."

I hear a snort at the other end.

"It's fine," I say quickly. "Graduation's not . . . not a big deal."

"You coulda died," she whispers.

"But I *didn't. Fuck.*"

"You watch your mouth."

This sets off a new gale of moans and sniffles. I put my head on the counter. Reach out and try to pull the spoon in with my foot. Oatmeal's gonna be cold now. Shit.

"Are you alone?" she manages. "You got your friend with you?"

"Her name is Mel, Mom."

"I know that."

"Then why do you keep calling her *my friend*?"

"I don't know."

I sigh. "She is here. We rented a house. We've been working on a project."

"How long you gonna stay down there?"

"Until the docs say it's okay to travel. Then we'll go back to New York, I guess."

"You'll stop here on your way back, won't you? You ain't been back in a while. You didn't even come home last Christmas."

True. Mel and I went to Montreal for work last December and just decided to stay through the holidays, ordering room service and getting drunk and watching the CBC. We rang in the new year at a bar called the Velvet Hammer, hepped up on absinthe and Ritalin, surrounded by transvestites who kept pinching our bottoms and screaming, "Girls' club! Girls' club!"

"Y'all come down here," Mom says. "I need to see you're alive."

I pinch my lips, too dumb and full-feeling around the ears to say anything but "Okay."

• • •

THAT NIGHT MEL SAYS, "I want to show you something."

I groan inwardly. Another appearance from our fuzzy, plodding nonproject.

"Come on," she says, and drags me into the living room.

There are two sketches on Mel's drafting table. She's taken an old lamp found at Goodwill and turned it on its side, training its light directly on the table surface. The rest of the room falls into shadow.

I linger in the doorway, not sure I want to see what she's done. She prods me. "Come on. It's not that bad. And if it is, then you say so, and I'll chuck it."

I sit at the table, look at the first sketch. It's a soft pastel sketch of a little girl, back turned, sitting in the light of a television set next to an empty La-Z-Boy recliner. The TV glow outlines the girl's silvery form, tapering to darkness at the edges. At the bottom, Mel has scrawled, *Sharon, 1994.*

The second sketch is a mock-up of a Warner Bros. sign-off, the hot red circle that surrounds Bugs Bunny with the cursive *"That's all Folks!"* above his head. But instead of Bugs Bunny, Mel has drawn Stroke Sharon—what I looked like when I begged her for a mirror. One side of my face is slack, the left eye dead, my head bald. My lips are drawn back into a crooked snarl, my mouth dark and sinister. It's grotesque. It's amazing.

In her best Mel Blanc impression, Mel reads what's she written above my head: *"Yeh-yeh yeh yeh* you're fucked*!"*

There's a deep well of silence before I start giggling. Mel follows. We sit there, cracking up. When one of us starts to calm down, we look at the picture and it starts all over again.

Something feels different, tonight. The sketch of Stroke Sharon—it has something that I want. I want to be able to feel this way all the time. To be able to laugh about the things that have happened to me, baggage and all, light and dark. To own it handily enough so that it could be funny and horrifying at once. Maybe this is the idea I've been looking for. Maybe this is something close.

When we quiet, I say to Mel, "My mom called me. She wants us to come to Kentucky to visit."

Mel's eyes go wide. Behind her there's a third sketch. It is another me, prestroke, full in the face and chest. But this sketch is unfinished, empty space filling the eye sockets. It is a half me, a ghost me come straight from her hand, staring us down as Mel says, "Oh, we have to go. Of course. We *have* to."

WHEN WE GET THE go-ahead from the docs a few weeks later, the weather is beginning to cool. We pack up the car and give Jesco the house keys. He flaps his hand at us. "Y'all are headed back to the big city, I reckon."

"Kentucky this time."

"Huh." He peers close at me. "Well. Y'all be safe. Don't get et up by a wildcat."

"Can't make any promises," Mel tells him. We pile in. We head north.

FAULKNER

I WAS BORN IN FAULKNER, KENTUCKY.

My parents grew up there, and their parents, and their parents. With each successive generation, the family tunnel vision thickened until living outside the perimeters of the triangle formed by the Bert T. Combs Mountain Parkway to the south, Interstate 75 to the west, and I-64 to the north was unthinkable. I have always assumed that my leaving is the reason my family doesn't like me, but it could be the other way around. It's a circular problem, a snake with its tail in its mouth.

My very first job was at the Faulkner County Library, an annex to the WPA building that served as the town's elementary school. It inhabited the basement, books dampened by the underground, carpeting the scratchy green found on outdoor patios. Mrs. Horsemuller, the county librarian and an epileptic, recruited me to keep an eye on the place whenever she had a seizure at her desk. She trusted me to pick her up (she weighed maybe ninety pounds) and carry her to the cot in the back office. Her husband owned Horsemuller Hardware down on Main and would stick his head in at lunch, whispering, "Was the little missus feeling sleepy?"

I'd reshelve the few books checked out but spent most of my shift paging through old yearbooks. I liked yearbooks from the smaller, outer-county schools best, back before consolidation: M. C. Mattox in Hollins, Purvis Manual in Shortridge, and Faulkner itself, the edge of tobacco country, where shipments piled with steaming coal still sped through on the five A.M. CSX train.

Faulkner was always more interesting to me in the past tense. Dad was class of '75, Mom '76, a time when girls in our part of the country were just beginning to stop ratting their hair. There were, in fact, precious few changes between the 1976 *Eagle* and the 2001 *Pride of the Tribe:* the White Dot became a Dairy Queen, wide-bottomed coupes were replaced with RAV4s. But the open, unfettered expressions of kids in portraits remained, as did the zeal for FFA and FCA (there were as many cows and Christians in 1976 as in 2001). The same twenty surnames are ubiquitous. Everyone is kin to everyone else, tributaries joining in marriage and forking off into nieces and nephews and cousins and step-cousins. The prom queen Mom's year was Denise Falwell, mother of my chief high school tormentor, Karly Ingram, who ended up leaving our senior prom because her boyfriend, Travis Cotter, got hammered and unsheathed the pimp cane he'd bought to match his tuxedo, revealing it to be a sword, which he swung around the gym to the strains of AC/DC until the police took him away.

I was from the town, like everyone else, but I could never shake the suspicion that I was merely a spectator. I haunted the yearbooks of the past yet failed to show up for my own senior portrait. *Not pictured: Sharon Kay Kisses.*

I was the only student from Faulkner to go to college out-of-state in ten years. When I got the Ballister scholarship, a frantically excited Mrs. Horsemuller called the newspaper and got me a front-page article.

Upon seeing the article, my father didn't say anything, but reached out and grabbed my head, something between an embrace and a noogie. This, coming from the man who typically responded to anything I said with a creased brow and some irritated head-shaking, who once, when my parents refused to send me to a gifted-and-talented program at Duke on the argument that it was too far away, turned and hissed, "You think you're too good to work this summer?" The article was clipped and thumbtacked to the bulletin board in his garage, where it was found when he died. The ladies at the laundromat where my mother worked had it laminated, and it was affixed to our fridge at home, where I was gratified to see how much it bugged Shauna. Though Mom did mutter, releasing me from a rare hug, "They did *not* get your best side, hon."

It seemed Mrs. Horsemuller was the happiest of all that I was leaving. When she heard the news, she hugged me hard, her skinny little limbs hot beneath the fabric of her sweater; then she dabbed at her eyes with the edge of a Kleenex, smiling.

Before I left for the last time, she grabbed my face with sudden ferocity. "Don't you come back here," she said. "Don't you dare."

When I said nothing, she shook my face for emphasis. "This place," she said, "is a bucket of sand crabs. One tries to climb out, the others'll reach up and pull him back down. Climb out of here. Don't you *dare* come back."

I'M THE YOUNGEST OF three. My brother Jared's a mechanic. He is sometimes called Red because of his hair, copper before it started to recede, but also because of his temper and his booziness. The red hair is a recessive trait; the Kisses crazy is dominant. He started going to bars when he was sixteen, stumbling home at four on a school night stinking of Budweiser, a problem of debatable size when our parents were waging war on each other. The town's sheriff was Mom's second cousin, and he found the idea of Jared kicking the shit out of people largely funny until Jared sent a guy to the hospital. The sheriff got Jared out of it, despite the brain swelling caused by my brother banging the guy's head against the concrete.

Jared settled down, had kids, started doing his drinking in the shed where no one else could see it (his wife is Britney, class of '98, a sly, mean girl with a moon face). Earning his good luck with quiet living. He and I have not had a conversation that lasted more than sixty seconds in a decade.

Shauna is between Jared and me. When she was a senior and I was a freshman, she wore a leather jacket and bolstered her ponytail so that it cascaded, a frozen latticework of curls, down the sides of her head. She was practical with an edge of wildness, one that pushed her to do things like get her first tattoo at sixteen—a small rendering of Tinker Bell on her lower back. I thought the tattoo itself was pretty stupid but was in awe of the gesture, Shauna's daring.

My sister was so organically of Faulkner that she seemed, at times, to be its quick, distrustful heart. Her barometer of what was weird and what was acceptable was dependably, heartbreakingly accurate. Bands I liked were weird (the Beastie Boys not *good* black music, or even *black,* Portishead like something out of a horror movie, Modest Mouse too far out of touch for any commentary other than "Guh"), the magazines I took pains to buy when in Lexington unbearably strange (*BUST,* back issues of *Mindrot, Spin*—could not find a copy of *Spin* within a fifty-mile radius of Faulkner in 1999), and the Doc Martens I purchased with babysitting money *most* certainly weird. "Brandon says them are dyke boots," she told me matter-of-factly.

"Tell Brandon he's a fucktard," I said.

But Shauna was also the one to call me crying when Dad moved out of the house my first year at Ballister. "Why ain't you more upset?" she whined. "Why ain't you mad at them?"

"I dunno."

"Well, why in hell not?"

"Shauna. Mom and Dad hate each other. You can hear them fighting from your living room. And you live *next door.* Don't you think this is for the best?"

"They're our parents," she said. "They're supposed to be to-gether."

Shauna also cried most openly at Dad's funeral the year after.

Jared took it hard, too, swallowing big enough to make his Adam's apple bob above his tie knot. I was surprised by my own sadness. I felt, as usual, adrift, uncomfortable in the crowds of my extended family. It squeezed at me, made me feel just alone enough to step out early, where Dad's brother Allen was propped against the building, breathing hard, fishing through his pockets for a smoke. "Whatter you studyin up there," he asked me.

"Visual arts."

"Visual *arts*." All jolly surprise, like I'd just said, "Mining for moon cheese." One of Dad's more bitter, KKK-leaning brothers. I'd started feeling conspicuous around Uncle Allen at perhaps age seven. "What in the whir-led is *that*?"

"Visual art. Like drawing."

"Like drawing, huh." He stooped and sighed, a Marlboro Red trembling between his lips. During the service, he had repeatedly wiped his mouth with a handkerchief, waiting until afterward for when he could start drinking, like every other Kisses in the room. I resented the gruff pat on the back I'd gotten from them all while Shauna got hugs, sympathetic hi-honey-how-are-yous, Jared warm handshakes and shoulder thumps. I resented the way Allen peered at me now, like I was an interloper. I resented the Amtrak I'd have to take back north, the two hours I'd spent on my ass in D.C. while they switched the engine from diesel to electric. The fact that I'd have to deal with this on my own while everyone else seemed to have someone supporting them. How long had it been since I'd actually had a conversation with Dad? Since he'd been interested in having a conversation with *me*?

I drew my own cigarette from my bag, a habit I'd picked up from Mel, lit up, and started to turn back when Allen said, "I always heered that art was for ugly girls and queers."

"Well, thank God for that, huh," I said, and walked away.

WE MAKE THE TRIP to Faulkner in two shifts, stopping in Georgia for the night to sleep. We break each hour so I can stretch my legs. They twitch and kick involuntarily, breaking into pins and needles if I sit in one position too long. Mel pulls onto the interstate shoulder to let me stretch, limp in place, jog. Each time, she idles, then very slowly moves away, making me jog to keep up. "Come on, Mamaw," she yells. "Move that ass. Your AARP discount won't cover Greyhound."

Today she pulls that stunt and I nearly fall down on I-75. Gravity still throws me curveballs covered in spit; no level ground is actually *level*. My left side can seize up with no warning. I take eight different pills in the morning and six at night—one for blood pressure, one for inner ear balance, a horse's dosage of Lexapro my Florida doc prescribed, calling it an "impetus for wellness." I look in the mirror every day, hoping that side of my face has gone back to normal, reinflated, but I still see my lips slope, a slack to my left eye giving me a look of partial, wan surprise. I am beginning to wonder if we left Florida too early.

Farther north, the sand creeps out of the soil and the mountains begin to ebb and flow. We make it through Knoxville to stop at a Chat 'n Chew in a county lining Kentucky. "I want pie," Mel says. "And I want to check my email."

"You want some waitress tail."

She gives me the finger.

"Good luck finding wireless down here."

"They're supposed to send Mom's coroner's report today," she says. "Finally."

I exhale, puffing out my cheeks. "Jesus. Sorry."

"It's fine. I don't care."

"Why don't we keep going. It's not that much longer."

"Screw these pigfuckers. I want my coffee and pie."

"I resent that term."

"I resent *you*."

The Chat 'n Chew is tinged with lo-fi nostalgia. Its parking lot is gravel, siding flaking from the outside, and the signage is posted with an ancient Mountain Dew ad promising to *tickle yore innards*. A table of local guys can be seen through the window, smoking and drinking Cokes. When we step out of the car, a chill breeze hits us, makes us hunch and hug ourselves. It's almost winter. So much lost time. The last I was out in the world, it was summer. We get the eye when we settle into a booth.

Mel is gratified to find a strong wireless signal. She purses her mouth to one side and clicks rapidly with her thumbs, stopping occasionally to push her glasses up her nose.

The waitress brings coffee and lemon meringue. Mel puts her phone down. "Press release on the Hollingsworth's out."

"Didn't that come out weeks ago?"

"They postponed it. Wanted to make sure you didn't bite it first."

"There's nothing about the stroke in there, right?"

"No, *Sharon*. I shouldn't have said anything to you about it being online. Everyone gets sick, but you're being awfully cagey about it." She rolls her eyes and licks pudding from her fork, one thumb still working.

"Sepsis," she says finally.

"Huh?"

"Kelly Kay. The official cause of death is sepsis. The wound got infected." She crams more pie into her mouth. "The report's pretty thorough, actually. One of the inmates stabbed her in the rib with, like, this super-sharpened toothbrush handle. So it's *not* an urban legend. They actually *do* that in prison. It's like if someone shaved the end of a screwdriver into a shark's tooth and then stuck it into you. Worse than a knife. Poison and pus and shit just bubbling up. They even have a picture of the toothbrush here. See? There's stuff on it."

I put my fork down.

Mel clicks her phone off and looks into her coffee. "Weird. Just when I got the word about the Hollingsworth? I thought to myself, *Hey, Mom should be hitting me up for cash any day now.* You know?"

"Why would she need money in prison?"

"Tampons and black-market lipstick? I dunno." She gulps her coffee down. "Probably booze."

"They sell booze in prison?"

"They sell everything in prison." She taps her fingers against the

Formica. "Didn't say anything about the reason for the fight. Any causes. I was kind of hoping it might say something."

"Mel." I make her look at me. "It wouldn't make any difference. Okay?"

"I know." She gestures to my plate. "You gonna finish that?"

Mel eats the pie. A few of the men at the table still stare at us. I palm my afternoon blood pressure meds and rise, looking for the bathroom.

When I pass their table, I hear the grandfatherly one with the John Deere cap perched on his wispy hairline lean over and say, "She must be the wife." The table erupts in snickers. I give him a dirty look. He shoots it right back, chuckling nastily.

When I return, Mel is smoking and ashing into a foil tray. "You can totally smoke in here."

"Yeah."

"What did Chester Molester over there say to you?"

"Nothing."

"Right."

"Just don't pay attention," I tell her. "We should get going."

She stubs out and rises, reaching for her wallet. The sky is gray. Sixteen-wheelers rumble off the interstate. Something else is said. In response, low and clear: "Dresses like a boy."

A guy at the table's edge, young enough below his cap brim to display fresh acne scars, calls over, "Hey. Hey."

We turn. He spreads his index and middle fingers into a V and waggles his tongue theatrically in the space between. "Y'all." He does it again. "Y'all."

The men chortle. The waitress making Mel's change shakes her head, a small smile on her lips. If we hadn't been there, she would have laughed with them, would have said, mock-disparagingly, "Y'all are just *awful*."

I grab Mel and drag her with me, opening the door. She turns before I can stop her, flips them the bird, and says, "Fuck you ingrates."

There's a beat of silence, then the kid yelps, "What?" The word is in two syllables. Something cold touches my spine. I know now that I'm *home,* and not in the soft-focus Hallmark sense of home-coming, but with the paralyzing fear of a rabbit about to get shot on a hillside: *Oh shit and goddamn, I am home.*

"I said eat it, Wonder Bread." Mel gives her crotch a quick tug.

The kid stands. His chair clatters to the floor.

We scramble to the car and dive in. Mel swings onto the road just in time for the group to emerge in my rearview. The kid in the hat throws a rock. It hits the trunk.

"Mel," I yell when we're on the road.

"What."

"Mel."

"What, goddammit."

All I can do is make fists and show them to her. I need to remind her of the world we are both from, where a man will hit a woman in public just as easily as he'll open the door for her. And if that woman is dressed like a man down here, he could do worse, and get a pass for it.

"That was stupid," I tell her. "That was really dumb."

"You're not wrong." She pats her pockets with one hand. "Did she even give me my change?"

We enter Kentucky and abandon I-75 at its very center for county routes: 52 to 82 up to Clay City, then Old Kentucky 11 and beyond—from there, it is an instinct operation, me giving Mel directives from memory. We pass mammoth paintings of patchwork quilts on barns. Cattle graze beyond barbed-wire fences, ponies saunter around mossy ponds. We crank the windows down as long as we can stand it, the dampness under our arms freezing.

There's change. On a patch of land east of Hazel Green where a fragmenting gray barn has always been is a blocky, castlelike elementary school. In the county over from Faulkner, the state road is more congested than it ought to be; we proceed to find a Lowe's there.

The turnoff to Mom's is just before Faulkner town limits. I direct Mel through the woods, past a large, flaking RC Cola sign by the bend, and finally up the incline into my mother's front yard. "Pull up," I tell her. "Keep going."

She looks out the window and swallows. "We're gonna fall back down the fuckin hill."

"No, we're not."

"Look at it out there. We're almost perpendicular."

"We won't fall," I tell her. "I've gone up this mountain in cars far shittier than this one. We will not roll. I promise. Gas, Mel. Press."

At the top of the hill, my mother watches, legs spread apart, hands on the backs of her hips. Her tennis shoes are puffy and pink. Through her T-shirt—one of those designed for older ladies, with ribbed stripes and a small bow at the collar's center—I see a new roll of fat above where her jeans button. New wings of gray around the crown of her head, streaks of it in her ponytail, more prominent jowls. All those Christmases and Thanksgivings I was breezing in and out, those lines must have been deepening. Here in the sun, I see myself in her face.

She sees me and her hand goes to her mouth. I didn't warn my family about my lack of hair, my thinness. Whoops.

"Whoa," Mel says. "That's your *mom*."

"I know."

"That's what you look like when you get mad."

"Thanks."

"Where do I park?"

I gesture around. Car skeletons are strewn throughout the yard. Our family has had a long-standing devotion to the American sedan, mammoth boats whose coughing tailpipes and wheezy engines elicited cusses from the men circling their hoods. It's a little woebegone car museum here: the Plymouth Duster, its more austere brother the Reliant K, the Pontiac Phoenix with its sloping pointer's nose. The incidentally sexual Buick Skylark—I recall a maroon '72 in a cousin's backyard propped up on cinder blocks, sad and bloated like a widow. Dinosaurs, all.

"Park anywhere," I tell her.

A new car sits in the driveway, large and humped, gleaming in the sun like the severed head of Snoopy. A PT Cruiser. There's only one person who would buy a monstrosity like that. Sure enough, the porch door bangs open and my sister, Shauna, still in the scrubs she wears for work, steps out. She stands behind Mom, hands on her hips, watching.

Shauna was once run over by a '77 Ford Granada. She was two years old, so tiny the build of the car missed her completely. Just sailed over her body as it dropped backward down the mountain and crashed into a ravine. I lied to Mel—if you leave a standard in neutral, it's totally possible to fall off a mountain. I made a decision to omit that information. Those synapses must be repairing themselves like gangbusters.

We pull in behind the Cruiser. I climb out while Mel pretends to fuss with our bags, head down, weirdly shy. I hold on to the car hood to stretch out my legs, shake my ankles loose. "Hi."

Shauna presses her hand to her mouth exactly like Mom. A tennis bracelet twinkles on her wrist. "Oh my *God*," she says.

Mom bursts into tears.

"What," I say. "*What*." I hold my hands up. "I'm fine. Really. I'm okay. Look."

Mom sobs, her hands grasping together. Her belly roll seizes.

"You look like a cancer patient," says Shauna.

I run my hand over my head. My hair's in a pixie cut. I thought it looked good. "Well, shit. Thanks a lot."

"I didn't mean it that way."

"Yeah? How did you mean it?"

She's silent for a beat. "I guess I did mean it."

Mom slings her arms around me. She breathes in waves, shaking. I hug her back. For a moment, I let myself sink into being held by my mother. It's been years since it has happened.

Shauna makes a move to join, but doesn't. She folds her arms across her chest, hangs back.

"You know," I say over our mother's shoulder, "the PT Cruiser is reported to fall out of alignment faster than any other car on the market. It's really poorly proportioned."

"So?"

"Just saying. You drive your kids to school in that thing. Thought you'd want to know."

"I'm surprised you know so much about cars. Living in *New York*, where y'all don't even need cars."

I feel Mom sigh. "Girls, will you all shut the hell up."

"Mommy's going through the *change*," Shauna whispers.

"I mean it," she yells.

We stand like that for a minute.

The Mazda creaks open. I unlatch myself and turn to find Mel crawling ass-end first out of the front seat. She thumbs over her shoulder, grinning uneasily. "Just putting the parking brake on."

I wave her over. "This is my business partner, Mel," I tell them. "She's the one I do the cartoons with."

Hands are shaken. Shauna takes a hard look at the smudged Docs on Mel's feet, her horn-rims. Mel takes a gander at the teddy bear print on Shauna's scrubs. Shauna's boobs are bigger than I remember. They look pendulous, middle-aged. This is hard information to process. Mom stands in the middle, sniffling.

"Nice to meet both of you," Mel says.

"Same to you." Shauna shifts, props her hands on her lower back. "How long y'all been working together?"

"About ten years? Little longer. Are you sure the car's okay there?"

"Ain't nothing gonna happen to the car," Mom says. She pulls a wadded pink Kleenex from her back pocket and swipes her nose. "You're fine."

The wind blows. There's a dark green smell, something sweetly mineral and fresh, coming from the dip in the land separating Mom's yard from where Shauna lives, her new house on the old Caudill property. It's the pines, and soil, and grass, the last fresh growth before the winter. Something else I've forgotten I know—the scent up here, the hills so much themselves you can smell it all the way back to your spine. The sun warms my head, close to bald; the wind cools it. I close my eyes.

My mother grabs me. "Sharon Kay. What's wrong."

"I'm fine. Just feels good to get out of the car."

Mel pokes me. Whispers, "Sharon *Kay*."

Shauna smiles wide at her. An outsider. She wants to see what she can get out of Mel. "You went to college with Sharon, right?"

"Yeah."

"In New York."

"Upstate."

Shauna nods, noncommittal. She's waiting to see whether Mel's going to make a big deal about having gone to Ballister, will judge accordingly. But Mel refuses to elaborate. She's making it her job to scale herself down for this visit—being, as she is, on business.

"Always meant to visit Sharon," Shauna continues. "But I never made it up there."

"That's a shame."

"What was it like?"

Mel shrugs. "Bunch of rich weirdos. I could take it or leave it."

Shauna lifts her eyebrows. "Are *you* a rich weirdo?"

"No. Just a regular weirdo."

"Uh huh."

"But not as weird as them."

Shauna crosses her arms over her chest. Family genetics mean spreading out is inevitable; we are an insistently lardy people. This is *me* in five years. Shauna's thighs are crying out for release from her pants. She squeezes them together, waiting for Mel to say something.

Mel looks over her shoulder to make sure my mother, checking the mailbox, is out of earshot. "We went to school with this one kid whose dad ran GM," she says low.

"Is that right."

"He used to have to start fires before he could come," she whispers. "Used to set little fires in the wastebasket in his dorm room, and then time himself when he was doing it with his girlfriend."

"No woman would put up with that," Shauna says.

"She would. He was rich."

This shuts Shauna up.

"He almost burned down this fifteen-million-dollar dorm on campus. He was in the bushes whacking it when the fire department came to hose it all down."

Shauna purses her lips. Mel has impressed her. "Well, I thought that place was real conservative, to hear Sharon tell it."

"I never said that." I turn to Mel as we go inside. "Have I ever said that?"

Mel shrugs. She's peering around the living room now, taking notes: fingers a pink doily on an end table, crouches in front of an old red-washed Sears studio portrait of the three of us as kids. I've been shoved into Jared's arms. A diaper shows below the ruffle of my dress. Shauna poses beside him, pudgy hands slapped onto his knee, told *stay just like that*. In a nearby photo, Jared's a toddler circa the Carter administration, haloed by crimson light; he stares, stunned, to the right. Behind his head, a transparency of his face gazes in the opposite direction.

"I can't believe I'm really here," Mel mutters.

"You cain't," Shauna says, sounding very much like Mom—half question, half demonstrated exclamation: a *what in the world is she saying?* to an invisible audience.

But Mel snaps to; she's leaving no room for this, which gratifies me. "No offense," she says. "I just had a hard time picturing Sharon having a family. It's strange to meet people who share, you know, DNA with her." She trails off. Peers at a portrait of my great-grandparents scowling at the camera lens in the sun of a tilled field, a pony tied to a post behind them.

Shauna shoots me a long, digging sort of look. I really should have prepared them for what I would look and sound like. It didn't occur to me that what I've become might require a warning.

Mom returns, balancing four Diet Cokes stacked in a tower, two glasses. Without asking, Mel steps into the kitchen and retrieves the other two. "Thank you, honey," Mom calls out.

"Mom, Mel said she always pictured Sharon without a family," Shauna says.

"Is that right." Mom plunks the Cokes down on the coffee table. She doesn't look up.

Mel glances at me. "I just had a hard time *imagining* you all. That's all I meant."

Mom looks up, smiles thinly at Mel. "Well, she's got one. Here we are."

Shauna gives me that look again. I use my middle finger to scratch the side of my head. "When's your hair gonna grow back?" she asks me.

"Shauna, that's like asking me when my fingernails are gonna grow. I don't fucking know."

"Watch your mouth," Mom says. She sees Mel looking at the portraits on the wall. "Would you like to see more pictures of Sharon, Mel?"

"Yes, I would," she says. "That would be lovely."

Mom slaps her thighs and rises. "I got a whole bunch in the bedroom. Let me go look." She hustles down the hallway.

"Get the Glamour Shots," Shauna calls after her.

Mel stops. "You didn't just say Glamour Shots."

"They made Sharon Kay wear a cowboy hat," Shauna says. "With *fringes*. She cried."

Mel hoots. "*Dude.* I have to see."

"I'll bet you were the only ten-year-old they ever made tape up her boobs," I tell Shauna.

She sighs. "I tell you Caelin wants em for Christmas?"

"I think you mentioned that."

She shifts forward to pop open her Coke, plucks her shirt out. "But she also wants these head shots done for pageants. Natalie— you remember Brandon's littlest sister? Her girls do pageants. They got Caelin wantin to do em, too."

"That's horrible."

"It's not *horrible*. I think it's kinda stupid, but she really wants to get em. So I told her, I said, you can only get the *one*. You gotta pick *one*. Cause they're expensive. But she's so good at it. You should see her shaking that little butt to 'Copperhead Road.' Cutest thing ever, I swear."

Mom patters back in, hands Mel something in a frame. It's the *Faulkner Gazette* article written right after I got the Ballister scholarship. I'm shocked to see the photo of myself at the bottom of the page—cheeks fleshy and pale, lips smooth. There's a heavy sheaf of bangs over my forehead. Seventeen.

"Whoa." Mel takes the paper, squints at it. "You were valedictorian," she says, as if it confirms something.

"She was." Mom straightens in her chair. "Got a full scholarship to UK, too. But she wanted to go out-of-state. Guidance counselors down to the high school still talk her up something terrible. I run into that one, what's her name, at Walmart the other day. Oh, I meant to say something the last time I talked to you, but the lady who ran the library, the one you worked for? She died."

I start. "Mrs. Horsemuller died?"

"Well, yeah, honey. She was old. And wasn't there somethin wrong with her?"

"She had epilepsy. Why didn't you say anything?"

"I done said I *forgot*. I'm surely sorry. It was maybe around the same time—" She makes a vague gesture with her hand.

"Jesus," I say.

"I saw her sometimes. She was real sweet. Always talking about how proud she was of you. She kept your all's movies at the library there in town."

Mel looks up. "You've seen our movies?"

"Some of em." Mom relents. "I'm gonna watch em all, now that I got the Internet up here to where it won't break. Sharon Kay sent me the one y'all did last. That big long one."

I cock an eyebrow at Mom. She rolls her eyes and sighs. "Well, Sharon knows I got the nervous-leg syndrome. Makes it hard to stay put for a whole movie. So I ain't watched it *yet*. But I saw the little short bit of it. It looked real interesting. The lady the movie's about, she's crazy, iddint she?"

Mel goes, "Oh yeah. That's Mom."

"Pardon?"

"That's my mom. A character based on my mom."

"Your *mom*."

"Yes ma'am." Mel puts the article down, plucks up a Polaroid: Shauna's ninth birthday. I am reticent and smeared with cake. Shauna screeches over a broken Polly Pocket beauty salon.

Mom clears her throat. "And what did your mom think about that?"

"I don't know. She's dead."

Mom looks at me. Another life preserver I could have thrown that I didn't. "I'm so sorry to hear that," she says.

Snow day 1989. Fifth-grade studio shot. Christmas 1994. Jared shows a pony for 4-H. Church Easter play 1990 (Methodist).

"Thanks," Mel says. "She passed on about six months ago, actually. She was in prison when she died. Sorry to say." Her voice is smooth and even; she is in professional mode, this is an interview.

She comes to the last photograph, freezes. Flashes it at me, wide-eyed. Summer before sixth grade. Me and Teddy Caudill on the trampoline in the backyard. Our arms are slung around each other's necks.

Mom stops, drink in hand. "Oh, look at that," she says, voice small. She reaches out and slides Shauna's cigarettes over.

Mel flaps the photo. "Cute kid. Neighbor?"

Mom closes her lips around a cigarette before muttering, "Mmmm hmm."

Shauna follows suit. Mel removes her own pack from her pocket. Soon the room is filled with haze. I see Mel flip the photo to the back, marking it with her thumb.

I lean over her, grab her smokes.

"Sharon, no," Mom yells.

Mel swats me on the head. "Smoke right now and it'll make you dumb."

This makes Mom laugh. I light up anyway.

Shauna rises. "Hold on, that's the bus coming. I want the kids to come over here. Mom's doing supper, Sharon."

"That's great."

Above the new television, an old family portrait hangs. I place it at 1986 or '87, that Sears crimson tint again. We are bunched together, Mom slim in the face, Dad standing behind her, nose not yet red with broken capillaries. I see Mel linger, comparing it to the old newspaper clipping of me, glancing between them. She's looking for demonstrable reproductions, line and shape. She's looking for a better way to draw me.

She straightens and looks to me. "Always pictured you as a fat kid," she says. I hear Shauna chortle from the kitchen.

SUPPER IS ALL OF Mom's specialties together, a spread for my benefit: fried chicken, mashed potatoes, cornbread, beans and weenies. Kent has crept in through the kitchen door while Mom cooks, silently lifts a hand to Mel and me. For dessert, Mom informs us that Kent insisted upon baking a pie. "He loves to bake. It's an apple pie with whattyacallit on top. Whiskey sauce. Iddint that something?" Kent hears this, shrugs.

Kent owns the laundromat where my mother has worked since I was in high school. He's a big, affable guy, lots of ropy muscle on top, potbelly jutting out just enough to be sociable. Likes NASCAR and, apparently, baking. Doesn't say shit. I've spent a few Christmas breaks silently watching *Jeopardy!* with Kent. Sometimes he whispers answers aloud. He's right often enough to surprise me. And he always, without fail, gestures to Alex Trebek as the credits roll and sighs, "Asshole."

I once asked him why he hated Alex Trebek so much.

He stopped to think it over before saying, "He's smug." Which shocked me so much I shut up.

The whole town had known about our mother's affair with Kent—it was the story that ruined my senior year. I have a clear vision of Jenni Bibbins and Karly Ingram hovering over their cold Bunsen burners in chemistry, giggling at me, neither bright enough to come up with anything to say other than *Yer mom's a skank*. I told

Mel this and it gave her a chuckle. "Right on, man. Funny how people think it's always the dude stepping out. I *respect* that. Lady wanted some dong for her tang? She went out and got it. Case closed."

I stared at her.

She sobered. "Well. Consider the source. You know my mom. Give me some credit for having the decency to put pants on in the morning."

I've never had a problem with Kent, but Shauna balked hard at the idea of him and Mom dating. The residual bitterness of knowing that Mom cheated on our dad with Kent hits Shauna in a sore place, though Mom cheated on Dad at least a few times that we know of— during one of their more monumental fights, he screeched the accusation at her and she was angry enough to bellow, *Yes I did, you drunk piece of shit, and I'd do it again,* not realizing all three kids were within earshot.

Mom has held her ground, however. Kent is here to stay. It is our burden to accept it.

Dad's death was a one-vehicle car accident blamed on slick roads, though the floor of the '95 Pontiac was strewn with beer cans and a half-shattered Beam bottle. He and Mom had been separated for over a year before the wreck. The divorce itself was never finalized; instead of a divorcée, she became a widow.

When I return to the living room, I am surprised to find Kent actually talking to Mel. He has told her that he has a brother living in Orlando. "Hot as hell down there," he says.

"Yeah it is. What's your brother do?"

"Runs a farm. Grows produce."

"No kidding," Mel says. "Spent part of my growing-up on a swamp farm."

I sit nearby and pretend not to listen. "Your folks' farm?" Kent asks her.

"My aunt Shelly did."

"Hard life, them farms."

"Yeah. Learned a lot, though."

I want to ask what, exactly, she learned when Caelin and Jaeden bang through the door, dropping backpacks on the floor, rummaging through Mom's fridge before entering with Yoo-hoos in hand to gawk at me. They are both uncomfortably fair, something alien from their father's side of the family, but when Caelin is informed that Mamaw has run out of chocolate Snack Pack, her displeasure is written all over her face in exactly the style of Shauna.

I make a point of gawking back. "Hey, guys."

"I thought Aunt Sharon was fat," Caelin yells.

Shauna calls, "Caelin, say you're sorry."

"I'm sorry," she says lifelessly.

"It's okay," I tell her. "Your mom says you want Glamour Shots."

Caelin's face lights up. "I did, but now I want head shots. I was in the Little Miss Mountain Rose Pageant and I won second place. I beat my cousin Kelsey. She cried." She twirls. "My pageant dress is in Mamaw's room. So's my bridge. Wanna see?"

"Bridge?" I crane my neck for Shauna.

Shauna rolls her eyes. "Flippers. Fake teeth. You can't have a girl up there with teeth missing."

"She's seven." I stop. "You're seven, right?"

"Uh huh."

"Seven-year-olds lose teeth."

"Well, them pageant runners don't seem to know that."

Caelin runs toward Mom's room. Jaeden creeps around the coffee table toward Mel, who is sifting through another box of photographs. "Think you could be a little more subtle with that?" I mutter to her.

She holds up her hands, cigarette dangling from her lips. Jaeden makes a grab for her iPhone. "How's it going, kid," she says.

"Can I see?"

"Do what you want to, man."

Jaeden flicks the screen. The phone lights, blares Mel's favorite Biggie track. *Fuck bitches, get money.*

"I don't care," Shauna yells from the kitchen. I see her hunched in anger, cellphone pressed to her ear. "You ain't seen my sister in like four years. The least you could do is plan for it and you didn't because you don't give a shit about your family." She pauses. "She could have *died,* and you ain't even getting off work to come see her. Marvin could cover you, you know he could."

Mom pushes Shauna hard on the hip, pointing toward the door. Shauna steps out, letting it bang shut behind her.

Mom sticks her head in. "Looks like Brandon's not making it," she deadpans. Jaeden barely looks up from the phone.

Mel leans over—"Hold up and I'll give it back to you," she says—and with a thumb flick so fast I'm not even sure I'm seeing it, takes a few shots of the Polaroids, then guides the phone to a Tetris program and hands it back to Jaeden. Looks to me, flashes a picture. Another shot of the old Caudill place—the small, squat white house, the crumbling front stoop, the chimney. The photo has yellowed; there are more trees surrounding the property. Pines brush the ground, slung low.

Caelin runs back into the room in full pageant regalia—pink dress sprouting crinoline, sock ruffles above patent leather Mary Janes. A thick red snake of lipstick runs over her mouth. "Mommy, I need my bridge," she yells.

"Hold on," Shauna calls from outside, then into the phone, "No, goddammit, not you, I was talking to your *daughter.* Mom? Get her the bridge?"

Mom ducks in, hands Caelin something. Caelin hunches, then spins around, revealing blindingly white teeth the size of Chiclets. She runs to the CD player she lugged out from behind the couch, presses *play.* "Copperhead Road" begins to twang loud. She turns, back to us, hands on hips, begins to line dance, shimmying. Mel and I glance at each other. Kent—we've forgotten he's there in the corner, ankle crossed over knee, *Faulkner Gazette* draped over his leg— coughs and shifts uncomfortably in his seat.

Shauna returns. "That son of a bitch." She tosses her cell onto the couch, then stands with hands on hips, watching Caelin dance. "Iddint that cute," she says.

• • •

JARED ARRIVES AROUND SIX with his wife, Britney, and their kids. They have three; the oldest is Melinda, who apparently had a growth spurt last summer. Boys lust for her, girls put up with her, and both make her unbearable at home. Shauna fills me in out of earshot. "She's gonna turn out like Britney. We all know it." I see her point: big boobs, oily hair, brimming with girl-on-girl antagonism. "Hey, Aunt Sharon," Melinda says, perfunctory, rolling eyes and giving me a loose, loopy hug. It makes me sad. I was fifteen when Melinda was born. Hers was the first diaper I ever changed. When she was two or three, she used to dance around to my Roxy Music CDs while I sketched her.

I ask her if she remembers this. She crinkles her eyebrow at me in such a way that I know not a lot has been said about her weirdo aunt in New York, but enough—just the right, damning details, probably from her mom—for her to draw a final disapproval. "Um, *noooo*," she says. And that's the end of *that* conversation.

When Jared sees me, he stoops over, removes his cap, and hugs me hard with one arm. "Hey," he says. "You look like shit."

"Thank you very much."

Red's hairline is feathering back. There are lines around his mouth. "Thanks for coming," I tell him.

"Well." Shuffling his feet and trailing off, he breaks with "Good to see you."

Jared married Britney when he was twenty-two. Britney was three classes ahead of me, and hung out with girls who did a lot of whispering and pointing at my boots, my hair; my sister-in-law now judges me in secret. She steps in as the other two kids—Bella, age eight with crippling ADHD, and Jaxon, four, whose name made me snort beer up my nose when I read the text message sent out at his birth—run in. I am somewhat entertained to see Bella, a little fat and a whole lot tall, smack the bejesus out of Caelin first thing.

"Hey, hon," Britney brays, giving me a hug, her hands flattening and nails pointing away as if she is afraid she'll get something underneath. I catch Mom wincing at the sound of her voice over her shoulder. For a split second, I feel bad for Britney. "Don't she feel *light* to you?" she whispers, in earshot, to Jared. "She feels so *light* when you hug her."

"I lost some weight," I tell her.

She lifts her eyebrows. "Well, you sure did, didn't you, honey." She turns over her shoulder. "Bella, Jaxon, say hey to Aunt Sharon."

"Hey," they drone. Neither remembers me or cares. Jaxon toddles to Jaeden. They nod to each other, click to something on Mel's phone. I hear the opening strains of *Dirty Duck*. Britney is drenched in Clinique Happy. I turn my head to the couch cushions and breathe for a minute before turning back. "Jared, Britney, this is my business partner, Mel Vaught."

Mel rises halfway, shakes hands with them both. She's plowed through nearly the entire box of photographs. A stack rests alongside for reference. She's going to take them into the bathroom to see if she can get some quick sketches. I know she is.

Mel catches sight of Jared's truck outside the window. "That the new Ford F-150?"

"Sure is."

Mel peers. "And in the new crimson. Damn. That is classy."

Jared hooks his thumbs in the loops of his jeans. "I'm pretty partial to the new colors, myself."

"Yeah, Ford's got really great color guys now. They had a hard time putting that one out on the market."

"Think I heard that somewhere," he says.

"The candy-apple red, the one they've had for years now? Ford thought if they put out two shades of red that people would complain one was too pink. But it's really popular. It's a nice job."

"It is." They stand there, admiring. Britney watches them sharply for a moment, does a quick study of Mel's haircut, Mel's shirt— a men's oxford, collar loose, sleeves pushed up—and her thought process is a seamless, transparent one. Watching her discover that Mel is a lesbian is one of the funniest things I've seen in a while.

Shauna strides in. "Guess who's not coming."

"But you *tole* him." Britney flips through her purse, comes up with Trident. She chomps down on a piece, offers the pack to Shauna, who takes it. I imagine Shauna's spent a few reluctant, drunk-on-wine-coolers-looking-at-old-yearbooks-now-how'd-*this*-happen nights with Britney.

"Yeah, I told him, but he don't give a shit. I guess."

"I guess." They both put their hands on their hips and stare at me. "So *little*," Britney breathes.

"I know. Mom almost laid an egg when she saw her."

"I'm right here," I say. "I can hear you."

"We know," Shauna says.

There's further sound from Mel's phone. Jaeden and Jaxon run around in a circle. From the corner, Kent ruffles his paper and mutters.

Mom pokes her head in. "Dinner's ready," she yells. "Y'all need to get in here and eat *right now.*"

SHAPE-SHIFTER MEL, SITTING AT my mother's dinner table laughing with my brother. Fast friends. His legs are spread, Coke nestled near the groin, and he nods to say something to Mel, like she's another dude at his shop. Red looks disconcertingly like our father with a paunch like half a basketball coming in above his belt, a decided crease to his forehead when he leans over his plate. Next to him, Shauna sets down her iced tea to yell at Jaeden, who is attempting to smear mashed potatoes into Jaxon's hair while Jaxon screams, soft and aimless, into his plate.

Mel mutters something to Jared, who guffaws, hiding his mouth behind his drink. They circled the truck for ten minutes before sitting down to eat, discussing the engine, the contours. I hear Mel tell him she misses seeing trucks in Manhattan. I always assumed she was being ironic when she said things like that. Apparently not. The whole thing leaves me testy.

Mom piles my plate high. I have forgotten that Mom is a bang-up cook, when she wants to be. It helps that most of this has been assembled with unspeakable amounts of lard. I'm careful with the chicken, still shaky with cutlery. I think of the solid month of my life it took me to relearn how to use a fork: the grip, the trajectory to the mouth. How much food I spilled. No one else would really relate if I tried to tell that story. It would just sound strange, and sad. No, I am a spectator here, a spectator to my own family, like I've always been. Kent's head is bent; he chews affably. Mom says something low to him. He pats her on the thigh. Shauna rolls her eyes. She lifts her phone to flick off an angry text. "Put it away," Mom says without looking at her. She does.

Mel catches my eye. Wiggles her eyebrows at me.

I look out the window onto the ridge, which extends into a deep drop of rocks and pines and underbrush before leveling out slightly farther down to the place where Shauna's house stands. To where Teddy's house *used* to be. I see a bare patch where our trampoline stood on the lawn, the grass there yellow and thin. Suddenly I remember Honus Caudill sitting in the back of his van, cleaning supplies at his feet. His eyes on me. The feel of him looking at me a sensation like being flayed open, organs exposed to the air.

Something happens. I leave my body—not floating this time, like during the stroke, with that deliciously airless vantage point over my head. This is a slow leak, a gradual darkening. Sound warps and cottons. The floor begins to shift. My heart speeds.

We should not be here. *This* is why I stayed away for four years; I knew, on the furry, subconscious level, that there was something here waiting to swallow me. I can feel the base of my spine curl in self-protection, an animal warning against the electricity of this place. How silly it is to assume that what we're dealing with is not something that will, in turn, deal with *us*.

You need to move away from whatever is here for you, I think to myself. Not toward it.

My chest constricts. A dark point in the middle of my vision spreads, grows deeper, more velvet. I can't draw a deep enough breath. The sounds around me begin to fade.

I drop my fork, make a small choking noise.

My mother looks to me sharply. Yells, "Sharon *Kay*."

"Huh?"

Everyone is staring at me. It's gone quiet.

"Are you all right."

"Yeah." I blink, take a few shaky breaths. Try to get my eyes to refocus. I pound my chest weakly. "Just—went down the wrong way. I'm fine."

"You look funny."

I go to Mel, trying to measure my breathing. She swipes her chin. *Drool.* I wipe.

"Just starin off into *nothin,*" Britney whispers.

Mom gives her a dirty look. "Hush," she says, and moves toward me. Reaches for my forehead. Feels.

Mel starts to get up. "You okay?" she says, low. "Want me to call Dr. Weston? I can." She grabs her phone, flecked with corn bits. My family stares at her; she's gone from good old boy to authority figure in three seconds.

"Don't," I say. "I'm okay. Really."

"Sure?"

"Yes."

She purses her lips, not totally sold. "Okay. But I can do it any-time if you change your mind."

I look at everyone. They're gaping at me. No one is eating. "I'm okay," I tell them. "For God's sake, let's please eat. Okay?"

Mom stares at me for a moment until she sits back, satisfied. "Everybody eat," she commands. And we do.

THE DISHES ARE CLEARED. Mom hauls out the pie and Bud Light. Everybody takes one, save for Mel and Jared. Britney wrings her hands when she sees me crack one open. "I'm allowed to drink," I say. "One's fine."

"Leave her alone," Jared calls from outside. He and Mel have gone to talk cars again; he's offered to show her some pre-Nixon Chevy skeleton down in the ravine. I step carefully onto the porch after them.

Kent's there, looking out on the ridge. He nods at me. There's a pipe in his hand, an old carved cherrywood job. A sweet, toasted smell drifts from the bowl. "The pie was great," I tell him.

He nods. "Glad you enjoyed it."

I turn to step off the porch when he says, "I watched your all's movie last night."

"You did?"

"It was real good," he says slowly. Turns the bowl of his pipe, taps at it. "Gives you a lot to think over."

"Thanks, Kent."

"You do all the drawings yourself? You and Mel?"

"We do. Well, we use a software program to help, but yeah, it's mostly just us."

He nods. "That is something. Lot of hard work, sounds like."

This is the most Kent has ever said to me directly. "It makes it better if you like what you do," I say.

"I reckon you're right. Good to have you all here." He steps back into the house.

I find Jared and Mel down in the weeds, smoking. They look up at me. "She looks all right," Jared says to her.

"I'm standing right the fuck here," I say. "Why does everyone keep doing that?"

Mel shrugs. Jared blinks as if he didn't hear me.

"Sharon's never brought anyone home, has she?" Mel looks at me. "You've never brought any guys home. Have you?"

"I just figgered she was a dyke," Jared says.

Mel caws and slaps her knees.

"Jared," I yelp.

"What? That's what happens in college, iddint it?"

"That's *exactly* what happens in college," Mel chortles.

"It is not," I say.

Jared holds out his hands. "Settle down. You don't wanna get Mom and them out here."

"You're right. I never brought anyone home," I tell Mel. "Guess why."

"Hey now. Your brother here, he's all right. He knows what's up."

Jared tips the bill of his hat to me.

"So," Mel says. "Sharon said something about Shauna's house down there being new? Like some weirdo lived there before and something happened, and they tore the house down?"

I didn't tell Mel any of this. She got it all from hours of Googling Faulkner, Kentucky. Looking up pictures of the property, now over ten years old. Honus Caudill, she pointed out to me, was the second search result after the Chamber of Commerce. She did as much research as she could, stopping when she came upon the same censored photographs of the girls, naked, with their eyes blotted out; she clapped the MacBook shut, put her hands in the air, and said, "That's it. Done. I'm gonna need to drink for *years* to get that out of my head."

I roll my eyes. "Honus Caudill," I say to Jared.

Jared grunts, "Sick fuck." Ashes with a backward snap of his wrist.

"So that's Shauna's house now, right?" Mel says.

Jared turns, peers in that direction. "Yeah, they knocked the old place down and rebuilt. She wanted to be close to Mom."

"To count the number of times Kent's car comes up the drive," I mutter.

Jared snorts. "Probably."

"Why'd they knock it down?" Mel asks.

Jared clears his throat. Says low, "Heard some of the stuff happened there."

"Really?"

Jared nods.

"Shit." Mel turns to me. "You were *there*, dude."

Jared snaps to attention. "What?"

"Sharon used to play over there. When she was a kid."

"No you didn't," Jared says to me. "Tell me you didn't."

"I used to play with Teddy Caudill," I tell him. "We were the same age."

His eyes are wide under the shadow of his hat brim. It's the first time all night I've seen the color of his eyes, that milky cornflower blue. "Fuck. Are you okay?"

"Nothing happened to me," I tell him. "I'm fine. We didn't see his dad that much." I snap my fingers at Mel's cigarette, glaring at her: *Shut up*. She hands it over.

Jared stares at me, shaken. I think of him fathering three kids, of him having a teenage daughter. Melinda with her long legs and smart-ass reflexes. Him not yet forty, but close. I have never considered my brother a worrier.

The screen door slams shut on the hill and Shauna hustles out, purse over her shoulder. "Girls, I'm a-goin to Walmart. Who's in?"

"I am." Mel stubs her smoke out on her shoe. "I wanna see Faulkner. Sharon didn't let us drive through on the way here."

"Sharon's ashamed of us," Shauna sings, sashaying down. "Wanna go, Red?"

"Nah."

Shauna pauses near us. "You still not drinking?"

"Sixty days."

I look at Jared. He tugs at the bill of his hat.

"Good for you, babe." She flicks her cell on. The light shines. She begins to toe carefully down the driveway in the dark. I see a large turtle plodding in the shadows. "I'm taking the good Chrysler cause I'm pissed at Brandon, so we gotta walk down. I can't believe you all were screwing around by that old Chevy. Rattlesnakes just *love* to nest in those engines. Bites ain't fun. Jaeden'll tell you."

We follow Shauna into the dark, whipping out our own cell-phones and squinting at the ground. Halfway down, Mel whispers, "I got weed."

I turn to her. "What?"

Shauna yells, "Hot damn. Let's go," and leans over to swat my butt before running ahead of us.

NIGHT RIDE

FOR MAXIMUM WEED CONFIGURATION, MEL TAKES SHOTGUN. I'M IN THE backseat, where I glare at her and Shauna's heads while we go the long way around Faulkner. Wind into the county's upper kingdom in a chain of high hills, homes tucked so deeply out of sight the only marker is a wispy gravel driveway the width of one car. There is a fingernail moon in the sky.

Still there: the abandoned water treatment facility, a dingy blue glass building, side spray-painted: MENIFEE COUNTY EATS IT HARD. Saplings break through the concrete parking lot. Not there: the house where the lady we called Old Moses once maintained an actual burning bush in her front yard. The population sign that, when I was a kid, was perpetually pocked with bullet holes; a sign reading HOME OF THE 1968 KY STATE CLASS AA STATE BASKETBALL CHAMPIONS.

I lean toward Mel. "I thought you quit smoking."

"I never said that."

"I thought you meant to."

"I said *cut down*. I never said *quit*. Besides, I think you're in the clear now. Relax."

She's right, but I still don't like it.

"What's Sharon bellyaching about," Shauna says.

"My wicked ways."

"Woo," Shauna hoots.

"Shut up," I tell them.

We sweep south and run parallel to the county line for five or six miles, finding ourselves on the parkway before we take an exit and head back toward Hollins Gap on U.S. 60's wide, dark vein. Shauna turns motormouth at puff one and Mel bends an eager ear, asking for stories about our high school, our parents. My shoulders loosen, my breathing slows.

"My family likes you better than they like me," I complain to Mel.

"Quit bein *stupid*, Sharon. She's being *stupid*." Shauna leans in and fiddles with the radio, steering with one hand, away from Randy Travis playing on Faulkner107.7. (*That's your hometown station, one oh seven seven the Tomahawk! Oooga Chaka Oooga Chaka!*)

We're cruising along the path of the northbound train now. Cars heaped with coal, steam rising from the chunks. Car after car, load after load. I let myself sink, stare at things I haven't seen in years. I do not remember where I was or what I was doing the last time I saw coal loads chug by. Maybe I was a teenager, saw it with eyes dulled by the desire to be somewhere else, anywhere else. How could I have missed this? This is the kind of beauty that gives you the fever wish to make things. How could I have *not* grown up wanting to draw? I feel a flash of shame. I used to hate it here. How could I have possibly hated *this*? This is *me*. I *sprang* from this place.

I am *real* stoned.

Shauna's looking at me in the rearview. Her teeth glow in the dark. "Sharon."

"Yeah."

"Why are you back?"

"I don't know," I stall. "Figured I was overdue for a visit."

She smirks. "Overdue for a visit, huh."

I have always hated having to decode whatever my family says. Everything is implicit with Mom and Shauna. Everything goes without saying. It feels like they're trying to trick me into making some sort of disclosure about myself that proves this point about me that they've secretly agreed upon. Every conversation, however minor, becomes another instance in which they are leaving me behind and I am running to catch up. It stings. Especially now, when *nothing* goes without saying. When I'm at my slowest and weakest. When I'm not even sure myself what I'm doing back here.

This all stitches together in my head, hot and itchy. I lean forward and say, "What exactly are you trying to say to me?"

"Nothing."

"No. We're not playing that game. You need to tell me exactly what the fuck you mean by *what am I doing back here.*"

"What *are* you talking about?"

"*Shauna.*"

"I mean exactly what I say, Sharon."

"You don't. I may have just had a stroke, but I'm not a moron and I never was."

There's a silence. Shauna finally breaks. "You hate being back here," she says. "We all know it. It's been, what, four years since you visited? My kids didn't remember you. Even when I showed them a picture. So why now?"

"Because Mom pulled out the crying act. And you know how that works *wonders* on me."

"That's not an act," she says. "She cried to me, too. This really upset her. You didn't even call her when it happened."

I feel a twinge of guilt. "I did."

"But not when it happened. Didn't you wait like six weeks?"

"Little hard to call when I couldn't talk without slobbering all over myself."

"Oh, you weren't that bad off," she says dismissively.

"You weren't fucking there. How dare you tell me it wasn't that bad."

Mel coughs softly. "She actually was in really bad shape," she intercedes. "She couldn't talk. For a while."

Shauna glances at her, then back at the road. "Really?"

"You think Mom was upset?" I tell her. "It took me a month to figure out how to walk again. It was so painful when I got up for the first time that they had to give me morphine. I missed being a vegetable by about two inches. I was *terrified*. And the last thing I do when I'm scared is talk to *you* people. Because you always seem to make it worse."

Shauna holds up one hand. "Okay."

"No, it's *not* okay. I am thirty-two years old and I had a stroke," I yell. "They don't even know how it happened. It happened because I am *fucked*."

"All *right*. I'm sorry. Good *God*."

We head back toward town on 460. Pass the country club, the Cattlemen's Association, the new Dairy Queen with a long line of trucks and SUVs crowding its lot. A few teenage girls, delicate necks rising from down jackets, flit between. Shauna stops at the four-way light at the Faulkner bypass. An abandoned Maloney's truck yawns open in a field.

"I didn't mean we aren't glad to see you," she says. "It's just that you don't like seeing *us*."

"That's not true."

She turns to another station. Bluegrass. She makes a face, flicks again. Springsteen. "Tell you what," she mutters. "I didn't know having a stroke could make a body so goddamn *mad*."

We pass the high school. Church of God. Tobacco warehouse. I shake my head, roll my shoulders in their sockets. Being high is suddenly uncomfortable. Mel reaches into her pocket for the additional joint and hunches below the dash to light up. A yarn of smoke curls above her head and expands. She hands it to me. Our fingers touch. It is a life preserver. Old life, new life. Mel is my familiar now, the comforting future in which I live.

Shauna takes us around the periphery, quiet. I feel myself getting back my drafting-table eye for the first time since the stroke, noting the dimensions of the courthouse, the Civil War monument on the cobblestone street, churches Methodist, Super Methodist, Seventh-Day Adventist. Old Kroger, new Kroger. Finally, we slope down into the slick ultralight of the Walmart Supercenter parking lot.

Shauna parks halfway back, shuts off the engine. "I ain't been this stoned since before Caelin was born."

Mel clicks off her safety belt. "Why don't I go in and get what you need. I gotta stretch my legs."

"All right." Shauna reaches into her purse, draws out cash. "Caelin needs her pageant nail polish. It's Revlon Quick Dry number 76. Magenta Magic. And I need a carton of cigarettes. Get the Marlboro Reds. I'm feeling bitchy."

"How much are they down here?"

"Carton'll be forty."

Mel takes the cash. "Damn. That's cheap. I'll get some, too. We should stockpile."

"How much are they up there?"

"Eleven a pack. Twelve or thirteen if you go high-end."

"Nuh uh."

"Yeah. They are."

"You're lyin," Shauna says comfortably as the door swings shut.

The parking lot is quiet. Music pipes in faintly through loudspeakers. It sounds like Amy Grant. I shift my butt on the seat, trying to stretch.

"Are you high?" Shauna asks me.

"Yup."

"Me too." She sniffs something back into her head and closes her eyes. "Tired. Sometimes I wish I didn't have kids. I mean, I love them and everything. But they just eat you alive."

She's quiet again until "I didn't mean to upset you."

"You didn't upset me."

"I did, though," she says. "You know, sometimes I feel bad about being mean to you when we were kids. Or just being . . . I dunno."

"Not sticking up for me?"

"Uh. Okay."

"Like when Brandon said I had dyke boots? Remember that?"

"You've thought about this some."

I don't answer.

"Well, I wanna divorce," she says. "So."

"Really?"

"He doesn't give a fuck about me. His kids barely see him. He's been screwing around with this girl who works at Nestlé." She stares out the window shaking her head, lips pinched. "I don't know what it is about Kisses women liking the ones who treat them bad." She looks at me in the rearview and raises her eyebrows. "We all seem to do it."

I shrug, uncomfortable.

"So fuck Brandon. If you see his car on the way out of town and want to slash the tires, go ahead."

"Pass that along to Mel. She loves destroying property."

"I like that girl," Shauna says. "I do. She probably had a hard time growing up, too. You got a lot of shit you didn't deserve, okay?"

"A lot of it came from our parents."

Shauna shifts. "Maybe."

"*Maybe,* huh."

"Sharon, they fought so much with each other, you think they had the time to concentrate on any of us?"

"They were better with you and Jared. You made sense to them."

"Are you saying I didn't get any of her bullshit? Looks like someone wasn't paying attention." She's getting louder. "She set a piss-poor example for all of us. And then she has the nerve to tell me not to fight with Brandon in front of the kids. Don't you think I wanna screw around like she did? But I don't. I got kids. I got responsibilities. They're watching what I do. Like we were."

She turns to face me. "Just cause Mom and I hang out don't mean we think the same way. She wants what she wants, and when she wants something, it's like everything else just falls away. She's always been like that. She won't ever change. I mean, have you ever been able to read Mom? She's so up and down. Something's wrong with her. Like something in her head."

Hearing Shauna say this makes me laugh.

She smiles thinly. "And you know what? I liked your all's movie. It was hilarious. And if she's so afraid to watch it, then her loss."

"She's afraid to watch it?"

"Well, she didn't say so, but that's what I think. She's afraid there'll be something about *her* in it." She rolls her eyes.

We both relax. There's a companionable silence in the car now. I wonder if I would feel unburdened, if I would feel somehow *loosened* from it all, by telling one more person, aside from Mel, to *be* with in it all. I figure now's as good a time as ever to find out.

"I'm back," I tell her, "because some things happened when I was a kid, some things I sort of forgot about that came back to me a few years ago. It made me want to see everything. To see how it would make me feel."

"And how's that going."

"Did you see my panic attack during dinner? Not so awesome."

"What kind of stuff did you remember?"

I take a deep breath. "When I was eleven, Teddy Caudill and I found a bunch of pictures of little girls that his dad took. Some of the stuff the FBI got later."

Shauna goes still. There's a pause in the music piped over the loudspeaker, a moment of almost complete silence before we hear an ad for a sale on Goodyear tires.

"You're joking. Right?" she says quietly.

I stare at her in the rearview.

She puts her face to the side without turning in her seat, waiting for me to say something. She inhales, exhales.

I wipe my nose onto my hand, rub my eyes. Outside, the automated Walmart doors part. Mel lopes out into the night, a stack of cigarette cartons tucked under one arm. She holds one aloft in her hand, triumphant. Breaks into a run for us.

W E CRUISE BACK THROUGH town. I try to see everything: the long downtown building that once housed Belk-Simpson on Main Street, the Faulkner Sundry Store, Cummings Lunch Counter, which retained its rattling bar seats and Johnson-era newspaper clippings on the walls until it closed.

The hilltop of Phillips-Stamper Cemetery hangs over everything. Our father lies at the western end, feet pointing toward the interstate. Small lanterns and floodlights have been placed on headstones, creating a glow on the rise in the dark, a hundred pinpoints of light. Mel cranes her neck to look, watching the hillside rise higher and higher above town, an outline of the city founder, his back to us, visible against the sky. There are stars. She curses softly in wonder, state-tax cigarette trembling between her lips.

"Pretty, iddint it," Shauna says.

"Dude. Right?"

I turn as we pass, trying to look as long as I can.

Something inside me shifts. I picture a deep, rich rendering of Phillips-Stamper, its purple girth, its lights twinkling on the slope, soft pricks against the night. How vibrant and full it would look. Like something you could stick your fingers into and *feel*.

There in the rushing dark, I am, for the first time in months, inspired. My chest opens. Adrenaline spreads hot down both legs. It's the opposite of what happened at the dinner table, that terrifying moment of shutdown. This is your chest hinging open and gasping with relief. This is air and light, this is blood flow and movement, the belief that I will overtake all this before it overtakes me.

This is how it happens. I am terrified, I fear for my life. But I fall. I fall.

THERE'S ANOTHER JOINT TO smoke. It is decided that we should park behind the D.P. Smith water treatment plant. We spark up, watching the tower of light and the water churn through the machines, everything glowing and moving. The whistle sounds. A guy walks past our window, calls, "Hey, Shauna." She lifts a polite hand, a tight-lipped smile.

"You gonna tell Mom?" Shauna asks me.

"I don't know."

I slide down in my seat, a shiver of shame running down my spine. *Shauna, whether you know it or not, you're all material.* But I close my eyes and see the Phillips-Stamper hilltop, indigo, slightly wavering on a frame. And despite my shame, I smile.

WE PULL UP THE drive at twelve-thirty. Kent's car is still parked there. "Guh," Shauna says. Pantomimes kicking its rear fender.

"Come on. He's not so bad," I say.

"He's still *him*."

Kent has gone to bed. Caelin and Jaeden are gone; Brandon picked them up, said something about the truck needing a new transmission, and took them home. "Well, he's paying for the fuckin thing," Shauna grumbles.

"You need to take this up with him. And y'all shouldn't be pickin at each other in front of the kids." Mom's in an old T-shirt and robe, a ripped pair of sweatpants cinched at the waist and ankles, ancient UK football symbol on the thigh. She stomps across the room to us, belly trembling. "What are you doing keeping Sharon up so late?"

"Sharon wanted to stay out. Sharon's a grown-up."

"It's true," I say.

Mom rolls her eyes and snorts. She's done with the cooking and hugging; we bug the shit out of her and she sees no reason to hide it. She turns to Mel. "So what'd you think of Faulkner."

Mel brandishes five cartons of cigarettes. "These are only forty bucks here," she says. "Kentucky's the *tits*."

Mom shakes her head. "The *tits*," she mutters. "Well, that's a new one on me, I'm telling you." She thumps out. I hear the fridge open and close. She returns and pushes a glass of water into my hand. Her forehead does not smooth until I drink the whole thing. "Shauna, go home and go to bed."

"I'm going." Shauna plops down on the couch. Her eyes are red. She glances at me. Raises an eyebrow. I nod. She nods back.

Our mother looks back and forth between us. "What did you all do tonight? I knew y'all didn't just go to Walmart. I knew y'all were gonna go out and screw around."

"Momma, *quit*," Shauna whines. "Just *stop*."

Mom exhales hard through her nostrils. She reaches deep into her robe and pulls something out: Caelin's pageant bridge, smeared with lipstick. She picks up Shauna's palm and slaps the bridge into it. "Brandon forgot this," she says, "but I think he's got the right idea because them pageants are sick, and you might just go to hell for putting her in one of em."

"Look who's talking," Shauna moos.

Mom grinds her foot into her leg. Shauna shrieks. "Y'all are drunked up or high or somethin. Need to behave yourselves."

"Quit," Shauna yells, and kicks her. The volume in the room doubles. Shauna lolls back, scrubs wrinkled, stinking of weed. They kick, feet aflurry. Mel picks a loose piece of skin from her bottom lip, staring. Goes, "Hee."

Shauna reaches in and slaps Mom's leg, half meaning, half play. Mom giggles and smacks her head. "Go, goddammit," she yells. She straightens her robe and gives her head a final tap. "Go home. I mean it." She turns to us, breathing hard. "Mel, I got you a bed ready in Shauna's old room. There's clean towels in there. And I got your old room ready for *you*." She takes the glass from my hands. "Out drinkin and druggin when here you just got out the hospital. Ought to be ashamed."

"I'm okay. Really."

Mom comes at me, grabs my chin between her forefinger and thumb. "Lemme see," she mutters, and pulls my line of vision directly in front of her. I get a close-up of the gray in her eyes—they were always gray, but are nearly transparent now—and the large pores around her nose. How much do I resemble her? I should ask Mel. Objectivity is the key when evaluating visuals. Distance. Parsing a whole down to its barest, most shape-based elements, passionless, exact. I try to turn to look, just to make sure Mel's there, but my mother makes a noise like "Aaaht" and jerks my head back.

Finally she lets me go. "Well, you don't look too crooked." She rocks back on her heels. Says to Mel, "When my uncle had his stroke, Sharon's great-uncle Zeke, I swear, half his face just went limp." Mom pokes my jaw, grabs a bit of cheek flesh. "Stayed like that for the longest time. Like that old-fashioned disease. What do you call it. Bell's palsy. Know what I'm talking about? Like that. They had an open casket for the visitation and all anyone could see was that half of face, like someone let the air out of it." Mom smooths my cheeks down hard with her thumbs. "Wife of his was a goddamned idiot, leavin it open like that."

I manage to duck out of her way. "Mom, you gonna be around tomorrow?"

She sighs. "Gotta pull day shift. Other girl's out sick with the flu."

"So at night?"

"Yeah." She looks to me, evasive. "Now, don't get pissy cause I gotta work. Sometimes you just got to."

"I'm not getting pissy. Who's getting pissy?"

Mel is staring at the family portrait again. Her lips are pressed together. She shifts her weight from one foot to the other.

Mom doesn't notice. "I'm going to bed," she grumbles. "I've had enough of y'all's bullshit. You and Shauna together just wear me out. Good night, Mel."

"Good night, Mrs. Kisses."

Mom flicks a hand at her. "Oh, I changed back to my maiden name," she says. "I ain't been Mrs. Kisses in years."

"What?" I say.

She shuts the door.

SNAP ON THE lamp. It is my childhood room, not a sign of me left. Underneath the bed, I find a stack of yearbooks and choose a paperbound elementary school volume from the bottom of the pile. Flip past Mrs. Monroe's class where my photo should be, going right for Mrs. Harrison, fourth grade 1993. I find Teddy in the second row.

I pull my sketchpad from my bag. The photo's a poor shot, over-exposed against a smoky-blue backdrop. The photographer clearly issued orders: body turned in one direction, chin tilted down to the other, a pose which has made Teddy slump forward, discomfort crimping his mouth. I work hard on the nose, the chin's delicate turn. A lot of tight, intense pencil work. Light-touch shadowing. Teddy would have made a beautiful girl. My hands are steadier than they've been in weeks.

Mel comes in damp and flushed from the shower. She rubs her head with a towel and looks over my shoulder. "Dude, look at pretty boy."

"I was just thinking the same thing."

She tilts her head to one side and cranks her pinky finger in her ear. "You know what? We should go find him. See the man Teddy Caudill in the flesh."

"I dunno," I say. "How did you get your information on him, anyway?"

She hangs her towel around her neck. "Jesus, Kisses, why haven't you learned to exploit Google like everyone else?" She shakes her head, smacking her palm against her ear, then rubs her hands on her shorts and disappears. Returns with a notebook she flips open. "Owns an art-movie rental place in Louisville called Weirdo Video."

"You're kidding me."

"No. They had a film festival there, and he was namechecked as the coordinator." She gives me the notebook. The address is scrawled across, barely legible. "The weird thing's that, of everyone you grew up with, he's probably the one who comes the closest to having seen anything we've done. Distribution sells us specifically to places like that. Art house, B-list, indie, whatever. How far is Louisville from here?"

I take the paper from her. "Three hours. Little more."

She shrugs and goes to town on her other ear, hopping up and down. "Well. Can you think of anything better to do tomorrow?"

THE GIRL WHO SHOWED
THE JURY HER TEETH

WAKE AT NOON DIZZY, ACHING FROM KNEES TO NECK. MEL IS ON THE back deck with coffee and a cigarette, a years-old copy of the *Faulkner Gazette* in her hands. I get a look at the front page. It is my senior portrait—she's rereading the story written when I won the Ballister scholarship.

She snaps the paper and sniffs. "You'll be gratified to know," she says, "that hog prices have risen two dollars per pound since your high school graduation. However, poultry rates have remained steady."

"Mom and Kent gone?"

"Yeah. Kent made us coffee before he left. Said there are biscuits in the freezer. Nice guy."

"I agree. Shame Shauna gives him so much shit."

"I'm guessing your sister doesn't change her opinions so easily."

"That's a kind way of putting it."

"She loves you." Mel hides behind the *Gazette*.

I shift. "Dude. This chair is really fucking hard."

"She wouldn't get so freaked out about the Honus Caudill thing if she didn't. She was genuinely disturbed by that. That's what you all were talking about while I was in Walmart. Right?"

"Was it that obvious?"

"Yep." She rattles the front page. "Get dressed. We got places to go."

I'M NOT SUPPOSED TO drive yet, but I offer to take the car down the mountain. Mel stares straight ahead, lips pressed together as I crane my neck and steer us in reverse down the hill to the main road. "Okay," she says. "Switch back."

"What, no thank you?"

"Thank you for scaring the bejesus out of me. Now scootch."

We take U.S. 60 to the interstate. A long line of kids riding ATVs cruise along the road shoulder. A few lift their arms in greeting.

I-64 west winds up and down through the hills, flattening as it passes Lexington. Two bathroom breaks and three carside jogs later, we arrive at 75's midsouth fork-off—St. Louis in one direction, Nashville in the other, Louisville in the cradle—get turned around taking a downtown exit, then ramble out Muhammad Ali Boulevard through blocks of fried chicken joints and Chinese takeout, houses with single red bulbs by the front door. "Did we just get teleported back to Brooklyn?" Mel says.

We make a turn, find ourselves on a block of Victorians, where we stop to photograph a jockey statue that has been painted pea green. Cut through Cherokee Park, nearly collide with an SUV on a turnabout, and emerge onto a tree-lined thoroughfare. The sidewalks are populated with kids in skinny jeans and square sunglasses. "Holy hell," Mel says. "Sorry, but if that was East New York back there, then this looks like—"

"Williamsburg. This is it. Bardstown Road."

"Jesus. Everything's a microcosm of New York now. It's ruined America for us." She rolls her window down and lights a cigarette, checking out two girls in cowboy boots at the light. "I spy with my little eye . . . an ironic mustache," she mutters.

And that's when I see it: a large, spray-painted marquee reading WEIRDO VIDEO. Above that, an R. Crumb–style fiend hovers, tongue lolling out, one eye askew, horny hand grasping at old-school VHS cassettes.

Seeing it makes it real. My insides twist. I feel my armpits. Soaked.

"I can't believe we're doing this," I say. "Remind me why we're here. Why did we think this was a good idea?"

"Because it is," Mel says. "Why not? He'll be glad to see you. And if he's not, then we leave."

"Let's go home. Let's get some pie, then go home. There's a pie kitchen up that way."

"Okay, *Cathy*. Let's all go ACK and shove our faces in some pie. Are you fucking kidding me?"

"Stop it. I don't like this."

Mel sticks her cigarette between her teeth and cranks the Mazda into a parking space. "Remember why we're here. We had to come to Kentucky to see it for ourselves. And we have to go to Teddy to see him, too. Whatever story we're doing here—it's incomplete without him. He was there with you *in that room*."

The image of Phillips-Stamper Cemetery flickers to mind, but dimmer than last night, weakened by the daylight, sobriety, my rising heart rate. "You know, I haven't technically given the go-ahead on this thing yet," I say.

"I didn't realize a formal go-ahead was required."

"For fuck's sake." I lean over and put my head between my knees. "I don't feel good," I tell her.

She hauls a bottle of water out of the back and hands it to me. I groan. Drink. Breathe.

"You're never going to get out on the other side of this thing if you don't confront some of it," she says. "You know I'm right."

I look around. It would take too much effort to run away.

"All right." She climbs out of the car, comes to my side, and opens the door. "M'lady. Let us sally forth."

The Weirdo Video exterior is a mosaic of broken glass—green Heineken and Ale-8 shards rendering Godzilla, a brilliant, plummy tongue, sparkling quartz for an eye. A bench studded with RC Cola and Nehi caps. Two boys are parked on it. The one in the Dinosaur Jr. shirt gestures to the one in aviator sunglasses holding *The Definitive Herzog*. A few cars line the employee lot, all European—a dented BMW, two newer-model Volkswagens with rainbow decals. A swath of bumper stickers reading STOP MOUNTAINTOP REMOVAL. Beyond: head shops, thrift stores, an old-school storefront catering to cotillions, white gloves and crinoline in the window displays.

I feel a strong, sudden affection for Louisville. It's too much city for where it is, stuck between the South and the Midwest, metropolitan pheromones forging a force field around its borders. It has no choice but to go off the rails and become its own entity, a mishmash planet spinning off on its lonesome.

We open the door and a blast of cool air greets us. A guy with dreadlocks sits at a counter, a container of noodles in front of him. He gives a little wave and stuffs in a mouthful. "Welcome to Weirdo Video," he chews. A television behind him plays something loud and stuttery. Rodney Dangerfield's face blinks.

A bald, lanky kid who looks about sixteen bounces out of the back room, throwing a wad of paper at Dreadlocks. "Dude, your dinner smells like ass."

"Shut up."

That's when I spot the trampoline by the door. It's a small version of the large one we had as kids—black base, blue liner. Someone's rigged an electric Domo doll, purple and ham-faced, to jump, getting about a foot of leverage before sailing back down.

"Psst." Mel is next to New Releases. She wags a DVD at me. It's *Nashville Combat*. "Check it out, baby," she sings.

Dreadlocks swallows before saying, "You should get that. It's awesome."

Mel and I grin at each other.

He stares. "What."

"It's awesome because *we made it,*" Mel says.

He looks confused. "You made it?"

"We made *Nashville Combat.* Me and skinny over there. This is our movie."

"No shit," the guy says. "You're Mel Vaught."

"I know."

"Wow." He pushes his noodles aside. "I've watched your cartoons for, like, ever. Like since middle school."

Mel leans over, shakes his hand, bobs her head. The switch has been flipped. "That's really cool to hear," she says. "That's great. So you're into animation?"

I hang back. It doesn't happen much, but when we're recognized, at a party or a convention, Mel always handles it more smoothly than I ever would. Providing she's not tanked.

The bald kid reappears from the back. "Ryan, we need to know where you strategically misplaced the invoices."

"Dude, I dunno. Ask Ted."

Ted. I feel my stomach surge.

Ryan gestures at us. "Look. They made *Nashville Combat.*"

The bald kid perks up. "Really? That movie is incredible."

"Thank you," I say.

He points to Mel. "Wait, are you Mel Vaught?"

"I am."

"Wow. You look just like her."

"Hey, thanks."

"So did all that really happen?"

"Yeah. Mostly."

"Even the *Grand Ole Opry* Riot?"

"Oh yeah. None of *that's* made up."

"Wow." He shakes his head. "That was a mindfuck to watch."

Mel shrugs. The wrinkles around her eyes bear in a little deeper. "It was a mindfuck to be there."

"So what are you all doing in Louisville?"

Mel points to me with both hands. "She's Kentucky-born and raised. Sharon, what the hell are you doing? Come over here."

They ask me where I'm from. I tell them Faulkner. "That's close to Morehead, right?" Ryan says. He turns to Baldy. "Didn't Ted live around there when he was a kid?"

At this, a tall, wiry man strides out of the back room. "Ryan, we really need those invoices, man," he says. "I don't want to have to perform voodoo to track them down."

Later I would realize that of all the good things my stroke did— sealing Mel and me back together, returning me, as much as was possible, to my family—giving me the ability to see Teddy clearly was the best.

The stroke slowed me down. For the sake of my own survival, I was forced to take in the outside world exactly as it was, without expectation or distortion, in order to exist in it without breaking myself in half. For once, I fought for realism, a state of mind that seemed the exact antithesis of who I was, what I did, but that allowed me to handle a toothbrush, go to the bathroom, walk without stumbling. I hated this—having no fantasy to soften the blow—but to survive, I did it. And sometimes, in return, the world gave me gifts.

So it is with Teddy. He is not subjected to any construction or treatment before I meet him. I no longer have the will to imagine what I want. The experience rises clean, without my greasy fingerprints all over it. When I meet Teddy, I meet him as he is.

I am surprised to find that I would know him, actually *know* this man, if I saw him as a stranger. The assertion of his nose, the sharp little chin, the pale skin on which I can see the faint outline of stubble as he stoops under the counter. This is the ghost of the boy moving through the world. This is his face, this is his body. He has become, as an adult, handsome. Square, solid, confident. A good-looking guy, looking for something as he dips behind the register, his shoulders shifting as things are socked and thudded down below. My entire body prickles.

Ryan ducks his head and shuffles over. "I'll get em," he says. "We got superstars in the house, man. Check it."

Baldy points to us. "They made *Nashville Combat*."

The shoulders stop. Teddy's head tilts. His eyes appear over the edge of the counter, wide, train on me. He slowly rises, face soft and open, a little anxious. I am amused to see that Ted Caudill is wearing suspenders.

"Sharon?" he says.

I nod. Give a lame little wave.

He doesn't move.

I scan my brain for something to say, anything. Feel it begin to fold up. Not again. *Fuck*.

He blinks. "Is that really you?"

"I had a stroke," I blurt.

Mel coughs. "Jesus," she sighs.

He comes around the counter and takes me by the shoulders, looking me hard in the face: first one side, then the other.

"You look exactly like yourself," he says slowly. "I'd know that face anywhere."

He puts his arms around me. We fall into each other.

It's like remembering how something tastes, hearing a sound gone unheard for years; touching him is a sensory experience I haven't realized I missed until it comes back to me, all that unfelt loss hitting me at once.

My face has disappeared into his shoulder. I manage to unearth it. Say, "I like your trampoline."

TEDDY SUGGESTS A BAR near Weirdo Video. Two high school guys arrive to take over the store and we head out: Teddy, Mel, Ryan, and the bald kid, whose name is Tatum. ("It's a girl's name," Teddy whispers to us, prompting Tatum to yell, "Shut the fuck up.") It's Friday night and Bardstown Road is alive with traffic. After-work crowds clog the bars, pack the pizza joints and coffeehouses. I spot a bookstore filled with people along the way. "Oh yes," Teddy says. "Very literate city we have here."

"Is that so."

"It's so." We've slowed down, falling into step behind Mel and Tatum and Ryan, who are lighting Mel's cigarettes and firing questions at her. I keep glancing at Teddy as we walk, unable to stop looking at his face. His accent falls in and out of shadow, the *A*'s still broad and unassuming, some of the words clipped, Midwestern-short. "So Faulkner's own superstar artist. Have they rolled out the red carpet for you?"

"My mom fixed me beans and weenies."

"Well, that's something."

Teddy's only a few inches taller than me. My eyes fall just short of his Adam's apple. I steal looks at it as we match pace. I feel him sneaking looks at me, too, fiddling with his little gold wire-rims, rubbing his five-o'clock shadow. He moves like one of those men who spent his adolescence with arms and legs too big for his body: slow, deliberate. He's got a great mouth. Pink and even. We're circling each other. *What happened to you? How did you grow up?*

I'm trying my best not to limp. "Do you ever miss Faulkner?" I ask him.

He grins. "Not really. Is that bad to say? My mom moving me up here was one of the best things that could have happened. I guess I didn't have much of a choice at the time, but it was completely for the best. Louisville is home." I feel him hesitate. "I already had this kind of, you know, *sense* of Faulkner. Like, kind of knowing that if I stuck around, the FFA guys were going to beat the hell out of me in high school? I didn't really *fit* into the scheme of things."

"I can relate."

"I'll bet you can." He looks me over now with open curiosity. Bruised, beaten, and from the past; it makes me feel self-conscious, a little exotic. He sighs and squints in thought. "Let's see. I moved here three days before I started the sixth grade."

"I remember. It ruined middle school for me. Broke my heart."

"Oh, mine too. I went through some solid Sharon withdrawal. Who else was going to force me to watch *Liquid Television* over and over?"

I bite my lip, hug myself. He *remembers*.

"So that's been about twenty years. I think that's right. Almost twenty years I've lived here, minus the four I spent in Lexington."

"You went to UK?"

"I did."

"I almost did, too," I say. "But Ballister happened. The chance to put that many miles between me and my family was too good to pass up."

"I read about you going to Ballister. That's great."

I feel my face heat. "You read about it?"

"I looked you up online, back in the day. Before Google. I Ya-hooed you. I Ask Jeevesed you. Does that creep you out?"

"It makes me glad." I lean in a little. He's wearing a wool jacket. I smell aftershave, smoke. I have to force myself to lean back. "They had a great art department back then. Still do. It's how I met Mel. That's where we started working together."

"And you ended up in New York." He looks to me again. I tuck my chin down and smile. He nods leisurely, hands stuffed in pockets. "Had you pegged for a New Yorker," he says.

"How so?"

He shrugs. Squints ahead of us. "I dunno. Let's call it self-preservation. You seem tough. That rough chuckles thing you and Mel have going on. Seems very big-city. Especially to *rubes* like us." He looks to me and his smile grows wider, goofier. It is unspeakably appealing when he turns on his dumb look, his put-on hillbilly face. The way he stretches out the word *rubes*. Is he flirting? I slip in another glance. Nah. Probably not.

"So how did you end up at the video store?" I ask him.

"I'm a film major who never made any films. See? It wasn't as useless as some might think, watching all the TV we did. You went the way of *Liquid Television,* and I went the way of—shit. I dunno. *Monstervision*? Stolen HBO? Something stuck for us, is what I'm saying. Something constructive."

"I like to think so."

"Me too. So I took a few business classes, climbed up the ranks to Manager Extraordinaire, then bought part of it out. We're surviving. Getting at the stuff so obscure you can't find it online. Putting on events. I figure the niche market's safe, for a while." He removes his hands from his pockets, twiddles them in the air. "Very grandiose, I know."

"That's great," I say. "You're a business owner."

He leans back and squints at me. "You look great for a stroke patient."

I run my hand over my head. "Heh *heh*."

"I just mean," he says hastily, "my mom had a stroke a few years back—a minor one—but it was enough to make her look pretty rough for a while."

"Is she okay now?"

"Oh yeah. Lives in a condo with her new husband. Goes to Florida a couple times a year. She blames the stroke on my dad. The stress he caused her. I let her have that one. I mean, she's not wrong."

"I remember your mom," I say. "Blond. Pretty. Drove something with a drop top."

"It was a Buick Reatta."

"Holy crap. It *was*. And it was red."

"Aren't they always red? It's no good as a memory unless it's red."

We laugh, still in step with each other, then let the silence spread and break while we search for something else to say.

"Well," I try, "I'm glad to hear she's bounced back. It's scary, getting to this age where shit's happening to our parents."

"It happened to *you*."

"It happened to me."

God, I want to smell him again. I wonder if I would have noticed Teddy Caudill in New York—objectively, were he simply a man who looked like Teddy Caudill as opposed to the real thing. That pretty boy's face is still pretty, with some well-placed lines around the eyes, a couple of feathery seams running nose to mouth. He's wiry-strong.

He makes eye contact. No one in New York has a face that open. I consider Louisville, and wonder how many baristas and bookstore clerks are after Teddy. How many come into his store in dresses and cowboy boots, hoping to see him.

Mel glances back at me, ticks her head. Ryan and Tatum are running circles around her, jabbering, poking each other.

"How are your parents?" Teddy asks me.

"Mom's okay. We're actually staying with her right now. She lives in the same house. A couple of years after Dad died—"

"Your dad died? Oh, Sharon. I'm so sorry."

"Thanks. It was a while ago, actually. My sister and her husband bought the property where you were and built a new house there, so they're next door."

His Adam's apple jumps as he swallows. "So they knocked the old house down."

"Uh. Yeah."

We fall silent. We listen to the back-and-forth between Ryan and Tatum and Mel—Mel holding court about some sketch technique and Tatum wagging his hands, saying, "Wait wait wait," and Ryan punching him in the back, saying, "Dude, shut up." We pass a head shop, a cupcake shop, another bookstore. A girl in front disassembles a sidewalk sale. She wiggles her fingers at Teddy, glancing surreptitiously at me. Something slick and familiar inside me turns over, hums. I nearly jump out of my skin. Holy shit, this is *jealousy*, all scales and forked tongue and lizard brain. The first stab of it I've felt since I got sick.

I smile wide, weirdly. I am returned to myself, new, rich blood pumping through my veins. Then I remember we're talking about my dead dad and I try to tamp the smile down.

Teddy changes subjects. "What I meant a minute ago is that you look really healthy, for a stroke patient. Didn't you used to have darker hair?"

"Yeah. I was heavier, too."

"You know what made me look you up in college? Your first cartoon. Or one of the first. *Custodial Knifefight*."

I hide my face in my hands.

"No. It was awesome. I saw your name in the credits, and it was so weird—it was like I had forgotten about Faulkner, in a way. I never forgot about you, of course. But seeing your name in print? It actually knocked the wind out of me. Like, *Holy shit. Sharon is out there in the world.*"

"That sounds pretty terrible, knocking the wind out of you."

"Not at all. It was a *glad* sort of unsettling, you know? I always wondered about you. Wondered where you'd ended up."

Mel and the guys turn toward a building decorated in the same fashion as Weirdo Video—glass mosaics, neon marquee. Above the door in a purple glow: A LIGHT IN THE ATTIC. They cluster by a rock garden to finish their smokes. "Don't steal her, shitsacks," Teddy says to them, opening the door for me.

"Thanks, *Ted.*" I poke him.

He cracks a lopsided smile and pushes his glasses up on his nose. "You're very welcome. You will have to excuse the associates, there. They are starstruck by the two of you. It's sort of cute, really."

"We're obliged."

A bartender waves to Teddy; Teddy confers with him and brings back a pilsner and a club soda. "I could handle a beer," I tell him.

"I'm sorry. I figured you probably couldn't drink."

"Oh, *can* she, though." Mel approaches from behind, delivering a soft noogie to my skull. "We call this one Rummy."

We sit at a table built atop an old Galaga console. Tatum asks how we started working together. "Art class, in college," I tell him.

"I just wanted to bang her," Mel says. I poke her, irritated. She guffaws. "Look at that. Look at how much that *scares* Sharon. It's hilarious."

"Is the Lite-Brite thing in the movie true?" Ryan asks.

Mel grabs a napkin, sketches a miniature Lite-Brite, requisite bulbs reading *Fuck You Ryan,* slides it across the table to him. This pleases him to no end; he demands she sign it, and she does. He sandwiches the napkin in between the pages of a book he's carrying.

Teddy's right. It's adorable, these two hanging on Mel's every word. And she's kind to them, is enjoying them. I keep it to one stern look when she goes in on a pitcher. Mel shape-shifter, Mel tightrope cruiser. I'm not sure how I feel about Teddy Caudill right now, but I'm fairly sure I don't want to be embarrassed in front of him.

We down first and second beers, dawdle on thirds and the greasy food we've ordered. Mel and the boys huddle to draw on napkins. Teddy and I are segregated at our own end of the table.

He's still giving me that curious look. "So," he says.

"So."

"I have to ask. Did you just see Weirdo Video driving around and decide to stop in?"

I shrug, feeling pretty loose. "No," I admit. "We came specifically for Weirdo Video. We wanted to look you up. Or I did."

He raises an eyebrow, puts a hand to his chest. "That's nice. I'm flattered."

This makes me dip my head. *Nice?* The fuck we are. There was a point in my life when I would have lied about that to myself in the hopes of creating a self-fulfilling prophecy. Teddy probably *is* a genuinely nice person. He has overcome adversity and has lived out his life doing something he loves in a place he has never very much wanted to leave. And here I come, this long-lost vestige of a childhood he has every right to recall as a perfect hell. But he welcomes me. Without reservation. He's kind and convivial and charming, when he doesn't have to be. Would I have as much grace, were the roles reversed? Probably not. And what did we come for?

We came to mine him for information. And when we get what we want, we'll go back to Faulkner. And when we get what we want from there, we'll leave Faulkner, too.

"We came to Kentucky to work on a new project," I say.

"Right on," he says. "I loved *Nashville Combat*. Obviously." He nods to Mel and his voice lowers. "It's about Mel, right? That movie is basically her."

"Basically."

He releases his breath in a long, slow whistle. "That's one way to grow up. And pretty fast, I would imagine."

I look over at Mel, sketching something else, Tatum and Ryan hovering over her shoulders. "You know, in this weird, backward way, she's maybe the most adult person I know."

He gives me that partial smile. "So what's the new project?'

I stop and look down at my hands. I can feel the support beams in my head start to shiver under the question's weight. I haven't been asked to verbalize a pitch yet; we don't really have a pitch to speak of. I try to imagine the synapses in my brain building a road, point A to point B. Question: answer. "Well, we're thinking it'll mostly be about my stroke. You know, my life before, my life after. How it's changed."

Is it a lie? Sort of. I try to negotiate with the writhing in my middle while Teddy tilts his head, continues to look at me, fingers peeling the label from his pilsner. That's a stare. That's a warm, interested stare. Shit. I only have so many chances to present myself honestly. So I take a deep breath and I start. Because talking to Teddy, in some way I can't articulate, is different than talking to anyone else.

"I was in a coma for about a week," I begin.

He folds his arms on the table and turns to me. "Wow. Okay."

"Yeah. They weren't sure I wasn't going to be a vegetable when I woke up. It happened really suddenly, this blood vessel breaking in my brain, and they're still not sure why." I trail off, shake my head. "I was really lucky. Anyway, when I was out, Mel found this sort of log I'd been keeping in my journal of every man I had ever been infatuated with."

"Industrious of you to write it all down."

I nod, pinch my lips. Try to look wry, or self-effacing. Something other than what I feel, which is embarrassed, with a hearty edge of shame.

"My life before the stroke was—complicated. I had a really hard time with guys. I had intimacy problems, I guess you'd call them. Spent more time imagining the relationships than actually *being* in them." I say this with difficulty. "I sort of made up stories and lived in *those*. Make sense?"

He nods. "I hear you."

"But because I'm a total obsessive, I kept this log. It's sort of embarrassing, really. But Mel found it when I was sick, and she thought it was really weird and interesting. She thinks it means something about me, the way I'm wired." *And here's the giant white space in the middle of the story. The one that features your creepy dad.* "So it's kind of a story about me making this list, or the story will be told through this list. That's how we might frame it. Still working it out."

"How many guys are on this?"

"Over a hundred."

His eyebrows shoot up. "Really? Wait. Okay." He holds his hands out in front of him. "You've been in a hundred relationships?"

"No. Like a tenth of those were relationships. Most of them, it's just, like—"

"Pining from afar?"

I shrug uncomfortably. I know too well what the next natural conclusion will be: *That's a fuckload of pining. What's wrong with you?*

But he grins, big and toothy. Says, "I'm the king of pining from afar."

I exhale, relieved. "Well, I may be competition for you, friend," I say. "Because I spent *years* making this list of my little failures."

He nods. I try to say something else, but it all falls apart. My mind blanks, my tongue seizes. I've got my hands in front of me, trying to sketch in the air what I mean. I let them fall, hit the table. "Talking is hard. Goddammit. Sorry. I'm sorry."

"It's okay," he says. "Don't apologize."

"I had lots of speech therapy. But there are still. Holes? Am I freaking you out? I'm freaking myself out."

"You're not freaking me out in the least."

"You're just saying that."

He clears his throat. "Hey, Sharon? My dad raped little girls and took pictures of them tied up asleep. You, of all people, should know—my tolerance for being freaked out's pretty high."

We both burst out laughing. I look down at my hands. "Okay, okay. Sorry."

"What are you sorry for? Stop saying that, would you?" He takes hold of my shoulder. "Hey. Really. You've done nothing wrong here."

Oh, but I have. I'm getting the feeling that I've done something very, very wrong just by coming here. Just by making Teddy a party to whatever's going to happen next. I clench my hands and open them. Look him in the face. "That must have been hell for you," I say. "And I'm afraid of saying the wrong thing. I don't want you to feel uncomfortable."

"Let me tell you something my aunt Nadine told me during the court case. Okay? You ready? I want you to take these words to heart. Take them to the *grave*." He leans in, puts his hands on my shoulders. Whispers, *"Sugarpie, it ain't your fault Daddy's a kid diddler."*

I clap my hand over my mouth. Teddy grins. Mel and Tatum and Ryan stare at us. "What are you looking at," Teddy says to them.

He gives my arm a quick squeeze, sudden and intimate. My breath catches in my throat. "In my experience, it usually makes it weirder to try to avoid the subject," he says.

He leans in, picks up his beer. There are glints of silver right above his ears, a little gray in his stubble. Every year that has passed between then and now is in the way he sits. Mel showed me the article the night before online—Honus Caudill spent a grand total of eight months in prison before, like her mom, he was stabbed by another inmate. Child molesters, she explained, tend not to last long in Gen Pop.

"And you say there's no rough chuckles in you," I say.

Teddy shrugs. "Well, I think I get what you mean, about your project. You make your head a hospitable enough place to be, why would you ever want to leave?"

I see something cross his face, dark and fleeting. It occurs to me that he might actually understand. That maybe he does something that feels like the List and puts effort into looking like he doesn't.

"I'm really glad you're here," he says. He reaches out, brushing my arm, and grabs an unopened straw. Taps the wrapper down to the tabletop, leaving a perfect crimped paper roll. The straw is inserted into his beer, beer suctioned up, dripped onto the paper. It unfurls, quick and alive.

"Look, it's a snake," he whispers to me.

Mel and the boys have left behind three empty pitchers and two plates of hot-wing bones, and have moved on to a vintage *Mortal Kombat* console. Tatum and Ryan watch the screen as Mel's shoulders flex under the denim jacket she has stolen from Tatum; she is winning. "Yeah, motherfucker," she hollers, then turns, lets rip her best Axl Rose, pointing with both hands. "Sha na na na na na yeah!"

"They're in love with her," Teddy says.

"She's been eating pussy since 1999."

"Oh well. Want to go for a walk?"

"Sure."

Outside it's breezy and chill. There's the smell of car exhaust and toasting leaves. We approach crosswalks and stop, waiting through two signals, talking, distracted. "So about this list," Teddy says, leaning over and jostling me with his elbow. "Am *I* on it?"

"You're number one," I tell him.

His face lights up. "Really?"

"Of course."

We've arrived at a little circular park. A sign posted at its entrance reads OLD EPISCOPALIAN BURIAL GROUNDS. Teddy leads me to a stone bench under some chestnuts. We sit.

"How did it happen?" I ask him.

He lifts his eyebrows. He knows, immediately, what I'm talking about. He takes a deep breath. "All of it? Oh Jesus. There's probably a pretty exhaustive Wikipedia entry somewhere." He rubs his palm over his chin and sighs, smile fading. I'm not sure whether he's joking. "Did you follow it at all in the papers? The trial?"

"I tried not to."

"What a luxury," he says. "I wish I could have slept through that part of my life. There's nothing more damaging to your sense of well-being than hearing about your parents' sex life in court. The whole unbearable, nasty story. All three-ways and body hair and 1970s key parties. Though that sounds pretty cosmopolitan for them."

"The seventies were gross," I whisper.

"The seventies were disgusting," he agrees. Then he goes quiet, picking at his jacket. "You know how being in our heads is sort of a refuge for us? Well, sex was sort of a refuge for my parents. And for Dad, it was an illness, something that made him dangerous. I think the weirdest part of the trial, for me, was hearing about these details from my *mom*. When she was giving testimony. Like, her acknowledging that she had always known something was wrong. That for my dad, it was more than, you know, swinging, having multiple partners. All in legalese."

"So you were there for the entire trial."

"Oh yes. I was twenty. I was there for it. The whole goddamned ordeal," he says. "Apparently Mom didn't think him having a thing for young girls meant he was dangerous, or a pedophile. That was her defense. Her argument? *All men do.* Can you imagine? But you remember that van?"

I inhale sharply.

He lifts his chin, looks ahead, not at me. "You do," he says. "He really committed to the cliché. Big gray van, tinted windows, rolling down the street. *Don't mind me. No child molesters here. Beep-beep.*"

We both laugh, a touch uncomfortably.

"I was three or four when he bought it. It's like, come on, Mom. The van wasn't a tip-off? The extended work trips? Or the fact that he always kept it locked? That wasn't an indicator? Well, one day she pried her way in. And under the passenger seat, she found a pair of panties that were very, very small."

I feel something cold and unpleasant shoot up my spine.

"So. In a move she can't quite describe to this day, even in *her* version of the story, my mom picked up and left. She claims she could barely take care of herself back then. Had undiagnosed hep C, drank a lot. But I think she was in panic mode. She realized that what was going on really was her worst suspicion. That she was married to a predator, a really sick guy. And her instinct said *run*. She says she planned to come back for me. Thought I'd be okay in the meantime. And I guess I was. Physically, anyway."

"The pictures," I say.

He turns to me, looks hard.

"You remember showing those to me?"

He shakes his head.

"I remembered those when I saw the news report back in college," I say. "It just hit me. Like I had forgotten. Actually, I think I had."

I can see his face drain in the dark. "I showed those to you?"

"You don't remember that?"

He shakes his head. Exhales. "No. Oh Christ. Sharon, I am so sorry."

"Well, what else were you going to do? You were a kid."

I see him swallow and close his eyes. "I can't believe I did that."

"Bound to happen. We were together all the time back then."

"We were." He speaks slowly, blinks rapidly. Takes a deep breath. "Your house was a refuge."

I toy with the zipper on my jacket. "Things had to be pretty bad for our house to be a refuge."

"Well, I knew I'd always get fed there," he says. "I wouldn't paw through things and find just *unspeakable* shit. Things like those pictures. Which, apparently, I showed you."

He covers his mouth with his hand. His eyes empty out. A necessary pause. The two of us, here, doing this—it feels like a miracle, a northern lights of human interaction. Two brain-dwellers of the worst variety, luring each other out.

He says suddenly, "Sharon, did he ever—"

"No," I say quickly.

He exhales, long and slow. His shoulders sag under his coat. He shuts his eyes, relieved.

"And you," I say, "you—"

"No."

The air has gotten colder, developed a light bite. At some point, the streetlights have flickered on.

"So your mom came for you," I say.

"She did. We moved here. And when I was a teenager, I tried to forget a lot of what I saw and heard in my dad's house. Did a lot of drugs. Read a lot of books. Watched a lot of movies. Just crammed my head with stuff to try to force it out. But it never worked. And, at some point, I realized what it was I saw, in those pictures. How wrong it was. Just what a trespass on someone else's humanity. I had a friend in high school who had something like that happen to her when she was a kid. It really fucked her up. Profoundly. She put the whole thing into perspective for me. I had to do something. So one day, junior year of high school, I got up out of my English class at duPont Manual, right there up the street, found a pay phone on Central Avenue, called the Faulkner Police Department, and left an anonymous tip. But they didn't have a search warrant or anything else they needed. So nothing happened."

"The arrest wasn't until a few years after, right?"

Teddy nodded. "He was in West Virginia. Tried to get a girl into his van. She bit his hand and ran off screaming. They traced his plates. When the police came to the house, there were bite marks that matched the girl's dental records. That girl was scrappy as hell. She testified. Showed the jury her teeth. There's a picture of it. It's pretty famous. She's probably in college by now."

"So that gave them what they needed."

"They raided the house, found something like what we found. You have to remember, this was pre-Internet, pre–deep web, really, so this was a very by-hand operation. There was a lot of just tangible *stuff* to go through, apparently. So much so that he was absolutely fucked by the sheer weight of the evidence. They connected him to a larger ring of porn distributors in the Southeast, something the FBI had been tracking for a while. And it ended up on the news."

We're close together on the bench. It occurs to me that I've been holding my breath. It's the kind of conversation that makes you feel an unspeakable closeness to another human being. For me, a person who has always considered herself alone, those conversations feel like a gift, someone trusting me with something private and valuable. My body reacts before my mind does: My stomach warms, I become weirdly golden between the legs, my breathing slows. I can count these conversations on both hands. Most I've had with Mel: the first night we met, and late, late at night, deep into work and bottles of vodka, when she'd talk about the way her aunt Shelly's house smelled, or her mom letting her drive the car when she was eleven, or when she lost her virginity, at sixteen, to the divorcée next door. I had one with my dad, on one of those nights before I left for college, when he was drunk and talking about his mother: how she'd actually, physically dig coal out of a crevice at their farm's rear acre for their furnace when his dad was passed out. Another one, a very long time ago, with Shauna—also drunk, on wine coolers—who told me, "Sissy, you suck. I love you."

And now I'm having one with Teddy. My body is lit from the inside out with Teddy, our talk. Maybe we're not wired to have many of these moments, as people. If we had too many of them in a single life, we would forget the heat of intimacy. We'd have nothing left to crave.

"I dropped what I was holding when I saw the news story," I say. "I vomited, actually."

"My sentiments, too," he says. He reaches into his breast pocket. Draws out a pack of Benson & Hedges. I take one and put it between my lips. He reaches over to light it for me, cupping one hand against the wind. His thumb touches my face briefly before the fire catches. We sit and smoke in silence. His arm presses into me.

"Thank God for moving," he says. "Louisville's a long way from a place like Faulkner. Can you imagine how much worse this would have been had I stayed there? I actually have some anonymity here. Strangers knowing intimate details about my life—doesn't much appeal to me. There were a couple of times after the court case when someone would see my last name and their eyebrows would go up. I went on a date once with a girl who was majoring in criminal justice, and she asked me, almost joking, was I related to Honus Caudill? And I told her he was my dad. Ruined the night. She couldn't get her head around it. I can't really blame her. It crosses your mind, when you go on a date with someone. What's going on with their bloodline? Could we have a kid together? Could the kid end up a socio-path? Or a sex offender?"

He flicks the ash from his cigarette and examines the cherry for a moment. "I think my dad knew it was me," he says quietly. "I think he knew I made that call."

We sit for a moment, silent, until I poke my elbow gently into him. "Hey you," I say. "You okay? Everything in one piece in there?"

He smiles tightly. "I have a good life. I'm in therapy, probably always will be. Which I think is a good thing. It's like I said earlier. You make your head a hospitable place to be, you might never want to leave it. But if you're trapped in there, you're doomed. I decided a long time ago that surviving probably meant achieving something in the middle. Something I could live with, that made me content. So, you know." His body relaxes. He is done. Turns to me with a slight smile. "Ongoing."

I reach out and take his hand. This is the sexiest guilt I have ever experienced. I'm a shit. He's going down the rabbit hole and I am looking for an excuse to touch him.

His hand closes over mine.

He says, "That's what makes what you and Mel do so staggering, you know? Mel has balls of steel, chancing the sort of personal dis-closure she did. I suspect there's a handling charge involved with that line of work, and it's probably too steep for me. There was a time when I thought I'd write, or make movies. But it hasn't happened yet. I'm not sure it ever will."

"You don't know that."

"I guess I don't. But I suspect no. I'm *veering* toward no. I might be a coward."

"You most certainly are not."

He looks sidelong at me. My stomach purrs. "Has it been tough for Mel? Making that, then having to talk about it in interviews and stuff?"

I flash on Glynnis Havermeyer's face, pale and shocked, as Mel ripped the microphone off the dash.

"She won't admit it," I say, "but yes. It's been pretty awful at times."

He sighs and shifts comfortably. "Well, I'm not surprised. Making a movie of your own life, there's some historic mangling involved, I'm sure. Do it enough, it might create a new truth. One that might be more damaging. Maybe you know something I don't. But."

Is this a judgment call? I can't tell. He's smoking his cigarette the way some country boys do, not between fore- and middle finger, but pinched between forefinger and thumb. It's quiet in the park. We hear traffic shift. The sky is a clean blue-black, no stars. We're still holding hands.

"So this new movie is about *you*," he says. "About the stroke, right? Is your family in it at all?"

"They might end up in it," I say. And here it is, one more chance for disclosure. "But probably not. It's in the first stages. Who knows how it'll mutate on down the line." I trail off lamely, gritting my teeth.

"Well, even trying something like this makes you a boss. So right on."

My phone vibrates in my pocket. I shift to pull it out, hand going into the space between us. "What it do, baby," Mel croons.

She's drunk, but with Teddy beside me, my reaction is softer, dulled. "Hey."

"Where'd you all go?"

"On a walk."

"They went on a *walk*," she repeats. I hear giggling. Someone makes a spectacularly loud fart noise. "Well, these two gentlemen," she says, words slipping and slurring, "have suggested we return to base. Watch some TV. Smoke some shit."

I turn to Teddy. "You ready to head out?"

"I live in walking distance," he says. "We could meet them there."

"We'll meet you at Teddy's," I tell her.

"Right on. Keep them legs closed." She hangs up.

We leave the park. Teddy offers me his arm. I take it.

"So Mel's gay," he says.

I laugh a little. Then a lot. "Yeah."

"No getting around that, I guess."

"Nope."

"But *you* date men."

"I do."

"Ever tried dating women?"

"Couple tries," I say. "Halfhearted, maybe. Wasn't for me."

"Did you and Mel ever date?"

"Me and Mel? No. No no."

"You seem like you even her out. Just the way you two are in a room together. Like you calm her down a little."

"As much as is possible."

"You two seem attached to each other," he says.

"For better or worse."

We turn down a tree-lined street, houses with porches on either side. "She's been good, through all this," I tell him. "It's changed her. She was in the hospital with me every day when I had the stroke. She leased out our studio in New York, she's kept our bills paid. She really came through."

We turn a corner and Mel and the boys are there, cigarettes dangling from their lips, playing Kick the Can in front of a rambling Victorian. "Here we are," Teddy says, and takes us all up a side set of stairs.

Teddy's apartment is old: dark wood, low yellow lighting. As we enter, he touches an oil lamp on the kitchen table and the place glows. A cast-iron skillet glistens on the stovetop. Books are stacked beside the door: a threadbare copy of *Ulysses,* a couple of Larry McMurtrys, a Harry Crews.

Mel spots the ancient record player console. She touches the doors and they swing open, little copper handles twinkling. The *Root Down* EP is already on the turntable. Mel mutters, impressed. She leans in, pulls something from the shelf, holds it up. The Oak Ridge Boys.

"Jesus," I say.

"No. Elvira." Teddy opens a cupboard and draws out peach

schnapps, bourbon, blue carnival glasses. Ryan and Tatum busy themselves with pruning through a Ziploc of weed at the table, placing seeds and stems in a crystal ashtray. "I'm inclined to make yours light," Teddy tells me. "I don't want to get the patient hammered."

Mel draws a record from its sleeve. Reagan Youth. "Dude, how do you even *have* this?"

Teddy looks over his shoulder, shrugs. "I dunno," he says, and grins. It is this surface note, sheepish and uncalculated, the opposite of cool, that hammers in the final nail. I decide that I really, really like Ted Caudill. A lot.

Sweet little drinks are produced, the bong fired upward. Talk resumes. Tatum brings out a VHS tape of cartoons pulled from New York public access in the early eighties, real basic pen-to-pad stuff, the kind of thing I used to hunt for in the city when I was at Ballister. When I ask Teddy, "Holy hell, do you really own that?" he says, "Of course," shrugs like it's nothing, like time *isn't* collapsing and universal circles *aren't* completing themselves and this *isn't* something that's been a foregone conclusion for years. We smoke, collectively reach a phase of fuzziness in which the room is one warm smear, a friendly blur.

Teddy and I end up sitting together on the couch, leaning into each other. "I love these old shorts," I say to him. "The old DIY ones. We used to watch these for hours, Mel and me."

"Me too," he says. "They reminded me of watching TV with you."

I feel his voice reverberating in my body. I can feel my head pleasantly unhinging itself as I sink into the couch. Whisper to him, "They're full of *ghosts*."

"*You're* full of ghosts." He starts poking the soft part of my thigh, making fart noises. When I laugh, it's a honk. I squirm into the tickling instead of away. Things are getting very stupid very quickly. My body's all surface, oil swirls on a bubble.

I moo, "Quit." Fold myself over, nose to knee.

He ruffles my hair. "Sharon, Sharon. Should I worry about you?" His Adam's apple jounces once, twice. I can almost breathe on it from here. I see Mel and the boys rolling their eyes at each other.

"Your accent comes back when you're drunk, Jim Bob."

"*Naw.*"

"Yes."

"You charmer." He twiddles his fingers into my belly and it starts up again. "That's how you moved up in the world. You just flattered the shit out of big nerdy dudes like me."

"Quit quit quit."

"Superstar comes home ticklish. Oh *no.*" He goes to my sides and it's a big, laughy, teeth-shining blur. I'm on top of him, he's on top of me. I feel my diaphragm go loose.

And that's when it happens. I pee. Just a little, but the valves release only a second before it happens. It shocks me into rolling back on my side of the couch.

I stand. "Hold up. I'll be right back."

Teddy sprawls, glasses askew. "You okay?"

"Yep. Where's your bathroom?"

I close the door and sit on the toilet, hand clapped over my mouth.

Peeing on a man you like is a deal breaker. I sneak a look down at myself, bony knees up, loose skin around my middle, the deflated slope of my breasts. For the first time tonight, I'm afraid of what might happen if I end up in bed with Teddy. Sex, since the stroke, has been a slow-moving, solitary preoccupation. I've had precious few orgasms in the past three months—some halfhearted attempts in the Florida rental house's grimy tub, an eventual, partial climax that was such a sad shadow of its former self that I wondered if I would ever get it all back: the joy, the envy, the pure, animal pleasure of arousal. Anything but this middling, vanilla nonfeeling. Can I even climb on top of someone without my inner-ear imbalance throwing me off?

I put my head between my knees and smell. Okay, not so bad. Pee-dappled as opposed to pee-drenched. I scrub at the damp spot in my underwear, zip up.

Outside the door, Teddy leans against the wall, mouth puckered in concern. "You okay?"

"I'm fine."

"I didn't hurt you, did I?"

"No no," I manage. "I'm—I'm on blood pressure meds that do some weird things when I, you know. Laugh and stuff."

"That's sad. You have a good laugh." He takes hold of my arms, rubs them briskly. "Sure you're okay?"

"Uh huh."

The hallway is dark and narrow. We hear the TV blare from the next room and look at each other for a long moment before he leans in and presses his mouth on me, dry and firm. Holds it there. I nudge back, touch his jaw, his ears, the back of his head. We sink in and open up to the kiss, hotter, faster, his tongue slipping in. I feel him exhale and run his hands along the length of my back. The floor shifts. Our bodies collide. I feel him harden against me.

There's shuffling nearby and we break apart. "Come on," he says, and pulls me into his bedroom: more dark wood paneling, books and CDs everywhere, the warm, sweet smell of his clothes. We fall onto the bed, him on top of me, me on top of him, rolling. I run my hands over the stubble on his cheeks, hot and prickling.

He says, "Sharon." Moves for the neck.

My entire body jolts.

Prestroke, my neck was kryptonite. There's this curve below my ear, back toward the nape, a square inch of pure nerve wildly responsive to all manner of kisses soft and hard, licks, bites, tongue traces, and at the right time, breath. For the few unsuspecting men with whom I actually went to bed, it was a happy surprise, the fastest way to make me lose my pants. From kiss one, Teddy seems to know, working his mouth down from the earlobe, transitioning to licking, to sucking. The pants are lost, I wrap my legs around him. I arch into him. I am me again. I am myself, in my own body. I have been returned.

He rolls on top of me to unhook my bra, lips nipping at the edge of one cup, and I'm grinding into him when my left leg seizes. I shriek.

It's my trouble leg. It stiffens up at least three times a day, falling asleep only to come alive with pain—it can't keep up. Before my body went apeshit, I never realized how much I enjoyed sitting over the drafting table with my left leg tucked under me, curling my body into its coziest shape while I worked. No question of me sitting Indian-style ever again. One more unanticipated loss. In addition to a number of sexual positions I assume have been rendered obsolete.

The cramp tightens. I make a sound in the back of my throat.

Teddy looks up, flushed. "What's wrong?"

"My leg."

"Oh. Sorry, am I—"

"No, it's—"

"Which one? What's—"

"Sometimes it cramps up."

I roll over and hum, holding the leg in both hands. I want to scream. This was going *so well*. Doubling up like this probably gives him an eyeful of my gut dough. Haggis McBaggis, gripping her gimp leg. An image to give legions of men reluctant chubbies. "It'll be fine," I say through my teeth. "Just gotta *sonovawhorethishurts* give it a minute to go down."

"Can I do something?" He scoots to my side, starts brushing hair from my forehead.

I rock and hum. Wheeze, "Just gotta wait it out."

"I could massage it. You think that might help?"

"I don't know."

"Let's try." He shifts down, puts both hands above the knee, begins to knead, thumb and palms pressing circles, making a *sssssshhhhhh* noise. "Right there?"

The muscles start to loosen. "Yeah."

His shirt has been unbuttoned and tugged out of his pants. His chest hair is coarse, darker than I expected. The cramp's grip starts to fall away. I reach out to put my fingers in his hair. He looks up, smiles. "Better?"

"Better. Sorry about that."

"A cramp once in a while's nothing to worry about." His hands move north. "That good?"

"Yes."

I lean back and feel his hands work up, strong grip, palms hot. Feel his lips join in, the softest contact working its way up and up until they meet fabric, press. The fabric is taken away. I close my eyes. I feel myself part for him. I close my eyes and I hear him tell me my name.

THE HEART LIVES AND DIES IN LOUISVILLE, KENTUCKY

WAKE UP IN A STRANGE BED NAKED AND MY FIRST THOUGHT IS *HOSPITAL.* Panic rises in my throat. *Oh God. It's happened again.*

Teddy rolls over and pulls me into him, muttering. Slides his hands down to cup my ass in a way I can only describe as polite, says, "Hey." Kisses that spot on my neck that makes my limbs spasm. From deeper in the house I hear the unmistakable bangs and clips of the Super Nintendo, two-player *Street Fighter,* Mel cussing, "Uh oh, lookit that shit. That's *right,* hussy." Then the grunt of the aerial kick, the call that sounds like "Shooore you can!" One of the boys glumly remarks, "Dude."

There's a thin line of daybreak glowing underneath the curtains. Teddy says something I can't hear into my shoulder. I arch my back. He reaches inside me. I need to remember the way this feels. Your memories will fail you, I think, a flutter of sadness closing my throat.

It will eventually disappear into its barest idea, an outline of itself. You have spent entire years knowing only the lack of what you are feeling right now. So feel this all you can. I turn and push him onto his back. Crane my head under the covers toward his hips, going lower and lower until I hear him gasp.

WE DRESS AND EMERGE to find a Murphy bed opened, Ryan, Tatum, and Mel scattered across it in their socks and T-shirts. Mel's arms are splayed across the boys, glasses pushed up to her forehead. She snores, mouth parted. Ryan is in a fetal position, fingers curled underneath his chin. Tatum's hands hang long and white, trailing nearly to the floor.

We stare at them for a moment. "Breakfast," Teddy whispers.

He leads me through the living room to the kitchen and closes the door, a frail oak scratched all to hell. The fridge is a listing Frigidaire icebox, at least fifty years old. A recliner sits inexplicably in the corner. I curl up on it and stare into the stove seam where two pilot lights glow. "The kitchen and the bathroom were part of the servants' quarters," Teddy says. His shirt is open. Two folds of softness eclipse his belly button when he bends to retrieve eggs. "This is one of the oldest mansions in the city. It was built by a banker whose granddaughter was killed by the Mafia and left in a ditch on Dixie Highway. He let the place go to hell after that. It was a crack house in the eighties. How do you like your eggs?"

"Sunny-side up."

"I had a feeling." He produces a spatula, a grinder of sea salt. He cracks the eggs. I wonder if I could cajole him into fucking me on the tabletop.

He tosses the shells in the trash, then comes for me, takes my face, kisses me. Presses his forehead to mine. There's the gassy flare of stovetop, a sizzle of melting butter. We smile at each other like goons. I never want to leave. We could stay here and live together in this creaky old apartment. Go to the farmers' market every Saturday. Have weird babies with psoriasis and stutters.

And then I remember the project. *Shit*. What did I tell Teddy about our project last night? What were the chances I fed him a few half-truths trying to get him into bed? I drum my fingers against the armrest. "Um," I start, "did we talk much about what Mel and I are working on last night? I can't totally recall."

"There are parts of last night that are spotty and there are parts that are still in very clear relief." His shoulder and elbow make circles above the bowl. The fork clicks. "We talked about it a little. It'll be about you? The stroke?"

"Kind of, yeah."

"It will be amazing, I'm sure," he says. "Go over big in New York with that string of boyfriends you have up there. All those hipster types with their slouchy ways. I'm sure you work your voodoo on them." He swishes his fork in the air. Yolk flies onto the countertop.

"Not quite."

"Modest Mabel over here. I've got homemade sausage in the fridge. Are you a meat eater?"

I wrap my legs around him and we commence to making out while the eggs scorch. There's a good, minuteless block of time, his hands well up my shirt, in which he whispers in my ear how happy it would make him if I stuck around for a few days. And just like that, I lose my courage.

IT TURNS OUT THE kids subletting our studio want to extend through the holidays. I propose staying in Louisville for a few weeks. "For research," I say.

Mel rolls her eyes. "Researching Ted's peen," she says.

But she's not the hard sell I think she'll be. She crashes with Ryan and Tatum, and after two weeks of general carousing with the boys, she is a convert. "This place is fucking *fascinating*," she tells me. Ryan and Tatum fill her in on the city's more destructive history and she follows up like a model student, spending hours at the university poring over photos of the 1977 tornado, rooting through the downtown cemeteries. At night, she and Ryan and Tatum drive around looking for abandoned buildings to explore, crossing the river into Indiana. She locates a regular weed dealer in Waterfront Park after three days and goes on long runs through downtown, platinum head bobbing and weaving through traffic. The city is a borderline zone—neither Union nor Confederacy, neither big nor small. Mel seems to master it quickly. She *gets* it, she tells me. She gets what it *is*.

"Let's try this," Mel says. She's sketching in the back room of Weirdo Video, waiting for the store to close so she can go out with Ryan and Tatum. She's sunk into what we're making already. Knowing it would make her more agreeable to staying—the baby with her bottle—I've encouraged it. "Be part of the great flight from New York. All those people flinging off their Brooklyn bullshit and migrating out to Detroit and Asheville and Austin? Well, for a quarter of the rent, why not Louisville."

When the first installment of the grant comes through, we have the check sent to Weirdo Video, cash it, and rent out a furnished carriage house at the rear of an enormous Victorian owned by a U of L professor. We convert the back into sleeping quarters for Mel and rig up the front as a workstation. Mel improvises, building a drawing board out of spare lumber and an old Formica tabletop, banding a handful of flashlights above the board for perspective.

After we finish setting up, Mel looks around appraisingly, hands on hips. "Okay," she says. "We can work with this."

MEANWHILE, I'VE UNOFFICIALLY MOVED in with Teddy. We're in the kitchen cutting vegetables for soup and I'm taking down a carrot, slowly, deliberately, when my cell rings.

I see the 606 area code for Faulkner.

I angle the knife fast and wrong, slicing my thumb open. "Crap," Teddy says. "Hold on."

I pick up the phone, consider letting it go to voicemail. Decide to answer. "Mom?" I say as Teddy bundles a wad of toilet paper and thrusts my thumb inside.

"Sharon, where *are* you all," she bleats.

I wince, hold the phone away from my ear. Teddy laughs silently. It's as loud as if she were in the room with us. I had described my mother's voice to Teddy as resembling the shriek of a thousand bag-pipes melting in Satan's taint. She's not proving me wrong. "You all have been gone for I don't know how long, and here I was thinking the *worst*. Y'all could be raped and murdered by the side of the *road*."

Teddy covers his mouth and doubles over.

"We've been gone two weeks," I say. "This is just now occurring to you?"

"You shoulda called me and you know it."

I squeeze my thumb, trying to stop the blood. "I'm sorry. We're still in Louisville. Some things came up."

"Oh," she says. Tones of blame. "You're in *Louisville*."

"Yes." I lean my head against the wall.

"Are you okay?" Teddy whispers. I nod.

"Who was that," Mom demands.

I hold my finger up and duck out into the hallway. "Funny story," I say. "That was Teddy Caudill. Remember? From next door?"

There's a wary silence. Then she says, in a tight, small voice, "Yeah, I remember."

"Well, that was him."

Her voice goes up. "That was him just *now*?"

"Yup."

"Well, what's *he* doing in Louisville?"

"Living. He owns a business. Mel and I are actually kind of thinking about sticking around here for a month or two. The people subletting our place in New York want to extend the lease, and we're really liking Louisville. We think it might be a good place to get a jump start on this thing we're working on."

There's a silence, then she counters, "Are you all staying with *him*?"

"Off and on. He helped us to rent out a space to work in."

"And that's all right with him?"

"Of course."

"I don't know," she says dubiously. "This seems like it happened awful quick. You sure you're not wearing out your welcome?"

"He invited us to stay, Mom. It's fine."

There's another minute of silence. Then she says, "I thought you come out here to visit with us. Did you really come out to hunt some boy down?"

"Holy hell, Mom. *Really?*"

When speaking to or about me, my mother has a very short range of tones: suspicion, resignation, exhaustion, singsong condescension, and, occasionally but memorably, disgust. She is not a believer in the power of tone—the argument *It wasn't what you said, it was the way you said it* earns the adjudication of "Bull*shit*"—but were one to judge from tone alone, my mother thinks I am the world's biggest twat. It's a weird sensation, knowing your family believes the worst of you. It makes you want to disappear a little.

Of course, the fact that she's partially right in this case doesn't make it any better.

"I know we're not real exciting or anything," she says, "but I would have expected you all to stick around a little longer. I didn't even know y'all were going to Louisville until you left. Kent had to tell me."

"We told you, Mom. The night before we left."

"Well, I didn't hear you."

"I don't have any control over what you see and hear."

"What are you *doing* out there," she repeats, and though I've already told her, I know she's asking a different question entirely.

MEL SUGGESTS A CHRONOLOGICAL format for the List movie, checking off items from first to last. "You are at the center," Mel tells me. "Just start from square one—the Faulkner stuff, growing up, Teddy—and then sprint out to one thirty-eight. Don't think about the guy, but think about what was going on in your life when you encountered the guy. We sort of chart your life *through* them. They're the buildup to the stroke."

"And then what's the resolution supposed to be here?"

"You'll tell me," she says. "We'll figure it out when we get there."

But when we start work on the guys, we quickly discover how *boring* it is. Instead, I find myself drawing the Phillips-Stamper Cemetery as I'd imagined it during our night ride—twilight, the sky in streaks of deep purple and vermilion, casting a shadow over Faulkner as it twinkles, light and wavering. "Whoa," Mel says. "What's *that*?"

We do Faulkner, we do Shauna's face. My father's face. The layout of my high school. The old Magnavox set I watched television on. Teddy as a boy. Teddy's dad's room. The red plastic ashtray on his bedside table. What a *Hustler* centerfold would have looked like in 1994. "The only difference between then and now," Mel says thoughtfully, "is bush. And implants. By 1994, all those adorable little tea-spout boobies would have been long gone."

"Do we have to start there? At the stuff in the trunk? I mean, I don't want that to be the launchpad," I say.

"We don't *have* to do anything," she says. "We can put the story about your mom throwing that ottoman through the window and spirits coming at you through the TV first, so long as it does what we want it to in terms of starting the story. First the fight, then the pictures. One discovery, then the other." Her eyes go wide and she starts rubbing her temples. "God, I sound like you, talking all this story technique shit. That's scary."

I think fleetingly of Teddy. I feel a final slice of guilt, oozing red, in my middle. "Sometimes I wonder if we maybe shouldn't take out the photo scene," I say. "Maybe it's too much. You know?"

Mel pauses for a moment, searching my face. She takes off her glasses and rubs at her eyes before looking back up. Without glasses, her face looks smaller somehow, her eyes lighter, vulnerable. "Do you ever think about the kind of person you would have become if you hadn't seen those pictures?"

"Let's not go down this road."

She puts her glasses on the drafting table. "Look. That story you told me is *brutal*. You saw pictures—*real pictures*—of little girls knocked out and tied up before you even knew what you were seeing. You were what, ten? You knew *nothing* then. You wouldn't even have had your first period yet. Once you see something like that, you can't unsee it. You were unwittingly exposed to the possibility of pain. Of violation. And I think a big part of you spent a lot of your life trying to feel something else." She leans in. Her eyes are wider. She's angry, I realize. She's furious. This has been curdling inside her. "Anything that *makes* you in that way, anything that makes you hurt and hungry in that way, is worth investigating. No matter how disgusting the source."

And there it is, in the middle of the room: a crystalline Mel Vaught reading of a life, fearfully, morbidly accurate. We both know she's right. She's right about the story, she's right about the shape. She's right about me. It's only two steps from drawing the Phillips-Stamper Cemetery to drawing Honus Caudill. My fingers are thinking on their own now. I bury my head in my arms and smell the wool on my sweater, seeing blackness running through it all.

I raise up. "Okay. Let's see what kind of story it makes," I say. "Try it out."

Mel has her way with the project, like she always does. I come in one morning, and she stops me, holds up one finger, waiting for my attention, then brandishes what she's made—a flipbook, thick but the size of an old address log. She used to make more of these, back in college. My favorite was the one of our old sketch prof McIntosh fellating a horse, then the horse kicking him in the face and braying, *"SHAZAM!"* For Fart's birthday one year, she made a flipbook adventure of a 1980s Ozzy Osbourne: taking blotter acid, then pulling on a sundress and snorting ants. At the end, Ozzy refuses to speak to anyone else on the tour bus except a blow-up doll with whom he spends a week conspiring against his bandmates. The flipbook's last page is a picture of Ozzy staring at the blow-up doll with what can only be called adoration. It is strangely beautiful. Fart teared up a little when she gave it to him. When people visit his apartment, he hustles them over, saying, "Look at this. My friend Mel made this for me."

The flipbook is me. It is a *Sharon flipbook*. It starts with Sharon the toddler, a scene from a Polaroid that Mel has stolen from my mother's house—me in bib overalls, holding a giant stuffed chicken I'd been given for Christmas. I start growing with the movement. Fat, then thin, then fat again. Breasts out of nowhere. Arms longer, nose longer, eyes sharper. Hair goes up, down, short, long. My entire life moving, my face growing, aging. Clear-eyed adulthood. The stroke is in the flick of three pages, so fast I start—I go from long-haired and top-heavy to thin, bald, lopsided. Mel did not hold back with the stroke face; it is there in twisted, distorted relief. Then the uphill climb. The face straightens, left side catching up with the right. The body fills out a little. But the eyes remain the same after the change. Smaller. A little warier, lacking in the quality that could have been mistaken for dumbness before when it was really the quality of one unburdened, a door that has not yet been shut.

"Do you see now what I want to do?" Mel says. "It's *you*. The whole story. The pictures. The stroke. Everything in between." She sends her hand on an arc through the air. "Your flight back up."

I sit down and flip through it, again, again, again. My throat starts to ache. It's a flipbook of someone losing something important to them, to who they are, and it is beautiful. Made with total care; total faith in the recovery of what is lost.

We begin making a storyboard on an old cork expanse Mel finds in the house's storage shed, posting sketches with summaries underneath: a little girl in front of a TV, cradling a bag of circus peanuts, reads *Friday night 4th grade. TGIF on ABC. Monday afternoon, school bus. Big girls steal backpack. Family dinner: Red comes home drunk, pukes in the bushes, Dad tells Mom to go fuck herself, Shauna rips up Sharon's drawing.* The plot turn: *Dirty gray van creeps up mountain. Front grill should look like a face (screaming/laughing).* Mel makes some oil-pencil sketches of the room: the spoiled carpeting, the drippy yellow walls. She sketches Honus Caudill's shoes, dark with insteps like open mouths, parked beside a porch door. The best is of me and Teddy, together, backs turned, facing a long, closed trunk that seems to stretch into infinity.

Mel's discouraged. I work more slowly than I did. My lines aren't as clean as they once were. My hands still shake some when holding a pencil. "All you need is practice," she says, brows coming low over her eyes. "Focus."

"I'm trying."

"I know you are."

"You don't act like you do. You act like I'm slacking off."

"I'm sorry. My intention is not to make you feel like a slacker. Just—treat it like a job, you know? When you clock in, clock *in*."

She doesn't like it when I leave for the day. "This feels slow," she says. "Does it feel slow to you? We can be patient with it, but that doesn't mean don't *push* a little."

For the first time ever, leaving work is the best part of my day. I live for the long, slow walk back to Teddy's, dawdling by the park he took me to our first night here, opening his apartment door using the key he made especially for me. Dropping the keys and massaging my hands, a pervasive ache from my palm to my thumb.

I run a bath and sink into the deep porcelain tub, letting my fingers prune up. I stare at them. There used to be something inside me that made drawing feel like a natural passage. I never knew this until I tried to draw without it.

Teddy walks through the door and makes me forget. Being happy makes work's shitfest a lot easier to handle. Who cares if I never draw again? We occupy our own universe. He likes to bring me antique sodas he keeps in the fridge—Moxie, Cheerwine, Nehi—and apply himself to my neck while I let the cold run down my throat. He recounts his day and I trace my fingers up the planes of his face, the chin, the cleft above his lips, the strange, soft little whorl where his neck ends and his earlobe, wild and unattached, begins.

He stops talking and he says, "How goes the project?"

"Rough."

"Oh, babe. I'm sorry."

"It's fine. Mel's all gung ho. I can barely keep up."

"She's a little hard on you, don't you think?"

"I can handle it," I say. I move my hands and find the bulge I know will be there, to cup it and hear the sound that comes from the back of his throat.

We fuck so long and so often that we make each other sore. We are getting to know each other's weaknesses, the triggers that make the world stop: tonguing a particular place on the collarbone, grinding against him while he washes dishes, palming him while he's on the phone to feel him come alive in my hand. We can smell each other on our skin when we're apart. "I'm not getting anything done," he teases me. "I'm having a contest with myself to see how often I can make you come. Doesn't leave time for much else." At night, we sleep deep, limbs thrown all over the other.

I have never had a life like this, where I felt so good so often, so perpetually safe inside my own head. I wake up with no headaches and no dream recall.

It becomes winter.

I'M NOT SURE HOW I keep justifying postponing telling Teddy about the project, but I do. There's always something else to talk about. There are stories about ex-girlfriends, and there's the graphic novel he's tried to start five times. There is the first apartment I lived in in New York and the time two middle schoolers tried to mug me on the L train platform. There was his first kiss in the eighth grade from a girl named Becky Walters, who tongued his face so hard she gave him a rash. How I met Mel. The cabin he dreamed of building in Henry County. Story on top of story; we lose whole nights of sleep talking to each other. We've missed twenty years of life with each other. We feel the need to catch up.

Most days, it feels wasteful to address anything that could spoil this. *When it eventually comes up, he will understand,* I tell myself. *You two will be so far into whatever* this *is that he will understand what you're doing. He'll understand why you're committed. It will be fine.*

One night, searching through the bathroom cabinet for Q-tips, I find a girl's scrunchie, a big, ruffled gold job of the American Apparel variety.

Before this, I haven't experienced what a sweet sea of land mines living with a lover can be. Are you moving into their territory, or are they moving into yours? Are there areas that are off-limits to you (his workspace, for example, stacked with store ledgers and videotapes and plans for the next film festival)? Are there *people* who are off-limits to you? What are the necessary, unspoken truths of the house, and how unpleasant will it be when you discover that they are to remain unspoken? Mel and I had known each other so well for so long; even our surprises had the feel of the well-worn. There are times when I have to remind myself that Teddy is *not* Mel, that I cannot live with him in quite the way I lived with her.

I pick up the scrunchie and bring it out, waving it in the air, nose wrinkled. Expecting to get a laugh.

Teddy looks irritated instead. "Okay," he sighs, plucking it out of my hands. "Where'd you find it?"

"Under the sink. That thing's the size of my head. Who'd it belong to, Pebbles?"

He grimaces and turns away from me. I see crimson rising up from his shirt collar. "Victoria. An ex. She works at the bookstore."

The girl on our walk to the bar, our first night in Louisville. That was bookstore girl. *Victoria.* I feel a twinge. Mystery woman's not so funny anymore with a face and a name.

Teddy softens. "I'm not trying to be evasive," he says. "But I did have a life before this, you know."

"I'm sorry."

"It's okay. It's just that you ask for a lot of information when you're not always forthcoming, you know? It feels a little imbalanced sometimes. Look. Watch this." He leans over, throws it in the trash, ties off the bag, and lifts it out of the bin. "Out of sight, out of mind. Okay?"

"I wasn't trying to pry," I say, but he's out the door and on the balcony, back turned, lighting a Benson & Hedges. Effectively ending the conversation.

That night, he comes to bed quiet before scooting over to me and saying, grudgingly, "I'm sorry."

"It's okay."

"I didn't mean to get as upset as I did."

"You were entitled to the way you felt. I was being a dick."

"No, there was no reason to get that irritated with you." He leans back into the pillows, runs a hand through his chest hair. "She and I broke things off not long before I met you. There wasn't any overlap, but it cut pretty close, time-wise. I guess I feel a little guilty about it."

I respect him for this. For sticking to his guns. For making an apology in the light when he could have snapped off the lamp and done it in the dark. I prop myself on my elbow and say, "You have a strong moral compass. You know that?"

He looks surprised. Says, "Well, so do you."

TEDDY IS A NATURAL manager. He changes the feeling of a room merely by walking into it. It's in the tone of his voice, rarely loud yet arresting, and in the easy, affable way he makes decisions. He is responsible, transparent. Living with him is quieter, more controlled, than what I am used to. It feels like I can share the reins a little. I no longer have to mind the clock and pay the bills for two people. Even for all the moments of self-consciousness, wondering how I sound or seem to him, it feels nice. He has incorporated me into his home, given me not ownership—not yet—but ground, the promise of a claim in the air, that delicious, foregone conclusion. It is new and exciting. Feeling older without fear of getting old.

We only really talk about the pictures one more time.

"I'm struggling with it," he tells me. We are driving out into the country. It's an unanticipated warm night, close to seventy degrees. He wants to show me an abandoned farmhouse that he loves close to the Indiana state line.

I ask how he's struggling.

"With the decision I made to show you those," he says. "It's a responsibility thing. I am responsible for exposing you to it. You said it yourself. Just remembering it was traumatic for you."

"You were eleven," I say. "Eleven-year-olds do not *make decisions*. In no way were you responsible."

"I disagree." He flicks a look over at me before returning to the road. He likes these conversations, the long, winding philosophical disagreements. "Eleven-year-olds make life-changing decisions all the time. They have all the weight and responsibility of any other human being."

"Those decisions are uninformed. Or they're informed by what's in front of them. Eleven-year-olds have no idea what the fuck they're doing."

"I know several people who have always been their own decision makers," he says. "From three feet high on. Present company included."

"Well, I've made some pretty shit decisions," I say. "So."

"I shared an incredible burden with you," he says slowly, "forced it on you, actually. And I'm having a hard time forgiving myself."

He's silent for a moment. It's dark. The hills are beginning to roll larger, giving our car the feeling of a boat on smooth and even waves. A college station is spinning an entire Wilco album we've discovered we both adored years ago, a soft song with a sweet radioed buzz, falling in and out of frequency. *Distance has no way of making love understandable.*

Suddenly there's a crack in the sky, a flash of pale orange light tearing down the horizon to the ground. "Heat lightning," Teddy says wonderingly.

I love this life. I love being in the safe, shadowy cell of this car, speeding by farmhouses spiked with the warm yellow of interior lamps. I can't remember the last time I felt such gratitude for what I have. I can't remember the last time I felt so lucky to be right where I was.

I reach over and take his hand.

• • •

W E ALL GET TOGETHER on Friday nights for dinner, Mel and the boys toting plastic bags from Kroger up the stairs and filling the kitchen with noise and flour dusting and splashes of tomato sauce everywhere, seemingly, whether or not the recipe calls for tomato at all. They kill a couple of six-packs while they cook and everyone's drunk by the time we sit down to eat. The meals are big, hot, yeasty affairs: homemade Sicilian pizza, frittata, meatloaf. Tatum makes dessert for every production, assembling it at home in a cast-iron skillet or an old-school blue-and-white Corningware dish. They are touchingly exquisite. A flaky apple pie so good it would have made Kent rip his hair out. Layered baklava that leaves us all sucking honey and olive oil from our fingers for two sweet days. "That's our lil treasure," Mel says, corking a wet willie into his ear. Tatum and Ryan follow Mel around the kitchen, deferring to her, looking to her approval for jokes, opinions, even the way they harass each other. Mel's always had disciples, the most striking of the New York followers being Fart—big, burly guys with a certain amount of social anxiety—but these two are a package deal, and she is good to them. We watch movies after dinner and I usually fall asleep on Teddy's lap, awake to him shaking me, saying, "Sweetheart, everyone's leaving," Mel and Tatum and Ryan behind him, bundled into winter coats, giggling at each other, cigarettes tucked behind their ears.

Mel and I both put on some weight. Our cheeks fill out and bloom up red. We're more polite, suddenly remembering all the staples of social nicety that New York makes you forget—opening doors for people, saying please, making brief, nonthreatening eye contact.

And our project, slowly but surely, is beginning to pick up. "See?" I tell her. "It's good, being here. We could live here. We could live here, and it could be great."

She shrugs, peering at the storyboard, glasses pushed up to rest on her head. "Maybe," she says.

T HE HEAT WAVE STRETCHES into the week after Thanksgiving. Teddy and I eat dinner at a Cuban restaurant downtown and walk along the edge of the Ohio River after, dark and rocky, skyscrapers looming behind us. We have been in Louisville for almost a month. Our studio will be vacant after Christmas. I'm trying not to think about whatever comes after this—after this walk, after this week.

"This is what makes me love Louisville," he says. "This view. I don't care that we're looking out onto Indiana. I really don't."

He smiles at me but brings his eyebrows in, like he's thinking. "What is it?" I ask him.

He shakes his head. Pulls me into his side. Then says, "We're pretty happy here, right?"

"Right."

We walk a little farther before he says, "I guess I want to know what you're thinking."

I feel my limbs loosen and glow. The warmth climbs right up through my jacket and into my face. "I'm thinking I'm done with New York," I say.

"Okay."

"I'm thinking I wouldn't be opposed to the idea of moving here."

"That's great."

"Maybe we could find some new subletters for the spring. I mean, I'd have to talk to Mel about it. But."

His face lights. "That's exactly what I was hoping you'd say."

"NO," MEL SAYS. "WHAT the fuck, dude. I mean, what. You wanna move down here forever?"

"Well, maybe," I say. "What's the problem? You love it down here."

"Sure," she says. "I'm into, like, the idea of an extended fellowship kind of thing. What we're doing now, basically. But our whole fucking *lives* are up there, Sharon. You wanna dump that for some tail? Really?"

"Would you mind not referring to Teddy as *tail*? Thanks."

"Sorry," she says. "Just—can we talk about this later? I've got something to show you."

She cracks open her MacBook. There's a file titled, "Sharon's Primal Scream."

"Oh no," I say.

"Oh *yes*," she says. "Don't decry it till you *spy* it, little lady."

I roll my eyes.

"I just thought this might be a good jump-off point for some of what we're thinking about doing. Like, think of this as you, right before the stroke. This would be *that* scene. Okay? Hold on." She shuts off the lights. Hits *play*.

I hear the opening strains of "Yakety Sax" and groan.

It's a montage: Sharon hits the ground running, grinning, Satan in her eyes. It pans out—I am chasing crowds of petrified men. There's me catching one and hugging him while scrunching my face and making a dying whale sound. Me in lingerie perched in the lap of a sobbing Santa Claus. Me calling into a radio station, hearts in my eyes, requesting Bread's "Make It with You" while a crying DJ stabs himself in the ear. Me springing from a dude's closet dressed in his three-piece suit, at which point he starts to bawl. Me doing the nasty with a despondent hobo, who grabs a nearby bottle and starts cutting himself. Me catching a grizzly bear in an embrace and making him hork. All with maniacally happy saxophones tooting in the background. My vagina morphs, becomes a Venus flytrap, eats and spits and dons a tuxedo and croons into a little peen-shaped microphone.

Midway through, a soft, low-grade scream commences, growing louder and louder until it rises above the music, and there's just me humping the air to shrieks, propelling myself with my cooch to meet the curve of the moon and, beyond that, one thousand humping stars, and I fly off into a neon night, a sweaty Lisa Frank stationery sheet of oblivion.

I make Mel play it over and over again. We laugh ourselves sick. It is the funniest shit I have seen in a long, long time. When Teddy arrives at six to pick me up, he has to tap the door twice to be heard.

I open up, giggling. "Hi."

"Hey." He ducks inside and kisses me, his cheeks cold, before looking up at the wall, where Mel's pocket projector has blown up the short from the Mac. The shot is me, glaze-eyed, tonguing the wino while he cries, *"NOOOOOOO."* "Oh, cool. Is this part of the project?"

Mel leans over and snaps the projector closed.

A weird silence settles over the room. Mel and Teddy stare at each other for a moment, small, partially open smiles on their faces, both politely waiting for the punch line—for Teddy to hear Mel say, *Just joshin ya!* and turn the projector back on, and Mel, for Teddy to realize she's being serious, to lift hands, to proclaim, *It's cool, no problem.*

I give Mel a look—*you could have been more subtle*—and tell Teddy, "It's not done baking quite yet. But soon. Can we go get food? I'm starving."

"Shoot," he says, and frowns. He's genuinely disappointed.

"Slow your roll, Pushy McGoo," Mel says. "You heard the lady. This ain't ready for screening."

Teddy gives Mel a hard look. She jumps over the couch and comes to him, lower lip pushed out. "Aw, I'm sorry," she says. "Bring it in, Theodore. Come on. Gimme some." She grapples him in a bear hug, thumping his back. Teddy rolls his eyes but returns the hug. And when Mel whips a candy cane out of her back pocket and hangs it on his ear, he laughs.

"When it's ready, you'll be the first to see it," she says. "Now you guys gotta leave, cause I'm gonna wank." She puts a cigarette between her lips. "So *git.*"

Teddy smiles until he shuts the door and we step outside. "Mel's funny," he says without conviction.

"She is." When I see him frown, I lean in and give him a tickle around the ribs, swooping in for contact. I'm feeling good after seeing the clip—good and a little itchy. I find myself wishing I could have stayed longer, to see it one more time. Maybe make some editorial notes.

"I'm sorry about what she said," I say. "She is the way she is. She's not going to change any more than she already has."

"It's fine," he says. "I totally get it. I do." He leans back and looks at me for a moment, the expression on his face unreadable. "Anyone ever tell you you get the sex flush on your face when you've been working?"

T EDDY THROWS A CHRISTMAS party at Weirdo Video and introduces me as his girlfriend. Mel and Ryan attempt to make wassail, ruin it, and spike it with enough rum that no one notices. As per usual, Mel is the hit of the party, a thousand new friends in a single night. She wears a Santa hat and lights firecrackers off a Bardstown Road side street. I'm so happy to be there that I actually help her, setting them up so she can light them and run to the sidewalk in time for the boom. We yell while smokeballs and jumping jacks spin and pop. "Oh hoooly night," she bellows, kicking burnt pieces to the curb. We're drunk and cold and we clutch and push at each other with our hands, our matching red claws ink-stained and knobby at the knuckles.

Teddy pulls me aside. "I think we should get Mel home," he says.

"What's the problem?"

His eyebrows fold into a concerned point. He has grown a soft, short beard. I feel it most keenly when he presses his face into my neck as I come, like he's listening for something inside. I reach for the beard, tune out. "Honey," he says.

"Hmmm?"

"She's setting off fireworks in the middle of a historic district. These people are touchy. She's going to get us picked up."

"It's fine." I twiddle my fingers in the swirl connecting sideburn with cheek stubble. From the corner of my eye, Victoria from the bookstore watches, her mouth a straight line, glass of fucked-over wassail in her hand.

"Will you please say something?" He puts his hands in my hair. Says into my ear, "Say something and I'll let you ride me in the stockroom."

Mel ducks through the kitchen to grab her duffel bag, which has inexplicably been filled, at some point in our travels, with fireworks.

"Mel," I say, then louder, "Hey. Mel. Stop." I reach out, grab her by the belt loops.

"Woo," she hoots, wiggling her eyebrows at Ryan nearby. "Look who's getting *saucy.*"

"Can I talk to you?"

Mel groans. "Go blow it out your peehole with that schoolmarm voice." She grabs *me* by the belt loops, jerking back and forth. "This is a *party.* Wow, your pants are super-loose. You need to eat more."

I guide her over by the stockroom. "Maybe give it a rest with the firecrackers."

"Aw, come on."

"You're going to get us all picked up. It's too much noise."

"What. Did Teddy offer you sexual favors in exchange for *controlling* me? He did, didn't he?"

My face flames. "No one wants to control you. We just want to keep everyone out of jail. Teddy's the one who lives here."

"He controls *you,*" Mel whispers. "This is where it starts. You'll become his *meat puppet.*"

"What?"

"He wants me to *leave,* man. That's what he *wants.* It irks the shit out of him when he sees you with me. He doesn't want you to have any kind of life that doesn't include him."

We're both swaying on our feet. Shitfaced is no way to have an argument. "That's not it," I tell her, "that's *not* it. All I did was ask you to stop lighting fireworks, okay? I don't want you to get hurt. That's it, dude. Don't make this a *thing.*"

We let it peter out, engage in some bro-grabs. Mel burps and moans, "That wassail was seven glasses of *mistake.*"

Teddy watches us from the corner, that weird, inscrutable expression on his face. Someone says something to him and he turns his head to reply, eyes still trained on us.

It doesn't occur to me until later that night in bed, Teddy snoring beside me, that maybe Teddy doesn't like Mel. And maybe the feeling is mutual.

I become convinced the closer we get to Christmas. It's not something I noticed at first, this strange tenor in the air between them; they do a nice job of putting up a veneer of friendliness, of cordiality. If there's something they both do well, it's *people*—getting a read on a room as soon as they walk in, putting forward just the right, subtle impression of peace and self-comfort, whether or not it is genuine. They find the same things funny. They both have an intolerance for lazy thinking. In any sane world, they would be friends. But they are not.

I try to tell myself, after every encounter, that the mood was lighter than it had seemed, that Mel and Teddy really do like each other. They're fine. They're the two halves of my life, stitching together. Any suspicion the result of my broken, neurotic brain.

It usually doesn't become fractious until the second bottle of wine peels the manners away. It starts with stupid stuff—which is the best Martin Hannett–produced album, Joy Division or Psychedelic Furs. The best David Lynch movie. The funniest Dostoevsky. The efficacy of the European Union. Tax penalties for the uninsured. But it devolves from there. It is during one of these exchanges that I learn Teddy is a registered Independent. Mel tries not to laugh. She fails. Another loud, sharp back-and-forth ensues over the many empty bottles on Teddy's kitchen table, each adopting their customary stance—Teddy pushing his glasses up his nose and flagging his hands in a trying-to-reason gesture of *Look,* while Mel folds arms across her chest, incredulous, smirking—all while Ryan and Tatum and I grimace at each other. Outbursts are always followed by weird little islands of silence, poisonous glances while shifting sitting positions or turning to fetch another beer. Friday dinners begin to end with something latent and unpleasant stretched over the top. Nobody likes Teddy or Mel very much after these squabbles.

THERE IS DRINKING. IT'S hard to ignore. Teddy drinks. He drinks when he comes home from the video store, and he drinks when we make brunch on the weekends, and he keeps a beer at hand when he's working at his laptop. When I'm sick, he makes tea with a shot and a half of Old Grand-Dad dumped in. He buys crystal tumblers and silver service trays for his bar, spends hundreds of dollars on Pappy Van Winkle bourbon and cordials that come in perfume decanters, and he takes evident pleasure in preparing outdated cocktails from the forties, humming under his breath, eyes warming as he mixes. He calls it his hobby, his weird little pet interest—*niche drinking*. He drinks and he drinks and he very rarely appears drunk, but I smell him in the night and it is alcohol sweating through his skin. Alcohol on his breath. Alcohol, seemingly, in his hair.

One night his mom calls him. His mom, he tells me, has problems with painkillers. She claims it started with a back injury, but he remembers orange and tan prescription bottles littering the bathroom vanity, her makeup table, the kitchen counter, long before. He recalls an intervention organized by one of her sisters on Christmas morning that ended with her locking herself in a bathroom. When his phone sounds off, his shoulders sag and I see a wary, glazed look in his eye, what I imagine I look like when my mother calls me. "I better get this," he mutters.

I pretend to answer emails while he takes his cell into the next room. I peek in once to see him hunched over, grinding one palm against his head. It gives me a queasy, culpable feeling to see Teddy in distress. I go sit in his bedroom, where I fall asleep reading.

I'm awakened by the sound of retching. Teddy is on the outside balcony in his boxers, shaking. The queasy feeling swells. I tuck myself into the wall in the dark, listening to the sound outside, cringing. It's that weird, transferable sort of shame when you feel the weight of embarrassment for someone else.

When I take him by the shoulders to lead him inside, his voice comes out trembling with cold. "I'm a failure," he says.

I wet a washcloth and begin to mop him down, looking away from his face. This is the trade-off, I tell myself, for a man so genuine, a man who feels so deeply. This is what you wanted, I remind myself as I sponge the vomit from his torso.

It occurs to me before I can stop it: We're head people, Teddy and me. We spend a substantial amount of our lives scratching around up there, realizing joyful, private milestones we'll never admit to on the ground. But there are the corresponding dark territories we'll never leave, tangled forests no one else can ever enter, where we will spend most of our lives alone. We may be lured out, once in a while, but we won't remain outside for very long.

Did I really expect him to step outside for me?

And then I think of Mel last summer, in exactly this position, sputum dribbling down her front. I think of her as I take Teddy's shoulders and gently tug, pulling him onto his side for sleep.

When I wake the next morning, he is already gone.

THE PROJECT IS CRUISING uphill, all pressed gas and increasing volume. But for the first time, Mel and I are not living in the same place while we're building a project. She alone falls into our standard work mode pattern—sleeping in fits and starts, smoking like a demon, funneling coffee at all hours—while I punch in at nine, do the day, and go home at six. "Where are you going?" she always yells.

"Bye."

"Don't *bye* me, turdlet. Get your ass back here."

"Bye. *Bye. Bye.*" I shut the door.

Tatum, that ingenious kid, has purchased himself a lightboard and has volunteered it for our use. It is moved into the studio and we get going, inbetweening on what we have posted to the storyboard.

To my horror, I find that I can't do it anymore—the rapid-fire production of images on onionskin, each shifted a fraction of a hair's difference from its predecessor, hundreds of pages granting an object its movement. It's close, fast work, the bare-bones first step of animation, period. Screw it up by a tenth of a centimeter and the whole illusion of movement is busted to pieces. When I try to get a rhythm going, my hands shoot with tremors, cramps. The pencil's a bucking bronco. All my subtlety is lost.

I let Mel take over the inbetweening, feeling a little guilty. But she doesn't mind—Mel was always our woman for this driving, hunched-over work. To watch Mel inbetween is to watch a sort of ghost birth in which a figure is born, light and quick and precise, in seconds, and then born again, the miracle finally evident only at fifty or a hundred pages, when it scratches its nose, or rolls its eyes, or blinks. What is tedious and overinvolved for me is just another day at badass school for Mel; her wrist arched and still like a pianist's, her hand twitching over the sheet, then turning for a fresh page: flip, scratch, done. Flip, scratch, done.

"It's blood-and-guts work," she said once. "Makes me feel like an animal. Like in a really good way. I get to turn my brain off."

She starts in earnest, sometimes breaking from an hour of cramped, close sketching to run high knees by the lightboard, sprinting in place, breaking out the squat-thrusts to keep from going batshit. Her color's high, her posture strong. She has Ryan and Tatum over for mini-lessons; they cluster near while she draws, points, exclaims. "It's called the principles of squash and stretch," she tells them. "It's sort of like reverb. Like bouncing a rubber ball—when it hits the ground, it flattens for a millisecond, right? Like goes oblong? And then it self-corrects." She demonstrates, then clears for the boys to take over, letting them stack onionskin to track their progress through the pages. She watches them scoot their arms to the left, tilt their heads, get kissing-close to the surface.

"You know," she says one day after they leave, "I don't think I'd mind teaching someday. Maybe I'd like it." She squints an eye at me. "Think I'm nuts?"

I am struck. "No," I say. "I think you'd be a great teacher."

She ducks her head and grins. I've hit her bashful bone. "Well," she says, turning toward the storyboard, pretending to rearrange something. "I'd be better than that fuckpants McIntosh, anyway."

In my absence, Mel has taken to texting ideas and findings, a steady stream of beeps for every time she used to lean over our desks and say, "Hey, check this out." A lot are links to videos. An early 1960s stop-motion cartoon ad for a regional ham product featuring pigs in a marching band. A series of Soviet cartoons from the seventies in an unsettlingly florid, psychedelic style. Some old NEA-funded Vincent Collins shorts, the trippy Bicentennial cartoon she's always adored. *We want a feel like THIS for the stroke scenes,* she texts.

Like spottier and more disconnected than Nash. Combat. Creepier. More confounding.

Cool. Let's try a draft, I text back.

Teddy has taken me to see *Paris, Texas* in an old theater downtown. Neither of us has spoken about the other night; in silent apology, he brings me a large, soft cookie from the concession stand. He glances at the phone, then at me.

I put the phone back in my pocket. "Sorry," I say. "Just Mel texting about work stuff."

"It's okay," he says.

Thirty seconds later, my phone dings. A cartoon short from a website entirely in Swedish. I hesitate, finger over the *play* button.

Teddy sighs and rubs his face. "Jesus Christ, honey, will you turn your phone off?"

"Okay, okay. Relax. I'm turning it off."

"I don't mean to get upset, but my God, it's like every two minutes with her. Don't you want to take a break from work when you get home?"

"I am taking a break." I put my hand on his knee, trying to tamp the fight down before it starts. "I don't draw at home. I want to be with you."

"You're not really taking a break if Mel is pestering you with work stuff at all hours," he says. "Your phone is never quiet. It goes off when we're trying to sleep."

It also went off once in the middle of sex. I started to move for it, him on top of me, then made the save and wrapped my arms around his waist. But he saw that I had to stop myself. And he saw that I saw.

He takes a deep breath, removes his glasses, polishes them with his shirttail. Turns to me. "I love that you guys are so invested," he says, "but there's a line you have to maintain between work and life. Just to keep yourself from going crazy. And I think that's something you need to work on."

This makes me grit my teeth. "I appreciate you thinking of me," I tell him, measured, "but there's no need for worry. I find our balance pretty healthy, honestly. First stages, we go a little overboard, because we're just getting into it. Later on the pace will become more even. This is pretty standard."

He shakes his head, unconvinced. Still polishing his glasses. I want to rip them out of his hands. *They're clean, goddammit, rub any more and the lenses will disintegrate.* "When Mel's like this," he says, "you know what she reminds me of? Did you ever read the Captain Beefheart biography?"

I sink down in my seat. "Nope."

"He used to lock his band up in this attic in his house for days on end. He was angry and irrational and he had insane mood swings, but he was brilliant. And he was their boss. So they put up with it. One of the band members told this story where he was really pissed off about a take they'd done that he wasn't happy with, and he just went on a rampage, breaking shit and yelling. And finally, he turned a water faucet on full blast and pointed at it screaming, "Play like *that*! Play like *that*!"

"Mel's not Captain Beefheart," I say.

"No. She's not." Teddy puts his glasses back on.

I open my mouth just as the lights begin to dim. It saves us from whatever I was going to say to Teddy next. I silence my phone instead. Tell him, "When you turn the work on, you can't turn it off, okay? Mel's just doing her job."

"She's not your boss, Sharon," he whispers. "She's your partner. You can stand up to her, you know."

I roll my eyes and cram the cookie into my mouth.

OUR PROJECT PULLS ITSELF together and begins to stagger around. It seems to happen quickly, though we both know it's the product of hours banked and material shorn, a million births and deaths.

We trim, weed, liposuction, force the thing onto a treadmill to run its belly off, knowing we'll have to do it all again. It's only the initial draft, but in Louisville, we get our first minutes—our project becomes a living thing with reflexes and breath, an animal, our cipher. It takes over. Always sitting in the room with us, refusing to leave until we finish its business. It eats and drinks and sleeps with us. It interrupts our sentences. It makes itself everything's point.

Around the first deep freeze, we start to pull twelve-hour work blocks, sketching and inbetweening. Fingers stronger, I join in: take upon take until it is the best it can be.

We bring Ryan and Tatum on as runners, drink fetchers, pencil sharpeners, careful not to let them see too much of the product until we're ready to bring it out into the world. Eventually we let them sketch a little for us. They're good. We're surprised at how good they are. It's only been the two of us for so long, we almost don't know how to handle the help.

We set up the laptop projector against a white sheet one night and watch the first ten minutes in silence, the room darkened. The storm scene, the throwing of the ottoman. We've been through it a thousand times, but I'm still struck by how profoundly creepy it is, how I can still feel it next to me after I've stopped watching. I mention it to Mel.

"Yeah, it'll do that," she says. She's chewing her lip in the shadows of the carriage house, thinking. "It's still the beginning. But it's there. It's on the highway. You know?"

"You think soon?"

"Yeah. Soon."

IT'S TWO DAYS BEFORE Christmas.

Teddy, true to form, has produced his holiday accessories. A vintage train set, a small, taxidermied reindeer. At some point, I find myself thinking that this might become grating: his attachment to the antique, to the quaint, to the rusted and enchanted. But for now, I'm still charmed by the brandies he's made for us, the little potbellied stove in the corner in which he's built a fire, wrapping a big block of coal in newspapers and feeding dried sticks into the flames. The sky purples at six now, going full dark by seven. It is snowing.

I clench and unclench my hands at the fire, wincing. My joints glisten large and red. "I had to draw myself all day today. It was weird."

He's at his desk, shopping for the store. He's been haggling with his favorite retailer, a guy in Berlin who sells what he calls "antique pleasure films" on Region 2 bootlegs. He shifts, looks up at me. "Won't hear many people say *that* about their day."

"Well, try and find as many people who are as self-absorbed as me." I turn, waggle my butt at him.

"Oh, you hush." He swipes at me. "Most people wouldn't be able to do that. I don't see how you can."

"Very uneasily. With lots of fuckups. It's hard to have that kind of outer perspective you need when it's, you know, your face. We've come up with lots of versions. It's just that Mel's not happy with any of them."

He turns back to the laptop, the glow filling his lenses with light. "Mel is a hard person to please."

"She's a perfectionist. It helps that she's right a lot. She doesn't believe in being dodgy. She doesn't believe in being afraid."

"Oh, she has her fears," he says, tapping at the laptop. It's irritating, the way he's so focused on the screen. I want him to look at me. "A person that given to acting out definitely finds fear to be a major motivator."

I leave the fire and stand beside the desk. "What do you mean by that?"

He shrugs. "I've known *Mels*. I mean, don't get me wrong, she's great. Amazing at what she does. But she's obviously got some issues. That really calculated flaying out of yourself?" He grimaces slightly, then says, bright and brittle, like he wants to change the subject, "It's complicated."

I flex my hand again, looking at the knuckles. Christ Almighty, they're huge. "You say that like you don't necessarily approve of what we're doing."

"No no," he says. "It's not that. It's just— Look. That sort of thing is really powerful. Writing about your own life? I have tried to write about stuff that happened to me. Stuff about Dad. The trial."

I think about the night we met again, talking in the dark. The way he focused on something in the distance while telling his story. "I didn't know that."

"Well, I did. None of it was very good. But I did it enough to make myself sick. I mean, my hair was falling out. I had insane IBS. I put myself through real hell, and it was because I was trying to *scene* these moments. You relive all this stuff when you do that. It's kind of like going into the wiring of your brain and twiddling around, you know? And it can change your memories. I mean, I actually *changed* what I remembered. I understand this urge, Sharon. You set out to eat the bear, but maybe the bear eats you. And I don't think Mel's the kind of person who acknowledges risk and acts anyway. I think she's the kind of person who ignores risk. And that is a dangerous, slightly self-involved thing to do."

I put my head down. It's like a needle going through my neck. Like reading that article the *Salon* guy wrote about *Nashville Combat* all over again, but with a greater echo. As it turns out, indictments are even more unpleasant when they're coming from the people you love.

"Hey," Teddy says, rising, voice filled with remorse. "Wait." He puts his arms around me. "I think what you guys do is great. I mean, you ever watch Ryan and Tatum with Mel? We're all fans. Okay? Me too. Especially me. I just want you to be careful, Sharon. If you feel like you're doing something adverse to yourself in making this, then stop. You're still recovering. Give yourself a break. Okay?"

"I'm not going to hurt myself." I say this into his chest, hot and muffled.

"I don't think you ever would intentionally," he says. "But you've got your blinders on when you work."

"I'm okay. I really am."

He pulls me in tighter, cupping my head in his hands. "I worry about you all the time. You know that?" he says. "All the time."

He lifts me up and puts me on the bed, rolls me on top of him. I feel his beard against my neck. It makes me forget how much my hands throb. He turns to take one of my fingers in his mouth, then spits it out. "Jesus," he says. "I just got a mouthful of ink."

I hold my hand up. He's right. They're splattered. "Sorry."

He tugs my underpants down with his thumbs. "I'm glad I met

you at thirty-two," he whispers. "Not twenty-two. I was rotten at this at twenty-two."

"I don't believe it."

"Yes." They're down completely and he lifts up my hips and there is the heat and slight sting of entry. We stop talking.

We live to reach the middle of each other, even after an argument. The best is when I straddle his lap, wrapping my arms around his head, his mouth to my ear. It feels impossible to be closer to anyone than I am to him when we do this, when I can clasp him inside me, pulling gently. And it is during lovemaking, sometimes rowdy enough to be called fucking and sometimes gentle enough to be called prayer, that we loosen our holds on ourselves enough to confess that this has never happened before, to either one of us, maybe not to anyone else ever, and we hope against hope, with gritted teeth, that there will be no end.

A FTER NEW YEAR'S, WE finally decide to let the boys see what we've made—the first fifteen minutes of whatever this project will be. We'll buy wine and Chinese food and invite them over to the carriage house for a screening.

We're anxious—or I'm anxious, anyway. I spend the bigger part of the morning in Mel's bathroom with the trots. What if Teddy doesn't like it? What if it upsets him? What if it's not good enough to convince him that I am above wrongdoing?

When I emerge, Mel is buttoning up a fresh flannel shirt. She offers me a very large joint. Says, "Dude. Relax. He'll love it." She wrinkles her nose, looks over my shoulder. "Guh. Gonna need an exorcist in there."

She sweeps the carriage house floor and sets her pocket projector against a clean white sheet hung on the wall. She leans into the bathroom, watches me apply eyeliner. "Don't be nervous," she says. "It's our first audience, and it's a good one. A smart one. They'll have good things to say."

They arrive, a burst of noise and cold from the outside—the boys, stamping snow from their boots, Teddy's icy face pressed into mine.

We eat, we drink. Finally, Mel ushers us over to the sitting area. Her laptop is ready to go.

Teddy's arm is slung around my shoulder. I feel good, loose. Excited. It's been a long time since Mel and I have had something new. I want Teddy to see it—to see how good Mel and I can be. I'm in my customary place, nestled into the angle under his arm, leg bent atop his. I can hear his breathing, feel the rise and fall, the echo in his chest when he speaks or laughs. He rubs my shoulder. "I'm excited about this," he says. "Really curious to see what you all have been holed up working on."

"I'm excited for you to see it, too," I say. "I know I haven't filled you in on much of it."

"You're a tough one to figure out, Kisses."

"Okay," Mel says. "We're ready. Go easy on us." She hits the lights. The projector glows. In the neon letters we favor: *The List*.

"Working title," Mel says.

The scene starts in my parents' living room. There is a storm rumbling outside, the faint sound of sirens tipping off. Me in front of the television, the glow illuminating my body against the dark. No internal monologue. These are the Faulkner scenes, childhood-mined. The colors are soft and whitewashed; it is dreamlike, lingering on single images, echoing sound. A this-is-the-space-your-brain-cannot-decode sort of work.

When the ottoman shatters the glass, the screen purples. Everything speeds up, becomes dark and fleet. The sound, fighting tracks we saved from the Kotex commercial, babbles.

There are laughs where we want laughs. There is silence when we want silence. Mel and I trade looks: *That was the way to go. Let's cut that. Let's adjust the color at the end.* We can't part with it now. We are completely in its service.

The next scene: the shift to summer. Teddy and I bounce on a trampoline, mouths open, eyes wide. A motor churns in the distance. Then a lingering shot we worked particularly hard to set: a decrepit silver van creeping up a mountainside, the sky shot with pink and brown veins.

I feel Teddy inhale. His hand, wandering through my hair, freezes.

Onscreen, the door to the Caudill house opens. We step inside. The door shuts.

I feel Teddy take his arm back from behind my head and drape it neutrally over the sofa. I look to him. He's staring at the screen. I see a muscle in his jaw work.

"Are you okay?"

He does not look at me. "Mmm hmm."

"You sure?"

"Mmm."

Onscreen, the trunk seems to pan out for miles and miles. It is a coffin, then a chocolate bar, then an enormous brick. It swells, looms over us. When Teddy's hand reaches up to unlock it, he has to strain, rising on his toes.

Later on, this will become a driving image for our movie, an encouragement of confrontation, of taking control of what haunts you, stealing its power: *Open your trunk*. It is an affirmation of why we made it, why we were so compelled to keep pressing forward. Repeated dozens of times in the comments sections of the clips on You-Tube: *Open Your Trunk*.

But I will never be able to watch that scene without feeling Teddy's chest against my face, rising and falling and then, when he watches his younger self unlatch the trunk, seize, as if he's been hit with something hard.

It finally ends.

Mel will tell me later that this first screening was when she knew the project was going to work. "You could feel it in there after the file had stopped playing," she said. "It was in the *air*. You could smell it. I practically went to sleep next to it that night."

But I don't notice any of this. I am too distracted by Teddy thrumming next to me, jaw clenched. By the time we reach the scene in which I take the Polaroids from his outstretched hand, images of the girls facing down, he is gripping his knees, breathing rapidly.

"That was awesome," Ryan says.

"Yeah," Tatum agrees. "It's gonna be even better than *Nashville Combat*."

"I need to talk to you," Teddy says to me.

"Is everything okay?" I ask him.

"Outside. Now. Please."

"What do you need to talk to her about?" Mel says.

"I need to talk to Sharon privately, Mel, thank you."

"Is it about the movie? Because if it's about the movie, you can talk to the both of us."

Teddy narrows his eyes at Mel and takes a deep breath. I hold up my hand. "It's okay," I say. "We'll be right back."

I follow Teddy out the door and into the carriage house's yard. We are surrounded by sprawling brick mansions penned in by high wrought-iron fences. It is ten degrees, icicles hanging from the oaks. There are no lights. I try to put my hand on his back. He shakes it off. "What the hell was that, Sharon?"

"That— What do you mean? That was the project. Or the start of it."

"And when were you planning on disclosing that *I* would be in this project?"

My mind goes white, empty. I stall. "I told you it was about me. I thought you might kind of infer—"

"You said it was about your *stroke*."

"Well," I say, "we started talking about it and decided that we'd start from, you know, Faulkner, and when I was a . . ."

I trail off. Teddy is staring at me.

"That boy character was *me*," he says.

"It never said that it was you. It never used your name."

"Bullshit," he yells.

I have never heard Teddy raise his voice before. It robs me of breath. I feel dread lace long, cold fingers up my spine. "It's not bullshit," I say weakly.

"Sharon. Do you think I'm an idiot? That is *obviously* me. You effectively co-opted my life in there." He stops, puts his hands on his hips, closes his eyes. "You've been working on this the entire time you've been here?"

"There's a lot more to it than what you just saw. Or there will be."

"Unbelievable. There's *more.*"

"You're angry."

He makes a sound close to a laugh as he pinches the bridge of his nose. "Yes. *Sharon.* I am angry. As I think any reasonable person would be."

"Okay. This is a problem." I try to put my hands on him again. His entire body tightens. It's worse than feeling him push me away. "How you feel is important to me. What can I do?"

He shakes his head and presses his palms to his face. "What can you do. Okay. The first step would be to *burn* what you just showed me."

"What?"

"You heard me. Burn it. Fucking trash it. Make sure nobody else ever sees this."

My voice comes out tiny. "All of it?"

He takes his hands away and stares at me. "Jesus Christ, Sharon, yes. *All of it.*"

My bad leg starts to tingle. I would do just about anything to get out of this situation—Teddy glaring at me in the dark, his voice venom on ice.

I glance back at the carriage house and see Mel's shadow, tall and skinny, through the curtains. She's watching and listening, Ryan and Tatum alongside. It's been over six weeks of work. Good work. Getting-lost-in-it, getting-lifted work. It's been, God help me, *revelatory* work. And it's ours. "That's unreasonable," I tell him.

He looks hard. "Did you just tell me I'm unreasonable? You— You're standing there staring at me like you're totally dumbfounded. Which seems pretty impossible. Is this why you've been staying with me?"

"Teddy. Of course not."

"Because I don't know anymore," he says. "Seeing what I just saw throws a lot into question, doesn't it? Did you— Wait." He dips his head to the ground, takes a deep breath. "You mentioned this project, the first night you came to the store. And then you never touched it again. Even when I asked you about your work, you avoided the question. Did you come to town to specifically solicit my permission?"

"No."

"Because if you did, I'm not giving it to you."

"I never asked you for anything," I tell him. "We do *not* need your permission. That story in there is mine. It belongs to me. It's not your story."

"That's such a weak argument. And moreover, it's a *lie*. It's my prerogative to say no. My entire life was fucking *traumatized* by what we just saw in there."

"Who's to say mine wasn't?" I counter.

He hisses, "I had to testify in court in front of those girls. I had to sit there and have them look at me, knowing that my father had ruined their lives. *And I don't want that to be in any story ever.*"

"Teddy." I try to take his arm.

He shakes me off, holding his hand out in front of him as if to keep me from getting any closer. "Don't wheedle me, goddammit."

My mouth closes. I hear my teeth click together.

"Maybe this practice of taking all your personal shit and publicly manipulating it until your life is explained sufficiently to your liking works for you. But I can't do it. And I won't. If you can sleep at night after putting something like that out into the world, then good for you, Sharon. If it makes you feel better, great. But you have no right to make that decision for anybody else. And just to be clear: Your pain is *nothing* compared to mine."

"That's not fair." My voice is high and loud. I scrub at my eyes with the back of my hand.

"I'm telling you now," he says. "Emphatically. Do not do this. Do not turn me into another *Nashville Combat*. You want an answer? This is it. *No.*"

"It doesn't belong to you," I tell him. As I say it, I can feel how flimsy it sounds.

"It does," he says. "People will see it, and they will know that it is me. They'll think I had something to do with this."

"I love you," I tell him. "I would never want to hurt you."

This is a fight, and it has every sound of a fight—the sharp shards bookended by concrete-thick silences. Teddy glares at me. The expression renders him unrecognizable. And for the first time since I've known him, I see it. I see Honus Caudill in his face, behind the eyes, in the slope of his forehead. It is the worst possible time to spot this, but I can't help it. I feel myself shrink under my wool coat.

The moment breaks when he turns to the side and rubs his eyes. When he looks up, they're pink, watery. He's crying. Oh fuck. I made him cry. "It bothers me that you could even consider this," he says. "Let alone execute it. You spent hundreds of man-hours carrying this out. What would make you think I didn't need to know about this?"

"If I didn't care what you think, you never would have seen this."

"That's your best defense? Sharon." His shoulders slump. He shakes his head miserably. "I never would have imagined that you could be this deceptive. Never."

"I did *not* deceive you." And this is where I lose it. A sob gasps out of my chest. I bend over, trying to cover it up. He does not move toward me.

"What do you call keeping something from me for months, then springing it on me without warning? That is *nothing* if not deception."

His voice breaks. I stay down. I don't want to see his face at that moment. I would never be able to wipe it from the inside of my eyes.

When I straighten, he has composed himself. Hands are back on hips. "You made a movie about Mel's mother. Who was stabbed in prison shortly thereafter. Correct? What did she think about *Nashville Combat*? How do you think that made her feel?"

I am silent.

"There's a lot of stuff about you and Mel out there, by the way. And a lot of it's not good." He goes to rub his face again, knocks his glasses askew. "You know, I'd be inclined to blame Mel for this if it wasn't so obviously your story in there. Mel's a jackass. She's a horrible influence on you. But you played just as big a hand in this."

"Don't talk about her like that."

"She inserts me as the star in her pathetic movie? I should be calling her a lot worse. To do this constitutes *theft*, Sharon. It makes you both *thieves*." He points to the door. He knows they're listening, too. "Are you admitting that you agree with Mel that I have no stake in this? That you and she are in accord in this decision?"

And the way he says this squirms under my skin so much—that big, sanctimonious *are you in accord*—that I snap. Scream, "*Yes*. This is what I do and you know it. We don't need your consent. Now or ever. This is not yours. It is *not goddamned yours*."

A light in the upstairs of a neighboring house flicks on. We both fall silent.

Teddy says quietly, "I wish you could hear yourself right now, so you could listen to the absolute bullshit you are trotting out." He points to the door again. Says louder, "All this proves is that *that* is the only kind of partnership you can do."

We stand there gazing at each other, our faces half in shadow in the January air, that heavy Southern wet that sinks the sinuses. Teddy is more right than he knows. I will push as far as I need to, to make this project get up and live. The damage was done the moment we watched the first scenes for ourselves. What's been the source of my happiness here? Teddy? Or was it really, truly getting back to work, getting *lost* in the work again, its gorgeous forward momentum?

We're finished. We both know it. We're just dancing now.

"I'm leaving," he says. He strides onto the porch, yanks open the door. "Car's leaving right now unless you want to walk," he calls inside, then jumps down off the porch and moves away.

Mel sticks her head out the door. "Teddy. Come on."

"Fuck you, Mel."

She looks at me. "Well. Fuck me, then."

A LITTLE STRANGE

ONE WEEK LATER, WE CLOSE UP THE CARRIAGE HOUSE AND LEAVE Louisville.

"We could rent a house in Faulkner," I say as we drive east on I-64. "We could do it cheap. Like three hundred bucks a month."

"Huh." Mel's drumming her fingers on the steering wheel, reading signs to gas stations aloud: Love's, Fast Track Waddy Peytona, Shell. "Do you really want to do that, though? I mean, we're more or less done down here. Those guys moved out on the fifteenth. The studio's empty. We could get more subletters, I guess, but it doesn't make much sense now. Do you not want to go back to New York?"

I can't go back. I can't do New York like I am, wounded, still limping. I can't do the dodging and weaving, the constant intimidation. I can't do the specific kind of loneliness that comes with being there. I think about the crowds of people pushing at each other as they climb from a busy subway station, all blank faces and swinging hands. My stomach burns.

"Not really," I tell her. "I mean, what am I going to do up there?"

"What do you mean, what are you going to do? Work. Go back to your life. Faulkner's a pipe dream. You would go crazy there."

"Maybe not. Peace and quiet. Cheap rent."

"All our real equipment's back in New York. We made do here, but the stuff we're going to need for the brunt of the work is up there."

I lean my head against the window. "I just can't do it anymore," I tell her. "It's expensive, it's cold as fuck, and I can't make anything decent up there. It seems like everyone around me is making amazing shit and I'm just treading water. I know that's not really the way it is. But still."

"Dude, everyone's a little marketer up there. Don't let it get to you."

"It still feels awful. I just keep imagining a roomful of Brecky Tollivers who keep telling me where they did their undergrad and won't stop tweeting to take a piss. I'm goddamned tired of feeling on the outside of everything." I'm just complaining now. But Mel keeps nodding.

"Teddy hates me." I look to her. "Right? *Hates* me."

She hesitates. It was Ryan and Tatum who fetched my belongings from Teddy's apartment. I could hear Mel outside on her cell talking to them as we packed up to leave. There were lots of *shut up dude*s and *right right right*s. Mel nodding with her bleakest *shit happens* face. Apparently they didn't know the boy in the clips was modeled on Teddy—had no idea, in fact, what had sparked our argument, until Teddy told them.

"He won't hate you forever," she says finally.

We pass Frankfort. Mel lights a smoke and flips the bird at a sign for Kentucky Republican headquarters. "You know what I would have done? Tell him *right after* he shoots his load. All those sleep endorphins swimming through his system. He would have been cool with anything then." She glances at me. "Joke, Kisses."

"It's my fault. My mess," I say. "The blame's on me."

"You were not making this to hurt him or anyone else. I'm sure he knows that, deep down. It's just." She shrugs. "His dad's a sore spot with him, you know? He struggles with it. You can tell. He saw all that stuff play out on a screen and freaked. He's not used to this kind of thing."

"Who is used to this kind of thing?"

She shrugs. "Artists and sociopaths? I dunno." She packs a smoke thoughtfully on the steering wheel. "Maybe I'm a little surprised that you never brought it up, but that's irrelevant. You weren't obligated to discuss this with him in the first place. We sought him out to see where and who he was now. That's all. I'm sorry if he feels offended. I hope he finds closure. And I wish him the best."

And that's that. She looks at me.

"I messed up, Mel. This is not something to feel good about."

"You did *not*. Think about whatever let you walk away. You didn't compromise with him. You are committed. Look." She pushes her finger down on the center console to punctuate. "When you take the things that happen to you, the things that make you who you are, and you use them, you own them. Things aren't just happening *to* you anymore. Make this thing because you are *compelled* to, and because it's yours. And do it whether or not it suits Teddy 'Fuck you Mel' Caudill or anyone else."

She merges onto the Mountain Parkway amid semis and RAV4s. One more night in Faulkner to pick up our things. Then back north. Another steely January hell in New York. Maybe I can wrap myself up in this thing. Spend a couple more seasons cramped in front of the drawing board, biding my time until my life comes to find me.

MOM'S MALIBU IS THE only car parked in front. We find her hunched over the kitchen counter pecking at a laptop, brow creased. A pair of reading glasses perches at the end of her nose on a beaded chain reading NANA up one side and MAMAW down the other. She looks at us, mouth a straight line.

"Hey, Mom."

"Well." She pushes herself back from the counter and lights a Doral. "Y'all have a nice time in Louisville?" Two smeared syllables: *Looo-vuhl.*

"It was okay."

"Now, how does a weekend turn into near on three months, again?"

"We ended up doing some of the project stuff there."

"Mmm hmm." She crimps her mouth like she's holding in a cough drop.

"I thought you'd be at work," I say.

"Off today."

"Oh."

She leans into the counter and stares at me. Something's simmering. "Melody," she says, "I need to talk to Sharon alone for a second. Could you go into the other room, please?"

Melody. Mel looks sidelong at me. "No prob." She steps out.

I put my bag down, pins and needles in my bad leg. "What's up."

She waits a beat, then spins the laptop around with a flourish. It is the wild orange-and-lime banner of Filming Forum. The article: "*Nashville Combat* Creators' Next Project: Life of Kisses?"

"I did a Google search," Mom says. "This popped up first thing when I typed in your name."

"You know how to run a Google search?"

"Sharon, I swear to God, do you think I'm stupid or something? Are you gonna explain this? Are you making some sort of cartoon out of us? Why'd they write this?"

I hold my hands out, take a deep breath. "This is a blog. The last movie did okay. They've been talking about us more. Someone caught wind of some gossip and they decided to post it. And our agent *let* them post it, because she figured it was good press."

Her bifocals slip down her nose. She fumbles them off. "So they just made it up? Well, that ain't legal, putting out lies like that about people."

"Well, it's not an out-and-out *lie*."

"So you are making a movie out of us?"

"It's not about you," I tell her. "It's about me."

"That *is* making a movie out of us."

"It is not. Why are you hell-bent on believing that anything that has to do with me also has to do with you?"

"Because it does."

"That's right. You're the goddamn center of the universe."

"Watch your mouth."

"It's not illegal," I say. "Publishing a half-truth on a blog is sloppy, but it's not illegal."

She exhales hard through her nostrils. "You best stop correcting me. I don't care if you've had a stroke or not, it don't give you the right to come in here and set me straight wherever the hell you think I go wrong. And after you disappear for near on three months."

I'd forgotten the bleeding, limping endurance race that is arguing with my mother. I raise my hands and let them slap down to my sides. "I don't know what to say to you that's not gonna hit a nerve, Mom. I piss you off with almost everything I do. Either that or I amuse you with how dumb, or weird, or pretentious I am. Why do you think I come home so rarely? Or why I didn't call you when I almost *died*? '*You had a stroke? Well, what'd you do that for?*'"

She blinks at me.

"Just once, I'd like to feel like I'm a part of this family. I've just had one of the worst weeks of my life. Would it kill you to ease up for once?"

"What happened," she demands.

"Listen to you! My God, your *tone*, Mom. It's like getting punched in the face."

"I'll talk if you quit yelling at me," she says. "I'll talk when you finish yelling at your mother."

I stare at her.

"Four years," she says. "That's how long it had been since you were home, before this."

"And I just outlined why."

"If I'd spent four years away from home, your mamaw would have died of a broken heart."

"Funny. You appear to be alive."

"You best shut that smart mouth up."

I feel my face flush. "Don't talk to me that way," I tell her. "And don't you dare pretend your interest in my life and what I do is larger than it actually is. You didn't come to my college graduation. You thought the first cartoons we ever made were a joke. There were second and third cousins who knew Dad was dead before I did. How was that supposed to make me feel? I never even got a fucking explanation from you for that."

"He wasn't your father," she yells.

Everything stops. My stomach settles somewhere around my feet. "What?"

The glow from the laptop flickers out. She reaches over and smacks it shut. She's gone too far to go back, and she knows it.

"What did you just say," I repeat.

Mom goes recalcitrant, now, her voice small and wavery. "He was mad at me," she says. "Daddy. But he loved you anyways. Loved you enough to sign the birth certificate." She starts to fidget with her glasses.

I shift off my bad leg, wobbling. Stunned. I hear Mel cough in the next room. "Are you being serious," I say.

"Sharon, please." Mom's voice breaks. "I'm so sorry."

"Who else knows."

"Nobody."

It's coming to me, in bits and pieces. I think of Allen, behind the church, during the funeral. I think of the great aunt who hugged Shauna, but merely grasped my hand, avoiding my eye. Dad at the dinner table, studying my face—at ten or eleven years old—as if trying to figure something out. His youngest, the most alien from him, the most distant. Whole worlds between us.

"No no," I say slowly. "You *know* Dad told people. He could get pretty chatty when he was wasted, remember? He told Uncle Allen.

That I do know. That stupid fuck had it written all over his face whenever I was in the room. Probably the rest of his brothers, too. That's why they were always such dicks to me. They were fucking mean, Mom. They were downright ugly to me when I was a kid."

"Buncha sleazy hillbilly assholes. You shouldnta paid them any attention."

"I was a *kid*."

"I wanted to protect you," she says.

"Well, you did a crap job."

"It was for your own good, to not know," she says louder. "How would it feel to grow up a little girl, knowing your daddy maybe wasn't yours?"

"It felt fairly fucking shitty, that's how."

She flaps a hand at me. "Oh, you didn't know."

"I always *knew* something was wrong," I hiss.

Her head is bent. I see a tear slide down her nose.

"So who was it," I say. "If you want to redeem yourself at all, you need to tell me."

She hitches in a breath, wipes at her eyes with both hands. Sniffs. "Walt Kroger. Used to deliver the mail," she whispers. "He's been dead a year. Maybe two."

"He was my father?"

"I don't know," she says. "There was a man from Owensboro out here with the extension office for a while. Then he went back. His name was Hatfield. Maybe him."

"There's *two* maybes? Christ Jesus, Mom."

She presses her hands to her face. Removes them. Blinks. "You remember the Caudills," she says. "Next door. Little Teddy, the one you used to play with."

My entire body goes cold. I shake my head. No. No no.

"Honus Caudill," she says. "That was his name. Could have been him."

I hear Mel exhale.

"Honus Caudill," I repeat slowly. "The *pedophile*. That one?"

She snorts harder. "Maybe. No one knew anything about him

then. I had no idea." She pulls out a pink Kleenex. Blows her nose. "Your daddy and I were separated. None of you know that, but we were, for a little while." She stops, takes a watery breath. "I was different back then. I'm not proud of it."

"You sure it wasn't Dad? You sure you didn't, you know, *accidentally* sleep with him while you were sleeping with *three other guys*?"

She rolls her eyes. "Oh, shut up," she mutters, making her way to the paper towels and tearing off a big hank.

"You don't get to tell me to shut up right now." I point over the rise, to where the Caudill house once stood. "Did *he* know?"

"No. Even then he was . . . a little strange. I didn't want him knowing nothing."

"How was he *a little strange*," I say.

She shrugs, says nothing.

"How," I scream. She jumps. "*How* was he a little strange? I deserve to know. You owe me this, goddammit."

"Good God, Sharon," she bleats. "He could get *rough* when you're not supposed to, all right? When he shouldn't have been." Her head tilts forward, her shoulders tremble. She's sobbing. "God bless it, I hope you ain't been with anyone who's done you that way. Trying to get you to do things you don't wanna do—"

"Okay. Please stop." I cover my face. "Everyone knows you'd let me get hit by a train and not do a fucking thing about it. Please stop paying lip service to this bogus mothering instinct that does not *exist*."

She lifts her head. Her face twists into a snarl. "You know what," she says, "you always thought you were just a little bit above the rest of us. Since you were little. We all knew it. They used to talk about it. Well, let me tell you something, honey. You most definitely are *not*."

"How in the fuck can you *project* that onto a little kid. That's sick. How dare you."

"I ain't projectin nothin, darling. I know an uppity bitch when I see one."

I hear Mel shift in the next room, then stick her head in, cutting her eyes at me. I hold my hand up.

"And Daddy did, too. Cause he didn't like it when someone looked down on him. And now the whole world's gonna look down on us, and that's exactly what you want. You ain't changed a bit. You're still a spoiled brat. And a mistake."

The room starts to spin. Sounds soften—only my mother, stationary, remains clear. She was searching for the worst thing to say, and she found it. Overshot her mark, even.

It's a moment before I can speak. "I'll tell you something that'll make you a lot sorrier," I yell. "If what you said is true, I just spent the last three months fucking my half brother."

She lets out a sound. Covers her mouth.

"That's right. I fucked someone I might be related to. That's my going-back-to-Kentucky story. So thanks for that."

"I think I'm gonna be sick," she whimpers.

"That makes two of us." I grab my bag off the floor. "Thank you for finally owning up to this. I'm going to need to shower in *bleach* before I can get this day off of me."

She hunches her shoulders, starts to warble again. "I'm so sorry," she says.

"Stop. You are no one's victim here." I point at her, make sure she's looking at me. "Don't ever contact me again. Do you hear me? Ever."

I stick my head in the living room. "*Mel.* Let's go."

Mel speeds past me with our luggage. "Right. See you, Mrs. Kisses."

IRREFUTABLE LOVE

WE DRIVE TO NEW YORK, THE ONLY PLACE LEFT FOR US TO GO: east, then north. Before we know it, we're on the other side, that long strip of Pennsylvania that is prelude to I-95, where the trip is more destination than origin.

On the way there, I keep Mel's flipbook in my hand. I watch myself grow up and empty out, over and over. I stare at myself in the rearview mirror. Do I look like Red? No. Do I look like Shauna? No.

I turn to Mel. "Do I look like—"

"Absolutely not. You do not look like Teddy. Stop asking."

We stop at a Love's in the Lehigh Valley. I stare into the restroom mirror, my mother's voice in my head. There's a very particular malaise that comes from being screamed at, when someone names you something terrible in an absolute fury—like something green and vital inside you has wilted. If she is just now calling me a *bitch*, a *mistake,* she must have felt this way for years. It was an ultimate judgment. I cannot pretend that it does not matter.

We cross the Verrazano-Narrows at midnight, power plants glowing in the dark, and up the Brooklyn–Queens Expressway. Moisture runs down my face. It hurts, seeing that cold, radiant skyline. We coast back into the city.

W E GET THE LAST installment of the Hollingsworth money and go to work cleaning the studio, filled with cigarette butts and half-empty beers and the stink of twenty-two-year-old dudes. It's numbly satisfying, having something to do.

Once we've made the place spotless, I am tapped. My mind is a frayed wire—no sparks, no heat. Everything—our cork wall for the storyboard, our drafting tables—is primed for work, except for me. "I don't know if I can do it," I say, curling up on the couch in a fetal position.

Mel squints at me, biting her lip. "We've already got a chunk, you know," she says. "It's not like we're starting from scratch."

I cover my head with my hands.

The next morning, she finds me on the couch again. I'm watching the trunk scene on my laptop: the soundless fluidity of my face, Teddy's hands. The quick slice of movement as the trunk is opened— how it seems fast yet deliberate, done with just the right amount of gravity. Mel was in peak form in Louisville. Maybe me too. The work is immaculate. No one walk or nose-scratch or cigarette flick like any other.

Mel flops down on the floor and laces her hands behind her head. Peers up at me, mouth screwed to one side.

Says, "Did I tell you about that article I read?"

She begins to tell me of a dancer she's read about who works almost exclusively with falling. The dances she choreographs are built of leaps from upper platforms and edges—the swoop, the plummet, the dive, the pitch. Dancers trained for the company have to first buck their natural fear of falling, correcting the body's self-protective horror of giving itself over to gravity. A fall is a fall, no matter how deliberate; it will never fail to stop your heart.

To practice, the dancers assume a plank position, as if readying themselves for a push-up, and then lift their arms, letting their bodies collapse to the ground. "It's a *controlled* fall," Mel says. "It hurts, but it trains you to deal with the fear so you don't start hyperventilating when you dive off a ledge. It's your body going against instinct."

"It's smacking your face into the floor."

"You're not afraid to walk, are you?" she says. "Every step you take is like a little fall. You're just so used to it that the fear's not there."

I give her my best *durr* face. Point to my cane, propped up by the door.

She rolls her eyes and climbs up. "Let's try it. Come on."

I slump over. Look at her through my hair.

"Come on, Kisses. Do it. Make sweet love to the *motion*. Become *one* with it."

I know what she's trying to do. I also know she won't leave me alone until I do it with her.

And that's how we both come to be on the floor, in plank positions, side by side. "Okay," she says. "One. Two. Three."

Nothing happens.

"Fuck," she says. "See? Your body doesn't want to do it."

"It means we're dumber than our own bodies."

"Let's do it just once," she says. "Once will be enough. Okay? On three."

We both take a deep breath.

"One. Two. Three."

Our elbows unlock at the same time and we fall. It feels like a mistake, like we really have jumped off a bridge together, and when I begin to move, I feel a split-second stab of regret. This is ridiculous. What have I done? I would give anything—*anything*—to go back, to have kept myself upright.

And then, there's a rush, so brief it's a blink. I'm falling. I have weight, and yet I am weightless, at the mercy of something larger than myself. It is reverse flight.

I have finally discorporated.

We hit the floor at the same time with a smack. We groan. Mel rolls over onto her back. Her lip is bleeding.

"Did you become one with the motion?" I ask her.

She punches me in the shoulder. Groans, "Mother*fuck*."

MEL TAKES OVER AN entire side of the studio and claims it as her Sharon Wall, blowing up each frame of the flipbook and posting them in chronological order. She keeps a sheet draped over it until she's done, then unveils it to me one evening with the warning, "Please don't puke."

When it is revealed, I freeze: Sharons from age zero to thirty-two, all present and accounted for. A progression of *me*s, each slightly different from her predecessor, a thousand tiny factors of difference comprising the new person awaiting fifty frames down. Each face has an expression, tight or loose, watchful or wan, that seems to barely conceal a complex system of inner workings: valves and pistons, desire and sad appetite.

I look at all those versions of myself looking back at me with a sort of expectancy. I feel something with long roots stir inside my chest. I would not be able to stand looking at this wall if I couldn't finish this thing. I would be too ashamed. Too angry at myself.

"Looks like a serial killer lives here," Mel says.

"A serial killer with one victim."

She pinches my cheek. Sings, "You're a special girl!"

MISSING TEDDY HAS BECOME a physical need. The heat of it moves through my bloodstream with nowhere to go but back around the track, tapering, returning. It feels like my body is digesting itself. I call. Hope he will have forgiven me. Grit my teeth against my mother's voice in my head. The ring always cuts off at the second or third beat, directs to voicemail: "You have reached Ted Caudill at Weirdo Video. For product and shipping information, please dial the store landline at 502 . . ."

I'm getting the old jitters, the adrenaline that was once with me all the time, nearly unbearable as my brain pumped away with the fantasy. But the fever is different now. It knows its only end is itself.

Nevertheless, it is this longing that finally lights the fuse for work. All that want, it opens me up, heats my insides so that it is impossible to sit still. I need to fashion a way out for myself, and this need clicks something crucial into place, bringing me back to my drafting board.

The fire catches. It's on. Someone hits the crazy switch and we go into hypermode, skull-first. Unstoppable. We are making this cartoon.

I'M USUALLY UP FIRST, around six. I shower, pull on jeans, and stumble downstairs to the studio. I make coffee in the French press, knocking yesterday's grounds into the garbage. Not clean? Don't care. More juice for the ride. Precious fuel. Jitters with purpose.

I take over the storyboarding corner, sequencing, filling in gaps. It's the final building process: seeing the whole, seeing the *holes*. Knowing when we're not done. Around noon, Mel steps in, half-awake, slurping the cold dregs of the French press, and looks to the board to check out the progress. She may know how to get us started, but I know how to keep her in her seat.

We start inbetweening in earnest, two mad cogs in a wheel, a perpetual-motion machine of the most badass proportions. We shift out drafting boards to face one another and each take a scene: flip, scratch, done, flip, scratch, done. Coffee cedes to Red Bull. Ashtrays fill with butts. We bust out the work-trance playlist: Wu-Tang, Nas, Funkadelic. We dance slightly as we work, whispering lyrics under our breath: flip, scratch, done. Flip, scratch, done. The dark comes and we segue to postpunk off-rhythms, an uneasy beat, Romeo Void,

Joy Division. Sometimes, my hands tremor without my noticing and I'll go through a whole run of a hundred tracings before I realize they're shit. I do them over. When Mel starts to flex her hands, I know she's getting tired. I tell her to break while I keep going, slower, bending close to the table to ensure it's right.

At the ten P.M. point, our stomachs are cramping and our hands are begging for mercy. We break. Mel pours the rum and cokes. I order tacos, Thai, sushi. I change into a long, threadbare maxi, what Mel calls my "eatin dress." "You putting on your eatin dress, Mamaw?" she yells.

"It's not a fucking eating dress. It's a *tunic*."

"Listen to her," Mel says to the empty room, flopping down on the couch. "*It ain't a fuckin eatin dress*. That thing's a eatin dress if I've ever seen one. Not *an* eatin dress. *A* eatin dress. Who cares if you slop gravy down the front? *It's a eatin dress*."

We've let our calluses soften. By the end of the first month, we both have to tape our fingers to catch the bleeding. Once, when she stays up late, Mel pounds a bloody smiley face on a piece of scrap paper and leaves it on my table. "Dude, this is gross," I tell her.

She grins, red-eyed and rabbity. Goes, "*Heh*." She got her hands on some coke; some nights, when she's super-juiced, she'll do a bump and work until dawn, greeting me when I wake up.

Throughout, the Sharon Wall remains intact. It's a hundred *me*s, watching me sleep, jerk off, eat bowls of oatmeal, sketch, do PT exercises. Watching the hair grow back down to my shoulders, get cut back up into a crew. Waiting.

I spend days lost in our world, sketching, editing. When I am inside our project, I am fluid, my identity negotiable. I don't want to go outside. I don't want to see anyone except Mel. I let a back molar rot completely. The pain is so intense, it finally forces me to leave the studio. I visit a Puerto Rican dentist to have it yanked for half price. I sweat in the examining chair, tears rolling down the sides of my face and into my ears, and still cannot wait to get back to the studio, back to the drafting board.

We're getting closer.

• • •

A COUPLE OF DAYS later, Mel pulls up in a Ford F-150 hauling a near-new, thirty-six-inch Cintiq, purchased from a Manhattan designer who sold it to pay off gambling debts. A top-of-the-line digital tablet in full HD, glimmering and sleek. Wide-screen, full and flowering pixel density. Full rotational possibilities. Zero lag time in line formation. She was probably drooling as she drove it down Knickerbocker.

Unilluminated, it resembles a very large, adjustable monitor. But lit from within, glowing and slightly blue, it becomes perfection, the ideal blank space waiting to be filled. It will make inbetweening faster; editing, a breeze. It will supplant stacks and stacks of onionskin with mere strokes on a screen. No more pencil tests, no more endless, endless drafts. No more recycling bins filled with castoffs, one out of every three drawings wasted. No more bullshit hours spent scanning drawings, impatient, one hand holding a cigarette, the other feeding sheets into the maw of the machine. We will sketch directly onto the screen from now on. A glowing, digital miracle.

We carry it into the studio and stare at it all afternoon, gawping, two monkeys with their first mirror. Wordlessly, Mel fishes two new digital pro pens from her pocket. Hands one to me. Tosses a case of detachable nibs onto the table.

"It's gorgeous."

"I know," she says.

"Should we be doing this?" I whisper.

Mel laughs at me. "We'll still keep some paper around," she says. "I won't torch the lightboard. Don't worry."

You can draw on paper and feel like a god, but it takes technology to make you truly divine.

It seems like cheating, the first time. But only the first time. I am shocked at the lack of guilt I feel. We start keeping the room dark at all hours to see the screen clearly, wipe it down to prevent a yellow nicotine film from building up.

The first part of our cartoon, we decide, will be old-method—

sketching, scanning, and editing from there. But the ending will be a new kind of baby, one born of the Cintiq. Our first paperless production. We've never used this much software before; we've never felt so wedded to a machine. But here we are. The Cintiq makes this the fastest project we've ever completed. Neither of us will argue with the results, which are not radically different. This story, we reason, is a journey. Movie Sharon will emerge into a crisper, more vibrant world. And so will we.

Stroking the screen, Mel says dreamily, "I've named her Carlene."

Days turn into weeks. I fall asleep on top of sketches and wake up with charcoal smeared on my arms and cheeks. Non-photo blue pencils roll next to spoons in our kitchen. There's a glare in my vision now, from the Cintiq, when I walk to the bodega for pop and cigarettes.

Mel starts cracking a fifth earlier and earlier, spiking her Pepsi as soon as night falls. She's doing it again. Getting drunk at the board, like she did toward the end of *Nashville Combat*. It worries me more than the coke: Drinking, for Mel, is not just a habit. It is the country in which she lives as a native, a part of her always there, even when abroad. It's subtler, sneakier. It's something that can take her away.

I don't like it, but she works quietly, the bend in her back growing more and more pronounced as she proceeds, outlined in the light of the Cintiq's screen. I go to bed at midnight. She's up until six. We overlap in ten-hour increments.

WE STRUGGLE TO NAME our baby. Discarded titles: *The List. Unlocked. Sharon's Stroke. Super Stroke!* Everything's stupid. Nothing works. "Why can't we just call it what it is and be done with it," I say.

Mel says, "I agree. Let's call it what it is. You drew what you wanted, right? So why not call it what you want most?"

We end up calling it *Irrefutable Love*.

• • •

THAT SUMMER, SIX MONTHS after leaving Kentucky, we finish the draft. Our cartoon—as it will come to exist—takes its first breaths.

It started with the men, but it ends with me. Mediums change. While the men of the List do surface in Sharon's legendary freak-out montage—that dark, heady universe-hump Mel had envisioned that would eventually precede the stroke scene—that is the only place for them, in this thing we've made. Real story told, I finally cut the dudes loose.

The festival blurb we will eventually use is this:

> *Irrefutable Love* (75 minutes). After a life-changing stroke, an artist experiences her recovery process as a hero's quest through the nightmare wilderness of her past. Animation.

Extended story: A girl and a boy make a dark discovery that forces them on a journey into the slithering, sick secrets of adulthood. We decide that our story is the girl's pilgrimage, and its shape is that of a parabola: the finding, the forgetting, the remembering. The descent into a life in which she consumes everything to fill the void blasted into her by the realization that this darkness exists, tamping the hunger down with food and sex and work and sheer hours of distraction, the more involved, the better. There are shots of the girl as an adult, at the drawing board, the closest she ever comes to hitting the truth of anything. Ailing on the inside and the outside, both pursuer and pursued. So much heat in her head. She shatters.

For the stroke, we try to envision what it would look like for a brain to break. We go textural for the creeper factor, using ripped pages from the KJV and defunct Houghton Mifflin grade school readers as backdrop and then smearing them with coffee grounds to simulate the oncoming storm, the thick, shitty haze that conceals everything. We envision the stroke as a night tour through a deep forest, a George Romero–Tobe Hooper monsterscape in which trees cry blood and faceless hunters watch, hands gripping blades, gory hammers. An abandoned murder house, frozen in a mid-1980s Christmas, provides shelter for one brief night. Dead Magnavoxes lie discarded in bushes, screens shattered. Ravens rise from a pond in one slick stream. Discarded love seats fill the clearings, stuffing and snakes emerging from their ripped bellies.

It is a chase. The woman needs to find her way out, become stronger, better, faster, before she is consumed. To survive means to escape. And when the footfalls come so close, she can feel the ground behind her trembling, she sees a rim of daylight on the horizon. She shakes off her limp at last. She runs.

The film is largely without dialogue. There is respiration and gut gurgles and sighs, footsteps in leaves. A wildcat screaming like a woman. In the forest, distant singing, too faint to hear the words. With scenes featuring me and the boy Teddy, we got two kids—the son and daughter of one of Donnie's friends—to talk gibberish over each other, a warm tangle of singing and giggling.

We wanted to create the experience of going through a tunnel—it has its bright spots, but for the most part the viewer is closed within, dunked in something dark blue and viscous for seventy-five minutes. I wanted to make something that made me feel the way I felt that summer we found the pictures. The summer I discovered that there were things that could wound me so badly, I might not be the same person after. The summer I also discovered that there were things that could keep me existing in the world, good things that made me forget.

Irrefutable Love is us making a place where redemption exists, a place where we can all be together. Me and the girls from the pictures. They are there to meet me as I crawl from the woods, scratched and bleeding. Their faces open up. They have eyes again. They part their lips and I hear cicadas, one or one hundred, impossible to tell. Their mouths open wide and the cicadas are loosed in a warm, iridescent stream, the rich alto hum filling the air. To forgive, to forgive. They hum.

I draw as I always have, maybe better. I draw what I'd most like to have. And we come to make a beautiful and horrible thing, a gentle beast with a deadly underbelly. It is funny/not funny. It is filled with ghosts. It is the happiest ending we have ever envisioned.

• • •

I T BECOMES FALL.

My life away from the drawing board has a spooky reverb quality. I often go a solid week without showering. I forget to pay our electric bill and Con Ed shuts off the power for a whole day. I sleep in fits and starts, never able to settle in for more than two hours.

My mother calls and leaves messages. I delete them without listening. When Shauna calls, I pick up. "Are you really making a movie out of us?" she says.

"No, it's not about you."

"What's it about, then?"

"It's about me."

"Well. *That* should be interesting."

"Maybe."

"You should make a movie about my dipshit husband," she says. "He's funny as hell to watch. You'd make a million dollars."

"I might take you up on that. When the teat of inspiration runs dry."

She giggles. "You say the weirdest shit."

"Completely involuntary."

"Why don't you pick up when Mom calls?"

"I am not talking to her, Shauna."

"She feels bad. Maybe she has a hard time saying so, but she's sorry."

"I find that difficult to believe."

"She's not sleeping at night. She got after Jaeden the other day for spilling something on the rug. And she almost never gripes at the kids."

"Did she tell you to call? She's sitting right there, isn't she."

"*No.* Oh my *God.* What do you think I am?"

"Sorry."

"You think Mom and I are, like, *besties* or something. Do you think I'm on her side about any of this?"

"So she told you what she told me?" I say. "About Honus Caudill and the other, what, *three* contestants for my paternity? She can go fuck herself. Period."

"Oh, I know. It's disgusting. If I were you, I wouldn't be talking to her, either."

It occurs to me that I shovel a lot onto Shauna. She probably gets the bad stuff from Mom, too. She lives right next door, after all. I never stopped to think about the shrapnel she might be catching in all this.

"You know what," Shauna continues. "She's probably wrong. I think she said that because she was mad and now she's too embarrassed to admit it. You don't even look like Honus Caudill. You know who you look like? Daddy's mamaw. The one who went crazy and stabbed her second husband with a fork."

"Didn't she have a Cro-Magnon eyebrow?"

"We should get a paternity test. Find out for sure."

"I'm afraid of what I might find out, at this point."

"I wanna come up for a visit," she says.

"You are welcome anytime. Come up and see Bushwick. The rats are little, but they're mean."

"I'd like to see that."

SECOND DRAFT. I SQUEEZE everything I can from my memories, but my memories start to change, like Teddy said they would. I picture the trunk and my brain generates a girl, eyeless, her mouth filled with cicadas.

It's lonely, finishing the movie. There's a space where even Mel cannot come in.

But I'm not sure Mel notices. Past a certain hour now, she calls it a day and steps out. She's seeing an undergrad from NYU who leaves blond hairs on her sweaters. She's also seeing an executive from HBO who always sends a car, a black Lincoln Navigator, to take her into Manhattan. "She's older," Mel says, and no more.

When Mel hits a distracted patch, she makes it count. The drinking seems weirdly lucid, nearly professional. Sometimes I catch her staring out the window of the studio, smiling faintly to herself. She leaves for the night more and more but always returns in the early morning. I wake to find her in the kitchen once, doot-dooing to herself, bellying up to the counter while she makes eggs. "Wakey, wakey, tickleshits," she greets me. "You want toast?"

"Where have you been." I fumble for coffee.

She produces the French press, pours me a steaming cup. "Dog track."

"You lie."

She spins around to replace the press, gets the half-and-half from the fridge. "Hanging out in Manhattan," she says. "Just rolled back in." She breaks off pieces of bacon, puts them in her mouth like buck teeth. Beams at me.

Later that day, I glance over her shoulder. She's scrolling through apartment listings.

O NE NIGHT I'M RUNNING the forest scene with the circle of girls through the editing program on the Cintiq when Mel strides in wearing new dark jeans, motorcycle boots, a men's tuxedo jacket. She is clipping on a pair of gold cuff links I do not recognize. "How's it going," she says.

I turn. "Look at you, fancy. Where do you think you're going?"

She shrugs and smiles down at her shoes, giving the cuff links a final tweak. "Figured I'd head out," she says. "There's this thing, in the city. Obligatory. The old ball and chain says so. You've got this scene, right?"

"Yeah. I've got it." Ball and chain? That's commitment for Mel. I watch her go to the fridge and pull out a bottle of water. "So does this old ball and chain ever come to Brooklyn?"

Mel wipes her mouth. "Not much. She's old-school. Still thinks you can't go past the Lorimer stop on the L train."

"That's old-school, all right." I turn back to the screen. Adopting a nonchalant tone, ask, "Do you think you could ever live in Manhattan?"

I hear her pause, swallow. Say, "Maybe, yeah. I mean, there are parts of Harlem that are cheaper than Brooklyn now. Could be okay. Why do you ask?"

I shrug.

"Well. Fart lives in Harlem. He loves it. Has his own little garden and everything." She finishes the bottle, deposits it in the recycling. Checks something on her phone.

Then looks up. "You know, the older I get, the more frequently I do things that surprise myself. I thought that, like, at some point, I'd really *know* who I was, right? But that's not the case. I've done all sorts of shit I never thought I'd do. So who knows, man. What, do you want to move to Manhattan?"

"Me?" I say. "No. I'm snug as a bug."

Mel rummages in the closet. Produces her good wool coat.

"It would be nice to meet this old-school ball and chain sometime," I say.

"Totally. I'll get her to come out."

When hell's a skating rink, you will. "Awesome."

She shrugs on her coat and gives my head a gentle tap. "Don't bust your brains out on it," she says. "It's coming together really well."

"Thanks," I say.

I'm restless after this conversation, scattered. I fall asleep on the couch, telling myself that I'm taking a break, that I'll get back up and work some more in a couple of hours, when the door opens and I hear the uneven *pat-step-pat* of Mel coming home. It's very early morning; there is a dark gray light coming in through the part in the curtains. There's the clink of keys dropping to the concrete; she hisses, "Fuck," and picks them up.

I rise up, groan, "I'm awake."

Mel peers at me, collar loosened. She's squinting, her hair's sticking up. "You scared the shit out of me," she slurs. "What are you doing up?"

"Taking a break."

She giggles. "Takin a *breeaak*," she croaks. She totters a bit, going from right to left, as if neither side is up to the task of holding her up.

"Are you all right?"

She makes duck lips, gives me the A-okay sign. "Little. Stomach drama. Think I had some bad wine. Scuse me." She weaves her way to the bathroom. A moment later, I hear the soft sounds of retching. I put a pillow over my head.

ONE NIGHT THE LINCOLN pulls up and lets Mel out. I'm at the window, massaging a cramp out of my leg. I watch her heave herself onto the sidewalk and stand, hands in pockets, as the car cruises back toward the BQE.

She grunts at me when she opens the door. Drags a chair across the floor, takes the ashtray off the sill. There's the click of the lighter, the chewy, familiar smoke. The Cintiq glows behind us, at rest.

"How goes it," I say.

"Eh." She taps her smoke to shake the ash. I shift to my side toward her—our version of *Wanna talk about it, champ?*

She's nearly done with her cigarette when she says, "I wore her down, I think."

"What happened?"

"Words were said. That car ain't coming back anytime soon. Let's leave it at that." She rises, rubbing the back of her neck with a pained expression. "Leg acting up?"

I think of the apartment listings, but keep quiet. I was tempted to log in to her laptop to look up her search history. I decided against it. Figured it was a step too shitty. Even for me.

She moves into the kitchen. The cabinet opens, shuts. There's the *snap-snap-snap* of the seal being broken from a bottle of Four Roses.

"It's all right," I say. "Are you okay?"

"Oh yeah."

She returns, drink in hand. Passes me a tube of Bengay. I lean over and pull up the seam of my pants. She squirts out a handful. We both massage my leg. I can feel her strong sketcher's fingers prodding into the calf muscle, the pressure points surrounding the ankle, below the kneecap, until my entire leg burns.

She takes a drink, makes a face. "Shit. Now it all tastes like Bengay."

"Thanks."

"You got it."

I wake in the middle of the night to a choking sound. I get up, shake out my leg, and stumble down to the studio. Mel is sprawled on the floor, palms splayed, neck craned over a puddle of vomit. She convulses, spews with a half sob, then looks up, teary.

"Jesus, Mel," I say.

"I *don't*," she says. "I told her. Couldn't *help* it."

Tries to finish, is cut off by another heave. On the table by the Cintiq, the Four Roses bottle holds half an inch.

I run a washcloth at the sink and drag the trash can over. I've never seen her this sick. Never seen her not swagger off a puke, stumbling away, yelling something incomprehensible. She's gray. I reach out, feel her forehead: cool and damp. I swab drool from her chin. She gurgles.

"You get. Older," she mutters, "and you think it's gonna get better."

"What?" I position her over the trash can.

She leans back. Tries to get up. Falls down on her ass. Groans. "You think it'll change. But it doesn't."

"Mel."

She closes her eyes, mouth open. She's crying. She's not even hiding it now. I go to push her hair back and she leans her head into my hand, the weight filling it.

"It just gets worse," she says.

"Don't try to talk," I tell her. She spits. I lean in, ignoring the smell.

Her body jerks forward. She retches, tucks her chin into her chest for a moment. Looks up. "Always gonna be like this," she croaks.

"No, it's not."

"You don't know," she mutters. "You never. Still don't."

She curls up and sleeps the rest of the night on the floor. This is it. I'm convinced she's finally achieved alcohol poisoning. I tip her onto her side and watch her breathe, long white hands curled into her chest. I survey the damage: blue pencils broken in half, chalk crushed, sketches ripped in two. A small crack at the Cintiq's corner.

I lie on the couch, sleepless, listening to her snore, watching her body for signs of movement. I think of Mrs. Horsemuller: *Is the little missus sleeping?*

I get dressed for physical therapy at eleven. She cracks an eye open as I unlock the front door. "You know you have to clean this up," I tell her.

She speaks into the pillow I tucked under her head. "Uh huh."

I turn and shut the door.

WE FINISH THE EDITS on Christmas morning, almost a full year after leaving Louisville. When we get the green light from distribution, we send it out for final edits.

The week we finish, I get a tentative clean bill of health from the doctor: sturdy enough to not have to return for three months. I can travel overseas, I can drive, I can—shakily—resume normality. When he gives me the news, I ask him, "Are you sure?"

Not a day passes when I don't lose my balance, or get a nosebleed, or look in the mirror to find part of my face slightly slack. My short-term memory is shot; my phone goes off six times a day warning me to take my pills. The studio is littered with Post-its reminding me of appointments, bill payments, deadlines. I am living a life punctuated with reminders that I will forever be in the woods, a medical bracelet wearer, the one who watches for impending death: a limp, a deep sneeze.

"You made it," the doctor says. "You survived a stroke to live a normal life. You should be happy. You should be *proud*."

I tell Mel the news as we do a final screen check. "Well, well," she says, turning to me, face thin and angular, lilac patches under her eyes. In retrospect, I will always wonder how much of the movie was a gift, of sorts—one that she made to me, or we made to each other, as much as anything we made was a gift for one another. She smiles, wide and creased. "Here we are."

The results are a perfect flow, neon and brazen: a high-color blur riot of growing up, a self that shuttles off into a bright and unknowable future. "Is it my imagination, or are we getting better at this?" I ask.

She turns back to the screen, the smile smaller. The screen reflects off her lenses, obscuring her eyes. "Either that," she says, "or just getting older."

THE EUROPEAN TOUR

W E TRY TO KEEP OUR EXPECTATIONS LOW FOR *IRREFUTABLE LOVE*. We're happy with it while admitting how weird it is, how hard it might be to sell. The ultimate fear, Donnie tells us, is that it is *inaccessible,* apparently the worst thing a movie can be. "Pitching it is going to be a nightmare," she says. "I mean, I love it. But it's a love I'm having trouble finding words for. It doesn't have a *hook.*"

"It's not a Hall and Oates song," Mel says.

Donnie has a point. It's not hugely accessible. I'm a hard sell, too. The first one to toddle out of parties, drunk and disenchanted, the one most worried about spilling something down the front of her shirt. That's what *Irrefutable Love* is about. I don't like *people,* goddammit. That's why I do *this* for a living.

But weird is our niche market, Donnie assures us. We'll start small. That's all. With that, we let it out into the world.

And one day our phone starts ringing.

There's no accounting for taste. Sometimes the truly unexpected will rise—the book, movie, painting that is the bespectacled boy in the back of the class, clumsy and asexual until he explodes in a flurry of revelatory pussy-wrangling. *Irrefutable Love* is that dark horse. Donnie sells it as *niche* but its impact goes further, sinking into the fandom of a certain landscape, a certain, bruised mindset. Mostly women, but some men, too. Those who fixate. It is a small but determined—and productive—group. It becomes the type of film other artists and writers comb the Internet for, looking for clips to send to friends. The kind of cartoon that elicits weird fan mail, naked pictures, phone numbers, letters confessing infidelities and childhood molestations and grand-scale thefts. Some staggering fan art. An Etsy store sells shirts and jewelry emblazoned with a half-opened trunk, an image of doom reclaimed, by the movie's end, as a power symbol. OPEN YOUR TRUNK.

For us, this is an outpouring. We are touched by it, but there's something about this kind of blind responsibility to others that scares the bejesus out of me. I'm still asked about the fan mail. *What's it like for people to approach you in public and burst into tears? How does it feel for perfect strangers to tell you their worst secrets?* "Weird," I usually say, and no more. Sometimes I cop out of answering at all. The best part of having a stroke is when others assume you can't talk.

L ATE SPRING OF THE following year, almost a full two years after we started. We do a mini-tour of western Europe to promote *Irrefutable Love,* releasing it in Berlin and Munich and at the Guggenheim in Venice. Budapest, Vienna, London. Berlin and London are cold as balls, but fun. Lots of meat and beer. Perpetually overcast skies.

We've already done the New York stuff, interviews for magazines and podcasts. We sell more DVDs of *Nashville Combat.* We're making a little money. A new wardrobe and some dental work for me. A decisive switch from GPCs to Parliaments for Mel. We stay in hotels and rack up frequent-flier miles. I read a lot. Go to hotel gyms. Check my blood pressure. Make a teary visit to a Munich doctor after a bout of violent queasiness turns out to be nerves. Live in a certain amount of fear.

"Dude, relax," Mel says. "You're all, like, bundled up. Squeezing together so nothing can escape."

"I wish we could talk about something without the inclusion of poop metaphors."

"You," she says, "are a chronic worrier." She thumbs through something on her phone, glasses at the end of her nose, chin tilted up. She's getting ready to go out somewhere with some women from a Swiss art journal she met the day before. "Sure you don't wanna go out? Be good for you. Find some nebbishy dude from a former social-ist zone to straddle."

"The Mel Vaught itinerary doesn't much appeal to me."

"Suit yourself."

"I'm just glad I don't have to share a hotel room with you on this trip."

I eat and drink a lot. I'm happy to let Mel be the life of the party, go out and make friends, pose for overexposed photos yelling into people's ears or humping statues or being embraced by slender, brightly dressed women, while I go back to the hotel to eat Kinder bars and watch *Cheers* with German subtitles.

There are moments when I have flashes of the old longing: in a plane taking off from a green countryside, smelling the moist under-ground of a foreign city's metro, seeing a man in a Paris subway flick his girlfriend's ear with his tongue. And there is the loneliness, a damp omission at my center. The movie takes off and I trudge along behind it, and Mel.

It's odd to live so sleepily, considering we spend our days being asked about Movie Sharon, heroine of *Irrefutable Love*—wildly, al-most violently emotional. The stupid sexual decision-making, the frantic hunt for something to grasp. When people connect with *that* Sharon, it shocks the shit out of me. *That's me too!* I'm told more than once, and I answer with *Hey that's great* before realizing what I'm confirming—about them, but also about me.

"Are you okay?" Mel asks me. "Feeling all right? Tired?" She insists on using the blood pressure monitor on me every night before she goes out. When my leg acts up: "Four hands're better than two," she says, rolling up her sleeves, muttering around her cigarette, and we labor over my calf with Bengay until the spasms subside. Once, a production assistant from a talk show on Channel 4 comes in to find us like that, my foot planted in Mel's lap, her brow creased over in concentration. "Uh, you're on in fifteen," he says.

Mel looks up. "All right." He shuts the door. She resumes.

I watch her for a minute. "People are going to think we're a couple," I say.

"I got news for you. They've thought that for years."

"Really? What do you tell them when they ask?"

She ashes her cigarette. "I tell them you wouldn't put up with my bullshit for five minutes."

But I have. And on this trip, as her nights grow later and her hangovers more painful, I do it again. Something has happened to Mel since the night of the Four Roses bottle last year; she has become thinner, sharper somehow, as if a part of her once soft has gone raw-boned from exposure. I watch her get patted down in Paris, praying she threw away her one-hitter. I listen to her throw up in Amsterdam. I try to will myself numb, covered in petroleum jelly, all concern slicking off. Ignoring how my entire body still knots when she makes certain noises or when she has that webby drunk cast to her eyes. It riles her to bring it up: Someone in a bar in London looked at her drink and said something good and snarky about how *Nashville Combat* obviously still applies, and Mel shoved the drink at him, saying, "This is *ginger ale*. So why don't you take that goddamn *quizzical* expression and shove it up your pooper, limey."

After Europe, we end up in San Francisco, a city neither of us has ever visited. *Irrefutable Love* opens to a bigger response than we could have imagined. The theater is packed. Students, cartoonists, some weirdo Hollywood types. A few of the older guys—those whose movies Mel and I were weaned on, guys whose names popped up in my college thesis—approach us, grasp our hands, tell us *well done*. We are rendered speechless that night. It is the apex of our hard work and sacrifice. We know it doesn't happen to everyone. But it's happening to us, and we are fortunate. We keep glancing at each other in amazement, Mel suppressing a grin, eyes huge, me giggling and adjusting the pants around my belly.

I only notice in retrospect, in pictures and video, how thin Mel is around this time, how her suits hang on her. But that night in San Francisco, all we know is that, up until its end, it is the best night on the tour.

The after-party is at the home of a wealthy, druggy animator who used to work for Disney but won money in an unspeakable lawsuit. (He winks and claws his hands at us: "Check it, babies. *Occupational arthritis*.") The place is a genuine mansion, a huge, creamy four-story. Ten bedrooms, more bathrooms, separate kitchens. It's packed with strangeness. People doing coke off a gaudy purple pool table downstairs. Transvestite strippers, one named Ronalda who keeps picking me up off the floor and twirling me around. Someone's potbellied pig is sprayed green and fed Velveeta and bologna throughout the night. I see two or three guys in suits and nice shoes smoking angel dust by an open window. The party is the biggest cliché I have ever seen. Later it will be embarrassing to explain what we were doing there.

I find myself in a quiet corner of the house trading stroke notes with a writer who tells me he was in a motorcycle accident when Mel happens by, a cup of something frothy and dark in her hand. "Sharon Kay," she croons, "with eyes of Drano bloo-ooooo. *Get it!*" She sways in front of us, puts her hands on my head, leans in. Blows a raspberry into my hairline.

"What do you have there, dear."

"Robitussin milkshake supreme." She waggles the cup at me, eyes sort of crossed and dilated at the same time. Her breath is a thick, noxious cloud of medicine cabinet. "Gonna toast the night with some *tussin*. Good for what ails ya."

"I'll pass."

"You're no fun, stroke girl."

Then something strange happens. I clear my purse from my lap, put my drink aside, smooth my pants over my thighs—I make room for her. And she plops down, slings her arm over my neck. We look at each other, then look at the writer, giving him the dumbest faces we can. "Whut," Mel says, and he just nods and smiles like this is normal.

Mel says, "Did you know you're talking to the most beautiful, brilliant woman at the party?"

"I do," he says.

She lays her head on my shoulder. "I mean me."

I smile at the writer. He's been giving signals I once would have devoured with my front teeth—the leaning in, the unceasing eye contact. But I'm already planning to go back to the hotel, eat a sandwich, order *Killer Klowns from Outer Space* on demand.

"You have no idea," Mel tells him. She leans in and gives me a hard, wet kiss on the cheek, then clambers off my lap and heads out.

"Boston tomorrow," I remind her. "We fly out at three."

She turns, points both hands at me. "Sha na na na," she agrees, and is gone.

The writer and I trade email addresses. To the best of my recollection, I am carrying it in my hand when some festival coordinator I barely know runs to me, face streaked and teary, screaming my name. A crowd is behind him. Someone close by dials for an ambulance—I swear to God, I can hear the three numbers being punched into the phone—and he drags me to an anteroom at the end of a huge hall.

Time warps. I hear my heartbeat in my ears on the walk down that hallway, pushed and dragged by the hand, the shoulder, and I dully realize that I already know what's happened, have imagined it thousands of times, and *goddamn it all I'm going to have to rebook our flights to Logan, she's gonna have to have her fucking stomach pumped again and this time I won't give her hell for it. I'll just let her sit there with it so she can become as disgusted with herself as I am.*

After all we've been through, I think, *she is still pulling this shit, as hard as she can.*

I'm shoved into the room by the hysterical coordinator and there is Mel, her head in the lap of some sprightly dressed girl, and her chest jumps once with effort, and then she is still. She is dead for more than a minute when the ambulance arrives.

SLEEPWALK

AM GIVEN VALIUM AND PUT ON A PLANE. I SLEEP THROUGH THE FLIGHT, climb out onto a cold, sandy tarmac in the dark, walk JFK's piercing Delta terminal. Donnie is at baggage claim, keys to her BMW in hand, face a soft, pale mask below her red hair.

She puts her arms around me. My knees give way. Then nothing.

WAKE UP ON the couch in Donnie's office, cocooned in her overcoat. Around me, there's a blanket that smells strongly of her pit bull, Wyatt, who gives me a conciliatory lick on the mouth. Donnie's voice drifts from the conference room. "That's way out in Flushing. Why would they take her there? They live in Brooklyn. The city morgue in Staten Island would have been closer. . . . No, we can drive out there, that's not the issue. What? . . . Well, if she's the only one who can do it, it's going to have to wait." Drops to a whisper. "This has hit her *hard.* She collapsed when she got off the plane. She had a *stroke* not too long ago. This is a health issue for her. Okay?"

Wyatt huffs, sticks his nose in my crotch. I push him away.

"We will get there when we can get there. I'm *sorry.* I'm working with limited resources here. We have put everything on hold to deal with this. Oh no. Thank *you.*" I hear her hang up. Mutter, "Dick."

She knocks softly on the door, pushes it open, and peeks in. "Sharon?" Her eyes are red. "Hey. You're awake."

Wyatt drops his butt on the carpet, drags his way back to me. Whinnies and pokes his nose into my ear. "Wyatt, no. Bad man," Donnie says. She picks him up, all seventy pounds of him. He hangs over her shoulder, beating his tail against her hip. She sighs and buries her face into his coat.

My thigh vibrates. I shift, pull my phone out. *22 new messages.* Donnie watches, her face pinched. "Hello?"

"Is this Sharon?"

"Yeah."

"Hey, Sharon, I'm calling from *Rolling Stone.* We're doing a short piece on Mel Vaught for our website and were wondering if we could get a statement from you."

I lie back down. The words are all ones I know, but they're not making any sense strung together like this. "Huh?"

Donnie shakes her head, holds her hand out.

"We're getting reports that Mel Vaught died of a heart attack stemming from an overdose. Can you confirm this?"

"Huh?"

Donnie lowers Wyatt to the ground, then takes the phone from me. "This is Donatella Sogn. Can I help you with something?" Wyatt climbs on top of me, smooches my chin. Doesn't protest when I roll over to spoon him. "Saying sorry doesn't mean dick, Brian. You should have been going through me in the first place." Donnie walks into the other room, voice trailing behind her. "We haven't seen the coroner's report yet. We know about as much as you do. We'll have a statement ready by this afternoon. That's the earliest it's going to happen."

Donnie returns, hands me my phone. "I don't want you worrying about anything. You're going to handle as much as you can and no more right now. If you see a call and you don't want to pick up, don't. Just give it to me. I will take care of it. Okay?"

"Uh huh."

"How are you doing?"

I shrug.

"How are you physically?"

"Okay."

"Any headaches?"

"I'm not gonna have another stroke, if that's what you mean."

"I just want to check in. You collapsed at the airport last night. Do you remember that?"

I sink farther into the couch. "Is this Wyatt's blanket?"

"It is. Sorry about the smell."

"He keeps sticking his nose in my snatch."

"He'll do that. Are you hungry?"

"Nuh uh."

"The kitchen is full of stuff. Fruit baskets and cheese plates. Someone brought a huge sandwich platter over from Citarella."

"I'm not hungry."

"It's there if you are later. Are you feeling well enough to go out?"

"Go where?" There's shuffling and whispering from the hall. Someone mutters, *She's awake.* "Who's here?"

Donnie rolls her shoulders, presses her palms into her neck. "Company people. Friends. You think you could run an errand with me?"

"I guess."

She sits next to me. "I'm very sorry to do this to you right now, but you were listed as Mel's next of kin. I have to take you to identify the body."

"Oh."

"They flew her back here. She's in Flushing. I have my car with me today, so we can go whenever you like." She leans over, takes my wrist. Her hands are hot. "You have to identify her before we can do anything in terms of arrangements."

I see the long, flickering hallway, smell the bleach and blood in the darkness. "Mel's mom," I tell Donnie. "We had to go to Florida. To identify her."

"I remember that."

"It was to make sure they had the right person."

Donnie blinks. "Uh huh."

I splay my hands out in front of me. I can't remember anything after the emergency room. I want to ask Donnie how I got here, why I don't remember being put on a plane in California to come back, what's happened in the meantime.

It all falls apart as soon as I open my mouth. It's from frustration that I tear up, pissed that I can't say what I mean.

Donnie picks up a wool shawl and wraps me in it.

DONNIE'S ASSISTANT WAITS WITH me, holding the shawl closed with her fist while Donnie pulls up to the curb. The ride over the Queensboro Bridge is mostly quiet. Donnie mentions *arrangements* again. She flicks the turn signal and wings the car onto a side street. "She hadn't chosen a method," she tells me. "She had a lot of stuff in place, but not that."

"What other stuff."

Donnie watches the road. "She did that next-of-kin document after her mom died. Made a will with a lawyer sometime after your stroke."

"That's weird. Considering I was the one who almost died."

"Act of faith? I don't know. You'd have to live to get the money. Right?" She glances over. Her eyes are still pink. "You didn't know that?"

"No."

She takes a long, deep breath. "A lot of us made wills when you had the stroke. And I'll bet even more of us will be doing it now."

I look out the window. "If she did all that other shit, she should have just picked if she wanted to be cremated or not."

Donnie blinks rapidly. Her Roman nose flares. "She was thirty-three years old. She didn't really think she was going to *die.*"

This shuts me up.

We pull in front of a new high-rise: OFFICE OF CHIEF MEDICAL EXAMINER, CITY OF NEW YORK/BOROUGH OF QUEENS. The guy at the desk is young, wears throwback Reeboks with his scrubs. Says only, "Name?" when we approach the desk. Donnie reaches out, takes my hand.

We're led down a hallway through double doors. I hear our foot-steps, the buzzing halogen lights. The hairs on the back of my neck prickle. I see the hot Florida parking lot, Lisa Greaph with her purple fingernails pulling the handle from the wall. The table within. The clavicle.

I start to sweat. Donnie glances at me.

It's an enormous room of stainless steel and linoleum, with a hallway leading to other rooms, cavernous, hyperlit. We follow the guy to a wall of drawers, the same kind we saw in Florida. The room tunnels, my ears cotton. It's suddenly harder to breathe.

He takes hold of the handle and pulls. The table extends. I bend at the waist. Donnie whispers, "Sharon, honey."

I close my eyes and tuck my chin in, trying to breathe. My lungs are collapsing. "I can't do it."

The morgue guy rubs his nose, distracted. Says, "You're required by law to identify the body as hers before we can release it. That re-quires *looking.*"

Donnie puts her hand on my back.

"She doesn't look, the body stays here," he tells Donnie. "Tell her to look."

She pulls me in. "Don't you dare talk to her that way. This woman was her partner. Have some respect."

He rolls his eyes.

Donnie rubs my arm. "Sharon."

I look.

Mel's hair has been slicked back from her face. She's blue from her forehead to her chin, skin sleek and glasslike. She is thin, so thin. Her collarbone is like a knife handle through the flesh. Her mouth is small and white.

I think about Dad. I think about seeing him in his casket at Damron Brothers in Faulkner, how he seemed so temporarily stilled, the air electric with energy unused. Maybe it was physics, maybe it was dumb hope, but I was never more sure of the unkillable quality of energy particles as when I looked at his dead body: *Life has to go somewhere. This can still be reversed. He doesn't have to be dead. He doesn't* have *to be.*

But here, Mel is the opposite of movement. Maybe because she was so constantly in motion, jumping and fidgeting and wriggling and flailing all the time. She was ADHD incarnate. She doesn't even look asleep. She is tapped, inanimate. Hard. There is no smell. This is not the body of someone who will talk or drink or dance or draw ever again. My belly starts to burn.

I turn quickly to avoid spewing on Donnie. She murmurs, gathers my hair back. When I straighten, she produces a tissue, motions to my mouth. I wipe.

The morgue guy grimaces and flips the sheet back up. "That's wonderful," he sighs, and pulls a walkie-talkie from his pocket. "We need someone in seventeen with a mop." He slams the drawer back into the wall. We hear a thump from the inside.

"Hey, goddammit," Donnie says. "Watch it."

"Now, please," he snaps into the receiver.

"If you bruised her, so help me God, we will sue you."

"No one would notice," he counters. "Alcohol poisoning with a DXM overdose? They can paint her up, but she'll still be blue."

"I'm reporting that cocksucker," Donnie says as she guides me out.

BACK AT THE OFFICE, I am repeatedly hugged. People keep springing up to give me their chairs. Someone has taken the clothing from my luggage, washed and folded it. It is understood that I will not be going home. A plate of food is put in front of me. Mugs of tea. Assistants and interns shuffle by, gawking. Donnie ushers away anyone showing even a prelude to tears.

I see all this from a strange distance. If I try hard enough, I can watch myself from the outside, like when I had the stroke. Will myself to float to the ceiling, look at myself breathe. Sit. Stare ahead. Nod when spoken to.

Fart comes by with a strawberry pie he's made. He tells me he grew up on a berry farm in Ohio. When he hugs me, he nearly lifts me out of my seat, clapping me on the back like a dude. Slips a fourth an ounce of bud into my pocket with a one-hitter. "We love you, hoss," he tells me hoarsely.

It occurs to me that I never slept with Fart. I wonder why. He would have been an excellent refuge fuck. A big old friendly bear fuck. Now I'm glad I didn't. It would have saddled this sweet moment with obligation.

There's a balcony outside Donnie's office. I take the one-hitter there, pack it, toke quickly. This is upper Midtown on the twenty-fifth floor. There's traffic and Times Square and the new Freedom Tower to the south, striking into the sky.

I can feel everyone's eyes on my back, but no one comes to join me. I inhale, wait to float out of my skin again.

THE FINAL CORONER'S REPORT: cardiac arrest caused by a combination of alcohol and lethal levels of dextromethorphan. Cough syrup.

The joke: Mel tried so many drugs—had, in fact, possessed such a zeal and lack of fear for substances—of course she would OD on something *legal*. Hick death. Something that would send a suburban fifteen-year-old to the emergency room. *Womp womp*. It is suggested in an otherwise reverent blog post that Mel would have found this funny. Which makes Donnie scream. But it's not wrong.

The cremation is in two days. There'll be a service the day after that. It's not a funeral, Donnie assures me. It is a *memorial*. People getting together to remember. No music, no hymns, no processionals.

I stay in Donnie's guest bedroom, falling in and out of sleep, sitting up every few hours to smoke a bowl and change the channel on the flat-screen. Donnie brings trays of food—poached eggs in little crystal perches, cups of tea and porcelain creamers, grapefruit split in half. "Eat," she says. I pick at everything while she sits at the edge of the bed, arms crossed, peering at the television. When she steps out, I feed Wyatt chunks of egg. Wyatt, my constant companion, my big spoony guy.

In a memorial gesture, Animacon airs our shorts, and then *Nashville Combat,* on its new cable channel. I cruise right past it and find *Saturday Night Live* reruns from the nineties. Smoke more bowls. Am unhappily rapt for hours.

Ten times a day, I turn—actually physically turn my body—to look for Mel, to tell her something, before realizing she's not there.

Brecky Tolliver comes to visit. I have no idea what time or day it is. It's the first time I've ever seen her out of a suit. "Sharon. Hey." She gives me a one-armed hug. Points to the bowl. I shrug. She picks it up and takes a hit and passes it to me. I toke. "What are you watching."

"Chris Farley."

We let that fartbomb settle before she takes the remote and turns to *CHiPs.*

I ask her, "So are you and Donnie, like, friends now, or something?"

"We're actually kind of seeing each other."

"Really. I didn't know that."

"Figured she wouldn't mention it."

"She plays it close to the vest."

"She does indeed."

"That's cool," I tell her.

"Yeah." Brecky clears her throat, toys with the remote. It occurs to me that she's nervous. "It was the panel discussion. She called me to apologize for Mel's—whatever. We got to talking. One thing sort of led to another."

I lean back into the pillows, take another hit. "I like knowing Mel's shitfit gave birth to a high-powered lesbian love unit. Does my heart good."

"Heh." Brecky scratches her head. "I could have been cooler about the panel thing."

"Dude. She dry-humped you in public."

"Well, I provoked her. I kind of can't blame her."

"I can. You know how she is."

"Uh huh." Brecky looks at me carefully. "How are you feeling, Sharon?"

"Shit. I'm. You know." I make a smoothing gesture with my hand.

We watch TV. She says finally, "I'm sorry, Sharon."

"So tell me how this works. Is Donnie the dude? What's it like when you fight? Who gets to scissor on top?"

"We don't fight much," she says.

"That's great. Everyone needs leeway from somebody. Milk of human kindness and all that."

She's quiet for a moment. Then she says, "She's usually on top."

"Well, that's nonnegotiable, isn't it."

"I'm sorry, Sharon."

"I heard you."

"I need to say it again."

"Okay."

She shifts. The bed creaks. "Look. I've never dealt well with envy, okay? Professional envy in particular. It's held me back from a lot of things in my life. It's a character defect. I know it. I've been working on it." She clears her throat. "It's made things very lonely for me at times. As I'm sure you can imagine. And that part of me made things really bad with you, but especially with Mel. I really regret the way I treated her."

I shrug. "All right."

"No. I— I did some things I'm not proud of." She takes a deep breath. "I think I might have knocked you all out of the running for a Hollingsworth. A few years ago. The first time you applied, maybe?"

"What?"

She shakes her head. "You didn't deserve it. I had some drinks with the board members one night and, I don't know, I said some things I shouldn't have. Like how I thought Mel would go off the rails and fuck up the grant if they gave it to you. There was something about Mel that triggered something—self-protective in me, I guess. She made me feel inadequate. But instead of dealing with it, I hurt someone else."

Brecky's face is tight, gray in the TV glow. She really is nervous. She made herself do this. Or Donnie harangued her into growing a pair and owning up. It's dark outside. I shake my head; my vision shakes with it. "Hey," I say. "It's cool." My mouth feels like it's filled with oatmeal. I am incredibly stoned.

"I lost a chance I'll never get back," she says. "I want to rectify this. I want you to know, if there is anything you need, anything I can do, you got it. I want us to be friends. And that counts for whether or not you want to work together. That's not an ultimatum by any means."

I take a deep breath and, for the first time in days, say what I mean. "If it makes you feel any better," I say, "you were kind of right."

It's the wrong thing to tell her, but I'm too stoned to correct the damage. Brecky tries to speak, sniffs, dips her head down. I freeze, not sure I'm actually seeing what I'm seeing. This is horrifying. Brecky Tolliver doesn't *cry.*

I lean over and take her hand. We both pretend to watch TV. I think, Mel's gonna shit when I tell her about this.

IT'S THE MORNING OF the memorial. I don't know what to do with this information other than curl up and throw the blankets over my head.

Donnie pats my back, softly pinching, trying to rustle me out. "I know, honey," she keeps saying, "but you have to get up. You just do."

"I can't. Tell them I'm sick or something."

"I won't do that."

"You don't get it. I can't."

Brecky stands behind her, kneading her hands. They're both in pantsuits again. Donnie has slicked her hair back, put on makeup. The TV honks. She huffs in frustration, snaps it off. "Up. Come on."

My voice comes out piss-poor tiny. "Uh uh."

Brecky speaks up. "Sharon, you're going to hate yourself if you don't go. It may not seem like it now, but this is what you really want to do."

"Fuck that and fuck you."

Donnie throws the remote down. "Don't *talk* to her like that."

I stick my head back under the covers.

Donnie rips the sheets from my body. "You will *not do this to me godfuckingdammit get up,* Sharon. Get up right the fuck now." She's red, crying. Leans over and picks me up like a little kid. Her arms are tiny, hot through the fabric of her jacket. My legs dangle down. I don't fight her.

I haven't climbed out of bed in three days. My limp nearly wings me into a wall. Brecky guides me to the shower, hands me a towel, a washcloth. "Don hasn't slept in two days," she whispers. "Her phone keeps going off."

"Don't care."

"Sharon, if you do this, I promise you I will get you out of there whenever you want. Okay? Just say the word."

I shrug.

She stands back, pats her pockets. "Do you have a cigarette?"

I look down. I'm wearing a T-shirt and underpants. Look back up at her.

"Right. Sorry."

"You gonna leave, Brecky?"

"Are you really gonna shower?"

"Well, I'm gonna start stripping. Stay or go."

Brecky leaves. I turn the shower on. Reach into my bra and fetch out the one-hitter and lighter. I smoke a bowl, watching the water hit the tile.

• • •

W E DRIVE TO THE Collective for Cartooning Arts in Brooklyn, a sprawling old mansion in Cobble Hill. The last time we were here, it was to accept the Newcomer's Award. I slit my own girdle so I could breathe and Mel made out with a cocktail waitress in an upstairs broom closet. *"Heh,"* I say to myself.

Brecky and Donnie exchange a look.

The block is stalled with cars. Crowds cluster at the entrance. There's a reaction when we arrive: groups parting, whispering. Lots of eyes on me. The high's wearing off and I can feel my bum leg, heavy, dragging slightly behind me. Brecky and Donnie tug me through, sometimes exchanging words with people. There's the interns: Jimmy the Fire Maniac, Indian John Cafree. Surly Cathie off to the side of the building, smoking a Black & Mild and twiddling with her cellphone. She uses it to salute me, a rueful little pucker to her lips. I think of her with the wild dogs in South Edgemere: *Okay, cunts, who wants to be first?* I am hugged and patted. My reactions are milky, on delay. The inside of my mouth is covered with fur.

We're led to the front of the screening room, where a projector runs a slide of Mel photos. Mel as a kid, dwarfed in a Def Leppard T-shirt. Mel as a high school senior, hair long and stringy, giving a clamped little smile to a studio photographer. Mel at Ballister, craned over a drafting table, brow nearly touching the surface. Mel and me clinking beers. Mel and me in the studio, her pointing to the Cintiq screen, mouth open, me frowning. Mel and me. Mel and me again.

A polished clay jar is at the center of a long oak table. Donnie stops to speak with someone. I creep toward it, flick the lid open.

"Sharon," Donnie calls.

I let the lid clang shut.

The service goes just as Donnie said it would. People get up to talk. Fart rises first, wearing a tie and khakis with sneakers. His hair is all combed down. He fiddles with his tie. He looks anxious.

"I met Mel my first year in New York," he says. "We were both doing freelance stuff, sketching for this sneaker company. It was maybe my first job out of art school. I knew, like, three people in New York. It was pretty lonely. And the day we met, she took me out drinking, and we stayed out until five in the morning. We were instant friends, you know? Like right away."

He shifts from one foot to the other, stares off into the middle distance, one hand in his beard. "She wasn't afraid of stuff," he says. "She wasn't afraid of anything. And she thought I had the right to not be afraid of anything, too. And I can honestly say that she's the only person I've ever met who made me feel that way."

His mouth crimps. I stare at him. It's as if I'm listening through a straw.

"She made me believe in myself," he says. "She believed I could do more than I actually could, which made me do more. She was a good friend." His voice cracks. He finishes by saying, very quickly, "My life will be less because she is not in it anymore."

He sits back down, head tilted forward. His back is trembling. Surly Cathie puts her red, calloused hand on his shoulder.

Donnie stands and begins to speak slowly and clearly, her eyes bloodshot. "I have never known someone who tackled life like Mel," she says. "She just went in, headfirst, without a helmet, pretty much all the time. Whatever she did. And when you met her, you saw it right away. But she was also one of the most loving people you could meet. It wasn't the most obvious thing about her, and you might not see it on first glance. I wouldn't want to hazard the guess of how many of you she called *motherfucker* the first time she met you."

There's a ripple of recognition in the crowd. Donnie smiles, for the first time in days.

"She loved hard," she continues. "If she loved you, she loved you the *most*. She would stick with you until the very, very end. She loved—" Donnie swallows. "She loved Sharon. Adored her. Of course. And she loved Fart. She loved John, and she loved Cathie." She closes her eyes. "She loved her mother, so much. If you knew her well, you knew that she did. What courage that took. What *forgiveness*. It takes a big, brave person to forgive. And she was big. And she was brave."

Donnie puts her hands over her eyes and rubs for a moment. I see her chest rise and fall. Starts to say something. Stops. "Sorry," she says.

I see her take a deep breath and smooth her jacket. She looks up. "I first met Mel and Sharon when they were twenty-one years old. They were kids. I was kind of a kid, too, just starting out. It was at a cartoon expo. I really liked their shorts. I thought they were smart, and funny. Mel was the one to chase me down and convince me to have coffee with them. And I remember her leaning forward across the table and saying to me, 'Believe in us. Just believe in us.' And I did. And I still do."

Toward the back, distribution guys stand in suits, Beardsley shifting awkwardly among them. I stare at him, numb, distantly enjoying his discomfort. It's all extremely smeary. I focus on one thing; the rest of the room collapses. I notice wetness coming down my chin. My mouth is open. Haven't remembered to close it in a while. Brecky passes me a tissue. People are looking.

One of the distribution guys—the head or second-in-command, a dude neither Mel nor I knew terribly well through our contract there—gets up, rummaging his hands through his nice suit pants, saying something about work left behind. A screen is pulled down, the lights dim.

A familiar sound snaps me back to attention. They're showing the last few minutes of *Nashville Combat*. A scene we worked over and over, rerecording the dialogue, drafting and redrafting, trying to get it just right.

It's set in a bar in Brooklyn. The first thing you see is Mel, and not the default Cartoon Mel, all spiky yellow hair and knobby knees, but *my* Mel. We decided drawing each other for the end was the right thing to do. My Mel is an airbrush shot glowing from within: thirty-degree nose on the profile, high Cherokee cheekbones, lanky body folded over the bar like a praying mantis. I've never realized before now how *right* I got her in that shot. It is so much Mel, so fluidly her—the lay of the shoulders, the way the mouth stills in thought. A glass of something warm and amber sits by the crook of her elbow.

It's one of the few scenes of the movie that has me in it. I'm coming into the bar to fetch her. It's the uncut scene. "November Rain" is playing in the bar. *Fuckin love this song, man,* she always said. *It's sadness porn. Skanky, melodramatic sadness porn.* But we both knew it meant something more. Both knew that if you were a child, and you watched TV in a room by yourself as we did, saw this video, heard this song, it struck something primal and private in you, the sense of being at your most alone in the anticipation of adult pain, a gray future memory. It was reassuring to be with someone else while you listened, so you were no longer the only one in the room, could be reassured that your adult life was not entirely the thing you had feared.

We weren't able to use the track in wide release. The rights cost too much money. But this is the private cut, the one distribution keeps in their library. *This* movie closes out on Guns N' Roses, the way the good Lord intended.

Mel's voice fills the auditorium—the end of the movie, Mel's adult self, ruminating on everything that has happened to her. There's a collective curling back of the audience. It's already slightly unsettling to hear the sound of Mel's voice. I feel a spark of something blue and hot at the base of my spine.

I spent years trying to outrun myself, Mel says. *Trying to make enough noise to drown myself out. It makes me ashamed to admit this. But it's okay to let yourself catch up. It's okay if you work to catch up to the things that have happened to you. You do it for yourself. But also for the people around you. The people who deserve to experience you, undiluted, honest. Your genuine self, given to them.*

My cartoon self takes her by the elbow, pulls her to the door. My voice: *"Come on,"* I tell her. *"It's time to go to work."* We leave together. The door swings shut.

Your life is the people who fill it, Mel says. *And nothing's good without them.*

The music ramps. I get the feeling of the room thinking the same thing at the same time: of Mel doing her ridiculous fucking Axl Rose shimmy-shaky snake. Her croon. Performed at a thousand parties. Her ghost is doing a staggering dance in the middle of the room. *It's hard to hold a candle in the cold November rain.*

A voice joins in, then two, then more. Then louder, people together, singing, an unreal thing, a thing that does not happen in real life but is happening *now,* and soon the whole room is in a trance, singing. Fart sings, Donnie sings, wiping her eyes with the back of her hand, Brecky sings with her arm around Donnie, Mel's drinking buddies, they all bellow it, we can barely believe this is actually happening. And the chorus extends into the credits, and we keep singing through Slash's guitar solo, the first one, that long, lonely tunnel between verses, and everyone is surprised that they know the melody, the song running like a vein underneath their thoughts for so long, the dim future for which we are all bound. We're singing it to Mel, trying to lure her out from wherever she is, because she's always the loudest when she sings this song. And if we sing loud enough, hard enough, if we don't miss a note, she'll come back to us, and all of this will end.

A CARAVAN TRAVELS DOWN the BQE toward Coney Island. The day has turned overcast. The twenty or so of us left close our coats, wrap on scarves, spit off the pier. The amusement park creaks behind us and a nearby housing project rises dull and red in the distance. Someone mentions keeping an eye out for police; scattering ashes from where we are on the coast is illegal.

"Is that right."

"I looked it up."

"Let em come at us, dude. Tell em to bring it."

"Mel Vaught's gonna be in the drinking water of everyone in Staten Island for a week."

"That's fuckin righteous."

Everyone's here now. The laughs die down. Someone sniffs. The waves beat and rush together. Donnie carries the jar from the service. She comes to me, presses it into my hands. "These are for you, sweetie," she says.

I shake my head. "What am I— I don't know—"

"You do whatever you think you should with them. Put them in the water. Keep some, scatter the rest." The jar is warm. It nearly slips from my grasp. Donnie leans in, catches the bottom.

I open the jar and look inside. The ashes are white, and gray, and black. I stick my hand in. Soft, mealy, little bits of stony matter. What I'm fairly sure is half a back molar. One of the bones is striped, mottled like quartz. I hold it up. Put it back.

I look to Donnie. She nods.

I tip the jar a little. The ashes stream down into the water. I wait, let it settle. Dust drifts up. I sneeze. God. This is so fucking lame. Mel would have hated this. Before I can stop myself I look up, expecting to see her beside me.

I take a handful and throw.

I take another handful and throw harder. The wind kicks up. The ashes come back and hit me in the front. I cuss, yell, throw more. Another gust and it all blows back. Mel goes into my mouth and nose and hair. The ash streams into the crowd and they cough and groan, and I scream and throw and Donnie goes, "Okay, Sharon, you can stop now, honey, *stop,* you're getting it all over yourself, Sharon, stop it *now.*"

I wrench away from her and fling Mel into the air, not even aiming for water. Donnie wrestles the jar away from me. I bend over and I scream until I can't hear myself anymore.

THERE'S A McDONALD'S OFF the boardwalk. Donnie hustles me into the bathroom to change into the sweatpants and Columbia field hockey sweatshirt she produces from her trunk. I am coated in ash—my hairline, the inside of my bra, between my teeth. I open my mouth and fish a piece of enamel out of my cheek. One of her teeth, a chip of it. I dreamily put it in my pocket.

Donnie is drinking coffee and smoking a cigarette in the parking lot. "When did you start smoking?" I ask her.

"I don't smoke. You have ash right there." She leans over, combs her fingers through my hair. Dust rains down. "Just shake. Don't worry about the shirt. Shake like a dog. Come on."

I lean over and wag my head from side to side. A group of construction workers stops to stare. Donnie smokes, stares back. They turn away.

When we return to Donnie's, the jar holding approximately one quarter of Mel is slipped into my luggage, lid secured with packing tape. It stays in that suitcase for the next six months.

I go back to our studio.

AFTER THE MEMORIAL, THERE is more press. Limited engagements for *Irrefutable Love* turn into longer runs. Movie theaters we didn't think would ever show the film do. The volume of articles and online chatter on it, and us, doubles, then triples.

I don't have to worry about money anymore. I keep getting checks. Now I'm getting Mel's share, too.

I dream hard, the first night back in the studio. We're at the morgue in Florida, just me and Mel this time, walking that long hallway that goes on and on. Then I blink and we're in the room of bodies, and we go to the drawer and Mel reaches over with long purple fingernails to tug it open. And instead of Kelly Kay being in the drawer, it is Mel. Live Mel looks at Dead Mel. And then Dead Mel comes to life.

Of course she does. Of *course* my subconscious is a big, crusty, low-budget horror movie, full of spooky shit lifted from all those grainy VHS dubs of *Motel Hell* and *The Slumber Party Massacre* rented from the rated-R section at Cornett's Family Time Video. If I'd had my dream as an idea for a cartoon, Mel herself would have made that fart noise she liked to make with her mouth and say that it sounded like something John Carpenter queefed out on an off day. The dream is embarrassing, but unsettling. Because everyone knows that a zombie's eyes are *always* empty. And Dead Mel's eyes, when seeking me out, are full. Sometimes with pleading, sometimes with relief. Sometimes with blame.

I stop sleeping.

• • •

THE SHARON WALL IS still up. We never took it down; it was a sort of motivation for us, making *Irrefutable Love,* and Mel protested when I tried to remove the sketches after on the argument that they were creepy. "Oh, come on," she said. "I like having a perpetual audience." And she bent over and shook her fanny at the Sharons.

A couple of weeks after the memorial, I sit at the drafting table, just to see what happens. I fix coffee, crack open a fresh pad of sketch paper. And nothing. Nothing happens. I flatline. I keep looking at the Sharon Wall—all those versions of me, still watching. Appraising.

I grab a bedsheet from my room and tack it up, covering the sketches, feeling a hint of triumph. When I'm done, I give it the finger.

I try it again the next day, thinking I'm just out of practice. And the next. And the next. I try doing all the things young artists are instructed to do when they're just starting out—carve out an hour a day in which to work, carry a notebook around to record ideas before they flit off into the ether. More nothing happens.

It's what I've always feared.

For years, we had a wealth of ideas. We had too many ideas. The visions were endless. This new blocked feeling is awful, a whole-body constipation. Everything is made of rock and nothing moves. The problem of what to draw, how to draw it, why—none of these are questions I can answer without her. I hold up my hand, wiggle it in front of my face. She took it with her. She robbed me.

Our drafting tables are still in the studio's center, back to back. I've been making a wide berth around Mel's, afraid to touch it. She left it clean. Nothing except a couple of pencils rolling off its surface.

I keep looking at it. It seems darker, now, the top duller. Is that a film of dust over the surface?

I stand up, knocking my chair backward, and run to the bedroom, grab a quilt from my bed, run back in, and throw it over her drafting table, draping it completely from view. Then I take it and drag it to the far wall. It could be anything now. A drum kit. A rocking chair. Fuck all.

I sit back down and stare at the board. My heart starts to pound, faster and faster. My vision narrows to a slim, dark tunnel. The table and blank sheet blur, the fuzz fades to TV snow, flurrying and buzz-ing, becoming indistinct. Bells chime louder, louder. The steady hum of the emergency broadcast system. I cover my head with my hands.

I push my drafting table to the far wall, too. I let it pile up with bills, newspapers, not quite able to bring myself to cover it with a blanket.

When I can't stand to be in the studio anymore, I rent an apart-ment in Park Slope on a quiet street with dogs and old people. I write the studio off as a workspace on that year's tax returns, in spite of the fact that I have nothing to work on. Work is on hiatus. Indefinitely.

Donnie sends me to a doctor. He prescribes Zoloft and Xanax. I gain back the weight I lost from the stroke, turning round and soft again. I sleep. Real, deep, gauzy sleep, nearly comatose. Stroke sleep. Sleep begetting sleep. I can't get enough. When I'm not sleeping, I crave sleep. Most days, it is enough to get up, change sweatpants, and transfer myself to the couch, where I turn on the TV and nap it all off.

It is strange and ultimately insulting how, when someone you love dies, just *expires* without warning, time does not stop. For weeks after the funeral, everything is in limbo. Obligations disappear, rou-tines crumble. It is enough to shuffle along the edge of one's life. When the call back to normality comes, I ignore it.

I don't answer the phone. I don't check email. I avoid going on-line at all until, one night, I make the mistake of Googling my name and am greeted with a shitstorm. Mel is being talked about, we are being *discussed,* in public and in private. Articles have been written, comment sections have become sinkholes of gossip, hearsay. There's the NPR interview gone to hell, the photos, the off-reels. I never knew just how many pictures there were of Mel licking people's faces, or using random objects to pantomime a wang, or, in our early years, flashing the shocker. That one half of the partnership is dead, of an *overdose, overdose overdose,* has doubled, tripled our search engine tally.

Mel is being made over large and transparent in legend, even while her smell still hangs in the studio, her cigarette butts still crushed in sundry coffee cups around the Cintiq, a pair of crumpled green Asics by the door. In death, she is changing. Disappearing.

I GET A STACK of mail from Donnie's office. A lot of sympathy cards I toss out. One from Florida in a soft pink envelope, a nice papyrus job. I know who has sent it before it's open. It is indeed a Lisa Greaph production. Her cursive is soft and gray and swooped. I've never seen the name *Sharon* written so beautifully. It almost makes me glad it is mine.

> *Dear Sharon,*
>
> *I read about Melody and was so sorry to hear this sad news. I know in my heart the love of Christ will find you and lift you up. "We know that while we are at home in the body we are away from the Lord, for we walk by faith, not by sight. Yes, we are of good courage, and we would rather be away from the body and at home with the Lord." II Corinthians 5:6–8.*

THERE IS A MEL that now exists only in my head. A faux Mel, a hazy stand-in Mel, a Mel more cartoony than the actual cartoons we made of her. This Mel in my head listens, pats me on the back, never pukes, never gets into fights. I forget the bad breath and sour moods, the drunkenness, the stupid dancing. It is idealized Mel, cheap, ill-made. And that cuts most of all. In my heart of hearts, I know how much she would have hated that.

The line between being fucked up and being straight enough to leave the house is becoming harder and harder to figure. I get my groceries delivered. Mail from the studio is forwarded. I don't even like to go out on the stoop. Each slant of sunlight is a visual warning against my new habits, my perpetual nighttime mind—the weed I now buy at the pound level from Fart's roommate, the Xanax I've started taking every day, sparingly at first, then ramping it, sensing a nearby boundary, getting just close enough to reach that zenith of fuzz, the mind's cable-cut snow. I want to wade through my apartment in a pool of yellow light. Decide I kind of know, now, what Mel was chasing after.

One night I run out of smokes. I decide to chance it, go out for some. I set off in my bathrobe and flip-flops. It's cold, but it feels good, bracing, to walk. I pass the bodega on the corner and keep going. I head west toward the water at Sunset Park.

When I hit Fourth Avenue, I cross without looking into a four-lane intersection. A sedan comes barreling toward me out of the dark. I'm so taken aback by the headlights, can barely believe they're coming at me like they are, that I have to stand and stare to make sure. The car honks. I hold out one hand. I know that will *make it stop*. It's just logic.

And for the first time in months, it happens: I am lifted out of my skin and into the space above so I am looking down at myself underneath, staring wide-eyed into the headlights. I see a few stray hairs blow in the breeze. I see the way my shoulders slump forward, like I'm lifting something heavy the wrong way. Who would it hurt, if it happened? Who would they call? What would I leave behind? A stockpile of stank weed. Two rancid apartments. Cartoons they'll have to censor pretty heavily, should they ever air them on cable again. A man in Louisville, Kentucky, whom I royally, inevitably fucked over. And family I don't talk to.

I sink back down into my body. The wind flaps my robe. Cool air rushes into my crotch. I forgot to put on underwear before I left the house.

The sedan screeches to a stop. The NYPD cruiser behind it is passing incidentally, slams on the brakes at the sight of my bush. I'm too dazed to protest or explain myself when I'm ushered into the backseat.

Except to tell the cops: "My hand stopped it. Did you see?"

Donnie comes down to bail me out. She greets me with a slip of paper: the number of an attorney. "You need to take care of this one yourself," she says.

We're outside the police precinct at Twenty-eighth Street. It's midnight. Brecky sits at the wheel of Donnie's BMW. She waves to me, fiddles with the radio. She doesn't climb out.

I struggle to pull the jeans Donnie brought over my thighs.

Donnie scrubs her face with both hands. Says, "I was looking in the mirror this morning. I just bought this under-eye cream, this fancy hundred-dollar Dior shit. It's supposed to tighten up the skin around there. Make the circles and lines go away. It's not working. I look like hell a pretty big portion of the time now."

"Never took you for the vain type."

"Shut up."

I shut up.

"You. Are making. Me old," she says. "You, and Mel, and everything that's happened. I have aged more in the past six months than I have in the past ten years."

"I'm sorry," I say.

"I realize that you're sorry. But that doesn't do much for me here. I can't do this with you if you don't at least *try* to move forward. Get some help. Get some of your shit together. Get out of bed in the morning, for starters. I have other clients. I don't want to have to worry about you getting creamed by a Mazda because you're too fucked up to walk."

"I understand."

She blows her bangs out of her eyes, bends at the waist, then straightens. "Do you realize how serious I am about this?"

I'm silent.

"Sharon, this is not like you threatening Mel with a bust-up and not coming through on it. When I tell you this, I mean it. Even if it kills me, even if I hate doing it, and by God, Sharon, I love you dearly, but if I say I'll do it, you better believe I'll do it."

I nod, too embarrassed to look at her. I watch the road instead, the traffic. An entire summer has passed. It's fall again.

She opens the car door for me. "Come on. We'll take you home."

• • •

TWO DAYS LATER I'M on my stoop having a smoke when a yellow cab pulls up and a frowsy, familiar head emerges, struggling with a suitcase. "Nuh *uh*," I hear the head say. "You near bout kilt me. You can just forget about a tip, bub."

The driver burbles something. What it sounds like when *fuck you* is said in another language.

"Well, same to *you*." She smacks the door shut and takes a look around. Squints up at me. There's a moment of delay before I realize it's Mom.

We stare at each other for a minute before I scramble up and run for the door. "Don't you move," she yells.

I slam the door shut and lock it.

"Sharon *Kay*." I can hear the wheels of her suitcase clacking up the stairs. She slaps the door with her hand. "Sharon Kay, I know you're in there. You best open up this door right now." There's a pause. "What in the hell are *you* lookin at?"

Donnie went behind my back. Called not Mom but Shauna, who then trotted across the mountain and blabbed to Mom. "Every single goddamn one of you have done me dirty," I tell her when I finally let her in. "Why didn't Shauna come up herself? If anyone had to come at all, why'd she send *you*?"

"Shauna's got two kids and an idiot husband to take care of. What do you mean, *I did you dirty*. No one's doin you dirty here. You're so hateful to me and I don't even know why."

"I'm a bastard," I yell. "Who knows why we do what we do?"

"Are you gonna hang that over my head forever?"

"Yes. I'm gonna hang it over your head forever."

"You're actin like a teenager. Just real immature."

"I lost the only family I ever had. I get to act how I want," I scream. Mom winces. We both pull back, surprised.

But I press. "You *lied* to me. Don't you dare act like that's a non-issue. I am entitled to act however I choose. And if you don't like it, you can leave. Get the fuck out of here. Go back where you came from."

She pinches her lips and goes quiet. "I'm sorry about Mel," she says after a moment. "That was so sad. She was real young."

I don't know how to respond to this. I sit down, cross my legs, run a hand through my hair. It's greasy, peltlike. I rummage through my robe pockets, locate a joint I rolled days ago. It's squashed, but I light it anyway.

"Smokin that stuff'll make you stupid," Mom says.

"Mission accomplished. But will it make me boff creepy old child molesters like *you*?"

She sniffs. "It'll make you walk out into traffic without your drawers on, that's what it'll make you do."

"Well, shit. Check and mate, *Mom*." There's a stem on my lip. I pick it off, flick it away.

"That Donnie sounded real upset on the phone," she says. "She's worried about you. A lot of people are."

"Go home. You flew up here for nothing."

"No ma'am. I wanna see the sights. I never been up here, whole time you've been livin here." She picks up her bag, wheels it into the hallway. "You got an extra room?"

"Nope."

"I'll put this in *your* room, then."

She disappears into the apartment, tripping and cussing and sighing over what she sees. I throw an empty Ensure can after her. It hits the wall.

It's sort of invigorating, feeling this angry. After all these months of surfing through the vanilla, I can almost appreciate being pissed off for its novelty.

"Where's the commode," she calls out. I turn the TV on, turn the volume up and up.

WHEN I FALL ASLEEP on the couch, she changes the sheets on my bed and sleeps there. The next morning, she cleans house, emptying ashtrays, tossing mossy soup cans, stomping at the roaches with her puffy mamaw sneakers. She mops floors and pokes at my ankles with the handle to get me to lift my feet.

"I think a roach just bit me," she says.

"Yeah, they'll do that."

Donnie calls later in the day. "Did your mom arrive safe and sound?" she chirps.

"I hate you."

"You'd be surprised how easily I can accept that."

"I was going to thank you for bailing me out of jail. But I think I'll skip it and just tell you to go fuck yourself, Donnie."

"Have fun with your mom, Sharon. Give me a call when you're ready to come back to work."

MOM FINDS THE XANAX on my dresser. She marches into the living room, holding the bottle. "What is this?"

I'm watching *Scarface.* "What's it look like?"

"Looks like *pills.*"

She strides over and taps me hard on the head with the bottle. "We sent you to that fancy-ass school for you to get out and get started on *this*?" She shakes the bottle. "You know what they call this? *Hillbilly heroin.*"

"Hillbilly heroin is technically Oxycontin. Xanax is a prescription antianxiety medication."

She whacks me on the head with the bottle again.

"You know what, that really hurts. Stop it."

She puts her face close to mine. Her eyes are watery, white-blue. Says, "You know better."

"I have a *prescription,*" I tell her.

"I don't give a shit." She storms into the bathroom and flips the toilet open, grimy and ringed. "Nasty," she mutters, and dumps the contents in.

I keep still. "Go ahead. I'm just gonna get another prescription. That's how it works when you're *under the care of a physician.*"

"You just try. I'll kick your ass up between your shoulder blades."

She finds Mel's ashes in the back of my closet and plunks them down on the coffee table while Tony Montana does Eskimo kisses with a big pile of coke.

"Sharon, is this drugs?"

"What the hell." I get up, grab them. "These are Mel's ashes."

Her eyes go wide. "Oh."

"Yeah. *Oh*. What, haven't you ever seen cremated ashes before?"

"As a matter of fact, I have not." She crosses her arms over her chest. She's in pissed mode, what she resorts to when she's wrong and she knows it.

"Jesus." I lift the lid, show her. Clap the lid back down. "How Baptist *are* you?"

"Sharon Kay, that's enough."

"I'll tell you when it's enough."

"It ain't sanitary, keeping those around your house."

"Leave. Them. Alone."

"Fine," she says. But it shakes her up. I can tell by the careful way in which she straightens the coffee table. Leaves the room. Does what I ask for once.

M Y MOTHER IS ALLERGIC to New York. She is particularly allergic to Brooklyn. The fact that flannel and high-waisted jeans are hot trends with the kids strikes her as both ridiculous and suspect. When homeless people yell at her, she is inclined to yell back. When I explain that there's a service that will deliver your groceries, and another that delivers cleaning supplies, and another that delivers pet supplies, she says, "I don't understand how people up here are so skinny but so lazy. I ain't wastin money on that shit."

She goes to a bodega and spends thirty bucks on detergent and Mop & Glo and Clorox wipes. She tries to haggle with the store owner. He tells her to fuck off. She pays up and lugs it all back to the apartment, then collapses on the couch, frowning at the red grooves the bag handles dug into her palms.

"Told you," I say.

The next day, I am persuaded to clean myself up and take her to Prospect Park. "I wanna see something while I'm here," she says. "And I won't quit until you leave the house for once. Don't need you getting to be a crazy old shut-in at thirty-three."

"I am old and crazy."

She leans in and swats me on the butt, hard. "Shut *up,*" she says, a weird, ragged edge to her voice.

Subway fares have risen twenty-five cents since I last rode. Swiping the MetroCard to get through the turnstile drives Mom batshit. She blows two minutes running the card through the slot too slow, then too fast, while a line builds behind her. I give the people waiting an empty look until they go to another turnstile.

"Haven't you ever used a credit card before?" I ask her.

"Don't get smart."

On the train, she suggests we go to the studio later. "Wasn't you all livin there for a while? Are people in there?"

"No."

"Maybe we should go over to clean. So you can work there again."

"It's not around here. It's in another neighborhood called Bushwick."

"Where's that?"

"Too far. Leave it alone, please."

"Well, I don't see no sense in paying rent on a place and then not having—"

"I said no," I shout. The car goes quiet. A couple of kids climbing on and off the seats stop to stare.

At the park, she starts wheezing at the quarter-mile mark. We make it to the duck pond before she lights a cigarette and holds up her hands, saying, "All right. I give up. I'm tired. I'll pay for a cab. Where's a cab."

We don't speak on the way home. She looks out the window, mouth pinched. We pass brownstones, cyclists. She grips her purse, knuckles pale.

I hear her in my room that night, Doral smoke curling from under the door. I don't know who she's talking to. Kent, maybe Shauna. It's not a conversation she wants me to hear. But I can hear it anyway, catch her say, wavery and close, "She *scares* me."

MY BUZZER SOUNDS. MOM goes to the box, presses the *talk* button, says, "Hello?" like she's answering a phone, then pushes *listen* like I've shown her. Turns to give me a triumphant look.

"Sharon?" It's a guy. Young. His voice is on the verge of cracking.

"Who is it?"

"Mom, you still have your finger on *listen*."

"Oh."

"Sharon. *Dude,*" the voice says.

I go to the window and look. It's Tatum and Ryan: one still bald, the other still overwhelmingly dreadlocked. Tatum sees me first. Slaps Ryan. They yell.

I run down the stairs, throw the door open, and they pile on. It's instantaneous—for two guys I barely know, I'm so happy to see them, I feel my throat go heavy, and I embrace them, letting them cover me up.

"WE QUIT OUR JOBS," Tatum says.

"We want to be animators," Ryan adds.

"Yeah."

"Ted was *pissed.*"

Tatum reaches out and flicks Ryan on the back of the head. "Fucktard," he whispers.

Already they're filling my living room: their boy smell, their messy, smeared luggage. "It's okay," I say. "You can mention Teddy. I'm not going to get upset."

I hear Mom hesitate, then she sticks her head in, all smiles. Ryan and Tatum may be suspicious, flannel-sporting, flat-in-the-accent, smelling-faintly-of-ganja boys, but they are still *boys,* and for her, that makes them the center of this particular four-person universe. She loves them unexpectedly and immediately. "Boys, we got that funny pop from around the corner."

"She means coconut soda," I tell them.

"Awesome."

"We'd love coconut soda, Mrs. Kisses." Ryan twiddles a dreadlock at her. Mom beams and claps her hands together.

"So this makes sense," I tell them. "You guys did a lot on *Irrefutable Love,* so there's one credit for your résumé. Weren't you VA majors in college?"

"I was VA. The Tater was film." Ryan stretches his legs, looking around. The room has been cleaned. I am dressed—it's sweatpants, but it's something. I'm glad for these things, now that they're here.

"That sounds like the right combination. So what made you decide to come up here?"

Tatum clears his throat. Ryan scrubs a place on his arm, squinting.

"Mel?"

They nod.

"Guys, it's fine. I'm not going to flip out if you mention Mel. Someone dies, it pushes you to do shit you were putting off. Understood. So have at it. Need an agent? I'll talk to mine. She'll probably be glad to work with someone who's actually doing something."

"You're not doing anything?" Tatum leans forward. He's the listener, the one who watches for signs. I see him scan the living room, examine the ashtray. He's the *me* of this partnership. But he's asking more questions than I ever did. Smart. It's because he's a dude, I think bitterly. They program them to navigate.

"I'm kind of taking a break," I say.

"Right on." Ryan waggles his head. "Everybody needs a break sometimes."

"So are you all working on something?"

"Yeah." Ryan palms out his phone, starts tracing through. "We can show you some stuff. It's about oversexed zombies who invent a secret aphrodisiac coffee. The coffee spreads worldwide and turns everything into a giant hump party. It's gonna be the tits."

"That's a sweet message."

"We think so. Mel helped us with it."

"You guys need a place to stay?"

"Uh huh."

Mom emerges with soda, plunks a Diet Coke in front of me. "Did I hear Sharon say y'all are staying with us?"

"Stay in the studio," I tell them.

Mom looks up. "I thought you didn't wanna go out there."

"No one's there. They might as well." I turn to them. "This is the work studio we're talking about, out in Bushwick. Stay there as long as you need. There's a couple of beds, a couch. There's stuff."

"Holy shit," Ryan says reverently. "That'd be awesome." He glances at Tatum, then back at me. His face is so earnest, so hopeful. This is a person who hasn't lost much yet. I get up and start putting on my shoes.

FRONT AND CENTER ON the sidewalk outside the studio: a sizable human stool. "Dude," Ryan says.

Mom turns to the boys. "I think y'all need to go back to Louisville right this minute."

Two raccoons stare us down from the stoop. Mom starts at them, hissing. They skitter away. "Gotta show em who's boss," she tells us, and strides up the stairs, cupping her hands around her eyes to peer in.

"Your mom is awesome," Tatum whispers.

I watch her sneeze. Take a layer of dirt off the window with her hand, wipe the grime off on the back of her Lees. "I guess," I say.

I unlock the door, bang it open with my shoulder. Mom's the first to step in. "Pee yoo," she bellows, throwing her purse onto the floor. "We shoulda come up a long time ago, Sharon Kay. Smells like shit in here." She disappears into the kitchen. Yells, "Sharon *Kay*. There are *mice turds* in here and I wanna know what you're gonna do about it."

"Your mom is awesome," Ryan whispers.

"So you've said."

"I'm gonna marry her."

"Gross."

"It's not gross. It's *saxy.*"

I sigh and put my bag down. The place makes me ashamed. I sort of care that Tatum and Ryan, two kids who looked up to us, are seeing my negligence for themselves. I care that Mom is seeing it. Balls, I'm starting to care that *I'm* seeing it. On the end table near the door, a Post-it note. One of Mel's old shopping lists. A dragon with clouds drifting from its nostrils burps *toilet paper popsicles Activia smokes.*

I carefully put the list back where I found it. Without turning, I say, "She's here because I freaked out on Xanax and ran into traffic one night."

The rummaging in the kitchen stops, then quietly resumes. The boys have their hands sunk deep into their pockets. Tatum rubs his head, looks out the window.

I nod toward him. "There's probably a mug shot online. Right?"

He shrugs. "The picture's good. You look pretty."

"That's sweet. But the fact remains, I got arrested for being fucked up and sashaying out into the road. And I wasn't fully clothed. Did I mention that?"

Ryan looks to Tatum and giggles. "That's kinda righteous."

"Yeah. Kinda." There's a heady, yeasty mold smell in the air. It's cold. A few monstertruck roaches skitter under the couch. I pass the little mirror Mel and I used to check our line work from the opposite perspective. There are silver hairs now, sprouting around my temples, my crown. I stop, stare. "This part of Brooklyn is sort of in the wilderness," I tell them, "or it used to be. Some coffee shops and stuff have popped up. You're about forty-five minutes away from Manhattan on the L train. There aren't many grocery stores around, so you might have to use delivery or take the subway to get what you need. But this place was good to us. It'll be good to you, too."

I swipe an old T-shirt draped over the back of the couch, wipe down the Cintiq. The crack in the corner is small, hardly visible. "You guys ever use one of these?"

Tatum's eyes go wide. "Those go for a lot. Like three or four thousand."

"More. But we got this one cheap." I draw back, finger the shirt. It's Mötley Crüe. One of Mel's. I bring it to my face, smell. Mildew and sweat and every empty day that's passed since. "Use it," I tell them.

Ryan is scuffling along the edge of the room, looking at our cork wall, peering out the windows. The Sharon Wall is at the end, still concealed by the bedsheet. He lifts the sheet, peeks underneath. Goes still. I hear him curse softly to himself.

I walk upstairs into the living area. Bedrooms. I stick my head into Mel's. The sheets are ones she slept in, the pillows tossed against the wall—we were packing, late getting to LaGuardia. Later, I hadn't wanted to move anything. There was half a hope in my mind that if I left the studio long enough, she would be there when I returned, twiddling at her drafting board. That when I came in, she'd glance up and say, "Well, where the fuck have you been? *Yore tardee.*"

I go back down. "Bedrooms are up top. We gotta clean them."

Mom emerges from the kitchen with a bulging Hefty bag. "I'm gonna call that place that brings cleaning stuff. And you best be callin an exterminator or a damn exorcist or something. I never seen so many cockroaches in my everlovin life." The door bangs shut.

I take the opportunity to ask, "So. How's Teddy. How's *Ted.*"

Ryan and Tatum exchange a look, do a mutual shuffle. "Uh," Ryan says.

"He's good," Tatum supplies.

"Yeah, he's pretty good."

A big, fatty pause. I put out my hands. *What.*

"He's getting married," Tatum says.

When I hear the words, my entire diaphragm goes cold.

In the two years since Louisville, I've put Teddy through the same old paces I put them all through, nursing a weird little fantasy scenario I acted and talked out, all those Xanax nights, a prized and private delusion: a we'll-go-through-hell-then-figure-it-out-and-end-up-together-with-killer-dialogue-and-a-charged-gasping-sex-scene narrative. I hadn't decided on exactly when I'd planned on reaching out to Teddy and implementing this reunion plan. But I was convinced that it would happen. In the infinite future, there is always time.

Old habits die hard. He had become less Teddy and more my brain's construction in the months between, but was still so palpable to me I could almost forget his real-life counterpart was out there in the world, living a life. If anything, it was a sign of further bounce-back from the stroke, a return to my old self. I could still make a Frankenstein. It was the only good news to be found. *You forget,* I tell myself bitterly. Anything vital and alive, even the way someone *loves* you, could never survive the hotbox that is your head.

The boys look on guiltily, Ryan wagging his dreadlocks in his face, when Mom bustles back in. "I just saw that homeless lady take a crouch in some gravel. In *broad daylight.*" She stops when she sees me. "Sharon. You're all gray. What's the matter."

"I'm fine," I tell her. "I just need to take my pills." I put my head down and beat a fast track to the bathroom.

We clean until midnight. I collect Mel's Post-its, her cigarette butts, pencils bearing her specific chew marks, and put them all in a box in her bedroom. "Just leave them for the time being," I tell the boys. And they nod, they don't ask questions, and they don't look at me.

I'm seething. I keep seeing Teddy's face everywhere I look. All of *this* happened—Mel dead, my arrest, the spiraling out of everything I've ever known—and he knew about it. It's not that hard to track me online. Ryan and Tatum knew, obviously. It was *news.* And not even a phone call? In my hour of need, *nothing* from this man, who occupied an entire world in my mind, even when we weren't speaking? I could still feel him *so strong, for Christ's sake.* He was with me *all the time.* And his life is proceeding without me, as if we had never happened?

Mom is sent back to Park Slope in a taxi. I take Ryan and Tatum to get tacos from a truck on Troutman and Knickerbocker. We're in the middle of Ryan trying a *cabeza* taco, then being told what *cabeza* means and losing his shit, when Tatum's phone rings. It's Teddy. We all know it. Tatum plays it cool, cocks his eyebrow, holds up a finger—*just a sec*—then ambles down the street, glancing at us over his shoulder.

We go back to the studio, picking up a bottle of Four Roses on the way. When I inevitably outdrink the boys and they collapse, I pick up Tatum's iPhone from where it rests next to his head and, with only a slim moment of hesitation, access the history and dial up.

Teddy's voice is fuzzy, craning upward from sleep. "Dude, it's late. You better be wounded somewhere."

I can't speak.

I hear him sigh. He's processing it. Knows who it is. Says low, "What are you doing?"

"You weren't going to call. What was I supposed to do."

He sighs. There's a murmur in the background. Someone beside him stirring, asking who it is. I feel a pang in my chest.

"Why didn't you call me," I whisper.

There's a pause, the creak of bedsprings. When he speaks again, he is in another part of the house with deeper acoustics. "I guess I really didn't know what to say," he says.

I feel a little of my anger slough off. He's being sincere, and there's no one as sincere as Teddy when he's being straight with you. That's the thing about sincerity. It never fails to feel like someone trusting you with a valuable.

"I'm sorry about Mel," he says. "I really am. It's absolutely miserable."

"Thank you."

"Does Tatum know you're using his phone?" I hear him rise and move elsewhere. The old kitchen. A door closes.

"He's asleep."

"Are you okay?"

"Ugh."

"I don't know what *ugh* means."

"Do you really care to know?"

"Did I not ask you, Sharon?" There's an edge now.

"Why didn't you call?"

"It's interesting that you seem to feel I *owe* you something, Sharon," he says, voice lowering to a hiss. "*That's* why I didn't call you. Your overwhelming sense of entitlement. Despite the fact that I was worried sick about you after you were arrested running through traffic in your goddamn *bathrobe*. You know, I actually went by the carriage house to apologize."

My stomach shrivels.

"You were gone. And thank God you were. Because you didn't deserve an apology. At the end of the day, it wouldn't have been worth the trouble. It would have set a really dangerous precedent, letting you get away with something like that."

"What did I do," I cry.

He grows louder. "You—" There's a pause, an intake of breath. A confirmation, if I ever needed one, that someone else is there, that he is engaged, that she is there with him and he doesn't want her hearing any of this. "You made a movie and you *put me in it against my wishes*. And it is *obviously* me, Sharon."

"Did you see it?" I ask him.

"I saw the parts I needed to."

In *Irrefutable Love*, Teddy is my young, nameless co-conspirator in opening the trunk, and he is also the unnamed man I meet in my journey through the forest, the man the boy became, the one with whom I climb into an oak's knothole and descend into a warm red cubbyhole, where we wrap our legs around each other and drift through the air, spinning lazily, a moment's respite from being pursued. I couldn't help it. He was, in a way, everywhere I looked; his face bloomed when I placed pencil to paper.

In the movie, he disappears, as if he were dreamed; I awaken outside the oak, the thunder of footsteps approaching, and am forced to run again. It was a section we'd considered cutting, of course, but at day's end, even Mel, with a peculiar, grudging twist to her mouth, had to admit that the scene added a certain softness to the whole— that it gave the journey out of the woods some hope, some solace.

"There's a version of me out there that I have no control over," he finally says. "Even when I specifically told you no, you went ahead and did it anyway. And when you did that, you chose Mel. Okay? Which is what she wanted all along. She could talk you into dancing on burning coals, Sharon. You could never say no to her."

I slide down to the floor, speechless. My mind flashes on him and Mel sitting across the table from each other in the kitchen, glowering behind their wineglasses. I know he's not wrong. I put my head in my hands and say the only thing I can think of:

"I can hear her."

"Hear who."

"Your *fiancée*. When were you going to get around to telling me about her?"

"Never. Not if I could help it."

I feel a cool wash of unpleasantness bleed through my belly. I can't see for a moment. It hurts that badly.

"This is why I didn't call," he says. "We are at an impasse, Sharon. There's nothing left to say."

We're at an *impasse*. If the man has one weakness, it is this: forever picking the wrong moment for sanctimony. I feel my temper spike through, hot and sharp. I go for the grenade. "You wanna know why I left Kentucky? My mother finally broke down and told me the truth. I'm illegitimate. And guess who my biological father is? Your dad. Because my life is just that much of a sideshow. We just committed biblical incest. You have a good one. *Ted*."

He makes a choking noise. I hang up.

In the other room, Ryan and Tatum blink at me sleepily. I hand Tatum his phone. "Sorry," I tell him.

"Is that true?" Ryan says.

"What, that Teddy's dad is also my dad? Maybe."

There's a moment of quiet, then Tatum spouts an incredulous chain of *dude*s. Ryan yells, *Gross, you did it with someone you're related to* and Tatum affirms, *Dude*.

I collapse into a chair, an empty gnawing in my chest. Teddy's right. He doesn't owe me anything.

•   •   •

B ACK IN PARK SLOPE, Mom comes into the living room and slaps my sketchbook down. "You've never drawn a picture of me."

"I drew you from the eighties for *Irrefutable Love*."

"I mean, like I am now."

"I didn't think you'd want me to draw you like you are now."

She narrows her eyes. "You thought wrong, sugar. Draw me."

I shrug. Feel around for a pencil. Limp over to the drafting board to pluck one out of the coffee cup.

"Don't see you using that thing much," Mom says.

"I'm taking a break."

It's weird, sitting with a sketchpad again. I finger the pencil, feeling ungainly. Could I *ever* really do this? I look at the pad, then up at her.

She stares back at me. Lights a Doral. "Well?"

She's lowered herself into the canvas Ikea chair she claims hurts her ass, crosses her legs. I do a survey. Sweatshirt, jeans, puffy sneakers, glasses on a chain against her chest. Her neck is a latticework of lines, folded skin. Deep webbing around the eyes, the seams linking nose to mouth, the hill where the chin ends and the neck begins.

Mom was beautiful when she was young. All milky and blond, none of the Kisses swarthiness. A very seventies kind of beauty, full and bawdy, an era in which imperfect teeth failed to impede sex appeal. We drew her in this way for *Irrefutable Love*—the tornado scene as the toppling point for my mother's prettiness, before she started to wear, long before I learned about line or contour or critically identifying those things in anyone. I feel badly for thinking this. But her face is better than pretty. It is an *interesting* face, one with depth and contour that requires skill, care in replication. It calls for a study. What Mel always said: The beautiful face is the simplest to draw.

"Come closer," I say.

She moves next to me on the couch. I fold my leg carefully underneath me, study her nose. "Been a while," I tell her, making preliminary marks, "since I picked up a pencil."

"Well, I reckon it's time to get back on the horse."

"Try to keep still."

"Can I still smoke?"

"Yeah. Just move your arm. Try not to move anything else."

She goes quiet. Mom has been in New York City for six weeks. She's no longer afraid to stay in my apartment by herself. We've both gotten used to her being there. I'm going to the studio later to watch *Wild at Heart* with Ryan and Tatum. It's nice to have plans, gives a warm sort of momentum to this sketch: Here are the things I have to get done before I go out and spend time with my friends.

"I'm gonna go back home," she says.

I stop. "You are? When?"

"Next Saturday. Kent got me a ticket. He says hey, by the way. He says when you come to visit again, he'll bake you all the pies you want. Between you and me, I think you're his favorite." She takes a drag, exhales a plume of smoke. The cloud tapers. She looks at me from the corner of her eye. "You're back on your feet. You'll be okay."

"I was always okay."

"I know."

I lean back into the sketch. The division, or melding, between chin and neck will be a challenge. I try to see if there's a common stream, a line to follow, and instead find five, all diverging. "Running out into traffic wasted," I murmur, "is far from the worst thing that's happened in our family. You people dance shamelessly with the devil."

She appears to give this a think. "You're right," she says finally. "Or you ain't wrong. Let's say."

She puts out her Doral, lights up another. She's got something to tell me, and she's going to stress-smoke it out. "I saw *Irrefutable Love*."

I halt, pencil trembling in my fingers. "You did? When?"

"Just the other night. Found a copy in your DVDs."

"Oh." It takes a force of will for me to put pencil to paper again.

"I liked it," she says.

"Really? What did you like about it?"

"It was funny. Real funny. Even when it was sad, you know? The sadder it was, the funnier it got. It was funny like you're funny. I knew it was you. You were all over that thing."

"I'm funny when I'm sad?"

"Yeah."

"Good to know I'm Steamboat fuckin Willie when I'm suicidal."

She sighs. "Don't get like that, goddammit. I'm trying to give you a compliment."

No wonder I'm so uncomfortable. "Sorry." More silence. More tracing.

"It was real inneresting," she says. "I have to say, I don't know anybody else who thinks the way you do, Sharon Kay."

"Heh."

"And you like shitheads."

"Come again?"

"You don't like good men. The ones you date. It don't seem like."

"Well." I fuck up the chin curve. Erase, try again. "It might be as much me as it is them. Or so I've come to believe."

"If they don't like you, they're shitheads," she says firmly.

I try tracing her neck again, the loose, silky swoop of skin there. Wait for her to finish. "I'm not sure," she continues, "but maybe there's something I shoulda told you, that I didn't. Somewhere along the way. And I'm real sorry for that. Because I think it's made a lot of trouble for you."

"Try to keep still." Neck, neck, sternum under the sweatshirt. Can't see a firm line for the back of her neck; it's all ponytail end, then spine. No line is straight.

"I didn't know y'all were staying with Teddy," she says. "I just figured you girls stayed out there cause there was more there than in Faulkner."

"Mom, why else would I have possibly stayed in Louisville?"

"I don't know." She grimaces, shifts her butt. "I was surprised you put that bit in the movie, about him. That was him, wasn't it? Finding them pictures. You all digging around where you weren't supposed to."

"What the shit. Did you just blame that on me?"

"Well, you were." Then, quieter: "Did that really happen?"

"Yes."

I see her swallow, her neck moving with effort. She closes her eyes. "Jesus wept," she whispers.

I can't do it. Her neck is fucked. I draw a deep gash through the page before ripping it out and crumpling it up. "What's done is done," I say. "At least I didn't reveal that we might be related. Give everybody something to whisper behind their hands about the next time you go to Walmart."

Mom pauses. "I'm sorry I told you that."

"I'm sorry you told me that, too."

"Because I don't think that's right." Her eye twitches. "I was thinking back on it later. And I don't think it was him. I really don't."

"I can't believe we're going over this again."

"I remember things," she says, "but it's like another person doing them. Like I was somebody else. I don't know. I got married real young. I was eighteen. I remember when you were eighteen. You were leaving home. Getting married was the furthest thing from your mind. I guess I thought your dad and I could leave together, though anybody woulda told you there was no way he was gonna leave for anywhere that wasn't home. It was stupid. I had your brother, and then I had your sister. And it made me happy, for a little while. And then it's like it all wore off. And I was stuck there. Like my life had been decided for me. The less I could do, the more I wanted. Wanted things I couldn't have and I wanted things I couldn't even think up yet, but I could feel myself wanting. And that feeling, it's like itching. Like to drive you crazy." She shakes her head slightly. "I just wanted and wanted and wanted. You ever felt that way?"

"Yes," I tell her. "I have." I feel something warm light my chest. It's maybe the first time in my life that my mother has put something into the right words for me. "That's kind of what I was trying to show. In the movie."

"I know," she says. "I know *you*."

My throat tightens. I lean over to pick up the pencil so she can't see my face. I bend down and start over.

"Teddy's a good guy," I manage. "But he's so angry at me right now. And he has a right to be. He didn't want me to make the movie. He didn't want me to put him in it."

"Well, you didn't. It's not about him. It's about you."

"He still hates me." I shift position. There's no way this picture won't offend her. "I messed that one up. He broke it off."

In a consoling tone, Mom says, "Well shit." Reaches out to thump my knee. "Forget *him*. Just forget him. You gotta do what you gotta do. He don't like it, he can go straight to hell. That's what I say."

This one is turning out better. I think I have a handle on the way her face comes together. "So did you like how we drew you in *Irrefutable Love*? Like you back in the day?"

She lights another Doral. "Oh yeah. I looked *good*."

"Did you really watch it all the way through?"

She rolls her eyes and coughs. "What kind of mother do you think I am?"

THIS IS BETWEEN ME AND
THE VOICES IN MY HEAD

NASHVILLE COMBAT AND IRREFUTABLE LOVE ARE LICENSED TO NET-
flix. We're nominated for some awards but beaten out by the
Pixar types, big, flashy Cineplex productions. We never stood
a chance—our loud, grainy clips next to all that slick shit, all that
money and shine. I go to the awards ceremonies anyway. I sit with
Brecky and Donnie and drink champagne and eat chicken.

I miss Mel then. Mostly because she would have yelled something
appropriate at the screen when the Disney logo rolled by, or spat on
the floor, or pissed on the red carpet outside, limo service guys drinking Diet Cokes, glumly looking on. I never noticed how big the silence was when Mel wasn't screaming into it.

It has been almost one year.

This is the second phase of losing her: going out into the world
and living in her stead. There is a *talking* of Mel back into exis-

tence. I watch in horror as Mel Vaught becomes a series of anecdotes.

Worst of all, some of the anecdotes come from *me*. Sometimes I get drunk and, with the right kind of people around—Donnie, Fart, Surly Cathie—it feels good to talk about Mel. Thoughts and recollections and discoveries, neutral and inflammatory. She is a mosaic, all shards and details without context. Her profile: strong, small nose, but, yes, a weak chin. Enjoyed making cats dance. Once owned a ginger tom, the late Mister Puddles, whom she made gyrate to Joy Division (*meow, meow will tear us apart again*). Sometimes smoked Parliaments, which she called P-funks. Rooted for Florida State, *not* University of Florida. Had a mallard bite her hand once in a petting zoo in Jacksonville and forever after fostered a hatred of ducks—always ordered it off the menu out of retribution. First concert: Rage Against the Machine, 1999, at the old Riverbend stadium in Cincinnati, a band that no longer exists in a venue that no longer exists. Loved explosives. Loved cartooning. Loved her friends.

Loved me. Apparently. Sides are taken. A drunken cartoonist named Hedgeberg stumbles up to me after an awards show in Austin bellowing, in front of a crowd, "She was in *love* with you and you *ruined* her, you *rotten cunt*."

"What in the hell did he mean by that?" I ask Donnie.

She shakes her head. Says, "Nothing. Doesn't matter. He's drunk." She looks as if she might say something else, but then shakes her head again, ushers me toward the car.

I go back to work, mostly because I'm boring myself shitless. Donnie wrangles some consultancy jobs for me in Atlanta, where I stay in a hotel by a loop exit for six weeks. Then I go out west for a few months, where some well-funded animators seek guidance. Los Angeles is a bright, hot blur. The sunsets are brown. My sinuses feel like dried elephant nuts. I stay in a sublet condo and make three thousand dollars in a day giving directives to guys young enough to waft off Proactiv fumes.

I carry my journal with me. I'm not filling it with much, but I keep it there, just in case. Did I ever have ideas, independent of Mel?

That I ever made anything at all was a miracle, a freak intersection of luck and circumstance. I even argue to myself that *Irrefutable Love* was the product of some sort of proximity buzz I got from her. Still, my eyes never cease to note the angle of the thing, color gradient, shadow, proportion. The line of beauty. The greedy part of me that wants *more*, always *more*, is still there, but the voice demanding the want is weaker. And now, when the universe says *no*, I'm more inclined to tire, sit back, and with a feeling of mild constipation say, *Okay.* It is the ache of a phantom limb.

I try to pretend that I'm not sleepwalking.

"You look great," people tell me. "You look *healthy*. You have *color.*" These are relative observations: My mug shot is a total Haggis McBaggis study if I've ever seen one. People are just surprised to see me with my hair combed and my titties put away.

Brecky Tolliver and I are friends, Mel. If you were alive, that fact alone might kill you. Brecky's first project goes into development right after the new year. She's shown me the schematics for a Civil War cartoon comedy, a project that, as is, looks super-dubious. But Brecky is wooing me, asking for advice, input. She does that a lot nowadays, trying to get closer. I shy away. Ours does not feel like an organic friendship. There is empathy, but there is no kinship. Something holds me back. It's petty. But I can't help it.

She convinced me to return, work with her on the show. "Be a producer," she says. "That, you can do. Come home. You're happier in squalor."

"There's no more squalor in New York," I tell her. I come home anyway. Three years after the panel, Brecky gets her wish: She gets me, slow, soft prize that I am. I go to big brunches at the apartment Donnie and Brecky now share on the Upper West Side. I wash dishes, talk to people a little, move on the periphery of things.

I let Tatum and Ryan take over the lease on the studio. They're good boys: dragging me out to Bushwick for movie nights, showing me their sketches. They work in the stockroom at distribution full-time, then part-time when they get a grant to do their own thing. It is touching the way they keep the studio rigidly intact the first six months, refusing to displace anything Mel might have touched. Despite my grumbling and face-scrunching, they insist upon unveiling and preserving the Sharon Wall.

As time passes, they break the place in, making it theirs until, shame-faced, Tatum moves into Mel's bedroom completely.

"I'll keep the bed," he says. "Don't worry."

"I'm only worried insofar as that's weird, dude."

It makes me miss her so much my rib cage aches.

THE CIVIL WAR CARTOON development deal is in the final stages, title pending. My first week back at an actual job means meetings and hemmed pants, eight A.M. commutes, coffee in little blue-and-white Greek cups. I enter the gray-and-white bizarro world of an actual *job*.

We have our first meeting with the network on a Friday. "People you'll never have to see again," Brecky assures me, and so I let her pitch and wheedle while I sit there and try to look busy.

Ten minutes into the meeting, I notice the lone female executive looking at me. Redhead, early forties. Armani skirt suit, pumps. Pretty. Well kept in the way of women who spend their lunch breaks at New York Sports Club. Her look is appraising. A little close for my taste.

I put my head down and try to scribble something on the legal pad Brecky smacked into my hands before we walked into the room. Glance back up. She's still looking.

After the meeting, Brecky falls into step with the two guys and the redhead approaches me, hand out. "Caroline Palik," she says.

"Sharon."

"I know," she says. "We met at the memorial service. Very briefly."

The memorial service. I put my head down, try to cram the legal pad into my purse. "I gotta tell you," I say, "I don't remember much from the service."

A couple of black Pilot pens clatter out of my bag onto the floor.

Caroline kneels down to pick them up, hands them to me. "I probably wouldn't, either, were I you. I suppose I wouldn't want to."

She tilts her head to the side, looking at me. God, I hate it when people do that. I'm supposed to say something, but I can't come up with dick. As I realize she's waiting for me to ask how she came to be at the memorial service, she explains, "Mel and I saw each other. For a time."

"Oh," I say, then, "*Oh*. Really? Wait a second. Did you work for HBO? Used to send a car for her?"

"That was me."

"Wow."

She lifts her eyebrows. "Wow?"

"I just never thought I'd meet you," I say. "She, you know. Didn't talk that much about that kind of stuff. Who she was dating and all."

I see something pull and set in Caroline's jaw. I have offended her.

"But it's nice to meet you," I say quickly. "Finally. At long last."

"Likewise. Listen, do you have anywhere you need to be at the moment? This is going to sound a bit odd, but I have something I need to give you, and I knew I would be meeting with you and Brecky today so I have it with me. There's a bar I like right around the corner. Mind stopping in?"

It's eleven in the morning, but I nod.

Caroline Palik has a Donnie-like quality to her. Less strident, maybe. Low-register finishing school sort of voice instead of that clarinet squeal. But when she walks in a specific direction, you are compelled to fall in with her, if not slightly behind. She leads me through Columbus Circle to a swanky, red-lit restaurant with leather booths and a polished oak bar on a quiet numbered street. She is carrying both briefcase and purse. She slides the briefcase under the bar, then produces a small suction cup from her coat pocket, which she discreetly licks—a kittenish move, *Mel,* I will never understand your taste in women—and sticks to the wall. She hangs her purse on it.

She looks to me and smiles. "I think Mel made that same face when she watched me do that. I told her Queen Elizabeth does it, too, but she didn't buy it."

"Natural-born skeptic."

"That's what made her so good." The bartender greets Caroline—they know each other. "What would you like, Sharon?"

"I'll have a Coke."

She turns to me with a thin, cordial smile. "Sure you don't want anything stronger?"

"I'm on blood pressure medication from a stroke I had a couple of years back," I lie. "Doesn't match well with drinking." I shrug off my jacket, irritated at my own impulse to explain myself.

"Mel mentioned your stroke. Your limp." She's not looking at me now—she has bent over to access her briefcase. When she emerges, her face is smooth, neutral.

"She talked to you about my limp?"

Caroline shrugs in a way I don't care for. "She mentioned it in passing."

I look around. We're the only people in the bar. "Did you say you have something for me?"

"Just a moment." She sifts through some files. Pulls out a folder. Puts it on the bar.

I open it up. Storyboards. Sketches. They're Mel's: her telltale lines, the tiny block handwriting, those wide, aerobic faces. Her storyboards were always messy as hell. This is no exception, all gummy with eraser residue, a thumbprint in clear relief in one corner. I've spent so much of my life looking at her notes, her schematics, adjusting and arranging. I know it's hers in a heartbeat.

"What is this?"

"Some stuff she left at my place before she passed," Caroline says. The drinks come. She puts her martini to her lips. Her hand trembles slightly. "I think she was working on it when you two were wrapping up *Irrefutable Love*. I called her to come pick it up at some point, but you'd gone to Europe. So into the desk it went. Forgive me for taking so long in getting it to you."

I flip through. New York scenes: the elevated train, rushing past our window. Our studio, strewn with clothes, ashtrays, the Cintiq glowing in the corner. The sketches are good. Not great. First draft, maybe second. There's no clear narrative, the presentation's fuzzy— those were always things I took care of. Things she would have had to learn how to do herself, for her first solo project.

The initial storyboards are of her and me, working. *2007.* It must have been *Nashville Combat,* the very beginning of development. We are bent over back-to-back workstations: curved, scowling book- ends. A TV in the background bears a faint etching of Dick Cheney. In the next panel, Mel tells me a joke. I laugh and the world blares red: trombones fart, flowers wilt.

She has written: *Her laugh. It was great. It was awful. It was a sound like Satan rubbing his thighs together. She was deeply embar- rassing to see movies with.*

In the next panel, we are designing a character named Mrs. Beav, who ping-pongs up and down the street, winging her crotch into random objects screeching, *"BEAV! BEAV!"*

"I think it should be BEEV," I am saying, a decided crease to my brow. *"I prefer the double EE to the superfluous A."*

She was brilliant, Mel wrote.

Next scene. We are getting dressed to go out somewhere. There are close-ups of me leaning over a sink, applying mascara in a mirror. I step out in a very hip, very snug pair of high-waisters. Panel one: Mel smirks. *"Look at you, making the strut in your mom jeans."*

"Shut up. I like these pants."

"You're like eighty percent pelvis right now. I can't even look at you."

"That's the jealousy talking. Jealousy over my super-cool pants."

"You pull them that high above your navel, it's a sign you've given up on life."

Last panel: I dump the pencil holder on top of her head, letting the shavings rain down.

She was beautiful, Mel wrote.

My entire body runs cold. There's a quality to these sketches I can recognize: the product that comes from the need to draw something out of your head. Every time she looked at me, she was studying me. The way my face moved, the way I looked when I spoke, when I thought. This is exorcism sketching: making a story so you can kill it and bury it. She was making this in order to put something to rest for herself.

My mind flashes on Mel, slumped over the drafting board, glasses pushed to the top of her head, brown-flecked coffee mug—her favorite, the one I got her that read KENTUCKY STATE TOBACCO SPITTING CHAMPION, no doubt filled with Jack and Coke—beside her. Mel worked her ass off as a matter of course. We both did. We both had our reasons. But I never thought to ask her for hers. A flare of guilt hits me so hard it is nauseating. It was callous of me, taking her investment for granted.

"I've never seen these before," I say.

I feel Caroline shift next to me. "You haven't?"

I can't lift my head. I rifle through the pages again. It is definitely a project, something to which she devoted time and thought. She was working behind my back, and Caroline wants me to know it.

"How did you two meet?" I ask.

"We met at Animacon one year."

"You mean she hit on you at Animacon."

Something in Caroline's face cracks, goes soft. She grins, showing her teeth. Rolls her eyes a little. "I guess. I gave her my card. She contacted me for development advice like a year later, maybe."

Page five. Dark hair, big tits. Round, anxious pupils at the eyes. It's me, a little ruffled, not all *Nashville Combat* ethereal—those were my salad days, the closest I'll ever come to sexpot—but still, better than I have ever seen myself look, ever. Jesus, Mel, why do you always have to make such a big deal out of my boobs?

"I assumed you knew about this," Caroline says. "I hated the idea of you working on something and potentially having missing materials." Her glass is empty. I notice her hand tremor slightly as she makes a flicking motion with her finger. The bartender comes, takes it away. Sets down another. "It's funny," she continues, "I've worked with writers and cartoonists for years, but my ideas about their process are still pretty abstract. You know?"

I put the file down and force myself to look at her. "She wasn't going to me with this. You know that, right?"

She straightens on the stool, shoulders back. "I didn't," she says slowly. "I had no idea."

I rub my eyes. Flip the file open again. "It's not obvious? Jesus."

She doesn't answer.

I wonder when Mel did it. Where. Not in the studio. I would have noticed. When had she planned to tell me? Was she going to employ the coward's gradual method, phrase it as *taking a break*— a prelude to dumping me for good?

I would have been completely blindsided, too.

"Who else knew about these?" I ask Caroline.

She stares down into her drink. I see her swallow. "No one. As far as I know."

"Right. As far as you know."

Caroline turns to me fully now, hands lifted. "Sharon," she says quietly. "Let's start over. I've wanted to meet you for a long time. I'm not trying to hurt you or ambush you with these. Okay? And if they *have* hurt you, then I'm sorry. That was not my intention."

"Am I supposed to thank you?"

She closes her eyes briefly. Her liner and shadow are perfect, drawn with a natural, knowing hand. Her lids are quivering. "I didn't feel good holding on to these. You are their rightful owner. They belong to you."

I shake my head. Restack the pages into the folder, splay my hands on top. "Do you not get this? If Mel had wanted me to know about these, she would have said so."

Caroline covers her mouth, seems to massage her jaw for a moment. "I get it," she says. "I get it now. I'm sorry."

She suddenly puts her face in her hands and vigorously rubs, making a growling noise, then looks up, wild-eyed. "*Fuck*," she says.

I stare at her.

"This is so uncomfortable." She holds up her hands. "Wow. I think I've fucked up here. Agreed? So I vote for a do-over. What do you say?"

The weird, spastic suddenness of this—it has an echo of Mel, something of her skinny ghost in its makings. It touches off the same thaw mechanism. I go from twat to docile, involuntarily, in three seconds.

Caroline smacks the bar. "You know what? I need another drink. My *drink* needs a drink. Let's get you something. Just one. Okay? Martin!"

The bartender appears from the back.

"Martin, would you mind dumping some whiskey into Sharon's coke? Just fill it up to the top."

The bartender laughs, but he hauls a bottle of Jack over and begins to do as Caroline says. She sighs, relaxes her back, lets herself slump a bit. Okay. I can see why you liked her, Mel.

"All right," I say, making sure to frown. "I could have one. I guess."

WHEN THE AFTER-WORK CROWD trickles in five hours later, we stumble into a booth. Caroline furtively cups an e-cigarette and watches me inhale a basket of chicken fingers and french fries. We are thoroughly, intensely drunk. I force myself to do a heel-toe-heel walk on the way to the bathroom to avoid falling down. The air feels like pudding.

"I get the shitfaced hungries," I tell her.

She tilts her head back, smiling. "Those are the best kind of hungries."

I offer her a chicken finger, holding it out to her. She declines.

"Mel used to get those, too," she says.

"Yeah, man. She could put it away."

"She could." Caroline drapes one arm across the length of the booth. She has rolled up her sleeves. "Though she was trying to watch it. She was worried about her blood pressure."

"She was?"

Caroline nods, looking down to screw a new filter onto her e-cig. "She was. Something her doctor told her. I told her cutting out the coke would probably be even better for her blood pressure. But what do I know?"

It's tough to swallow my mouthful. Doctor's visit? Coke? What the fuck was going on with her? What was I not seeing?

I can't bring myself to ask. I pick at my fries. Say, "Sorry for being such a bitch earlier. You didn't deserve that."

"Don't worry about it."

I eat another fry, chewing tastelessly, before asking, "So why'd you two break up?"

Caroline gazes at the ceiling and narrows one eye, as if taking aim at something. She has unraveled, through the course of the day: her hair loose, blouse untucked. There are lines around her eyes and mouth, an increased webbing at her neck, but in spite of—or because of—these new layers, it occurs to me that Caroline Palik is a complete knockout.

"I cared for Mel very deeply," she says finally. "I was willing to put up with a lot of things to be with her. Things I wouldn't have tolerated, really, in anyone else. I'll be honest, there were some really late nights, there was some unpredictable behavior. There were more substances than I was comfortable with."

"I thought she'd slowed down with a lot of that stuff," I say.

Caroline gives me a close, unreadable look. I go quiet, feeling foolish. Behind us, a large, down-coated group comes in from the cold, laughing, stomping their feet. It has begun to snow.

"Was that it?" I ask.

She grimaces. Fiddles with the band of her watch. "This is going to sound strange," she says.

I shrug.

"There was this quality of—what would you call it. Distraction? It felt as if, sometimes, she was only thirty percent there. And then, other times, it felt like there was something else in the room with us. Just sort of hanging there. And it seemed like she was okay with that. Like it was normal for her. But I could never get comfortable with it. And it's a hard thing to call someone out on, you know? Like, *Mel, please take this ghost out of the room.* Couldn't very well tell her *that,* right? It would have sounded ridiculous. It sounds ridiculous now.

"And when I saw the project she was working on," she says, "it, well. Kind of made sense, a bit."

I think of Mel's storyboard. The sketches of me. I feel my throat constrict. I am culpable here. And this is Caroline's kind way of telling me that she also thinks I am culpable.

"We never dated," I insist. "Really. I know that might be hard to believe, because she dated half the women in New York. But it's true."

"Oh, I know," she says. "I know." She puts her hand on top of mine and squeezes hard.

I study my fries, no longer hungry. When I come to, I am talking. "I feel guilty. Like someone more thoughtful than me would have been able to see what she needed and given it to her. And the last couple of years were all about *me,* you know? My stroke, my family, my breakup, my bullshit. And I was constantly worried that she thought I—wasn't good. Or as good as she was. I'm such an asshole."

Caroline gives me another close, inscrutable look, and again I feel like a toddler. But she says, "Are you kidding me? She *adored* you. She didn't think of your problems as *bullshit.* She felt like they were her problems, too. She referred to you constantly. I felt like I knew you, even though we'd never met. She even *drew* you. You know that? Not just those." She points to my bag, where I stashed the folder. "When she was doodling, on takeout menus, the *TV Guide.* Your face came out."

"Really?"

Caroline's forehead wrinkles. "Sharon, have you sat down and watched that last scene in *Nashville Combat* lately? The part they showed at the service?"

I shake my head.

"Watch it again."

Being with Caroline is both sweet and painful, a weird, hazy event that could only occur in the portion of my life that I have come to refer to as *after.* It is a glimpse into an alternate reality, into a Mel I might have recognized but who would have been a stranger to me—

my partner, gone total, unquestioned adult. It is a chance to savor grieving with another person; for the rest of our lives, we'll have to do this by ourselves.

And because Caroline is a person who elicits others to follow— a quality that would have been interesting to see Mel operating from under—I match her drink for drink. It grows later. Arms linked, we climb onto the sidewalk and prop each other up until one of Caroline's car service guys, someone she also knows by name, cruises up, and she deposits me gently in the backseat with a dry, hard kiss on my cheek.

S TILL DRUNK, I DIG *Nashville Combat* out of the back of my closet and put it into the DVD player.

Mel's drawn me hot—breasts round, hair liquid black, mouth red and wide. Luminous in a way I could never, in real life, hope to be.

I make a sound when I realize it. Better than reading Mel's face was reading her work. Mel would only draw someone she loved that way, with that sense of skin-glow so difficult to capture, the hours melting into each other as you poured your whole being into the sketch. What she loved was always embedded there, immovable as line or shape or color.

It was her weight, her burden, that had tethered her to the chair, to her board, to make what I was seeing right now. My body runs ice-cold with the knowledge of all I didn't see, the things I had never known.

S HAUNA CALLS ME ON a Friday night. "What are you doing."
I'm lying on the couch in my underpants watching *60 Minutes*. "I'm at home," I say.

"Let's meet up."

"Cool. You got vacation time coming up?"

"I mean now. Like, right now. Like in a couple of hours."

"Are you okay?" I ask her.

"I'm fine. Why?"

"You sound weird. Like you're out of breath."

"We're getting a divorce," she says. "*Finally.* Me and Brandon. Like I filed the papers *today.* Like I kicked his lazy ass to the curb *tonight.*"

I sit up. "Really? Dude. I'm sorry. That's rough."

"No it ain't," she says. "I'm happy as hell. Let's meet up. Right now. I'm serious. I'm in the car. I'm driving up. I just passed Huntington."

"Seriously? Where the fuck are your kids?"

"They're with Mom. God. What kind of mother you think I am? Listen, I been thinking about this and we're never gonna get a straight answer out of her, so I think we should just get you a paternity test. Okay?"

"What time is it?" It's been a long day. We drafted show episodes with a roomful of writers and sent the first schematics to Korea. It was also the first day I went into work wearing jeans. When I got the tilted-head-prickle-eye from Brecky, I told her, "This is how it's gonna be, dude. I am what I am."

"It don't seem like you want to," Shauna says, sounding hurt. I hear rushing behind her. The low-level murmur of the radio dialed low. She really is on I-64. I'll bet she swipes the good car in the divorce settlement. She'll bitch at him until he bends like a straw. "Don't you wonder? Don't you want to know?"

"I have a job now," I say. "Like a job I have to show up to. I can't just leave New York whenever I want."

"Tomorrow's Saturday."

"It's Fox. I gotta go in."

"Are you in front of a computer? Go check and see what the halfway point is between New York and Faulkner. I got a friend who's a nurse who'll run the lab tests. All I need's a cheek swab. Come on. Let's see if you've won the lottery and you're not a Kisses."

I end up renting a car and driving down. Our agreed-upon halfway point is just past Columbia, Maryland, off Interstate 68, at an all-night Love's with an attached Denny's. When I pull up, Shauna's already there, leaning against a Chevy HHR, smoking a cigarette, looking slickly tan under the parking lot lights. She sees me pull in, runs over to the driver's side, and knocks the window hard with her left hand. Her wedding ring has been replaced with a massive ruby and cubic-zirconia wrap, a weird triangle-swoop stone on a wide band. Her nails are purple.

I roll down the window. She leans in, grinning, and juts her hip out. I see a couple of truckers give her the once-over. "Hi, baby," she says.

"What color of nail polish is that?" I ask her.

She grimaces. "I dunno. Purple something. Purple Rain, I think?"

I slap the steering wheel. "God *damn*. I *knew* it."

"What."

"It's— Nothing. Probably too weird to explain."

"Sometimes I think I don't see enough of you," she says. "And then other times I think it's just enough." She retrieves a plastic bag from her pocket, pulls out a swab, pinches my cheek. "Say *ah*," she commands.

I open up. She takes a quick, triumphant swipe. "There. That's all you had to do, angel baby." She drops the swab into a plastic cup, puts the cup in a Ziploc bag. "Well," she sighs. Leans against the car.

"Well," I say.

"At least now we'll know."

"Certainty's not a bad thing."

"We'll never get it from Mom," Shauna says. "Between you and me, I think she's goin senile."

"If I turn out to be a bastard, will you buy me a Grand Slam breakfast?"

A WEEK LATER, I get the text from her:

> Lab says . . . you are officially a Kisses. Sorry? ☺

W HEN TEDDY GETS MARRIED, I send him a wedding gift—a water-color skyline of Louisville, painted by an artist in New York. It is a softer Louisville than the one we drew for *Irrefutable Love,* that jagged lifeline struggling against the sky, the Ohio River gray and indifferent beside. This Louisville glows with the water, the view curving the bend of Interstate 64 as it stretches, out and out, into the west.

I am beginning to understand what I did to Teddy, what he was trying to tell me, when I look at Mel's sketches. Finding yourself in a world someone else has made is a theft that is difficult to put into words—the magnitude of your life, smeared to their order, your voice impersonated or, worse, winked out altogether.

I know what Mel and I did with memory. We ran our endurance dry with our life stories, trying to reproduce them, translate them, make them manageable enough to coexist with. We made them smaller, disfiguring them with our surgeries. We were young. We did not know what we were doing.

I am protected by my forgetting: What I can recollect is subject to my own personal slash-and-burn, my inability to *lay off*. It is not in me to be able to leave well enough alone. Thank *God* I forget. Thank *God*.

I want to tell Teddy that I had no alternative. I had to make what I made to survive, to move forward with my life without the shadow of that goddamned trunk hanging over me. But now I'm aware enough of the cost for it to keep me from sleeping at night.

All I write on the card is this: *Congratulations. I am so happy for you.*

THIS IS THE YEAR I meet Danny.

It happens at Animacon. He's just moved to New York from Los Angeles to write and work PR for a media blog. *ReAnimator* has just launched its list of the top thirty adult animated films of all time. *Nashville Combat* is number 12, *Irrefutable Love* is number 7; he's assigned to write a story about it, and me. When I meet him, he's eating. He lifts his hand, a wad of bagel in his cheek, and he says, "Good morning, Sharon Kisses. Are you ready to be interviewed?"

I'm a good five minutes into the interview before I realize Danny is cute. Sort of medium height, substantial five-o'clock shadow, big brown eyes (even in distraction, I am still forever a sucker for the kind of moony, chocolaty eyes you can fall ass over cranium into). Nice hands. Sweet little teeth. And those five minutes ultimately work for me, because it means a window of coherence before my hormones descend and scramble my shit to pieces. A first impression in which I actually, unknowingly, have some game without getting in my own way. Snapping off some solid one-liners, some thoughtful ruminations about Brecky's stupid Civil War show.

I ask Danny out to a bar afterward with me and Tatum and Ryan and some of the old crowd. On the way there, as we cut through the squirrels chattering in Washington Square Park, I elbow him and say, "You know what they call those where I'm from?"

"No."

"Limb chicken."

He guffaws, and I discover what will be my kryptonite with Danny: When he shifts from neutral to amused, his face transforms. Something lights from within, his spine straightens, neck snaps back, and he lets rip: "Heh *heh*." And it feels like an accomplishment, the ultimate payoff. I like what I do to him. I feel myself leap to attention between my legs.

I spend the rest of the night trying to make him do it again. I watch his face, watching the way he watches me when I'm dancing with Surly Cathie—hands deep in pockets, face serious, searching. I can't remember the last time someone looked at me so closely.

At the end of the evening, when the group splinters, I take his hand. Tell him, "My place's this way."

He says, "Okay."

We spend the following month cocooned together.

Making him come is even better than making him laugh. When he's inside me, I take his face in my hands and I have him look at me, so I won't forget what it feels like to be watched.

It's the first time I've been inseparable from someone since Teddy; a honeymoon rush. It helps that Danny is so easy to be around. He's worked PR long enough to have adapted aspects of his job as primary mode of operation. As a result, he is the most informed person I know—about the news, about celebrities, about stocks. He is ravenous for information. He knows the public story of Vaught and Kisses, things about me that I have not told him. Yet he does not insist on having his way with the conversation.

We pass a throwback theater in Alphabet City and see a movie poster for *Tank Girl*. "Loved that movie when I was a kid," he says.

I say, "People used to tell my old partner she looked like Tank Girl."

"Lucky her."

"Yeah."

"You hungry?"

We fall in together. He lets me be. Doesn't pass pointed looks at the drafting table, heaped in a shifting tide of bills and papers and Post-its. Is perfectly content to let me watch TV in my underpants while he writes, researches, makes calls. Lets me leave work wherever I leave it. Only once did he try to push the career issue, suggesting that I start a Twitter account. In response, I drew him a picture of the Twitter bird getting fisted by the hammy, hairy hand of Truth.

"Noted," Danny said. He folded the picture and put it in his pocket. Later I found it tacked on his bulletin board.

We move in together, into the bottom level of a house in Bay Ridge. I am surprised to find myself comfortable. It's the first place that has felt like home since the studio. I am settled, and strangely itch-free.

"I had seen you before, you know," he tells me. "You were with Mel Vaught. At some Animacon thing. You all were doing stuff for *Nashville Combat*."

"You're kidding me."

"Oh no. I noticed you, for sure. But I was too scared to talk to you."

"Why in God's name were you too scared to talk to me?"

"Every time I saw you, you were surrounded by, I dunno. Light. And people. And noise. I just thought, there's no way. There's no way I could ever slip into that woman's orbit."

"Really?"

"Of course." He puts his arms around me. "You're *all* light and noise."

"I'm not," I say, and he pulls me in, muffling my voice into his shirt. "I'm the most alone person I know."

A FEW MONTHS AFTER Danny and I move in together, *An Uncensored History of Modern Cartooning* is released. It's a big oral history of animation during the past thirty years, filled with process and technique and gossip. It receives positive reviews in the *Times* and *Kirkus:* informative, though perhaps more salacious than necessary due to the many anonymous, let-the-shit-fly quotes within. Glynnis Havermeyer is a co-editor. She called Donnie early on to see if she could interview me.

I made a fart noise. "Not on your life. Tell her to suck it."

"You don't want a chance to give your voice?" Donnie asked me. "We should probably consider this a warning. If you don't talk, people will gladly talk *for* you. You and Mel are going to figure pretty heavily into this book."

I told her I didn't care.

She sighed. "Well, forewarned is forearmed, I guess."

Forewarned I am, but it doesn't do much good. The week the book comes out, I find myself pinned to the wall with needling stares at work. I spot a copy sitting on the coffee table at the studio before Tatum whisks it out of sight. Everyone's got a copy in their bag, whispers about it over drinks. I block it all out—a practice at which I have become fucking *super*—but am caught off guard when I walk into our apartment to find Danny lying on the couch reading it, marking his place with his finger, looking up at me expectantly.

I know the book's general spin on Vaught and Kisses, more or less. Mel Vaught, brilliant addict/erratic cutup/blabbity bloo, gone from this world, leaving her quirky, lesser partner to while away as a shut-in, getting tubby and running out into traffic without her pants. Beyond that, I don't care to know the details.

Later that night, when we're cleaning up after dinner, Danny asks me, "Do you miss her?"

I nod. Hope what I'm not saying will be enough to create that space of wordlessness people are supposed to recognize as the *forbidden zone*, that deep well of hurt human decency demands you not touch when speaking about the dead.

But Danny presses. "You don't talk much about her."

"Yeah. Well." I shrug. Turn my back. Pretend to scrub the counter.

Danny sits at the kitchen table and looks at me, hands on his knees. All big, sincere eyes. Waiting. He knows I'm shortchanging him.

"What. What do you want me to tell you," I say. "What would you like to know that's not in that book?"

"Wasn't going to mention the book. Wasn't even going to bring it up."

"Come on. I saw you reading it." It's louder than I mean for it to be. "You might as well. How many hillbilly cough-syrup jokes did they let slide through editing? Or is that too *gauche* to include in a book of that caliber?"

He rubs his face and sighs. "Jesus, Sharon."

It's a fight. We don't have many, and we don't have them that well, going back and forth on an uneasy sort of equilibrium. Sometimes our happiness does not lessen the feeling of sand running out from underneath my shoes, me constantly changing positions in order to stay on land. We're not even comfortable enough with each other to argue. When we're upset, we hit a wall. No one makes a move. Just thick, world-ending silence.

"I wish you'd let me in a little more," he says. "My girlfriend's a superstar and I have close to no idea about that part of her life. I don't feel like I know Sharon the cartoonist."

"Dude. Do you really want to?"

He clears his throat. "I don't want to feel like an intruder when I'm asking you questions about yourself. It feels like you had this entire life before I met you that I'll never have access to. I mean, your best friend died and you almost never talk about it."

I turn away from him. Go to work vigorously rinsing forks, water full blast. "That's not my life now."

"That's not the point. It feels like you're trying to keep something from me. It's always kind of felt like that. What don't you want me to know?"

"Could we not keep going in circles about this? There's nothing I don't want you to know."

He comes behind me and shuts the faucet off. "Okay. Let's talk about the damn book. It says things about you that are really disquieting, Sharon. And considering the fact that we are sharing our lives with each other, it worries me some."

"I don't plan to read it," I say.

"Maybe you should take a look."

He holds it out to me. I heave a sigh. Take it from him with two fingers.

Sharon Kisses laughs like a goat. And when she's on a panel, she always wears a push-up bra. It's like two terrified honeydews peeking out of a wrinkled Costco bag.

"Why are you shocked? You see that every night."

He rolls his eyes. Turns the page.

Page 343:

You think she's the *stable* one? Sharon's totally bizarre. There's a reason their cartoons are so, you know. Visceral. Maybe she was stable in comparison to Vaught, but that's not really saying much. She's super-impulsive, too. She used to. Well. How do I put this. *Couple* in random places? The worst I heard about was her having stand-up sex with a guy in a carousel in this, like, abandoned amusement park in New Jersey. Just picture that for a second. Like, sex during which you can hear the retching of a crackhead from the old Tilt-A-Whirl. It's not hard to see connections, is it? Like, you have to be really unhinged to make the sorts of *things* they made.

I grunt, throw the sponge I've been using in the sink. "That's *Fenton*," I tell Danny, "and he's a grade-A dick. Just an incredibly nasty guy Mel managed to piss off, one way or another, so now he's out for blood. He used to work for Glynnis. Now he's a cultural critic for some blog. He should also get a fucking medal for most ticlike usage of the word *like*. That's millennial journalistic integrity at its best." I turn to the fridge and haul a bottle of Ketel One out of the freezer. "Besides, this is New York. I've heard of sex in worse places."

I'm dumping the vodka into a tumbler of orange juice when Danny reaches out, gently takes hold of my wrist. "That doesn't bother me," he says. "If watching *Irrefutable Love* didn't make me jealous, you think *that* would?" He flips the page, points. "Right there."

I don't think many people understand what that was like for her. Sharon and Mel had each other. No spouses, no partners of note, no close family members. They were each other's family. Of course she's not the same person. When something like that happens to you, you move a little slower, a little more cautiously. That's what you do when you've been wounded. I think stopping work, for her, is a protective mechanism. If this is what you do, it's part of who you are. It's as natural as walking or breathing. I definitely got the sense that Mel was the one who had the big ideas, and Sharon was the one who kind of kept things moving.

I wince before I remember that Danny is watching me.

Who wouldn't be just totally lost after something like that? No one knows if she'll ever draw again. It would surprise me, in fact, if she did.

I have to stop and put the book down, it hurts so bad. Oh God. Please, let this be Brecky on a bad day. Just Brecky running her mouth, *ruminating,* and not Donnie. *Please not* Donnie. Because that would finally do it. That would lay the last, lethal hairline fracture on my heart.

I close the book and hand it back to Danny, careful not to look at him. Pick up the screwdriver, now slightly warm. "When I got up this morning," I say, "I wouldn't have given two fucks about somebody flapping their jaws in some stupid book. But now that it's ruined my day, someone's getting the boots."

"This is something you love," Danny says quietly. "Sharon. Look at me. You think I don't know that this was your life, before we met? You think I don't see you *not* drawing anymore? I see it. It's an omission, and I can see it. I can see the gap, in you."

I shrug.

"If you've given up something you love so much," he says, "and you haven't said a single solitary word about it, I take that as a sign that something is very wrong. It makes me worry about what might be happening to you on the inside. It makes me worry that you might regret what you're doing with your life right now, later. How that regret might spread to other parts of your life."

He goes quiet. The silence in the room is unbearable.

I say, "What. You wanna hear more *Penthouse* Forum stories about me fucking in the abandoned Funlands? Is that it?"

He leaves the room.

Danny's right. He knows nothing. I've kept it all from him—the terrifyingly fossilized middle of me that used to spread and contract like a living thing, when I sat down to work. About Mel. My memories are disintegrating, slurring together. I watch an interview of us online from years ago, both of us college-sprung and round-faced, *babies,* and I hear her say the words, "I'm Mel Vaught," and it raises the hairs on the back of my neck. I'm forgetting the sound of her voice. The way she coughed. Her footfalls. All sensory evidence that she'd even been a person, evaporating. A part of me can't help but crawl deeper inside in response. I can't take another part of myself grinding to a halt.

This is the first real fight I've had with Danny. It turns my stomach inside out. Some of the worst vomiting since the stroke, so much so that Danny breaks his silent treatment to stick his head in and grudgingly ask if I'm all right.

I find him in our bedroom at midnight, hunched over his laptop. I sit behind him and rest my forehead into his back.

I say, "Okay. Ready?"

I tell him everything. I tell him about going to Florida to identify Kelly Kay's body and I tell him about the fight Mel and I had in the Times Square subway station. I tell him about the stroke and the hospital and about Teddy and about my mom. I tell him about Mel and me and the cold, dirty, lonely year we put in on *Irrefutable Love*. I tell him that meeting him felt like waking up from a long, dark sleep. It's the longest I can remember talking in months.

I show him the sketches Caroline Palik gave me. He pages through them slowly, nodding as if it confirms something for him.

"I'm sorry," I tell him. We're lying on our bed, holding hands. It's two in the morning now. We will turn off the lamp, I will climb on top of him. The sex is where we really forgive each other; the compromise that can only happen when he is inside me. "I'm not the greatest at talking about myself. Irony enough, considering what we made our stuff about."

"I think you should do something with Mel's project," he says.

We both understand that I am not totally forgiven. But for now, I have been given concession.

I CALL DONNIE. "THERE'S something I need to show you."

She drives over from Manhattan with a warm, fragrant bag of chicken tikka masala and naan. She has business to discuss: *Irrefutable Love* has been excerpted in a documentary about fantasy and feminism, and permission is needed. Someone else wants to option it into an off-Broadway play. "A play? How in the fuck do they expect to do that?" I ask her.

"Never underestimate what people can do." She looks around the apartment. "It looks great in here. Much better than the studio. No severed body parts. No smeared feces on the wall."

"Okay, how crazy do people think I actually am? I should have gone on record for that goddamn book."

"I'm kidding," she says, pulling plates out of the cabinet and ripping the bag open with a gesture of finality—she's as sick of talking about the book as I am.

After we eat, I show Donnie the sketches. She goes through them slowly, glasses perched on top of her head. "Yes," she says. "These are Mel's, for sure."

"It was about me. You don't find that a little weird?"

"Frankly? No. She adored you." Donnie leans back, folding her arms across her chest. "Okay. So what's next?"

"I don't know," I say. "I feel weird even looking at these. I'm not sure how much *my story* this is. It feels . . . private, I guess."

We look at each other. Our kitchen is clean, well lit. Danny's cat clock hangs on the far wall, a smiling Felix staring glassily off into space.

"I guess the main thing," I say, "is the fact that, when I look at these, I don't really know what to do with them. I used to be able to look at our stuff and see four or five scenarios I would just *sit* with, you know? And a couple would usually stand out as best options. I'd try them out, work with the strongest choice. But I look at these and just flatline. Because they're not mine." I lean back, scrub my eyes with my hand. Say very quickly, "I look at these and all I can think is *she kept these from me.*"

Donnie gazes at me levelly. "Look at them long enough and you won't think that anymore," she says. "You can make this your project. You two had to have diverged at some point, right? You and Mel were not one person, Sharon. You were fifty percent of that partnership. Just think of this as another collaboration. You don't have to be Mel's conduit or anything. Pick it up from your end and do *your* work, as you always have."

I pull the last of the Ketel One from the freezer and take a look around our kitchen, our apartment, a place I never would have thought to put myself a year ago. "I guess I didn't think about it that way."

Donnie pulls a couple of tumblers down for us, then leans against the counter, arms folded across her chest. "Would you be willing to try to work on this?"

"I guess I would be willing to *try.*"

"Fair enough." She takes the vodka from me, pours a half inch into each glass. "Things we can think about. What you're doing on your own will be a departure from the way you worked with Mel, so you might want to think about bringing in some help. Brecky, if she can? Or Ryan and Tatum?"

"Someone in that book said I would never draw again. Did you see that?"

Donnie rolls her eyes. "I did. I didn't pay much attention to it. Of *course* you will draw again. Surrendering work *period* was never part of the plan."

"I wasn't aware that we had a plan."

"Oh, there's always been a plan. You're not just going to make a full stop here."

"I've never done anything on my own before," I say.

"Sure you have."

"Storyboards, maybe. My senior thesis. But that's it, man. That's the extent of my solo stuff."

"Hey. *Irrefutable Love* was yours. Mel facilitated in development, but that was *your* idea." I start to protest. She holds up her hand. "This is how we need to start seeing your track record, Sharon. Get in the trenches and get to work, and you'll surprise yourself by how much of this you can handle on your own. When you're ready. You'll know when you are."

She mixes the screwdrivers, hands me mine, and turns toward the sink, where she starts to scrub our plates. She hands me a drying rag. She knows I am afraid. "You and Mel were moving toward this anyway," she says. "This is what happens. People grow up. Do you remember what we talked about, before your mom came to stay with you?"

"When I flashed my beaver at the policeman?"

"We talked about your needing to be *present,*" she says. "Starting this project up and sticking to it will be a big part of that."

At that moment, Danny walks in through the front door. Donnie reaches out and squeezes my arm before greeting him with a hug. She always liked Danny, from the very beginning.

I SPREAD THE SKETCHES out on the kitchen table and examine them, one by one. What was Mel trying to make? Of all the stories I had ever envisioned for myself, I never saw *us* as a story. I never saw us ending. But she had. What was this story? How did it end?

There are storyboards of me at work on *Irrefutable Love*—looking at the Cintiq, an expression of total absorption on my face, and in the background Mel watching me. There are perspectives of Mel leaving the studio, looking through the windows from the street at my figure craned over the drafting table. This is a different Mel than the one I saw and heard in the home we shared together—this is a raw Mel, quiet, sad, a Mel who saw more than I ever thought she did. A Mel who circled me, looking for a way inside.

Finally, a single sketch of Mel, packing a box. She has drawn the essentials going in: alarm clock. Coffee grinder. Her charcoals. This is the box you pack when you are leaving for good, when you need to make as much fit as possible. I'm in the background, but I'm a shadow. Already a ghost with no face.

THE CIVIL WAR SHOW is titled *General Malaise*. The test episode passes approval with the network and we are given the green light for a six-episode season. Brecky gets us office space on Twenty-seventh near Madison, one of those Flatiron corridor streets that goes dark and empty after ten P.M. "I'm promoting you to the head of the art department," Brecky says. "You get your own department. You're the boss now."

My first decision as executive animation producer is to hire Ryan and Tatum as my head storyboard revisionists, my second-in-commands. With their help, we hire my very first staff of storyboard artists—Luke, Marlon, Dave, Jay, all fresh from SVA. These are young, young guys. Two of them have twirly mustaches, until Jay shaves his off. They all wear a revolving selection of bright sneakers and large watches and can do swift, scary things on their phones. They don't remember Reagan and they don't remember what a dial tone sounds like. They're the new generation. They scare the hell out of me.

They are *bros;* I am not their *bro.* I am their (guh) *mother figure.* "It's true," Brecky says. "We are in that age range now. Whether or not we'd be fit mothers for anyone."

I'm hanging out the office window, a Doral from a pack Mom left at the old apartment smoldering in my hand. "Fuck that shit. They already have mothers they don't listen to. Can't I just be a benevolent authority figure?"

"You can be whatever you want," she says. "This is your department."

But the boys don't scare me nearly as much as Caitlyn, our color key artist and the sole woman on staff, all of twenty-four years old. When Tatum introduces me to her, he says, "Caitlyn's parents grounded her for watching *Custodial Knifefight* when she was in middle school. She's a huge fan of yours."

Caitlyn blushes wildly. I lean over and shake her hand. Tell Tatum, "Stop embarrassing her, shitfit."

She smiles tightly at me. Says low, "Call me Cate. Please."

The older I get, the more the memory of how my head roiled and heated and spat from about age fourteen to thirty fades: becomes a little more brittle, a little more distant, and hence more dangerous. But I remember enough to look at Cate and feel a little sorry for her. She is the lone woman's voice in what I'm sure will become a big, senseless sausage party, which makes her even more nerve-wracking to be around. One look over her shoulder tells me how good she is, already a pro. You could destroy us all, I think, and you don't even know it yet.

I'm easily a decade older than everyone else in this room. This, I imagine, is what makes them listen to me. I fall into the boss role while willfully expending as little effort as possible. More days than not, I wear Danny's old sweaters, or baggy flannel shirts that trail almost to my knees.

I clock in at nine. Heft my bag on my shoulder at five-thirty and address the room: "See ya, nerds." And I go home.

The kids stick around after hours, like kids do, with that fire in their bellies. I encourage them to do it, to use the workstations and the large Cintiqs in the off-hours (though they all have their own smaller versions now, the size of iPads, something they can slip into their fancy leather portage bags and take back to Williamsburg with them). They all have their passion projects and they all pull them out at six with fixed, singular expressions on their faces, overflowing cups of coffee in their hands, getting ready to work a night shift of their own design. They have the glazed, immutable gazes of those in love.

I am bone-rattlingly, eye-wateringly envious at first, can feel the dry clutch of loss in my throat as I walk down Broadway to the R train. I try not to think about what I'm missing, try not to remember what it felt like to anticipate the blossoming of an idea. Instead I tell myself to savor the smaller dependables: getting in out of the cold into our warm, safe apartment. Spending an evening with Danny. Cooking a particularly complex soup. I try to appreciate the feeling of neutrality: a quiet, grateful life.

In stride with *General Malaise*'s Civil War setting, and as my private metaphor for leadership, I put Stonewall Jackson's farewell quote to Robert E. Lee at Chancellorsville on the office bulletin board: "SO GREAT IS MY CONFIDENCE IN GENERAL LEE THAT I AM WILLING TO FOLLOW HIM BLINDFOLDED."

Then I post a Mathew Brady print of Richmond, Virginia, gutted at the Siege of Petersburg, after which General Lee fled, right underneath.

"There's something there," I tell the team. "That's the end of season two or three. Lee on the run. Maybe pantless. Probably pantless."

"It's weird to walk in and see that every day," Dave says.

"You're not wrong," I tell him.

I like spying on them from my office. Dave and Jay are Fart types, big, stolid guys with quick fingers and absolute ease with new CGI programs that resemble NORAD control boards. They don't work with each other, are not *partners,* but they are friends. I watch them leave together and return together every day at lunch; once, coming back from the Duane Reade around the corner, I see them walking out of the basement of an Episcopal church. An NA meeting.

Marlon and Luke, on the other hand, are partners. Marlon's the asshole of the pair, the dandy who buys clothes he can't afford and toys with girls way out of his league. Luke's the nerd, the super-studio sketch stud, quiet with stony, solid resolve; skills that will get him hired anywhere he wants later on. Luke puts the ideas to paper. Marlon yells out the scenarios, flapping his hands, pecking on his iPhone, always dancing a little. It's not until I see them in action that my old ghost, the one that always whispered about the weight of Mel's talent throwing mine off the scales again and again, is finally put to rest. My God, we were a *real* team, I think.

Marlon and Luke are on the same side of the room as Cate, facing my office, and they talk more to each other than to her, who doesn't say much at all. She is delicate and milky, seeming to disappear into her down coat when winter arrives. It's obvious she works; her work is written all over her body. For hours at a stretch, only the top of her head, dark blond and bent forward in concentration, is visible, occasionally tilting to the left or right to work out a crick in the neck, a single solitary arm coming north to push the sleeve back and reveal her hazardously thin wrists. As the months progress, she wears support cuffs on both. I think of the host of the San Francisco party, his Disney lawsuit, the way he clawed his hands at us. Once or twice I see her eyes come up, above the board, to look at me. When I look back, she ducks down like she's been shot.

Marlon and Luke have a project in the works and they're deep into it. They go out for Taco Bell and forty-ouncers of Colt 45 before they start in on the night shift.

They're weirdly shy about whatever they're doing. I run into them in the elevator at eight-thirty one morning, fresh from bagels and cigarettes. They have clearly not slept. "You gentlemen look like shit," I tell them.

They giggle. "Yeah," Marlon says, "we were working on something way urgent."

I raise my eyebrows politely. "Were you."

"It's early stages," Luke says quickly, wagging his hands. Marlon shuts up, obedient. Luke gives me a small, pensive smile. "We're still kind of figuring stuff out."

"I got you," I say, and we step out onto the floor. I turn toward my office. "That's exciting. Let me know if I can help."

They don't need my help, as it turns out. They land a Hollingsworth. They are the new wunderkinds, come from out of nowhere. I give them big hugs, tell them I'm springing for pizzas. Search myself for useful advice I could pass along to them.

"Don't have a stroke," I tell them. "Or try not to."

The room is loud with chatter and backslapping—someone has put the press release from the Hollingsworth website up on the projector—and I am the only one to spot Cate out on the balcony, tugging her coat around her shoulders. I slip out into the cold without anyone noticing, pull the door shut behind me. I'm wearing a cardigan I reserve only for work, hanging it on the back of my door at night when I go home. A pack of American Spirits is tucked into the pocket; Danny and I "quit smoking" together. Meaning that now I only smoke at work, out on this little balcony, sometimes with my drafters, sometimes alone.

Cate's shoulders are hunched. She turns slightly to hide the fact that she is crying. "Hey," I say. "Is it okay if I—" I pull out my smokes.

"No," she says. "Go ahead."

I light up. For a brief, uncomfortable moment, I am still before I reach over and thump her on the back. "You know, you're doing good work in there," I tell her. "I probably don't say that enough. I definitely should say it more with you."

Cate's shoulders sag. She puts her hands to her face, her knuckles red and knobby. "I don't know," she says. "I've just been feeling really bad about my stuff lately. Like, what else can I *do*? I don't do anything but work, you know? I apply to fellowships and I send stuff out to contests, but nothing sticks. It feels like screaming into a void. You know?"

"I know."

She sniffles. Points to my cigarettes. I slide them over to her. She picks one out and lights up, takes the shy, wincing drag of a non-smoker. "It makes me feel like shit," she says, "not being able to be happy for Marlon and Luke. They're my friends. I should be able to be happy for them, but I can't. I applied for the Hollingsworth this year, too. And I didn't get it. Why not me? I'm talented, too. I work just as hard. Right?"

"You're right," I say. "You are just as good. It is true."

She wipes her nose with the crook of her wrist, cigarette cocked up and out in a spidery gesture that suddenly reminds me of Mel. What did Mel and I do, when we were rejected for the Hollingsworth, NEA, NEH, whatever? Went out and got hammered. Bought one of every weird Middle Eastern candy bar at that bodega that kept live chickens in the back, and made each other finish every bite. Held our own private *Ren & Stimpy* marathons. We kept each other upright, kept each other working. I was lucky, I realize. Luckier than I ever really knew. From age eighteen on, I had a partner, a kindred spirit. I had a friend. Someone bound and determined to keep me from the worst in myself. Someone to keep me from doing what Cate is doing right now. In a roomful of guys who have already partnered up, formed alliances, Cate is alone.

She continues, "My ex-boyfriend just got this huge contract with Marvel. They're calling him a *phenom*. And he's totally mediocre, Sharon. I know that sounds mean. But even *he* knows it's true. He's not worth the money they gave him. I just wish I could stop feeling so bad. I want to stop wanting these things I can't have. And I wish I were more excited about what I'm working on. It deserves excitement. It deserves, you know. Love. Attention. It deserves to feel as important as it is."

I put my arms around her and pull her in. She is tiny. A Midwestern girl, probably, perpetually underweight as a kid, with parents who worry about her all the time, even in their sleep. A nurse and a claims adjuster, I imagine. I place them in Kansas. Maybe Missouri.

She huddles into me, shivering. "What do I do?" she says. "I'm getting knocked out so much, I feel like I'm bleeding."

I tell Cate what I know: That she's good. That she's going to get even better. I could tell her that she's actually better than Luke and Marlon, and when Marlon leaves to take a higher-paying gig at Nickelodeon in a couple of months, he won't really be missed. But I don't. I tell her that the little things that break her down, day after day, don't matter, because she draws like an absolute bastard and because she is in love with this thing that we do. Because it keeps her alive. Because she is the truest version of herself when she does it. The work will always be with you, will come back to you if it leaves, and you will return to it to find that you have, in fact, gotten better, gotten sharper. It happens to you while you are asleep inside. The world in which we work is a place where no one is a ghost, a world in which the potential for *anything* walks and breathes, alive. And this is reason enough to have faith. To keep going. I tell her, I know what I am talking about.

At six-thirty I clear out, wordlessly holding my hand up in the air as I walk toward the elevator. "Where you goin, boss," Marlon yells.

"Home."

"You don't work late?" he says. "Nothing secret holed up in your office? No *Irrefutable Love* sequels?"

"Nah."

Dave shifts in his chair, pushes his glasses up his nose. "What do you do at night?" he says, shy. This is what they talk about, I realize. They wonder about me. If I work on anything anymore.

I smile at Dave. "I plant my ass on the couch and eat a bag of Funyuns. Good evening, gentlemen. Lady." I nod at Cate and walk out the door.

Danny's working late. I've got our apartment to myself. I've put my old drafting board and stool in the mudroom at the rear of our apartment, a hopeful gesture. It comforts me to know that it is there, my station. Ready for me when I'm ready for it.

Tonight, I put Mel's sketches up on the bulletin board above the desk and I stare at them for a long, long time. I'm not looking for answers. I'm not looking for absolution. I'm looking for a feeling: not nostalgia, no cheap, tin-foiled remembrances, but the element that will bring her back into the room. A distant sniff. The sound of a foot slipping out of a shoe. A smell from far away.

I sit down and I finish Mel's story, again and again and again, toying with a hundred different endings, an infinite future in which we have all the time in existence to live out our stories. It is my own personal shoestring theory, each narrative fraying at the ends to make for a thousand more stories in which we both live. In one, the stroke kills me—not as sad, of course, because Mel lives. In another, we make *Irrefutable Love* and we take it on tour, going to Europe, going to the West Coast, but in this world, we opt out of San Francisco's party and return to New York to find the studio lacking enough space to hold the both of us. We cease to have ideas together. In this world, we return home to find our way separately, each forgiving the other for the things she could not give. In this world, we see each other occasionally: a friend, a touchstone to whom we both return, the heartbreak we both bravely revisit.

I work steadily into the night, gray sky deepening to black, Brooklyn dimming to a single light hovering above my drafting board. I work through Danny coming home and putting his hand on my back, through my wake-up alarm and the first jogger to clap down our block. I work until the night dies and the morning is born at the waterfront, that familiar itching at the base of my spine ramping, the adrenaline peaking at the unspooling of images. The hunt for that hot and nameless thing is on, and I am certain only that the old impulses are not dead, that the voodoo does not die.

ACKNOWLEDGMENTS

This book was written in part with the support of a graduate scholarship from the Jack Kent Cooke Foundation. I am grateful to this organization for their faith in, and active encouragement of, my abilities.

The Animators had an incredible team propelling it forward, and I owe a debt of gratitude to many. Bonnie Nadell, Austen Rachlis, and the team at the Hill Nadell Literary Agency: Thank you for seeing something in me, and for seeing this book through.

The Random House team: Caitlin McKenna, my brilliant editor—this is a better book because of you. My publicist, Lucy Silag; publicity associate Melissa Winters; my marketing directors, Alaina Waagner and Jessica Bonet, for their expertise and kind guidance with all things media; and Danielle Siess, for the photography work. The super-sharp copyediting and proofreading team: Beth Pearson, Jennifer Prior, Annette McGinn, and Kathryn Jones. I'm lucky that I've had the opportunity to work with all of you.

Those kind individuals who read, advised, supported: Emily X.R. Pan, cheerleader and pillar of strength. Liz Rodriguez, Eliza Martin. NYU folks who read this in its earliest form: Jessica Amodeo, Matt Shaer, Gabe Habash, Julie Buntin, Cliff Benston. The team at *Bodega,* which published an early excerpt from this book: Cat Richardson, Lizzie Harris, and Melissa Swantkowski. Artist/designer friends who provided technical details: Sarah Bednarek, Annelise Capossela, Ashley Howell, Tabitha Mund. Greg Johnson, for the eatin dress. Slater Ferguson, for Custodial Knifefight.

Susannah Kemple, editor/adviser/friend extraordinaire. I'm lucky to have you in my corner.

The teachers: Chuck Wachtel, Irini Spanidou, Darin Strauss, Rick Moody, the Lillian Vernon Creative Writers House at New York University. Thomas Marksbury, Nikky Finney, Gurney Norman. Dan Rowland, Lisa Broome, and the Gaines Center for the Humanities at the University of Kentucky.

Glenna Whitaker and Randy Whitaker, for their faith and support and understanding. Faron and Tametha Sparkman and Shane and Kim Sparkman, for taking me in as family.

And Warner, of course—this is for you.

ABOUT THE AUTHOR

KAYLA RAE WHITAKER was born and raised in Kentucky. She is a graduate of the University of Kentucky and of New York University's MFA program, which she attended as a Jack Kent Cooke Graduate Scholar. She lives in Louisville. This is her first novel.

kaylaraewhitaker.com

ABOUT THE TYPE

This book was set in Sabon, a typeface designed by the well-known German typographer Jan Tschichold (1902–74). Sabon's design is based upon the original letter forms of sixteenth-century French type designer Claude Garamond and was created specifically to be used for three sources: foundry type for hand composition, Linotype, and Monotype. Tschichold named his typeface for the famous Frankfurt typefounder Jacques Sabon (c. 1520–80).

ABOUT THE TYPE

This book was set in Sabon, a typeface designed by the well-known German typographer Jan Tschichold (1902–74). Sabon's design is based upon the original letter forms of sixteenth-century French type designer Claude Garamond and was created specifically to be used for three sources: foundry type for hand composition, Linotype, and Monotype. Tschichold named his typeface for the famous Frankfurt typefounder Jacques Sabon (c. 1520–80).